THE COALITION

A NOVEL OF SUSPENSE

From the fiftieth floor of an office building in Denver, Colorado, a long-range assassin calmly watches a procession of black Lincolns. When the motorcade pulls to the curb in Civic Center Plaza, a prominent leader steps from one of the vehicles and takes the stage to make an important speech. Moments later, a loud BOOM echoes through the Plaza and the man slumps to the platform like a stringless marionette. The mysterious sniper, whose very existence is unknown to the international law enforcement community, has just assassinated U.S. President-elect William Ambrose Kieger.

In the aftermath of the shocking political crime, the shooter escapes and a Task Force is swiftly assembled, headed up by Special Agent Kenneth Patton of the FBI's Denver Field Office. A ten year vet in Domestic Terrorism, the unconventional Ken is driven to solve the crime by both professional and personal motives. His search leads him to a secret society whose diabolical and far-reaching plot threatens the very highest levels of the U.S. government. Yet the group's motives, secret membership, and ambitious plans remain elusive. Can Ken and his team uncover the plot in time to save the day? Can they beat the countdown on the clock and catch the assassin and the shadowy group in the background pulling the strings? Or will time run out?

Praise for Bestselling, Award-Winning Author Samuel Marquis

"A promising thriller writer with a fine hero, great research, and a high level of authenticity."
—Donald Maass, Author of *Writing 21st Century Fiction* (for *The Coalition*)

"Marquis is brilliant and bold…It's hard not to think, 'What's he going to come up with next?'"
—SP Review - 4.5-Star Review (for *The Slush Pile Brigade*)

"With *Blind Thrust* and his other works, Samuel Marquis has written true breakout novels that compare favorably with—and even exceed—recent thrillers on the *New York Times* Bestseller List."
—Pat LoBrutto, Former Editor for Stephen King and Eric Van Lustbader (Bourne Series)

Praise for *The Coalition*
Winner Beverly Hills Book Awards – Political Thriller

"*The Coalition* has a lot of good action and suspense, an unusual female assassin, and the potential to be another *The Day After Tomorrow* [the runaway bestseller by Allan Folsom]."
—James Patterson, #1 *New York Times* Bestselling Author

"This ambitious thriller starts with a bang, revs up its engines, and never stops until the explosive ending...Perfect for fans of James Patterson, David Baldacci, and Vince Flynn, *The Coalition* is a standout thriller from an up-and-coming writer."
—Foreword Reviews – Four-Star Review

"An entertaining thriller about a ruthless political assassination...Marquis has woven a tight plot with genuine suspense."
—Kirkus Reviews

"*The Coalition* by Samuel Marquis is a riveting novel by an uncommonly gifted writer. This is the stuff from which blockbuster movies are made! Very highly recommended."
—Midwest Book Review - The Mystery/Suspense Shelf

"Reminiscent of *The Day of the Jackal*...with a high level of authentic detail. Skyler is a convincing sniper, and also a nicely conflicted one."
—Donald Maass, Author of *Writing 21st Century Fiction*

"Author of 2015's *The Slush Pile Brigade* and *Blind Thrust*, novelist Samuel Marquis has accomplished something rather rare. In *The Coalition*, Marquis has injected fresh air into the often threadbare genre of political conspiracy and assassination thrillers."
—Dr. Wesley Britton, Bookpleasures.com (Crime & Mystery)

"Marquis knows his stuff: [his] conspiracy is prescient and plausible, and well-drawn. Each one of his characters has uniquely interesting motivations. If you're in the mood for an engrossing assassination thriller with a unique twist, *The Coalition* is a very good place to start."
—SP Review – 4.5-Star Review

"*The Coalition* is an entertaining conspiracy story driven by the diverse motives of a varied and complicated cast of characters."
—IndieReader Book Review

Praise for *The Slush Pile Brigade*
#1 *Denver Post* Bestselling Novel
Award-Winning Finalist Beverly Hills Book Awards

"This high-energy, rollicking misadventure will change the way you look at the publishing industry forever. The plot is unpredictable...twists and turns and counterturns abound. So, too, does the humor...The dialogue is superb...Marquis laid the groundwork as a thriller writer with *The Slush Pile Brigade* and hopefully his following novels build up a James Patterson-esque empire."
—Foreword Reviews – Five-Star Review

"There's a lot going on in Marquis' book, as the author smartly builds off a solid premise...A fresh concept and protagonist that breathe life into a conventional but exciting actioner."
—Kirkus Reviews

"*The Slush Pile Brigade*, by Samuel Marquis, is a hilarious and exciting read filled with one crazy turn after another...The author slams on the accelerator early in the story and doesn't let up, forcing the reader to flip the pages frantically. And once it's over, it's still hard to catch one's breath."
—SP Review - 4.5-Star Review

"Twists, turns and double crosses in literary theft quickly expand to threaten the globe in *The Slush Pile Brigade*, a promising debut from an up-and-coming thriller writer."
—IndieReader Book Review - 4.5-Star Review

"Marquis makes the whole bewildering journey entertaining with his quirky friends who accompany Nick on his mission. The fact that Marquis himself wrote a novel called *Blind Thrust*, bring out the book-within-a-book theme, and the New York City scenes and dialogue feel authentic throughout. Read *The Slush Pile Brigade*...for the enjoyable romp that it is."
—BlueInk Book Review

Praise for *Bodyguard of Deception*

"*Bodyguard of Deception* grabbed my attention right from the beginning and never let go. The character development is excellent. Samuel Marquis has a knack for using historic details and events to create captivating and fun to read tales."
—Roy R. Romer, 39th Governor of Colorado

"Readers looking for an unapologetic historical action book should tear through this volume."
—Kirkus Reviews

"As usual, Marquis's descriptions are vivid, believable, and true to the time period...*Bodyguard of Deception* is an intriguing launch to his new trilogy. Warmly recommended."
—Dr. Wesley Britton, Bookpleasures.com (Crime & Mystery)

"Old-time spy buffs will appreciate the tradecraft and attention to detail, while adventure enthusiasts will enjoy the unique perspective and setting for a WWII story. A combination of *The Great Escape*, *Public Enemies*, a genuine old-time Western, and a John Le Carré novel."
—Blueink Review

"The world hangs in a delicate balance in the heart-pounding *World War Two Trilogy* opener, *Bodyguard of Deception* by Samuel Marquis. Put together with an intricate plot to follow and a commitment to realistic detail, there's a lot going for the read...a wonderfully nail-biting experience with good characters and solid intrigue."
—SP Review – Four-Star Review

"A fast-paced, riveting WWII espionage thriller. *Bodyguard of Deception* is as good as the best of Daniel Silva, Ken Follett, Alan Furst, and David Baldacci and brings back fond memories of the classic movie *The Great Escape* and Silva's finest novel, *The Unlikely Spy*."
—Fred Taylor, President/Co-Founder Northstar Investment Advisors and Espionage Novel Aficionado

"*Bodyguard of Deception* is a unique and ambitious spy thriller complete with historical figures, exciting action, and a dastardly villain. Fans of prison-break plots will enjoy this story of a loyal German struggling to save his homeland."
—Foreword Reviews

By Samuel Marquis

THE SLUSH PILE BRIGADE

BLIND THRUST

THE COALITION

BODYGUARD OF DECEPTION

THE COALITION

A NOVEL OF SUSPENSE

SAMUEL MARQUIS

MOUNT SOPRIS PUBLISHING

THE COALITION

MOUNT SOPRIS PUBLISHING

Trade paper: ISBN 978-1-943593-08-8
Kindle: ISBN 978-1-943593-09-5
ePub: ISBN 978-1-943593-10-1
PDF: ISBN 978-1-943593-11-8

Second Mount Sopris Publishing, premium printing: May 2016
Cover Design: George Foster (www.fostercovers.com)
Formatting: Rik Hall (www.rikhall.com)
Printed in the United States of America

To Order Samuel Marquis Books and Contact Samuel:

Visit Samuel Marquis's website, join his mailing list, learn about his forthcoming novels and book events, and order his books at www.samuelmarquisbooks.com. Please send fan mail to samuelmarquisbooks@gmail.com. Thank you for your support!

ATTENTION: ORGANIZATIONS AND CORPORATIONS
Mount Sopris Publishing books may be purchased for educational, business, or sales promotional use. For information, please email the Special Markets Department at samuelmarquisbooks@gmail.com.

Dedication

For my mom, Anne, and my wife, Christine, and our children, Sam, Clapton, and Cassidy, whom I cherish.

The Coalition

A Novel of Suspense

Let us not despair but act. Let us not seek the Republican answer or the Democratic answer but the right answer. Let us not seek to fix the blame for the past—let us accept our own responsibility for the future.
—John F. Kennedy

Sniping is poetry in slow motion, up until you pull the trigger.
—Unknown

SUNDAY

CHAPTER 1

THE MOTORCADE SWEPT IN FROM THE WEST. Five equally spaced Lincolns, each the same: sleek, jet-black, with U.S. government tags, bullet-proof windows, and tinted glass to conceal the identity of the occupants. The caravan stretched nearly a full city block as it rolled up Colfax Avenue, police escort fore and aft. In the third vehicle sat an august-looking gentleman donning an English-cut, double-breasted suit. He was scheduled to give a speech in the Civic Center Plaza in sixteen minutes.

On the fiftieth floor of the Union Plaza Building, from behind a reflective office window, a woman watched the procession with detached interest through high-powered Leupold binoculars. The woman was unusual in several respects. A pair of perforated black leather gloves encased her nimble hands. She wore a special disguise and was fluent in six different languages. And concealed in the hardcover carrying case at her feet was a Barrett M82A1 .50-caliber semiautomatic scoped rifle, broken down into five separate components. She was intimately familiar with the lethal weapon; for more than a decade now it had been her closest companion.

The woman was of Italian heritage, but with her clever disguise, polyglot mastery of languages, and surgical alteration of her Roman nose, it was impossible to tell. Her given name was Angela Ferrara, but years ago she had forsaken her real name for aliases. Her current alias was Skyler, no last name. She also had a *nom de guerre*—Diego Gomez—a fictitious name created by her control agent. The invented Spanish assassin remained a mystery, a phantom of the files in the hands of the international law enforcement community.

For her own security, Skyler was determined to keep it that way.

She continued following the black motorcade through her binoculars. The motorcade turned right onto Bannock Street and pulled to the curb behind the speakers' platform in the western end of the plaza. To the distant west, beyond the jungle of glass and steel of downtown Denver, the snow-shawled Rockies stretched toward an unseasonably warm mid-November sun and periwinkle sky. Skyler had spent the last few hours periodically gazing at the shimmering mountains, her eyes drawn like a magnet. They brought back pleasant childhood memories of family vacations hiking and skiing in the Dolomites of her native Italy.

Before her life had changed—drastically.

The car doors opened. The man and his handlers emerged from the Lincolns. Skyler took in the chiseled face captured in countless photo-ops, noting the famous boyish smile, as the man shook hands with party loyalists.

Five days after winning the presidential election, William Ambrose Kieger was returning to the home state of his vice-presidential running mate, Katherine Fowler, to pay tribute to the people of Colorado who had played a pivotal role in his capturing the White House. Fowler—the two-term, red-meat senator from the Centennial State—was in Colorado Springs today giving a similar speech in support of the president-elect.

But Skyler didn't care. She was here to do a job. In fact, she was here to kill, just as Don Scarpello and Alberto—the heartless bastards—had long ago killed her inside.

With notepads, microphones, and cameras in hand, the claque of awaiting pool reporters called out questions from the rope line to Kieger and his growing entourage. Still smiling, he playfully answered a few of them as he moved toward the speakers' platform, protected by a phalanx of Secret Service agents.

Setting aside her binoculars, Skyler opened the case on the desk. She smiled confidently to herself as she pulled out the sniper rifle's lower receiver and set it on the floor. The lower part of the weapon contained the adjustable bipod, magazine feed, trigger, and stock. She took the metal bolt and carrier and attached them to the lower receiver with an audible click. The upper receiver housed the barrel, various springs, and the scope mount. She pulled the upper section out and joined it to the bolt carrier group and lower receiver. Then she withdrew the fluted Krieger precision single-point cut-rifled barrel from the upper receiver and locked it into position. Finally, she adjusted the length of the lower receiver's bipod to exactly eight inches.

The man and his coterie continued toward the speakers' platform. When the group reached the security checkpoint behind the platform, it was funneled through a bank of magnetometers.

Skyler reached for her custom-fitted Brügger & Thomet baffle-type sound suppressor. It was a critical component of today's operation, for it would substantially reduce both the muzzle sound signature and ground echo, either of which could give away her position to the Secret Service countersnipers stationed on the rooftops in front of her. With several quick turns of the wrist, she screwed the suppressor into the threaded barrel.

The crowd roared as the man took the stage. Even through the glass, Skyler could hear the sound filtering up. She reached for her binoculars again, training them on the plaza below. She watched as the man shook hands with several local dignitaries before being escorted to a chair on the left side of the platform. Another man, whom Skyler recognized from her dossier as Colorado Governor Jackson Stoddart, stepped forward to the podium to make the scheduled introductory remarks.

Somehow, the whole scene seemed oddly incongruous to her. Here she was about to wreak bloody death and mayhem in the plaza and the damned place looked like a carnival: the shimmery festiveness of the crowd packed onto the grassy lawn; the multicolored richness of the banners and American flags ruffling in the crisp autumn breeze; the hundreds of balloons, arranged like clusters of grapes, festooning the platform. Everything seemed out of place, like stage props brought to the wrong movie set.

Setting down her binoculars, Skyler reached into her case again and withdrew perhaps the most critical item: the Leupold Vari-X III long-range M1 sniperscope. The Leupold's maintube was a monstrous 30mm diameter, allowing for the generous range in elevation and windage adjustments required to account for bullet drop and wind drift. She slid the sniperscope into position on the upper receiver, and only then did she step back to admire her handiwork.

What lay before her was a lethal rifle almost five feet long and weighing slightly less than thirty pounds. Fully assembled, the "Light Fifty" was a bit dated and far from gracile, but like a fine old wine it was still in a class of its own. One of the most accurate long-distance sniper rifle in existence, in the hands of a master shooter the weapon was capable of upper-body hits beyond a half mile. Skyler had paid over ten thousand dollars for the military rifle on the black market and thought it well worth the price.

As Governor Stoddart spoke on, Skyler pointed the muzzle directly at the eight-inch-diameter hole cut in the reflective window. The diamond glasscutter and hydrofluoric acid solution had etched a nearly perfect circle. The circular pane of glass, held in the hole by clear tape, would not be withdrawn until just before she fired and replaced right after. It would take the Service an hour or more to find her position after the fatal shot. By then she would be long gone, leaving behind only the clues she intended found.

That was the plan.

But sometimes even the best laid plans go awry.

CHAPTER 2

WHEN KIEGER launched into his speech—a speech Skyler knew would take between twelve and fourteen minutes—she took time to study the countersniper positions once more through her binoculars. Teams were posted on the seven tallest buildings surrounding the plaza: the State Capitol, Judicial Building, Public Library, Art Museum, *Denver Tribune* Tower, Petroleum Building, and Adam's Mark Hotel. Because of their close proximity, the countersniper and spotter on the twenty-story hotel posed the gravest risk.

Taking a knee to make her final scope adjustments, she nestled the heavy-duty Kick-Eze shoulder pad on the stock against her shoulder. She then sighted the soft target's head and upper torso through the scope. The heavy black lines of the duplex reticle converged from all sides of her circular field of view. The thick lines pointed to a thinner crosshair centered on Kieger, who came through so clearly, Skyler could see his lips moving, his auburn forelocks riffling in the breeze.

She felt the tension pick up inside her. Though the professional's professional, she was not so brazen as to be overconfident. This was the biggest assignment of her career, and getting out alive was going to be precarious despite her meticulous planning. She had taken out powerful businessman, government officials, "most wanted" terrorists, and rival snipers—a total of fourteen individuals in Europe, the U.S., Canada, and South America. But never before had she faced such a sizable security detail.

All of Skyler's targets in the past had been men. She hated men—how the hell could she not after what Don Scarpello and Alberto had done to her?—and wanted to kill them all. But she had never harmed a woman or child, accidentally or otherwise. Nor would she ever kill a man in front of his family. Which was why she was relieved that Kieger's wife and three children were not present for this political event. If they had made an unexpected appearance, she would have had to scrub the mission.

Still keeping her eye on the scene below, Skyler took a minute to carefully adjust the angle click elevation and windage dials. Then, with the calm of an experienced diamond cutter, she tweaked the low-profile knob on the side of the scope's turret to make the parallax adjustment. When finished, she had not only corrected for the bullet drop and prevailing wind drift, but had even better resolution of her soft target. Next she turned the power selector ring until the upper sixteen inches of Kieger's body filled the opening in the scope's duplex. With her target perfectly framed, she read off the distance-to-target number on the rear of the power selector.

Eight hundred twelve yards. Nearly one-half mile—in a stiff crosswind no less.

It will be a challenge. But you have risen to many such challenges before. Stay true in your hold.

She reached for the ten-round magazine on the floor. With a firm upward movement, she clicked it into place in front of the trigger. The magazine was packed with .50-caliber Raufoss hi-explosive-incendiary-armor-piercing cartridges; each one was six inches long, green- and silver-tipped, and cost more than one hundred dollars on the black market. A single HEIAP round would not only be an immediate kill with a hit on any portion of the target's head, chest, or torso, but the shrapnel would leave behind a difficult—not to mention misleading—ballistics story.

After chambering the first round and dry firing the rifle with the safety on, she scanned the room to make sure nothing would be left behind except what she wanted found.

Then she went through her mental checklist.

Only one last thing remained.

Skyler took out her rosary and kneeled down to pray. Closing her eyes, she pressed her hands together into a steeple and brought the string of crimson beads to her lips with her fingertips. There was no need to ask forgiveness for what she was about to do; she knew that it was unforgivable, that righteousness was little more than a stepping stone to hypocrisy. Nor did she plead for a keen eye or steady hold, or pray for a clean escape. Instead, she surrendered herself unconditionally before God, in all her imperfection, and gave Him praise. She concluded her supplication by kissing the rosary again and declaring, in a soft voice, "Glory be to the Father."

Now she felt cleansed, purified, but not absolved.

She knew she would never be absolved.

The preparations were now complete: mind, body, and rifle were ready.

It was time to fulfill the contract.

Skyler's heart quickened as she pulled the glass from the window and again brought the stock of the rifle to her shoulder. She locked onto her soft target; his image in the scope was unwavering, crystal clear. She heard the distant cheer of the crowd, the president-elect's baritone voice broadcast over the loudspeakers. The sounds mingled with the noisy traffic on Colfax and Broadway.

Her throat went dry.

Our Father who art in heaven...Once you fire, close the hole quickly. Don't give the countersnipers time to lock on.

Calmly, she moved the rifle a fraction of a millimeter to the right, until the thin crosshairs of the calibrated reticle were lined up directly on Kieger's heart. Inside, she felt a palpable sense of danger. Her job demanded absolute perfection; there were no second chances.

Thy kingdom come...Project the bullet to the target.

Breathing in a controlled rhythm, she tightened her left hand around the buttstock and visualized the lengthy parabola the bullet would take in its travel path to the kill zone.

Give us this day our daily bread...Control your hold.

Her finger curled confidently around the trigger, as it had so many times before. There was no wobble or quiver; her hands were steady as a surgeon's.

And lead us not into temptation...Don't think—just feel.

Holding steady on the target, she willed herself into an almost trance-like state, the sniper's cocoon. With a world-class shooter's discipline, she summoned all her resolve, every ounce of concentration and professionalism she could muster, and channeled the energy into the shot.

The field of fire turned preternaturally calm, noiseless.

Her mind was totally lucid and unencumbered: no anger, no fear, no guilt, no doubt.

There was only the rifle, her soft target, and the invisible arc connecting them.

"But deliver us from evil. Amen," she murmured aloud, concluding her prayer.

And then, gently, she squeezed the trigger.

CHAPTER 3

TO FBI SPECIAL AGENT KENNETH GREGORY PATTON, it was all too sudden, too jarring and unexpected to be real. One second, President-elect William Ambrose Kieger—the enormously popular moderate Republican—held the audience before him in quiet rapture; the next, there was a loud *BOOM* and a puff of smoke and wet pink cloud of blood and tissue flew out his back.

Good Lord! Patton gasped in silent disbelief, unable to process this sudden and unusually grisly sensory input.

Then he saw the president-elect's body twitch once and his arms fly out helplessly, as if he were groping through the darkness.

He saw blood spray over those standing closest to the podium, like crimson paint spattered across an empty white canvas.

He saw the poor, luckless leader lose the unwinnable battle with gravity as his legs buckled like a stringless marionette and he slumped to the wooden platform.

He saw a nearby Secret Service agent go down hard, blood gushing from his torn pant leg.

But despite what his eyes told him, he couldn't believe that what was not supposed to happen was actually happening. The violence seemed too horrifying to be real. The world seemed to move in slow motion, as if he was caught up in a terrible nightmare.

And then the realness of it all came crashing home as he heard an urgent voice slice through the horrible incubus, summoning him back to reality.

"Pathfinder down! Pathfinder down!"

Suddenly, the world around him began to roll forward at ridiculous speed as the plaza turned to bedlam. He saw six Service agents rush to the president-elect, who was sprawled face down, his back opened up to expose a gruesome, spongy mass. He heard a collective shriek of horror and saw people recoiling from the scene in panic, running in every direction, staggering, colliding, the pandemonium spreading like a contagion as it moved through the frenzied crowd.

When the shot was fired, Patton and his five-person FBI team were fifteen feet away from the speakers' platform, next to the press bleachers. They were here in a supporting role to the Service—which was in charge of Kieger's personal protection detail—and their assignment was to control the ingress and egress of pool reporters from the press bleachers. Suddenly, those very reporters they were supposed to control jumped from the bleachers and flooded toward the platform. Patton and his team struggled mightily to hold them back, but the numbers were too many, the collective force too great, and they were, ineluctably, swept up in the tidal wave.

Up on the speakers' platform, the Service had formed a human barricade around Kieger to shield him from further gunfire. Four agents reached down to lift him up, their faces contorted in a collective rictus of desperation.

"Get Pathfinder out of here! Move it!"

Still struggling in vain to control the reporters, Patton jerked out his Saber hand-held radio and tried to contact the Secret Service command post. But all he got was the hiss and crackle of static. Meanwhile, the four Service agents carried Kieger's limp body to the north side of the platform, leaving behind a trail of bloody footprints. In the chaos, Patton was swept up again and pushed forward to within a few feet of Kieger as paramedics came rushing up carrying a stretcher. Still clinging to a shred of hope, he searched for any sign of life as the president-elect was transferred to the stretcher.

But there was nothing—not a goddamned thing.

"Move it! Get him to the ambulance!" a Secret Service agent barked.

The paramedics hoisted the stretcher and were off and running, the Service clearing a chute out in front to the waiting ambulance. The agents were relentless, using both agility and brute force to accomplish their objective. But Patton could already tell that it was all in vain.

Suddenly, his radio squawked to life, a clear urgent voice from the Service command post.

"Bureau One, this is Command!"

He keyed the mike. "Command, I read you!"

"Proceed to Colfax Avenue and post your team in a line from Bannock Street to the east side of the Annex Building! Block the escape of any potential suspects fleeing northward along Bannock. We're getting Pathfinder the hell out of here!"

"I copy. Do you have an isolation on the shot?"

"That's a negative, Bureau One. Get your team moving. Now!"

Patton quickly radioed his team and relayed the instructions. Then he blazed off, fueled by pure animal adrenaline and a sense of patriotic outrage that burned inside like a wildfire.

CHAPTER 4

WHEN SKYLER SAW the bullet strike her target, she knew it was a kill. Everything that followed was like a fast-forwarded Zapruder clip as she replaced the window glass, disassembled her weapon, and made her getaway.

The expertly crafted weapon in her hands was not something to leave behind. It wasn't just a gun—it was the source of her power. In the unreal world of the assassin, she was as powerful as any man, more powerful even, and with her Light Fifty and a few explosive armor-piercing rounds, she was invincible. As proof, she need only look down in the plaza below.

First, she removed the ten-round magazine and extracted the two cross pins on the lower receiver of the rifle, one forward of the magazine, the other adjacent to the butt plate. Next she pulled back the charging handle until the bolt head was withdrawn and cleared away from the barrel extension. Though nervous, she worked quickly and efficiently; the countless hours spent blindfolded breaking down and reassembling the rifle were now paying off. With a few more flicks of her wrist, she detached the upper and lower receivers of the gun, removed the bolt and carrier from the lower receiver, and collapsed the barrel into the upper receiver. She had now disassembled a lethal, 57-inch semiautomatic rifle into five separate components, each of manageable length. She placed the sections of the rifle into her hardcover carrying case and snapped it shut.

She slid the case into a compartment on her custom-designed baby stroller, a critical component of today's masquerade. All other items used for the assignment—the card-key decoder and other electronics devices, hand tools, suction-cup gadget, binoculars, and hydrofluoric acid—were already hidden within another compartment. She checked her watch again as she moved to the door of the office; less than sixty seconds had passed since the fatal shot.

At the door, she took a final glance around the room. Earlier, she had planted evidence to keep the law busy—and perplexed. It was all part of the game. Her eyes passed over the items on the floor first, which lay near her firing position, then the little display on the windowsill. A ghost of a smile appeared at her mouth.

My little parting gifts ought to make things interesting.

Ten seconds later, she was at the service elevator, which she had electronically disabled. Here too she had left behind a little surprise for the authorities. She pushed the stroller inside, reactivated the elevator, hit the button for *Parking*.

As the elevator plummeted to the garage fifty-two floors below, she removed her gloves, stashed them in the stroller, and examined herself in the elevator mirror. She was pleased with what she saw. Her blond wig, dyed eyebrows, blue contact lenses, and white facial powder masked her Mediterranean heritage perfectly and gave her an Aryan appearance. She wore an oversized pink dress that draped past her knees. The garment, though not quite a maternity dress, was larger than normal, like those worn by women in the ensuing weeks of childbirth. Beneath the dress was a synthetic waist pouch that gave her a prominent tummy, lending her a distinctly *mommyish* look, an air of maternal innocence. She appeared pudgy and harmless, cute and wholesome.

The light for the thirtieth floor lit up as the elevator continued its rumbling descent.

Now for the final part of her disguise—the baby. The animatronic infant in the stroller was surprisingly lifelike, with rosy cheeks and a pacifier in its mouth. It was obscured by a hood and covered with pink blankets and a wool baby cap, so that very little of its face was exposed. One would have to peel back the hood and peer inside to see the baby was not real. Skyler reached into the stroller and flipped the control switch on the little anthrobot, which began wiggling gently beneath the blanket and making faint sucking noises. Together, her maternal disguise and fake baby would be the perfect foil. The cops and federal agents swarming the streets below would not suspect a woman pushing a stroller with a baby. They would be looking for a man.

A certain kind of man.

Suddenly, she felt the elevator slowing down.

Looking up, she saw the fourteenth floor light up as the elevator shuddered to a halt. Her heart lurched in her chest. She tried to scramble around the cumbersome stroller to press the *Close Door* button, but was unable to reach it in time. The doors began to part and there was nothing she could do to stop them. Instinctively, her hand latched onto the grip of the Swiss-made SIG-Sauer P228 concealed in her thigh holster.

The door opened all the way.

She stood face to face with a casually dressed man and woman. Two young professionals, who had come in on a Sunday to get some work done, but were now, by a monumental stroke of misfortune, standing before one of the deadliest assassins on the planet.

They were close and the lighting was good, so they would be able to give the police an accurate description, even with her disguise. They were most likely heading outside, where they could point her out or describe her to the authorities within a matter of seconds, thwarting her escape. Though Skyler was reluctant to kill them, failing to do so could pose a serious risk.

And that was unacceptable.

No one knew what she looked like or her true identity, except her control agent, Xavier. Most of her killings over the years were attributed to Diego Gomez, her fictitious male alter ego, and that was the way she had to keep it. She would be breaking a cardinal rule of her profession if she allowed them any chance to later identify her.

You know what you have to do—there's only one option.

The woman smiled refulgently when she saw the baby in the stroller. Skyler knew, by their relaxed expressions, that they were unaware of the chaos in the plaza below.

They started to enter the elevator.

CHAPTER 5

THE NICKEL SLIDE of the noise-suppressed 9mm semiauto glinted murderously in the artificial light as Skyler stood up on her toes, raised the weapon above head height, and pointed it slightly down, so the shot would appear to have been fired by a much taller person.

She dropped the man with a single shot to the forehead.

The woman screamed as her companion fell back into the hallway.

Skyler jammed her foot against the door, keeping the elevator from closing. She knew she had to kill the woman too. But for a brief instant she couldn't bring herself to fire. She had never killed a woman before—her targets were always evil men—and the very thought of killing a fellow female sickened her.

But you can't just let a witness get away!

The woman stood there paralyzed with fear, unable to run or speak.

Skyler's mouth, full and sensual on most occasions, curled into a primal frown. She had to act quickly before the woman screamed for help or started to run. She was an assassin; she could not imperil herself by showing sympathy toward some total stranger, even a kindred female.

Biting her lip, Skyler stood up on her toes, raised the gun high, and squeezed the trigger twice.

The woman collapsed on the carpeted floor, two red stains on her blouse.

Lord, forgive me for what I just did and for what I am about to do.

Locking in the *Emergency Stop* button, she stepped to the man, took aim at his head, and fired once more, execution style, to make certain. Then she repeated the process with the woman.

There, it was done.

She looked at her hands and saw that they were trembling.

A voice called out inside her: *Get a grip, Angela! Don't lose sight of the objective!*

She looked at her watch. This unanticipated interruption had cost her critical seconds. *Damn!*

Feeling a stab of panic, she picked up the spent casings from the hallway and elevator. Then she released the *Stop* button and hit the button for the parking garage.

As the elevator hurtled down again, she cursed herself and wiped the floor buttons clean of her fingerprints. Not only had precious time been wasted, she had been forced to kill two innocent people. Worse by far, one of the victims was a woman. In all her years as an assassin, Skyler had prided herself in the fact that she had never produced collateral damage. She had terminated only those specified in her contract, and had never found herself in a position where she had to kill a bystander. Though she had wounded men standing close to her targets—invariably bodyguards or members of a personal protection detail struck by exploding fragments—none of these men, she had later learned, had died from their wounds.

But now the circle had been broken and she hated herself for what she'd done. Only cowardly terrorists killed woman or children; only zealots, amateurs, and street thugs murdered non-specific targets. Still, she couldn't allow what had happened to affect her judgment. She had fulfilled her assignment, and her sole task now was to escape.

Her rental car was two blocks away, which put her four blocks beyond the current Secret Service checkpoints. Once the Service gained control over the situation, they would undoubtedly expand the radius of the perimeter. She had already calculated that it would take her slightly under five minutes from the time she fired the fatal shot to reach her car. Checking her watch again, she realized that she only had two minutes left to meet her goal, which meant she was a minute behind schedule.

Fortunately, it was a Sunday and the Sixteenth Street Mall was overflowing with people. The feds and cops couldn't stop every person on the street until they had set up a perimeter. With all the confusion, it would be a full fifteen minutes before that could be achieved, since no one would be able to pinpoint the firing position.

The elevator came to a halt; the doors opened. She pushed the stroller into the underground parking structure and headed for the steel door leading to the exit ramp, paying no attention to, but very much aware of, the disabled security cameras above her. Radiant shafts of sunlight slanted through the exit door's panel window.

She picked up her pace.

If she made it to her car in the next two minutes, she would be miles away before anyone had a clue what had happened. She didn't need to run. All she had to do was walk at a steady clip, pretending to be a mother pushing her baby in a stroller. Then she would drive to Colorado Springs, board United Flight 457 direct for Los Angeles, and relax in her first-class throne with a much-needed glass of Cabernet.

That was the plan.

But Skyler knew that sometimes even the best laid plans go awry.

CHAPTER 6

POSTING HIS TEAM in a line from Bannock Street to the east side of the Annex Building, Special Agent Kenneth Patton took position next to a hundred-year-old oak tree and scanned the area for someone who didn't belong. Someone slipping quietly away from the scene. Someone more deliberate and controlled than those around him, yet possessing the chilly air of menace of a professional killer.

Then he thought of John Wilkes Booth, Oswald, Sirhan Sirhan, Hinkley. They didn't look like cold-blooded killers. So if an assassin wasn't trying to sneak away, how could you tell if he—?

His eyes darted down the block to his team members. Did they see anything? All five agents had drawn their standard-issue FBI firearm—a Glock 17 nine-millimeter semiautomatic—and kept them cocked and unlocked, with the noses pointed into the ground, as they too scanned the area. But they didn't appear to see anyone suspicious either.

Beyond, he could see the frenzied crowd pushing through the barricades guarded by the riot police and Secret Service. It reminded him of a 1950's B-horror flick, the way the pandemonium spread inexorably in all directions.

He scanned the rooftop of the City and County Building and the Annex. The Service countersnipers and spotters were gesturing to one another uncertainly and barking into their radios.

Damn, they don't know where the hell the shot came from any more than I do!

He was jarred from his thoughts by the sound of screeching tires. Turning, he saw a pair of Service vans tear down the street, knocking over orange cones and blocking a knot of hysterical people from making a hasty retreat. Further up the street, two canine-squad cops struggled to keep a pack of bomb-sniffing German shepherds under control.

Come on, people, get it together goddamnit! I need an isolation on the shot! Or at least a possible!

He continued to scan the area, but he felt useless, standing on the corner, waiting for somebody suspicious to materialize. It seemed unthinkable that, right here in the plaza, there was a veritable army of law enforcement people, yet no one seemed to have a clue where the shot had come from or what to do.

Precious seconds were ticking away, lost forever.

With no one in his immediate vicinity, he raised his binoculars and looked toward Bannock Street. President-elect Kieger was being transferred from the stretcher to the waiting ambulance. Even from a distance, Patton could see his face was as white as a burial shroud. He shook his head at the sheer craziness of it all. For him, the loss was deeply personal. He believed in William Kieger and what he stood for and had been looking forward to January 20 when the forty-fifth president of the United States was supposed to be sworn into office.

His radio squawked again. "Bureau One, this is Command!"

"Read you, Command. Where do you want my team?"

"Proceed to the high-rises north of the secured area, set up a perimeter at each building, and await further instructions. Service teams will be moving into the downtown area simultaneously."

"I copy. What's our objective?"

"To block all escape routes out of the Sixteenth Street Mall."

"You've got a rough iso on the shot, then?"

"Not yet. We're vectoring in now."

"Do we have a green light for take down?"

"Affirmative. If threatened shoot to kill!"

"Copy that! We're on our way!"

He quickly assembled his team and reissued the instructions, making sure each agent was clear on the assignment and wouldn't set out alone, hot-dogging.

Then they bolted across Colfax to an orchestra of shrieking sirens.

Reaching the sidewalk on Cleveland Street, Patton glanced back at an ambulance, a pair of Service vans, and three police cruisers careening wildly around the corner, like a roller coaster yawing out of control. Seconds later, a hundred feet further down the block, he looked back again. The vehicles had disappeared, the swirling red of their flashing lights but a nightmarish memory, the drone of the sirens receding into the background like a dirge.

His mind reeled with a pair of questions that he knew, if history was any indication, might never be answered.

Who the fuck did this? And why?

CHAPTER 7

AT THE CORNER of Cleveland Street and Sixteenth Street Mall, they flashed their FBI creds to the two cops at the checkpoint. Shoppers were as thick as grasshoppers in the trendy outdoor mall, the vast majority unaware of what had just happened in the plaza three blocks away. Patton halted the team at the barricade and issued instructions in a tone of controlled urgency.

"Heiser, you take the Petroleum Building. Stolz, you got the Adam's Mark." He pointed to the brown hotel with the thin vertical windows. "Rassenfoss, take the Trade Center. Seal the exits until the Service gets there. No one gets in or out. No one!"

"Got it!" Heiser said, and four of the agents were off and running.

"What about me?" asked Special Agent Tom Weiss, nicknamed "Wedge," a big solid kid who had played D-I ice hockey as a right winger at Denver University. He was the handiest with a Glock, but also happened to be the greenest of them all in terms of actual field experience.

"You're coming with me, Wedge," Patton said. "We're going to seal that big mother."

He pointed to the shiny, chrome-blue Union Plaza Building two blocks away. Stretching to the clouds, it dwarfed the surrounding buildings. It seemed a good candidate, but he knew the shooter would have to be one hell of a marksman to pull off a shot from that far away and high up.

Quickly crossing the street, they ran past the United Bank Building, darted through a short walking tunnel, and emerged into bright sunlight spilling onto a paved courtyard. Patton posted Wedge at the front entrance of the building, facing the mall, and ran around to the rear. He pulled out his Glock and checked the doors. They were all locked.

Turning around, he scanned the area. There were fewer people in the downtown streets now that he was off the mall: a father in chinos and a polo shirt walking with his son along the sidewalk; two women with close-cropped hair and nose rings, holding hands as they crossed the street; a homeless man pushing a shopping cart; a group of elderly tourists coming out of the Brown Palace Hotel; and...and a blond woman pushing a stroller up the parking ramp to the Union Plaza Building.

His own words came back to him like an announcement over a PA system. *No one gets in or out.*

NO ONE!

He sprinted down the sidewalk toward the woman with the stroller, passing several picnic tables of fabricated rock on his left and the concrete ramp on his right. The woman was now on the sidewalk, heading north perpendicular to Patton.

He ran toward her carrying his gun.

Before he had a chance to identify himself, she brought the stroller to an abrupt halt and threw up her arms.

"You can take my money, but please don't hurt my baby!" she pleaded, her terrified voice carrying an unmistakable New England accent. She pulled the leather bag from her shoulder and held it up in surrender as she edged protectively in front of the stroller.

"Here, take it—just don't harm my baby!" she repeated.

Patton was taken aback, but quickly realized that she thought he was a mugger, despite his navy blue cap with "FBI" emblazoned in bright gold lettering. His eyes turned down, guiltily, to the pistol in his hand. "I'm sorry—I didn't mean to scare you."

"You mean you're not going to rob me?" she asked incredulously.

He was winded and deeply disturbed by what had just happened to Kieger. Still, he managed a polite half-smile as he slid his piece into his belt clip. "No, ma'am—I'm with the FBI. Can you tell me what you were doing down there?" He pointed down the exit ramp.

"The wheel of my stroller got caught in that crack, and I had to turn it to push it out. The stroller almost got away from me." She pointed to the gaping crack in the concrete a few feet behind her. "What's this all about?"

Patton looked down at the huge crack and wondered if he was being paranoid. *Come on, you really think this woman has anything to do with this?* Looking up, he appraised her more closely, taking in the honey-blonde hair, soft-blue eyes, and full-lipped mouth. He could hear the baby making sucking sounds beneath the hood of the stroller. The woman had obviously given birth only a short time ago, for she was still flabby around the waist beneath her rumpled pink dress. But even with the extra weight, she was uncommonly beautiful.

"There's been a shooting. We're sealing off the area."

"Oh my God, how terrible."

"Have you seen anyone suspicious?"

"No, I'm supposed to meet my husband in a few minutes. We're visiting from Boston." Her face turned fretful. "Do you think it's safe with a...with a *gunman* on the loose?"

Suddenly, his radio crackled again.

"It's me, Agent Weiss! Two guys are about to come out the front

17

door...I can see them through the glass! They're...they're wearing uniforms...maintenance workers or something! What should I do?"

The rookie was clearly agitated. *Shit, this could be it—I'd better get my ass over there.* "Just calm down, Wedge! Stop and hold 'em—I'll be right there!"

"Okay, but—"

"Just hang tight! I'm on my way!" He turned back toward the woman, who looked at him with a combination of dumb puzzlement and fear. He couldn't waste any more time with her; he had to get to the front entrance, and fast.

His voice was now clipped. "You'll be fine, ma'am. Find your husband—I gotta go!"

He dashed off.

Skyler gave a little smile of triumph, continued two blocks away to a parking lot, calmly took apart her stroller, and stuffed it in her rental car with the rest of her belongings.

Then she drove to Colorado Springs.

CHAPTER 8

BENJAMIN BRADFORD LOCKE pulled his Cadillac Seville into the parking lot of the American Patriots headquarters, took his designated spot bearing his gold-embossed nameplate, and quietly turned off the ignition. Stepping from the plush vehicle, he hit the door-lock button and sniffed contentedly at the salubrious late fall air. The ornate spires of St. Mary's Catholic Cathedral loomed majestically to the northwest, like sharply faceted emeralds against the pastel dusk. Beyond the church, Pikes Peak and other rugged granitic massifs stretched toward the heavens, reminding him of one of the major reasons he had moved to Colorado thirty years ago. The mountains tugged at his soul and made him feel closer to God.

He started for the front entrance. Colorado Springs was pleasantly serene on this late Sunday afternoon. Across the street, an elderly woman with a purse was getting into her car, but there was no one else around. Locke waved to her and smiled. She waved back and slid her plump derrière into the driver's seat. He continued on to the front door of American Patriots—or AMP (pronounced A-M-P with each letter sounded out individually like F-B-I)—as the reputable, charitable, not-for-profit Christian organization was known in abbreviated form by its countless loyal members and the national media.

Out of nowhere, he heard the sound of running footsteps. Looking up in startlement, he saw a sudden blur of movement across the street: the elderly woman was under attack. A dusky-faced man with a ragged beard and disheveled street clothes had pried open the driver's side door and was engaged in a tug-of-war with the poor woman over her purse.

"Stop that at once!" yelled Locke.

The thief paused a moment to look at him, appraising the threat from across the wide street. He quickly decided that the distance between them was too great and jerked harder on the purse, struggling to tear it from the surprisingly tenacious woman's arms.

Locke looked around. The street was deserted. It was no use calling out for help—he would have to stop the thief on his own.

Resolute as a guided missile, he dashed across the street to help the woman, who was screaming at the top of her lungs and clinging to her purse as if it held her entire life savings.

"Help! Help me!"

Locke hit the far curb just as the man ripped the purse from her hand. The feisty woman, who had been dragged several feet from her car, tumbled to the asphalt parking lot as the thief jerked himself free from her talon-like clasp and darted down the sidewalk. But Locke had been anticipating the thief's next move and the American Patriots' director and former Crimson Tide defensive end, still spry on his feet at sixty-two, was in position.

It was a classic clothesline tackle. One instant the thief was blazing down the sidewalk like a locomotive, purse in hand and ecstatic at his good fortune; the next he was down on the pavement flat on his back, the purse separated from his hand like a fumbled pigskin.

His head hit the pavement with a sickening thud and he lay totally still.

Locke made sure he was down for the count and no longer posed a threat before helping the woman to her feet, picking up her purse, and handing it back to her.

"Here you go, ma'am. It's all over—you're safe now."

"I can't believe that just happened. Thank you…thank you for coming to my aid."

"It was the least I could do."

He inspected the woman from head to toe to make sure she hadn't been injured then surveyed the thief again lying on the pavement. The bedraggled man—who was probably only thirty but looked a decade older—was still out cold. Locke hoped he hadn't hurt the poor fellow, even if he was a thief.

"I don't think he'll be stealing from anyone again anytime soon," he said to the woman.

"Thanks to you he won't." Her expression abruptly changed. "Oh my God, it's you! You're Benjamin Locke!"

He smiled bashfully. "Yes, ma'am."

"I don't believe this—I was just saved by Benjamin Locke? This is *such* an honor!"

"It was nothing really. I'm just glad I could help."

The woman hugged him. "Bless you, Mr. Locke. Bless your precious heart. You are an inspiration to millions of people!"

Locke felt mildly embarrassed. "Thank you, ma'am."

"I can't wait to tell my friends and family that I was saved by Benjamin Locke!"

"Actually, I'd prefer it if we could keep what just happened between ourselves."

She looked at him with puzzlement. "Keep it to ourselves? But what about that dangerous thug? He robbed me. Why we've got to get him off the streets. He must go to jail for what he's done."

"I understand how you feel, ma'am. But I would prefer it if you would let me handle the matter in my own way."

She eyed him curiously.

"I believe there's a way we can solve this matter that is best for everyone. Here let me help you to your car."

Her momentary confusion gave way to complete trust. "If you say so, Mr. Locke. By the way can I have your autograph? I'm an American Patriots member you know?"

"I didn't know that, but I am glad to hear it." He escorted her to her car and signed his autograph on the cover of an Air Force football game day program she handed him from the front seat.

She clutched it to her chest like an anniversary present. "I'll treasure this for the rest of my life! This has been such an honor!"

"I'm just glad you're all right."

She glanced down at the thief lying still on the sidewalk. "What will happen to him?"

"Don't worry, justice will be served. I promise."

She smiled at him with absolute faith and trust. "Whatever you say, Mr. Locke. I know you'll do the right thing. You are a saint."

"What is your name, ma'am?"

"Why it's Elizabeth Gardner," replied the elderly woman coquettishly.

"Well, Mrs. Gardner, I'm sorry that all this happened."

"Oh no, this has been the greatest day of my life. Just getting the chance to meet you in person means the world to me!"

He couldn't help but feel a little sorry for her. After all, she had just been mugged on the street and here she was fawning over him as if he was Brad Pitt. "That's awfully kind of you to say, Mrs. Gardner. Good day to you."

"No, good day to you, Mr. Locke. And thank you again for everything!"

She smiled ebulliently, as if touched by an angel, and drove off. Locke politely waved goodbye and stepped over to the thief in the tattered clothes, who was just coming to. The man looked up in terror through his tangled thatch of beard and started to back away like a crocodile along the sidewalk.

Locke held up his hands to show he posed no threat. "I am the last person on earth you should be afraid of, son. I want to give you a second chance."

The man licked his cracked lips and stared incomprehensibly at him, as if he didn't believe such kindness was possible in the world, especially for someone like him.

"Are you without a home?"

Squinting warily, the man gave a barely perceptible nod.

"That is not an excuse for what you did. You have sinned against your fellow man here today. But what I want to know is whether you want a genuine shot at redemption?"

Now the thief looked around nervously, as if calculating his chances of escape.

"You can't run away forever. So I'm going to ask you again. Do you want a second chance?"

The dirty vagabond licked his lips nervously.

"It's a simple question. I am offering you a chance to atone for your sin, to live and prosper as a contributing member of society instead of living on the streets and stealing and begging from others to survive. The question is do you truly want a second chance in this life?"

The man pulled nervously at his ratty beard, thinking it over. Locke saw how deeply torn and filled with self-doubt the poor fellow was. But he could not help the man if the man would not meet him halfway.

"I know what it's like to be without hope and to think that no one cares for you in this world. But there are people like me who do care. And God Almighty cares. Do you know who I am?"

The man shook his head.

Good, it's better this way. "I want to offer you a job—a good-paying job." He pointed across the street to the historic, Empire-era, ten-story brick building with the massive pine trees in neat, tidy, carefully-raked planters. "Do you know what that office building is?"

Again, the thief shook his head.

"It belongs to American Patriots. We are a not-for-profit organization dedicated to helping American families. I want you to join our flock and help you get back on your feet. I think you can do it. Do you want to give it a try?"

The man looked across the street at the imposing building. After a moment tears came to his eyes. "I…I'd like a second chance."

"I think you deserve it, my son. And so does the Heavenly Father. He is rooting for you right now just as I am."

The man stroked his beard thoughtfully, the emotion welling up to the surface. "Do you…really…really think I can do it?"

"I know you can. You can do anything you put your mind to. You show up tomorrow at eight a.m. to the third floor—and you will have a second chance. The job will pay twenty dollars an hour and we will train you and assist you with housing. We will help you get back on your feet and bring out the best in yourself."

The thief rose up from the pavement and shook off the dust, a touch of newfound pride on his haggard, bearded face. "I'm going to do it. I'll be there—8 a.m."

"What is your name, my son?"

"Brown...Peter Brown. But my friends call me Pedro."

"Well, Pedro, this job will not solve all your problems. But it will give you a fresh start."

The thief's lips quivered ever so slightly. "That's all any man can ask for," he said with feeling.

CHAPTER 9

"WHATCHA GOT FOR ME, SPECIAL AGENT? Tell me you haven't been playing fiddle while Rome burns to the ground," growled Henry Copernicus Sharp, assistant special agent in charge of the FBI's Denver field office. He stepped away from the silver Lexus he had just navigated down from Steamboat Springs. Now, three hours after the shooting, the pedestrians had cleared out of the plaza, leaving behind only Secret Service and FBI investigators and the police. A stone's throw away at the speakers' platform, crime scene technicians worked methodically behind the yellow tape as the last streaks of sunlight faded over the snow-capped mountains to the west.

Before responding to his boss, Special Agent Kenneth Patton pulled up his collar, not so much to fend off the stiffening breeze as to protect himself from Henry Sharp, whose ability to intimidate was legendary throughout the Rocky Mountain Region's FBI field and resident offices. Patton and the other young agents in the Denver office referred to him as 'Wyatt Earp', behind his back of course, on account of his irritating *I'm-God's-Fucking-Gift-To-Law-Enforcement* and *Everything-Has-To-Be-100%-By-The-Book* personae.

"We've shut down the whole downtown and have a dozen units in the field," responded Patton to his boss's querulous inquiry. "A Service crime scene search team's working the speakers' platform. DPD's handling all the checkpoints. And Joint Bureau, Service, and DPD squads are canvassing witnesses."

"Tell me you have something on our shooter."

"We know where the shot came from."

"Are you going to tell me or do I have to guess?"

He pointed to the towering office building a half mile away. "Fiftieth floor of the Union Plaza Building. We've got an ERT up there right now."

"I take it you got brass?"

"No, no casings. But there's a hole in one of the office windows the size of a soccer ball. The line of sight's clear and the preliminary trajectory and blood spatter analysis point to the shot being fired from up there."

"Who's on the fiftieth floor?"

"The floor is leased by Front Range Investment Advisors."

"So the shooter cut through the window?"

"Used some kind of special cutting tool and glass-dissolving chemicals. We're still searching the building to make sure he's not hiding out somewhere."

"Who are you liaising with from the Secret Service?"

"Agent Taylor, Frederick Taylor. He's the lead investigator attached to the personal protection detail. We'll be talking with him in a minute."

They were stopped by two cops at a checkpoint. Flashing their FBI creds, they walked over to the yellow tape and stared at the speakers' platform. Six Service crime scene investigators labored in silence: a photographer, a computer mapper, two ballistics extraction techs, and, in the grass nearby, two magnetometer sweepers. Patton grimaced at the sight of the heavy bloodstains on the platform. He glanced at Sharp, thinking he would probably be having the same reaction. But all he saw was a look of cold analytical detachment.

"Pick up any suspects?"

"The Service is holding eight men for questioning. Two maintenance workers who were in the building at the time of the shooting—and six others."

"What about the person who works in the office? You talk to him or her?"

"Name's Lee Wadsworth Brock, investment manager. Seems like a regular business guy." He quickly told him about the hair samples and campaign buttons he'd found in the office. Sharp responded with a grunt, then, with no visible change of expression, asked, "What about eyewitnesses?"

"We've tracked down six employees who were inside at the time of the shooting, but they didn't see anything. We're still completing the floor-by-floor search and canvassing witnesses."

Sharp gave a nod and stared off in silence at the technicians. The Montana native looked more like a cowboy than a senior FBI agent. His face was tan and angular, his frame lean and rangy, and he had a full mustache that ran out parallel to his upper lip and was tapered on both ends, like a gunfighter in an old tinny daguerreotype. Yeah, Wyatt Earp all right, only without the Boss of the Plains hat and Colt .45 Peacemaker.

"All right, here's how it's going to work, Special Agent. The attorney general's spoken with both directors. They've decided the Bureau's going to be the lead on the case, with the Secret Service in a supporting role."

"Is Washington calling the shots?"

"No, it happened here and we have the staff to run it, so it'll be handled out of Denver. We'll be getting support from other field offices though as the need arises."

"Who's going to be the case agent?"

There was a moment's hesitation, a narrowing of the eyes. "Will's giving it to you."

He felt a little twitch pass across his face. The message was clear: His boss Wyatt Earp didn't think he should be given the case, but his boss's boss—Will Nicholson, the special agent in charge of the Denver field office—very much did. In fact, the SAC was giving him the opportunity of a lifetime and Patton decided right then and there that he would damn well take advantage of it. Will Nicholson's message too was clear: *Catch the governor's killer, Ken, and the Domestic Terrorism desk is yours!*

In fact, Patton had already applied for the DT supervisor's job. But he was unlikely to land it without having won another big case. He had put away Stump Jurgens, the mosque-burning white supremacist, but that was six months ago. He was also facing stiff competition from more experienced agents at HQ and other field offices. Will Nicholson and one of the Denver office's two assistant special agents in charge were big supporters, which normally would have given him the inside track over his rivals. The problem was, Henry Sharp didn't like him and he was the ASAC whose opinion counted most, since the Domestic Terrorism squad fell under his authority. Plus, as stellar as Patton's performance had been over the years, he had logged only a decade with the agency and didn't have an advanced law degree, as many of those competing against him did.

Unfortunately, the career board that approved promotions would take all these things into account. The negatives might be enough to offset his outstanding record and favorable recommendations. But if he caught the man who had assassinated William Kieger, that would put him over the top. He would be the next supervisor of the DT desk if he brought in the president-elect's killer—dead or alive.

With these thoughts weighing heavily on his mind, he posed a question: "Where is Will?"

"Nepal."

Shit, that's right—the trek. "How'd you track him down so fast?"

"You can thank CNN. Will heard about the assassination only a few minutes after me. He called in from some small town. Hasn't started off on his trek yet."

"Is he going to cut his vacation short?"

"He'll be back on Wednesday or Thursday. It's going to take him a whole day just to get back to Kathmandu. Until his return, I'm in charge, and I'm warning you right now, the heat's gonna be turned up on this one."

"Just tell me how you want it handled, Henry."

It took Sharp five minutes to lay out the assignments. Patton would be the case agent. He would manage the day-to-day operations of the task force, keeping in touch with the lab techs and other specialists and compiling their findings, while working closely with the Secret Service. Because of the case's high-profile, everything he found out was to be reported to two separate levels within the FBI: John Sawyer, the supervisory special agent of the Domestic Terrorism desk; and, until Will Nicholson's return, Sharp himself, who would, in turn, report directly to FBI Director Sidley. However, as the case agent, Patton would have substantial control over the case. The Bureau's approach was to let competent agents do their jobs as they saw fit, allowing them to focus on the investigation while others ran interference with the media, politicians, and watchdog groups.

Sharp looked at his watch. "I've got a press conference in an hour. What else you got?"

"Prelim ballistics. Looks like the assassin was using heavy caliber stuff."

"How heavy?"

"Fifty. That's what Eric Kronebusch, the Service team leader told me." He pointed to a walrus-mustached man bending down to examine the wooden platform.

"Fifty caliber, huh. What is this guy a buffalo hunter?"

"That's not all. The shooter used an explosive cartridge. Military ordnance, not available at your average gun show. Fragmented on impact like a grenade."

"Wasn't taking any fucking chances, was he? Anything else?"

"Just one thing. I talked to two of the Service countersnipers. They think the shot that killed Kieger was one in a thousand."

"Meaning our guy got lucky?"

"No, meaning he's a world-class shooter."

CHAPTER 10

FROM THE PLAZA, they drove to the Union Plaza Building, where they were met by Agent Frederick Taylor of the U.S. Secret Service and three other suits. *Unhappy times,* thought Patton as they exchanged greetings. The Service guys all had the same expression: a combination of intense focus, guilt, tarnished pride, and bitter anger. For some of them, most notably the guys in the personal protection detail, this wasn't just about losing a presidential candidate to a sniper's bullet—it was about having your whole career flushed down the toilet and not being able to do a goddamned thing about it.

The two senior agents, Taylor and Sharp, shook hands. Fred Taylor was mid-fiftyish and fit, with a shock of white hair that deluded one into thinking he was older than he was. Patton knew all about him. He was a legend in the law enforcement biz, having knocked John Hinckley, Jr. to the ground in 1981 in front of the Washington Hilton Hotel. The swift response prevented Hinckley from squeezing off a sixth and, possibly fatal, shot at President Reagan.

When they were finished with the introductions, Taylor escorted them to the security control room in the basement of the building, posting his men outside the door. High-tech surveillance gadgetry was neatly built into the rows of cherry cabinets lining the walls. On one wall, there were eight flat, oversized video panels, and on another were eight more. All but two of the control monitors in the panels showed color images of the interior or exterior of the building.

A bald man wearing a fluorescent green golf sweater and a look of worry stepped forward and introduced himself as the property manager. Next to him stood a tall, cadaverously thin man in a gray suit. The property manager introduced the second man as chief of security for Security Systems, Inc. A third man stood behind the other two, but the property manager didn't bother to introduce him. He wore a light-blue uniform bearing a Security Systems logo.

With the preliminaries completed, Henry Sharp stepped forward in his patented Wyatt Earp pose, looked the chief of security squarely in the eye, and demanded a rundown on the security system. Patton pulled out his iPad to type down notes, acutely aware of the frisson of tension gripping the room.

"It's a state-of-the-art electronic security system. We have sixteen security cameras that feed the control monitors you see here. Two at each main entrance. Four covering the lobby and elevators. Two in the loading/parking garage area. Two on the roof. Three covering the power and maintenance floor. And one for this security area. Everything we have is high-resolution color video."

"What about the individual floors?" asked Sharp, leaning in close and crowding him.

The property manager fielded the question. "Only three lessees have additional security cameras. They're on the twenty-fifth, thirty-eighth, and fifty-fifth floors. One's a software company, the other two are insurance. They have their own internal security that monitors the recordings. Front Range Investment Advisors—that's the company leasing the fiftieth floor—doesn't have any cameras."

Patton pointed to the two blank screens. "Why aren't those two showing anything?"

The security man and the property manager exchanged a look. "Those two cameras are down," said the property manager guiltily.

Patton looked at Sharp, saw his patented frown. "What part of the building do they cover?"

"The loading/garage area," the uniformed security man replied. "They've been down since this morning, around eleven. I called the repair people, but they're still not here yet."

Now he understood why they were so tense, the uniformed guy in particular. "Do you know what's wrong? Is it the cameras or the wiring?"

"All we've been able to determine is that the cameras aren't working. We don't tamper with the hardware—we just call in the repair people whenever there's a problem."

He made a note on his iPad. *Cameras disabled. Shooter or accessory?*

After another uncomfortable silence, Taylor switched directions. "How often do you record over these tapes?" he asked the chief of security.

"Every seventy-two hours. We have continuous recordings since Friday morning."

"So if the assailant entered the building between Friday and today, and left right after the shooting, he should be on film."

"That's correct, with the exception of the footage from the parking garage after eleven a.m."

Sharp looked intently at the property manager, causing him to retreat a half step, and again took over the line of questioning. "What do you have to do to get inside the building?"

"The entrance doors on Seventeenth and Eighteenth are open from seven in the morning until seven at night on weekdays, except holidays.

We have a security guard and information desk staff member in the lobby during business hours. But there's no official check-in point at the two main entrances. Access during non-working hours, weekends, and holidays is by a card-key system."

"What about once you're inside the building? What would you have to do to get up to the Front Range Investment offices on the fiftieth floor?"

"During normal working hours, all you'd have to do is take the elevator to the fiftieth floor and get past the receptionist."

"What about during non-working hours?"

"That would be more complicated, but not impossible. The individual floors can be accessed in three different ways during non-business hours: a card-key, a keypad, and an ordinary key."

Now the security man spoke up. "Front Range Investments has a keypad system. Each employee receives their own six-digit code when they're hired."

Sharp held up a bony hand, signaling that he had heard enough. "We appreciate your cooperation," he said without a hint of sincerity. "But we're going to need more from you. First, the videotapes. Second, a list of all companies in the building and the names of all employees along with their job titles and phone numbers. Third, a list of all employees who entered the building after five p.m. Friday. I'm guessing your card-key system records the code number of all personnel entering the building on weekends?"

"That's correct," the property manager replied.

"The last thing we need is a list of all maintenance, security, and other building support personnel. Again with titles, phone numbers, the works."

Sharp pulled out a pair of business cards, offering one to the property manager and another to the security man. Patton and Taylor followed suit.

"Obviously we need everything by yesterday," said the ASAC.

"We'll get right on it," said the property manager, looking relieved to be finished with Henry Copernicus Sharp.

"Call Agent Patton here when you pull it all together. Got it?"

The nervous property manager started to nod, but was interrupted by a knock on the door.

Patton turned and opened it. Standing there was Agent Weiss.

Jesus, Wedge, you look pale as a ghost.

"We've found something," said Weiss. "It's bad—you need to take a look."

CHAPTER 11

WITH TURBOFAN ENGINES RUMBLING, the 747 streaked across the night sky like a giant falcon. From her first-class seat, Skyler handed her empty wine glass to the steward and peered out the window. Beyond the flickering starboard lights loomed a curtain of blackness sprinkled with stars. Soon she would be back in La-La Land: the world of movie stars and broken dreams, white sandy beaches and traffic jams, endless sunshine and toxic air pollution.

A place of striking contrasts, not unlike Skyler herself.

She had been living in an apartment in Venice Beach for the past three months. But she would be moving on again soon, now that the Kieger contract was complete. Her control agent, Xavier, arranged her "safe house" accommodations, depending on where she wanted to live at any given moment and her contractual obligations. But with her assignment complete it was now time for a little R&R. She was thinking of a vacation to Bora Bora; the Society Islands were supposed to be wonderful this time of year.

Today marked her fifteenth contracted kill. Yet surprisingly, even after all the killing she didn't think of herself as a murderer. She was simply an extension of her gun, a mechanical robot that pulled the trigger. The real murderers were the evil men who hired her. They were the ones who gave the orders; all she did was execute them, and if she didn't, someone else would.

All the same, she regretted killing the woman and her companion at the elevator. Though she had been forced to—there had been no choice considering they could identify her—she still felt anguish over the incident.

Still, it would not be until later tonight, when she was asleep, that the true haunting would begin. When the nightmares came—and they always did—she would quake with shame. With sweat pouring from her body and teeth grinding, she would see the faces of her victims, one after another. They always came through clearly, framed in the perfect circle of her sniperscope with the crosshairs centered on the forehead. When she squeezed the trigger, the smooth, clear faces would explode in a spray of blood and she would gasp for air and leap up in her bed, covered in sweat.

It was strange how she always saw the faces blowing open when it was her custom to shoot for the heart. She thought it was to remind her that the people she killed were actual human beings, tangible and alive. Real people with real faces, real emotions, real lives.

The bad dreams usually came the first evening after a contract and gripped her for two or three nights. It was on those nights that she hated herself for what she did and wished she had never become an assassin. And it was on those nights that she prayed to the Holy Father—not for her own redemption, but for the souls of those she had killed.

CHAPTER 12

THERE WERE two bodies, a man and a woman, slumped against the floor outside the service elevator, their white bloodless faces frozen in expressions of mute horror. Patton could see instantly that they had been shot at close range. Both bore small entry wounds and gaping exit wounds, splattering off to comet tails of dried gray brain matter and blood. Standing at the scene of carnage with him were Sharp, Taylor, Weiss, another FBI agent, and a cop. But out of all of them only the ASAC, his boss Henry Sharp, looked unaffected by the grisly scene.

"This can't be a coincidence," he pronounced. "Got to be the same guy who took out Kieger."

"Do we really know that for sure?" inquired Patton mildly. "Our shooter could have had a spotter, or there may have been another accessory."

"Did I ask your opinion, Special Agent?"

"No, sir. All I'm saying is it might not have been a lone gunman."

Ignoring him, Sharp looked pointedly at Weiss. "Who was first on scene?"

"Me, sir."

"Touch anything?"

"No, sir. I came straight to Agent Patton. Officer Johnson and Agent Williams remained here to keep the area secure." He motioned toward the uniformed cop and FBI agent next to him.

Sharp squinted at them. "You guys touch anything?"

They shook their heads.

"I'll call in a crime scene team," Taylor said, pulling out his cell phone.

"And the ME," Sharp reminded him, referring to the Medical Examiner. He turned back to Patton. "Where are my gloves, Special Agent?"

Feeling like a serf, Patton pulled out two pairs of latex gloves and handed a pair to his boss. After donning their crime scene gloves, they knelt down to take a closer look at the corpses, making sure not to step in any splattered blood or tissue. The blood was a glossy iron-black patina, cracked near the edges. Patton withdrew a fiber-optic penlight and, with Sharp looking on, shined it on the dead man's face.

There were two small entry wounds—one in the forehead, the other between the eyes. Patton carefully turned the man's head sideways to expose the back of the skull. There wasn't much left; a jagged exit wound much larger than the entry borehole, and a semihard lump of brain and tissue. They turned their attention to the young woman. There was a large bloodstain on her cream-colored blouse at her heart. Patton could see two neat bullet holes in the fabric. The woman also had a small entry wound in the forehead and a large, ragged exit hole on the back of her cranium.

Hollow point? Heavy caliber for sure.

"I don't see any skin abrasions or other signs of a struggle," said Sharp. "Looks like they came upon our perp by surprise as he was making his escape."

"We should take a look at the elevator. That will confirm it." Patton hit the elevator button. A half minute later the doors opened up. They stepped carefully inside and locked in the *Door Open* button. There was a cryptic blood spatter on the left side of the elevator door as one faced out. It looked like his boss was right: the victims had come upon the shooter by surprise and he had gunned them down from inside the elevator.

"No brass," Sharp mumbled after looking around.

Taylor walked up and stopped outside the elevator. "Maybe our guy wasn't using a semiauto."

"Either that or he picked up the spent shells after he made the kills," Patton said, thinking this a more likely alternative. Empty shell casings, if recovered, could be matched to a murder weapon, based on the firing pin and ejector markings on the casing.

"No, he wouldn't have had time," said Sharp emphatically.

Patton disagreed, but didn't bother to challenge him. He knew that Wyatt Earp didn't like to be challenged.

They took a minute to chart out a rough trajectory path of the shots. The aerial spray patterns, though partially obscured by the bodies and heavier tissue, angled away from the elevator, suggesting both victims had faced the assailant just outside the elevator when they were shot. There were no drag marks across the marble floor; the bloodstains and spray patterns implied the deceased had been shot where they had fallen. Which made perfect sense, thought Patton, if they had surprised the killer at the elevator.

But why, he wondered, would the shooter have let the elevator stop and the doors open in the first place? Was he distracted or preoccupied in some way? Why didn't he just hit the *Door Close* button and not let them in? After all, he had been in a huge hurry to escape. It was odd. But more importantly, it was just the kind of unforeseen circumstance and unanticipated evidence trail that might actually help them nail the perp.

Five minutes later, the ERT arrived and quickly secured the area with yellow crime scene tape. When the team began setting up, Patton took Sharp and Taylor to where the nightmare had begun.

CHAPTER 13

THEY STARED OUT the fiftieth floor window in silence. The Secret Service crime scene unit was busy down in the plaza. Powerful lamps illuminated the half dozen figures laboring inside the yellow tape. From a half mile away and fifty floors up, they looked like fastidious ants.

While they stood gazing down at the platform, five ERT technicians quietly went about their business in other parts of the room. They had finished the photography, mapping, and sampling, and were now performing the final evidence vacuum sweep and preparing for fingerprinting. The e-vac was a small, powerful vacuum cleaner equipped with a special filter for retaining fibers, hairs, and other miniscule bits of evidence. Patton turned to watch a technician pull out a filter and place it in a labeled evidence bag. Meanwhile, another technician cleaned the vacuum, inserted a new filter, and began vacuuming a grid area on the other side of the room.

Over by the desk, an ident technician in a navy-blue FBI cap was rummaging through a fingerprinting kit, making sure he had the necessary supplies. Next to him, a woman was busy calibrating a compact, laser-fingerprint scanning device. The fingerprinting was the last thing done at the crime scene. Whatever usables could be obtained would be captured digitally, transmitted electronically to the lab, and checked against the digital records in the FBI's Integrated Automated Fingerprint Identification System.

All of this activity was being supervised by the team leader, a rotund older man with a nimbus of silvery auburn hair. Everyone in the Denver field office knew Timothy "Red" Romer; he had logged forty-five plus years with the Bureau and had even met J. Edgar Hoover himself on several occasions.

Sharp turned away from the window and pulled Red aside. "What can you tell us so far?" he asked as Patton and Taylor came walking up. Again, Patton couldn't help but feel a whiff of tension in the air in the presence of the assistant special agent in charge.

"I shouldn't tell you a durn thing 'til we're finished, Henry," the old curmudgeon fired back at Sharp, drawing a barely concealed smile from both Patton and Taylor. "But seeing as you're my boss, with the indisputable right to fire my ass, I suppose I can give you a little preview."

Grinning mischievously, the red-haired veteran led them to the corner of the room where three evidence kits lay on the floor, pulled out a small glass vial, and held it up for all to see.

"Agent Patton found these hair samples on the floor near the window. Definitely human head hair—by the looks of 'em blond Caucasian."

"How do we know they don't belong to the guy who works in this office?" asked Sharp.

"Because we've already checked and Lee Brock's hair is black," responded Patton.

"Okay so we can eliminate Brock." The ASAC turned back toward Red. "I've got a press conference in twenty minutes. What else have you got?"

"It's not so much what we've got as what we're gonna get. Once we complete a microscopic exam of the hair samples, the lab folks will be able to tell us the sex, what part of the body the hair is from, and race. Then hopefully after that we'll complete the DNA fingerprinting."

"Why hopefully?"

"To get reliable DNA results we need a complete hair bulb, the actual root of the hair, and the sample has to be fresh. If the hair's too dried out or starting to decay, it's useless."

"How do these samples look?" asked Taylor.

"The hair strands found by Agent Patton look to be complete strands and also fairly fresh so I think we're in luck."

That wasn't good enough for Sharp. "We've got to have DNA. You're going to have to find a way to work your magic, Red. What else you got?"

"Let's take a look at the glass." He returned the vial to the box and pulled out a small, circular plate of glass with duct tape, enclosed in a labeled plastic bag. "This is the portion of the window that our shooter removed." He pulled the glass out of the bag, holding it carefully by the duct tape. "Quarter-inch thick, reflective coating. Our guy used a special glass-cutting tool and some kind of acid bath to cut the hole. You can see the fluid here."

"Get any usables?"

"We're holding off the fingerprinting until we've swabbed the glass at the lab."

"Well, have you seen a cut like this before?"

"Not like this. This guy's a pro all the way."

"Why do you think he chose this room to shoot from?"

"On account of the clear line of sight, I reckon."

"No, there's got to be something else," said Taylor. "The drop is crazy."

"That's a fact," agreed Red. "But that in itself tells us a lot."

"What do you mean?" asked Patton, intrigued by the wily old veteran and the way he stood up to Sharp instead of being scared shitless like every other supplicant in the Denver field office.

"It tells us we're dealing with a world-class shooter. Think about it. Whoever this guy is, he's so goddamned good he can shoot through an eight-inch hole fifty stories up and a half mile out, in a stiff crosswind, and hit something no bigger than a watermelon. Our boy's got talent—scary talent. I've never seen or heard of anything like it before in all my life."

At this, Sharp's mouth curled into something resembling a smile. Now that was unusual: Patton couldn't remember seeing the ASAC actually smile before. "He may have talent," allowed Sharp, "but we're still going to nail this bastard. We're going to take him down and put him away for the rest of his natural life."

"I'll drink to that when it actually happens, cowboy," pronounced Red. "Here, let's take a look at this over here."

He set down the glass and led them to the window sill where four campaign buttons had apparently been placed. Off to the left, a green button for Mason Schumacher and the Green Party. To the right of this, two red, white, and blue campaign buttons: one for current Democratic President Gregory Osborne, the other for Senator Fowler, who was now the Republican president-elect. And six inches further to the right, clearly separate from the rest, a large red button with blue lettering that read AMERICAN PATRIOTS.

"Agent Patton pointed these babies out to me when I first got here. I agree with him that they were planted. You can see the dust has been disturbed recently. My ident guy will go over this area carefully as soon as you're done looking. Agent Patton here wanted me to wait until you'd seen it."

"Lee Brock told me the buttons weren't there when he left work on Friday. He says he has no idea how they could have gotten there. So I'm thinking they were planted by the shooter, or an accomplice. Either to make some kind of political statement or to mislead us."

Sharp didn't respond. He studied the buttons for several seconds, pulling at the tips of his cowboy mustache with his fingers in the way Patton always found irritating. "We need to find out which one it is, and I mean pronto, or the director's going to have all of our asses."

"I'll put Hamilton on it," said Patton, referring to Dr. Thomas Hamilton, the field office's criminal profiler.

"That's the best idea I've heard from you yet, Special Agent," snorted Sharp. "Apparently you're not as dumb as you look."

"Coming from Henry, kid, you should take that as compliment," said Red with a grin. "But you fellas don't need a durned shrink to tell you what's going on here." He pointed to the button furthest to the right and looked Patton in the eye. "American Patriots. If I were you, young buck, that there's the clue I would start with."

"Why's that?"

"Must be a reason our shooter put that one six inches from the others. It's like it's supposed to stand out."

Sharp frowned. "Let me get this straight. Are you saying this is some sort of calling card?"

"Might could be."

"But it doesn't fit," argued Taylor. "Why would a right-wing Christian group want to assassinate a fellow conservative? It doesn't make any sense."

"Does this day make any durned sense?" asked Timothy "Red" Romer rhetorically.

Not at all, agreed Patton, studying the American Patriots button closely. *But you, Red, are right about one thing: AMP is definitely the place to start.*

CHAPTER 14

WHEN SKYLER OPENED the door to her third-floor apartment, the alarm chirped softly until she input a string of numbers and disarmed the system. She flipped on the light switch, locked the door behind her, and conducted a thorough room-by-room search to verify that there had been no intrusion during her absence. Even after over a decade in the game, her vigilance never waned.

Tastefully furnished but not luxurious, the apartment told an enigmatic story about its occupant. There were no personal documents, no bills or letters of any kind. There was no phone; the only one Skyler used was her secure coded mobile. There was not a single photograph of her or anyone she knew in the apartment, including family members. To an investigator or nosy landlord, her past would appear as an empty canvas.

The furniture was antique, dominated by classical styles no more feminine than masculine. Though she lived here alone, both male and female clothing hung in the closets, and the toiletry articles were for both sexes. In the built-in bookcases, modern male action-adventure novels vied for space with feminist manifestos, woman's literary fiction, and poetry. All of the books were in English, though Skyler's first language was Italian and she was as fluent in Spanish and French as English.

The walls were covered with outstanding enlarged photographs of California's diverse landscape: foamy waves crashing at Big Sur; the glacier-carved sculptures of Yosemite; the starkly splendid desert foliage of Joshua Tree; a street car topping a hill in San Francisco; a squadron of sea gulls streaking across the Pacific. The works showed a skilled artist, meticulous yet sensual; but they said nothing about whether the person behind the lens was male or female, white or colored, American or foreign. Skyler's photographs fetched generous prices from discrete dealers in the U.S. and Europe, but she sold her work only rarely, under a pseudonym.

After carrying her bags into the bedroom, she walked into her office and logged onto her computer using three different passwords in sequence. The computer was equipped with the latest antiviral, antitampering, and encryption technologies, courtesy of her control agent, Xavier. She went into her email and clicked on a message from the Frenchman, as always carefully encrypted. She pulled up a jumbled assortment of letters and symbols that looked like hieroglyphics. With a few clicks of her mouse and two additional passwords, the text was unscrambled in English.

CONGRATULATIONS. MARK
SUCCESSFULLY RETIRED AND CONTRACT FULFILLED.
EXPECT TRANSFER OF BALANCE 11/11.
WILL ADVANCE TO ACCT., LESS EXPENSES,
BEFORE CLOSING.
CIAO.

Smiling, she deleted the file and logged off the computer. Her thoughts turned to the shower she had been dreaming about the past hour. Killing always made her feel unclean, and she wanted to wash away the filth. She walked into the bathroom and took off her clothes. Before boarding her flight in Colorado Springs, she had removed her blue contact lenses and exchanged her blonde wig, pink dress, and inflatable tummy pouch for the attire of a power businesswoman.

Now standing before the mirror was an olive-skinned woman with dark amber eyes and hair of like color falling to gently sloping shoulders. A woman with a slender nose, high cheekbones, subtle cleft chin, flat stomach, and supple upturned breasts. A woman with muscular arms and legs, but without the cursed bulk and rigidity of the overzealous weightlifter. A woman who could pass for not just an Italian or ethnic American, but a South American, Mexican, Spaniard, Greek, or even someone of Arabic persuasion to the casual eye. Of all her features, only the nose had been surgically altered. The classical Roman profile had been reduced to conceal her Italian heritage and lend her a more generic look.

Skyler turned on the shower, taking a moment to adjust the knobs before stepping in and closing the cloudy glass door behind her. Once wet, she took a bar of soap and lathered her body, feeling a tingling sensation as she rubbed her breasts. Her nipples grew hard and she began to feel the hot hand of desire take hold of her body. She probed her lower extremities, working her fingers inside, and felt a burning fire in her loins. Consumed with her assignment the past few weeks, she hadn't had time to think about sex; but now it was very much on her mind, as she stroked herself, gently touching her clitoris and quietly moaning.

How long has it been? Two months at least. Too damned long.

She continued to fondle herself, letting the water shoot onto her hard breasts as she probed with her fingers. She was aroused, but masturbation was never totally satisfying. She wanted a man badly and, despite the inherent risks after having just fulfilled a contract, she simply had to have one tonight. She decided to handle the matter in the usual way.

She would pick a dark, handsome man and bring him back to her apartment, handcuff him to the bed, and fuck his brains out until she was satisfied. Then she would toss him out into the night, like a piece of broken furniture, and see the wounded look on his face as he realized he'd been taken like a whore. At that point, she would feel triumph.

Deep inside, she detested herself for her dependence on men; unfortunately, they were the only ones who could satisfy her. Her hatred of the opposite sex was so strong that she had several times had oral sex with women, but they could never fulfill her needs. She had to have hate in the equation, and she could never bring herself to hate any woman enough to achieve orgasm. The power and control was what got her off—the sexual conquest and retribution, relived again and again, for what Don Scarpello and Alberto had done to her.

It was the same reason she was a contract assassin.

CHAPTER 15

SHE HIT THE STREET dressed to kill. A black Calvin Klein slip dress clung to every curve. Black fishnets climbed up her tall legs. Her feet brandished a pair of sleek black heels that would have perhaps looked a tad sleazy on most women, but not her. A double strand of exquisite Indonesian pearls dangled from her throat. Her silky black hair was slightly damp and smelled of avocado and lemon. All in all she looked ravishing—in a dangerous way.

She walked down to Ocean Front Walk, hung a right, and was greeted by a soft, cool zephyr that caressed her face and tasted of salt. The crescent moon shone on the rippled Pacific. Sliding past Muscle Beach, she heard soft voices in the shadows and the familiar rumble of waves rolling onto the sand.

Venice Beach, California. The perfect hiding place for an assassin. In Skyler's line of work, one had to have reconstructive facial surgery on a regular basis, hide out well beyond the reach of the law, or find a way to be anonymous. Skyler chose the latter. In Venice Beach, she had no problem blending in. The place was like an open-air carnival, with so many different kinds of people that keeping track of anyone was a formidable task. There were artists, hustlers, anarchists, businesspeople, surfers, panhandlers, fitness freaks, street-theater performers, druggies, and others who defied definition. To many, Venice Beach was simply a giant, happy insane asylum along Southern California's sandy coastline where life was resplendently askew. It reminded Skyler of Paris's West Bank and the Ponte Vecchio of her native Florence.

Two policemen in dark-blue shorts approached her as she neared Windward Avenue. Sensing danger, she shifted her purse containing her SIG-Sauer from her left shoulder to her right. But the cops were busy talking and, despite her revealing attire, showed little interest in her.

She stopped on the beach pavilion in front of the old St. Marks Hotel and stared up at a large, illuminated, graffiti-disfigured mural facing the ocean. Entitled *The Rebirth of Venus* in tribute to Botticelli's original in Florence, the painting showed an angelic-faced woman in skimpy shorts, a shoestring top, and roller skates racing out of a seashell. Skyler broke into a smile. She had gazed up at the mural hundreds of times before, but it still brought her joy. It reminded her of growing up in *Firenze* as a little girl—

before her world had been turned upside down.

She checked out a couple of bars before settling on The Pumphouse, a Prohibition-era speakeasy cluttered with 1920's pictures and memorabilia. A four-piece band kicked out inspired jazz-blues fusion in the corner. There was a surprisingly large crowd for a Sunday, only a couple of open tables. She received wolfish stares from a pack of men at the bar, but fortunately she saw no familiar faces, except the bartender. Skyler ordered a Chardonnay from him and searched the room for the man who would satisfy her needs for the evening.

It took her less than a minute to find him.

He sat alone a few tables from the small stage, nursing a glass of white wine, which Skyler took as a good sign for it suggested sophistication. He looked to be in his late-thirties and was dark and winsome, like Alberto, except he appeared less aggressive, sensitive even, by the thoughtful way he studied the saxophone player and guitarist during their solos. By the way he carried himself, she could tell he was not law enforcement, which was critical for tonight's enterprise. He had full crescent lips, jet-black hair combed back, and a bronze Mediterranean complexion. The nose was long and narrow, and his chestnut-brown eyes seemed somehow both penetrating and soft. He wore a white cotton shirt, tan chinos, and a light dinner jacket, which gave him the appearance of a handsome college professor, the kind that stirred the hearts of young coeds.

She waited until the song was finished before approaching him. When she asked if she could sit down, he smiled politely but nervously, stood up and helped her to her seat. Skyler was both surprised and pleased by this gesture; most men were so self-absorbed these days that seldom did they remember basic social graces. She reminded herself that she wasn't here for a relationship; she just wanted a man to fuck, someone with enough talent to satiate her desire.

His name was Anthony Carmeli and he said he was a "not-very-good" Hollywood producer, though Skyler wasn't sure she believed him. She offered no information about herself except her fake name, always managing to deftly change the subject when necessary as she had learned to do over the years. They listened to the music and talked for half an hour, Skyler feigning interest. When she invited him to her apartment, he looked surprised, embarrassed even, but he accepted. They left the bar quickly. Skyler scanned the faces on the way out and saw no special interest from the patrons.

She led him down the boardwalk, well lit from the glow of the lights. Palm trees rustled in the sea breeze and wind chimes jingled from one of the verandas, mingling with the gentle roar of the waves. The sounds were peaceful and rhythmic; for a fleeting moment, Skyler felt something resembling romance in her sheltered heart, walking with this handsome man who seemed pleasant enough.

But then she reminded herself, again, that what she was about to do was only for sexual gratification. There was no real romance—and never would be for her. Since Don Scarpello and Alberto she hated men—the whole damned lot of them. There was no room left in her heart for love.

When they reached her apartment, she considered opening a bottle of Firestone Chardonnay, but decided against it, not wanting to waste any more time than was necessary to achieve her objective.

"I believe I'll have you right now, Anthony Carmeli."

He looked uncertain, so she pressed her body close to his and slid her tongue into his mouth. Then she took his hand and led him to the bedroom. She made him undress first then slapped a pair of handcuffs on his wrists and shackled him to the bed. Though surprised at first, his look turned to one of silent amusement, which was different than the others. Usually they got all excited, like salacious schoolboys, when she cuffed them to the bed. She quietly undressed as he lay there submissively, his penis growing large at the sight of her exquisite, perfectly lubricious body. She could tell he had no idea that she was totally in control, that any satisfaction he received was secondary to her own.

"You're not going to hurt me are you?" he posed half-jokingly as she pulled off her lacy black panties and tossed them on the chair.

"Yes, I am going to hurt you," she said, repeating Don Scarpello's words from two decades earlier. "But you will like it."

CHAPTER 16

LIKE MOST NOT-FOR-PROFIT ORGANIZATIONS, the American Patriots headquarters in downtown Colorado Springs contained no electrified fences, guard dogs, motion detectors, or armed security personnel. What the conference room on the tenth floor did possess, however, were electronic surveillance counter devices common in South American drug cartels, well-funded terrorist organizations, and legitimate government spy shops around the world.

The steel walls were more than six inches thick, meticulously soundproofed, and contained copper and zinc coatings to guard against sophisticated directional microphones. As an added precautionary measure, hidden speakers were mounted in the walls and at the windows to produce background electronic chaff in the ten- to twenty-decibel range. This so-called "white noise" effectively filtered out the sound of voices and rendered even the most sophisticated eavesdropping gadgetry useless. The phone was equipped with a pre-programmed controller that automatically swept the line for wiretaps. Embedded in the ceiling was a similar device that scanned for eavesdropping devices in the room twice daily. And to top it all off, the room's secure phone, supercomputer, and audiovisual feed for teleconferencing were equipped with next generation anti-tampering protections and high- and low-frequency modulators that electronically distorted voices, rendering them unrecognizable.

In the conference room on the tenth floor, staring straight into a teleconference camera carefully trained on him, the legendary Benjamin Bradford Locke made his concluding remarks. The high-definition screen on the wall projected not only his image but the images of nine other men, transmitted from nine different remote locations. The teleconference attendees on the other end had followed security protocols every bit as rigorous as those followed by the illustrious Locke himself. The cloak-and-dagger precautions were not simply to avoid the inconvenience of public scrutiny, for what these important men—and others around the country just like them—required was absolute secrecy. After all, they were a clandestine society.

They called themselves simply *the Coalition.*

Two minutes later a chorus of cheers echoed through the room and the teleconference was brought to an inspired, resounding conclusion. As his assistant turned off the video camera, Locke stepped to the window. From his vantage point on the tenth floor of American Patriots headquarters, he had a sweeping view of downtown Colorado Springs and the towering Rocky Mountains beyond. The brisk autumn wind howled and rattled the double-paned reflective window. With all the shaking and scratching, Locke couldn't help but feel an undercurrent of tension and vulnerability at the hand of Mother Nature, despite the positive outcome of the teleconference.

He stood at the window in ponderous silence, quietly inhaling and exhaling. He looked like a larger-than-life statue. By any standard, the former Vietnam intelligence operative, descended from ancient Norsemen, was no ordinary man. His prominent cheekbones, jutting jaw, robust shoulders—all appeared to have been chiseled from Pikes Peak granite. The artificial light in the room brought out the deep stormy-gray of his eyes, which, when combined with his thick owlish brows, gave him a quiet, focused intensity. But his sublime gift was his titanic size: it gave him an aura of almost mythical power, as if he had been unleashed upon the world from the gates of Valhalla itself.

He sighed at the sight of the city he had come to love like a warm hearth in wintertime. After a moment, his thoughts turned to his speech. Thinking about his Christian comrades-in-arms, he felt a powerful sense of brotherhood. He had some issues with a couple of his colleagues— actually, one colleague in particular—but at this epic moment in history that was irrelevant. Today's success had brought them together as one—as a unified team with a singular purpose—and that was what was most important.

But would it be enough? Could they actually pull off the greatest coup in the history of the nation? Was American hegemony truly a thing of the past or were the country's brightest days ahead of her? Would the grand republic continue to be a second-rate power to the Chinese, or could the Coalition truly succeed in restoring her to her former glory in a single bold stroke? There were also still many loose ends. Would he and his sanctified brotherhood succeed in tying them all up to ensure that their ultimate goal would be met?

Turning away from the window, he looked questioningly at Gregory Powers. Perhaps his young assistant had some answers. In any case it was time for a postmortem of the teleconference.

"Your thoughts, Gregory, on Phase Two Main Strike?"

The young man cleared his throat nervously. "Are you worried about Ares, Mr. Chairman?"

"Should I be?"

"I don't think so, sir. You heard Mr. Truscott. The virus will be released 'in the wild' and has been programmed for maximum dispersal. Team Bravo will infiltrate the subject's apartment at 0800 and Ares will be released from his terminal."

Locke steepled his long, bony fingers on the conference table. "That's not what concerns me, Gregory. What I am concerned about is whether the virus will produce the desired result. As we all know, the key to the whole operation is not to implicate President Osborne in too heavy-handed a way. The goal is to establish a thread, a connection. If we can do that, then everything else will fall into place."

"I think everything's going to fall neatly into place, sir. Your plan is brilliant."

"It is not my plan, Gregory. It is *our* plan for we all had a hand in its formulation and execution."

"Of course, sir. My apologies."

Locke rewarded his cyber-savvy strategic services director with a little nod of approval and paused a moment to examine him in the artificial light. The face before him was young, inexperienced, and anxious, yes, but also determined and focused—making Gregory Powers look mature beyond his years.

"What about the virus itself?" asked Locke, brushing away a fleck of dust from his well-tailored Brooks Brothers suit.

Again, Powers nervously cleared the phlegm from his throat. "Once the virus is released, it can't be stopped by conventional antiviral protection software. Within minutes, it will have spread to hundreds of thousands of PCs via email. By the end of the day, we expect more than twenty million systems to be infected."

"I just wish we were more certain the FBI won't be able to track Ares back to us."

"The virus will be transmitted from the subject's own computer. His name will be cryptically embedded in the source code and his unique programming signature will be all over the virus. There will be no viable suspect except him."

The lad knows his stuff; he is undoubtedly one of my best hires in recent years. But why is he so nervous? Is it me or does he have misgivings about the operation?

"How long, Gregory, will it take for the feds to track down the source of Ares?"

"Colonel Heston said it would take three to four days."

Locke looked at him intently. "I know what the colonel said. I'm more interested in what you think, Gregory."

"Again my apologies, sir. I believe three days tops, which still means that by the time the feds track the source down, the subject will have been eliminated."

The Apostle, thought Locke, picturing the iron-hard face of the Coalition's top contract assassin. A short-range specialist who was always on call and able to take the field at a moment's notice. Though no less vital to the ambitions of the Coalition, the Apostle was a different animal altogether than the internationally renowned yet mysterious long-range sniper they had hired to assassinate President-elect Kieger, the Spanish contractor Diego Gomez.

"Forgive me, Mr. Chairman, but I do have one question."

"Yes, Gregory."

"Well, sir…how do we know that *she'll* do what we want?"

"Kieger's replacement, the vice-president-elect?"

"Fowler's now the president-elect, sir. She's already been sworn in."

"Yes, yes, hard to believe, isn't it? And come January 20, she will be the leader of the free world and commander in chief. The first female president in the history of our great nation—this is truly a historic moment."

"It most certainly is. But what I was driving at, sir, is what guarantee do we have that she'll come through as expected?"

Locke could tell that his scrupulous understudy had given this some serious thought. "Come now, Gregory. We are not talking about some unknown quantity here. We personally groomed this woman during the primary. She is *exactly* what we want in every respect."

"Yes, sir, but what about the money?"

"Consider it a twenty-million-dollar insurance policy going forward."

"Forgive me, Mr. Chairman, but doesn't that show a lack of faith? I mean, that's thirty million dollars total including the ten we put in her coffers during the primary. It seems like a lot of money for someone who should be 'in the bag' so to speak."

"It is a lot. But, in the end, it's the only way to guarantee the senator's—excuse me, the president-elect's—commitment to *our* platform. Politicians, Gregory, have a nasty habit of getting amnesia when they take office. The only way to secure their loyalty is money—and lots of it. That Katherine Fowler is the ideal person for the job has never been in dispute. But that doesn't mean she won't need additional motivation—or a little reminding from time to time. Her stands on the issues were clear during the primary and the general election, but how will she fare once she takes office and the special interest groups sink their teeth into her? How about a few years from now when she starts thinking seriously about her place in history, her memoirs? We can't afford to have our handpicked candidate go soft on us now can we? We need to give her another sizable contribution, one that will secure her loyalty for years to come.

"Trust me, Gregory. A contribution of thirty million dollars will buy us considerably more than mere access. And let's not forget, we still have Mr. Frautschi." He was referring to Peter Frautschi, Fowler's campaign manager during the primary and her closest advisor. "He'll keep us abreast of matters and control her for us if and when the time comes. Look at what he's done for us already. Tomorrow we have a meeting scheduled with the president-elect. Think about it, Gregory. William Kieger—God bless his poor departed soul—hasn't even been buried yet and already we have the ear of our next president."

Powers slowly nodded. *Another lesson learned,* thought Locke.

"You truly are brilliant, sir. Everything's proceeding according to plan."

Locke rewarded him with another approving, paternal smile. The young man returned the smile through perfectly stacked teeth the color of ivory. Locke was amazed at how much he looked like a young Ralph Reed.

Suddenly, the large video-projection screen flickered to life and the images of four members of the Coalition's Executive Committee reappeared in four separate computer windows.

Good heavens, what do they want now? wondered Locke.

CHAPTER 17

UP ON THE SCREEN, there was Senator Jackson Beauregard Dubois, R-Louisiana, white-haired, craggy-faced, stringy as an old-time sharecropper, chairman of the Senate Judiciary Committee, which made him one of the most powerful—and feared—men in Washington. There was Joseph Truscott, former CIA deputy director of operations and current consultant to a host of security firms, his face harshly angled, eyes hollow and opaque. Locke called him *Skull Eyes*—though he didn't dare say the name to his face—and considered him the one Executive Committee member of the secret organization that was a potential threat to his authority. The two other faces up on the screen were Colonel Caleb S. Heston U.S.A. (Ret.), currently a highly paid consultant to a large defense contractor based in Colorado Springs; and media and tobacco magnate A.W. Windholz, president of United Broadcasting, which owned two-hundred radio stations, nine major newspapers, and three highly profitable cable channels and was the largest Christian radio broadcaster in the country.

Powers punched at the computer keyboard in front of him. The video camera in the room came to life and zoomed in on Locke, transmitting his commanding, leviathan image back to the four men at each of their remote locations.

"Was there something else, gentlemen?" inquired Locke mildly.

It was Senator Dubois that responded. "It's about Gomez, Mr. Chairman."

"Very well, proceed."

"Well, Mr. Chairman, we all agree the asset has handled the Kieger business with the utmost skill. We wondered if perhaps we should consider bringing him on board full time."

"Are you suggesting he join our little…organization?"

"I reckon so, Mr. Chairman."

"If I may, Mr. Chairman," said Colonel Heston.

"Proceed, Colonel."

"Well, we've been assured the asset is one of the best assassins in the world. Based on today, I've seen nothing to dispute that. It might be in our best interest to take someone of his caliber into our fold, so to speak."

"Some of our wet operatives are just plain sloppy, Mr. Chairman," Dubois quickly added. "Not the Apostle, of course—he knows how to buck a bull off a bridge—but the others. They leave MOs behind so the police will recognize their personal signature. Frankly, I'm concerned about their professionalism—or lack thereof. Is it possible Mr. Gomez would be interested in working for us on a more full-time basis? Like our friend the Apostle?"

"Your thoughts, Mr. Truscott?" asked Locke, looking up at the stoic image of the former intelligence director, his main rival to the Coalition chairmanship. Skull Eyes would be the one to know. He had made the arrangements for the assassination, having done so through Gomez's control agent, Charles Xavier, former ops director of the French intelligence service. Xavier, once a great foe of the ex-spook, was now an unlikely ally.

"I don't think Gomez would be interested," Truscott said after some deliberation. "This man is one of the world's best assassins precisely because no one knows what he looks like. He only takes on enough work to meet his needs, and it is high-end work at that."

It was true, Locke reflected, as he recalled the sparse details in the dossier put together by Skull Eyes. No one except Xavier knew who the protean Gomez was or what he looked like, and the control agent guarded the man's identity zealously to protect his most valuable commodity. Gomez was in various law enforcement databases, but all the photos and artist's sketches were of marginal quality and different from one another. He might as well have been a ghost. He supposedly only took on no more than one contract a year, and they were always big time marks for which he was amply compensated. He only worked in Europe, the U.S., Canada, and South America where he could blend in. He never came under the watchful eye of the Mossad or other Middle Eastern, Russian, or Asian intelligence services that might try and take him out. And he supposedly had no set MO.

"Pros like Gomez," Truscott said, "aren't going to take on small-time wet work. There's too much risk relative to the compensation. I recommend that we continue to call upon him for high-profile sanctions, but don't extend an offer for him to join the organization. If we ever crossed him, he might come after us."

Now there's a terrifying prospect, thought Locke. After a minute's more discussion, they agreed that Diego Gomez would be retained on the A-list of assets, but would not receive an offer to join the secret society. The Apostle would remain the sole assassin on the payroll who was an official member of the Coalition.

As they were about to wrap up the teleconference, the secure phone on the credenza rang.

Gregory Powers and the four powerful men up on the screen tensed.

"It's all right," Locke said, as he rose to answer it. "I think I know who it is."

He picked up the phone and talked for several minutes, while Powers and the others looked on anxiously. When Locke was finished, he hung up and turned around slowly, his expression one of grave concern.

"We need to get Xavier on the line," he said. "We've got a problem."

MONDAY

CHAPTER 18

AFTER THE THIRD FORAY, Skyler was exhausted. She wanted to sleep and didn't want Anthony Carmeli, supposed Hollywood producer, in her bed any longer. He had satisfied her immediate needs and there was no longer any use for him. She hated the way men sometimes liked to lie around afterwards, stroking her hair and talking in affectionate tones, presuming an intimacy that, for her, didn't exist.

At 2:20 A.M., she booted him out, making it clear that this was a one night stand and she never wanted to see him again.

Usually, the men she exploited went away feeling like whores. But sometimes the younger ones thought it was a thrill ride and wanted to come back for more. She had devised a way to make sure that didn't happen, by claiming to be with the CIA Domestic Resources Branch. Once she disclosed to them her fictional occupation, they usually wanted nothing more to do with her. She might as well have told them she was HIV-positive.

When she commanded Anthony Carmeli to leave, she noted the usual hurt, but he was somehow different than the others. He seemed like a genuinely kind and caring person—and this made her feel less triumphant and more hurtful than usual, as if she was a schoolyard bully.

After bolting the door behind him, she studied him from the window as he passed under a street lamp. His head hung low and he walked slowly, placing one foot in front of the other tentatively, as if he didn't fully comprehend what had just happened. She couldn't help but feel a little sorry for him. As he moved out of the yellow glow, he looked back up at her and their eyes met. Skyler pulled the curtain across the window with a quick jerk of her hand. She wasn't about to waste her time on some foolish man who represented nothing more to her than a sex object.

And yet she couldn't help but feel a touch guilty.

Turning off the light in the living room, she heard the computer chirp in her office. She walked into the room and brought up an encrypted message in legible English.

CONTRACTORS UNHAPPY WITH YOUR OUT OF
SCOPE STUNT. HAVE RENEGED ON BALANCE OF
PAYMENT. BEING CUTE IS NO WAY TO CONDUCT

BUSINESS. YOU SHOULD NOT HAVE LEFT THAT SOUVENIR BEHIND. I WILL RECOVER THE BALANCE BUT THIS IS GOING TO COST YOU. DO NOT CONTACT ME. I WILL KEEP YOU ADVISED OF SITUATION. FUCK YOU FOR THIS.

She read the email twice, cursing out loud both times. Xavier was obviously referring to the American Patriots' button she had left behind at the crime scene. But what was the big deal? Collectively, the four buttons would prove more of a distraction than anything else, leading investigators in four different directions. It wasn't as if she had pointed an accusing finger at AMP in particular.

The more she reflected, however, the more she realized that leaving the buttons behind had been foolish. She had violated standard operating procedure by making improper use of the dossier on the men that had hired her provided by Xavier. So far, she knew of only three men involved. From the dossier she knew about Joseph Truscott, former CIA deputy director of operations, current consultant to a host of security firms, and one-time rival of Xavier; and Benjamin Locke, leader of a powerful religious-conservative organization in Colorado Springs called American Patriots. The third man was a high-level field contact she had only spoken to over the phone and whose identity had not been revealed.

It was customary for her to receive dossiers on contractors, but the information was for protective purposes only. The dossiers were not supposed to be used except in the event of a double-cross. Under such circumstances, it was critical to have background on the men who took out the contract. That way, if they refused to pay, tried to take her out, or were caught and tried to strike a deal with the authorities, there were options open to Skyler and Xavier both. But for the current assignment, the contractors had done nothing to violate Xavier or her.

She was the one at fault.

The main reason she had left behind the buttons was to stir things up and confuse the investigators. But there was an additional motive behind the AMP button: to make sure the contractors understood that the assassin they had hired knew about them. The Kieger hit was the biggest of her life, with tremendous risk, and the button was to serve as a thinly veiled threat and protection against a double-cross.

Now, however, it looked as though her ploy had backfired.

Cursing herself, she deleted the file and logged off the computer. Turning off the light, she went to the bathroom, put on some facial cream, and brushed her teeth. Then she kneeled down next to her bed as she had since the age of three, prayed to the Heavenly Father, and went to bed.

For an hour she slept heavily. Then the demons came on like a firestorm.

The nightmare was different than the others. First she saw her father's business partner, Don Scarpello—*"Yes I am going to hurt you, but you will like it"*—gleaming in brutal triumph after taking her against her will when she was a girl. Next she saw her former lover Alberto—the Genovese freedom-fighter who had trained her and later ordered her death—cackling at her through clever brown eyes. Then she saw the innocent man and woman she had shot at the elevator. Finally came the men she had killed over the years, one by one, standing before her as they had the moment before their unexpected demise. Their ghostly images were framed in her sniperscope, crosshairs centered on their faces. In the next instant, there was a little *pop* and their heads exploded like melons.

Before the last man fell, she jerked awake gasping for air. Touching her body, she felt sweat beneath her chin and arms. Her teeth ached from the grinding. It took several minutes to bring her breathing under control and steel her shattered nerves. There was no hate left inside for her victims; she felt only a profound guilt and hatred of herself.

Fetching a glass of water from the kitchen, she gulped it down like a healing potion. Returning to her bedroom, she pulled a rosary with a small silver crucifix from her bedside table. For several seconds, she stared at the figure of Christ, nailed to the holy cross in humble surrender. Kneeling next to the bed, she clutched the rosary with trembling fingers, her lips quivering.

Then she said a prayer for every one of the people she had murdered—the last for the woman at the elevator.

CHAPTER 19

LATER THAT VERY SAME MORNING, an undercover freelance journalist named Jennifer Odden set foot in her office at American Patriots just as her telephone rang. She thought it might be Tom Stokes, managing editor of the hard-hitting, non-partisan monthly news magazine *The New Constitution.* He had said he would catch up with her at the beginning of the week on her secret piece. *Good old Tommy.* Flicking on the light, she tossed her JanSport daypack on the credenza and made a beeline for her desk, picking up the phone before the third ring.

"Hello."

"Is this Ms. Jennifer Odden?"

The voice was clipped, businesslike, with an unmistakable upper-class East Coast flavor. She didn't recognize it. "Yes," she answered after a moment's hesitation.

"I'm Reid Farnsworth Lampert, the new managing editor. I've taken over for Mr. Stokes."

Her jaw dropped. "Tommy's quit? But I talked to him just last—"

"Mr. Stokes didn't quit," Lampert cut her off. "I've taken his place."

Something about the man's insolent manner, smug tone, and cavalier dismissal of the well-liked Tom Stokes made her picture him as a multiple-generation Ivy Leaguer with a bloated trust fund, raised by nannies he tormented incessantly.

"But he's been with the magazine for the last twelve years. I can't understand how this happened."

"It's been in the works for weeks, but with a strategic move of this magnitude, we had to conduct the negotiations in the strictest confidence."

Jennifer saw a pair of AMP employees—the enemy in her way of reckoning as well as the subject of her story—walk by her office. Not wanting to be overheard, she quickly pulled the telephone cord around her computer monitor and closed the door. Returning to her desk, she slumped in her chair, wondering what she had done to deserve the likes of Reid Farnsworth Lampert. She had spoken to him less than a minute and already she wanted to smack him.

"Ms. Odden, what Mr. Stokes failed to understand is that we've entered a new era of investigative journalism. To compete with the blogosphere and tabloids, we have to bring a certain *edge* to our product."

He made a burbling sound, as if clearing phlegm from his throat. "Now I'd like to move on to the reason for my call. I need you to bring me up to speed on this story of yours."

A certain edge *to our product? Jesus, what rock did this pompous fool crawl out from under? What's with this Miss and Mister crap? And how in the hell did he manage to steal Tommy's job?*

"I don't have all day, Ms. Odden. I need to know where you stand with the story."

She felt harried and on the defensive, but she forced herself to plod forward. "Well, so far I've put together Part One...how AMP was formed, its purported mission and organization—"

"I already know about that, Ms. Odden. Mr. Stokes *did* brief me before his departure. What I want to know is where you stand with Part Two. What goes on behind closed doors? Who is Benjamin Locke and how did he rise to the pinnacle of the religious right movement?"

Jennifer took a deep breath, hoping to restore her own equanimity. What he seemed to be asking her was not so much to bring him up to speed, but to 'sell' her story, to justify it as newsworthy. "Okay, here's what I've got so far. American Patriots is not a charitable organization dedicated to giving Christians an active voice in government, it's a front for partisan political—"

"Oh, spare me the claptrap," Lampert interrupted rudely for the third time. "What I want to know is how they do it."

"I'll tell you how they do it. They've carved it up into two different divisions."

"A political division and a religious division."

"That's right. But what you don't know is that the political division is supposed to account for only ten percent of the organization and is required by the FEC to report its income sources and expenditures. Like a political action committee. The religious division, on the other hand, is supposed to make up ninety percent of the organization and be a non-partisan, tax-free entity. Which means it can't conduct political activities. In reality, there are no lines between the two divisions. More than seventy percent of the organization's resources are going toward electing hardcore conservatives to public office, not religious activities. In short, AMP is hiding behind a cloak of religiosity. Why? To pay minimal taxes. That way it can raise more issue-advertising revenue to help put its hand-picked representatives into office. Both at the state and federal level."

She was met with silence. When Lampert finally spoke, his voice was skeptical. "The proof is in the pudding, Ms. Odden. And I still haven't heard any proof."

She was prepared for this. "It all starts with the voter guides and congressional scorecards. Fifty million were sent out for the primary and another sixty million for the general election. The voter guides list candidates' positions on Christian conservative pet issues, while the scorecards give numerical scores to candidates based on their voting records in the House and Senate. What I've found is the religious division is just as involved in the preparation of the voting materials as the political arm. In fact, staffing requirements are such that they can't get out all election materials without the help of the religious staff."

"So they're bending FEC rules."

"No, they're flagrantly breaking them. The materials aren't just to educate voters—they're blatant attempts to influence votes. They're deliberately stacked in favor of hard liners over moderate Republicans, Independents, and Democrats. Not only that, the voter guides grossly distort the issues, misrepresent and even falsify opponents' positions, and deceive voters about whether candidates replied or not."

"How are you sourcing all this? You know we need at least two independent sources before we can even think about going to print."

"I have something better. I've kept copies of all draft red-line strike-out versions of the voter materials to show how they've been altered to fit the AMP agenda. When you see the drafts and finals side by side, you can see what's going on: a pattern of deceit to achieve a desired political result."

"Documents are best because they can't change their story. But is anybody willing to go on record?"

"I haven't approached anyone. That would blow my cover."

"You have people on tape though, correct?"

"Yeah," she replied, realizing he must have learned this from Tommy. The truth was, by posing as a loyal AMP employee while actually trying to uncover the organization's dirty little secrets, she really was something of a spy. She routinely taped American Patriots employees with a microrecorder that looked like an ordinary pager, discovering, in the process, that what her co-workers said was far different than what appeared in the AMP mission and policy statements. The recordings were useful in capturing the true political nature of the organization, since the employees had no idea they were being recorded.

"What exactly do you have on tape?"

"I've got several high-level employees, including Locke himself, boasting that the voter guides and scorecards are deliberately distorted to have a partisan impact. What makes what I've told you news is AMP is expressly advocating GOP candidates for state and federal office. By coordinating the distribution of its voter guides and making thousands of phone calls instructing voters whom to vote for, it's using its political muscle for the sole purpose of getting rabid right-wingers elected. Most of this is being done by the religious division to avoid paying taxes. Bottom line: American Patriots is a patently illegal political action committee masquerading as a religious organization. And that's what the public needs to know."

Jennifer stopped right there, confident she had made her pitch. The line was quiet for several seconds while Lampert sorted out all she had told him. The silence was excruciating and she felt as if all her cogent arguments were slipping away.

"This piece seems to have possibility and yet it still needs something more. What else have you got?"

"I've managed to get my hands on draft and final versions of the Republican Party platform presented at the convention in Houston in August. It was written largely by Locke and his assistant, the rising conservative star Gregory Powers. Obviously if AMP is writing, editing, and re-writing the GOP platform, it's only reasonable that the group be regulated as a PAC, not as a religious organization."

"No politician adheres to the party platforms anymore. Look, Ms. Odden, I'm looking for the big hook here, and I'm just not hearing it. AMP has to be involved in something more than election law violations and aggressive politics. What we're looking for here is the misappropriation of funds, elected officials being strong-armed into taking stands they oppose, direct linkages between political payoffs and public policy. And behind it all, we need someone we can hate: a larger-than-life Nixon or Cheney. The problem is everyone seems to love Benjamin Locke. He is incredibly popular. Ultimately, what I'm looking for—and what Mr. Stavros is counting on from you—is a *real* vast right-wing conspiracy that sells. Unfortunately, I'm just not getting that from you."

"All right, I'll get some more material."

"It's a little late for that, Ms. Odden. Senator Fowler—I mean President-elect Fowler—is the only game in town right now. A violent political assassination. The first woman president in the nation's history. A country in crisis. Everything else is bloody being frozen out."

"Don't tell me you're pulling my story before I've even finished it."

"I have no choice. The Kieger assassination is just too hot right now. And besides, you're already out there where it all happened. I need you."

She felt herself burn with anger now. "That's not going to work for me. I have a written contract for this story. Tommy and I wrangled over it for a month with Legal."

"I don't think I need to remind you, Mr. Stokes is gone. I, and I alone, decide what *is*, and what *is not* a story, as well as when to print it. The magazine will fulfill its contractual obligations, if that's what you're worried about. Just not right now."

"What do I tell Benjamin Locke and everyone else at AMP?"

"You don't *tell* them anything. You wrap the story up and hand in your resignation."

She felt a wave of panic. "You can't pull the tent stakes now. I've penetrated the computer files as far as I can go, but I still haven't tracked down all the hard copy files. There's a special fileroom that only certain employees have access to. I think I can get in, if you give me a chance."

Now his voice held piqued interest. "Did you say fileroom? What kind of fileroom?"

Somehow she had known the prospect of dirty little secrets locked behind closed doors would intrigue him. "Fileroom E. It's supposed to house the human resources records, but the word is there's other stuff in there. Proprietary stuff, like financial and lobbyist records."

"Why can't you get access?"

"It has a cyber keypad. I have four of the six numbers, but I'm still trying to get the last two."

He gave a nasally chuckle. "Tommy was right—you truly are quite the spy."

"Look Reid," she said, hoping to appeal to him as a human being, though she wasn't sure he fit into that category. "You have to let me finish this story. It means everything to me."

"Never call me by my first name again. It's *Mister Lampert* to you. How much time would you need?"

"One week."

"I'll give you until Thursday."

"But that's only three days. I'm going to need more time. This is a five-part—"

"Do you want me to make the deadline Wednesday, Ms. Odden?"

"Okay, okay, I'll get it done," she said quickly before he had a chance to change his mind.

"That's the spirit. As my grandfather, Princeton Class of '27, used to say, 'Where there's a will, there's most certainly a way.' Ta-ta, Ms. Odden." He hung up.

Jennifer collapsed in her chair, cradling the phone on her chest. She had just dodged a bullet, but now she was confronted with a far bigger problem.

How the hell was she going to get into Fileroom E?

CHAPTER 20

WHEN SPECIAL AGENT KENNETH GREGORY PATTON looked up at the American Patriots headquarters, he was reminded of the foreboding castle in Orson Welles' *Citizen Kane*. It wasn't the ten-story brick structure itself that gave him pause, rather the ominous cumulus-laden sky that served as its backdrop and the knotty pines twisting in the gusty wind. The roiling, black storm clouds bearing down from above gave him a vague feeling of claustrophobia, which was intensified by the howling wind and scratching sound of the branches against the building, like a persistent ghost.

As they neared the entrance, Patton looked at Fred Taylor, wondering if he felt it too, but the senior Secret Service agent's face was inscrutable.

Patton opened the front door and they stepped inside. A spacious marble-floored lobby opened up before them. They walked to the bank of elevators and took the elevator to the tenth floor. On the way up, an instrumental version of *Amazing Grace* trickled through the overhead speakers. Though Patton had always liked the song, something about this particular version gave him the creeps. With the droning synthesizers and high-pitched string instruments, it sounded like something you might hear in the compound of some twisted New Age religious cult.

Stepping out of the elevator, they came to a reception area. A platinum-blonde woman with a shiny gold chain around her neck bearing the inscription WWJD—*What Would Jesus Do?*—smiled at them with bland efficiency from behind a teakwood desk.

"Can I help you?"

"I'm Special Agent Taylor with the Secret Service and this is Agent Patton with the FBI. We're here to see Benjamin Locke."

The receptionist smiled pleasantly. "Good morning. Do you have an appointment?"

"For nine o'clock," Patton said. "I spoke with Mr. Locke earlier this morning."

She looked down at her planner. "Hmm. I don't have you on my list."

"This is a federal investigation, ma'am," Taylor said stiffly. "We'd appreciate it if you'd call Mr. Locke right now and tell him we're here." In a fluid motion, he pulled out his creds and held them up for her to see. An official picture ID card flew up first, followed quickly by a gold shield. It was meant to be intimidating, and judging by the receptionist's face, Patton could tell that the desired effect had been achieved. He didn't even bother to take out his own.

"I'll call Mr. Locke now." She smiled nervously and reached for the phone.

While she made her call, Patton and Taylor looked around. The reception area was well furnished, but not lavish. There were a pair of tan leather sofas and a glass table in front of the desk. Patton scanned the magazines on the table: *Christian Quarterly, American Hunter, Family Focus, Conservative Chronicles, Colorado Business, The American Spectator,* and *Rising Tide,* the magazine of the Republican National Committee. The employees in the nearby cubicles and hallways were all carefully groomed and neatly dressed in the kind of business suits one would find in a mid-grade law office. No Armani, but no polyester either. Two men watched him from the doorway of an office; they looked suspicious, disapproving even, and for a fleeting instant, Patton felt like he was in the midst of a lost Indian tribe. This was getting weirder by the minute; Kafkaesque was the word that came to mind.

Ignoring the stares of the two men, Patton studied the color prints on the walls. They showed spectacular mountain and ocean vistas with pithy quotations from the Bible at the bottom, almost like commercial product plugs. "Rejoice in the LORD, O you righteous!" (Psalm 33:1). "Many are the pangs of the wicked; but steadfast love surrounds him who trusts in the LORD" (Psalm 32:10). "Arise, shine; for your light has come, and the glory of the LORD has risen upon you" (Isaiah 60:1). Patton was trying to figure out if there was a hidden meaning in one of the quotes when he heard heavy footsteps coming up from behind.

"Sorry to keep you waiting, gentlemen. I'm Benjamin Locke."

When Patton turned around, the room seemed to shrink by half. The renowned Christian leader swallowed the reception area and sucked the air out all at once. Though Patton had seen Locke on TV, he had never met the man in person and was wholly unprepared for such an awesome and charismatic physical specimen. For a moment, he felt like a little boy again, gazing up in stupefaction at those giant statues of the mythical Civil War generals at Gettysburg.

They shook hands. "We appreciate your meeting with us under such short notice, Mr. Locke," Patton said, unable to take his eyes off his host as he was gripped by the big man's bear-sized paw.

"Anything I can do to help with your investigation," Locke said through a disarming smile. He introduced himself to Taylor and said, "Please follow me, gentlemen."

They padded obediently behind him down the hallway to a conference room with ornate paneling and a polished table, both mahogany. Locke took a seat at the head of the table; Patton and Taylor sat down next to each other to his right and pulled out their computer tablets. A tubby secretary with blood-red lipstick and a bulldog's face surveyed the two federal agents suspiciously as she poured fresh coffee into the pot on the credenza.

Just for kicks, Patton winked at her.

She did not wink back.

CHAPTER 21

"I THINK IT'S A TRAGEDY, a terrible tragedy," said Locke, and he meant it even though he firmly believed that the assassination had been necessary in order to save America from herself and her enemies. "President-elect Kieger was a good man and honorable leader. I was fortunate enough to work with him on a number of occasions. My heart goes out to his family and all those whose lives he's touched. I can only hope that whoever is responsible is tracked down and justice is swiftly served. But I know you didn't come here to listen to me lament a true statesman's loss. How can I help you with your case, gentlemen?" He smiled at the younger man, the FBI agent Patton, who had called him early this morning to set up the meeting and whose picture he had seen on page three of today's *Gazette-Telegraph*.

"Well, as I said over the phone, Mr. Locke, we'd just like to ask you a few questions. It shouldn't take more than a few minutes."

The silk tie at Locke's throat felt a touch constricting, but he resisted the urge to loosen it. "It might help if I had a better understanding of the circumstances surrounding your inquiry. Is this regarding my professional association with William Kieger, or is there something else?"

"I'm afraid we can't comment on that," Taylor said. "This is an ongoing investigation."

Locke gave a look of polite deference. "I understand."

"We appreciate that," said Patton, who began typing at his iPad. "I'd like to start with promotional buttons. You know, like those given out at campaign rallies and other events. You have buttons like that here, don't you?"

Locke feigned a look of puzzlement, as if he couldn't understand what possible relevance such items could have in the case. But inside his mind was grinding along in another direction. *So that's it, then—they are here because of the damned button.* "Yes, we have the kind of souvenirs you are describing," he answered in a helpful tone. "To the best of my knowledge, they are given to all new members upon joining our organization."

He watched closely as both agents jotted down notes on their tablets.

"And how many members are there?" Patton asked.

"More than twenty million."

The two agents looked at one another, their eyes saying *dead end*.

"Would employees have access to the buttons?" asked Taylor.

"We keep them in boxes here at headquarters, and at all the chapters. It's quite easy to get one's hands on such items."

"How many employees are there?" Patton asked.

"Five thousand. And another fifty thousand volunteer activists at our more than three hundred chapters around the country."

"Are the buttons given out at political rallies or other special events?" asked Taylor.

"All the time."

"So what we've got," Patton said, "is more than twenty million of these things out there."

"It would appear so."

The questions continued for another minute. Locke answered them in his most cooperative tone and strived diligently to appear accommodating. But deep down he wondered: *Is there any way this nonsense could point to the Coalition?*

"The reason we're asking you about this, Mr. Locke," Patton said, "is because an American Patriots' button was left behind in the room where the fatal shot was fired."

"One of *our* buttons? I can't believe it. But how do you know it was...left behind?"

"We're sorry, but we can't tell you that," Taylor said stiffly.

"Are you suggesting the button may have been put there by one of my employees or a member of the organization?"

"We have to consider it a possibility," Patton said. "It's also possible the killer isn't affiliated with AMP, but has some personal reason for bringing attention to the organization, like revenge. Or maybe he has no connection whatsoever and planted a clue to mislead us." His expression narrowed slightly. "Why do you think the button was left behind, Mr. Locke?"

He felt their eyes heavily upon him and, again, resisted the urge to loosen his tie. He decided the best response would be to appear mildly affronted. "I don't have a clue, gentlemen. You're asking the wrong man. I have no idea what goes on in the mind of an assassin. And the truth is I don't want to know."

That seemed to satisfy them. But inside Locke felt a growing anger. He was furious at Gomez for leaving the damned clues behind in the first place. Phase One had come off so smoothly, why did he have to do it? It made no sense. What was he trying to prove? All he had accomplished with his stupid prank was to forfeit the balance of his payment. The Executive Committee's vote on the matter early this morning had been unanimous.

Patton typed a note on his iPad and looked up. "Is there anyone, presently or formerly with AMP, who might have a grudge against the organization? Someone with a military background?"

Locke did his best to look surprised. "Agent Patton, we are a Christian organization. The individual you are describing is not the kind of person who joins our flock."

"We understand. But we'd appreciate it if you'd have your human resources people look into it. Every group has its fringe element. More often than not, it's this element that poses danger."

"Of course I will do what I can."

The agents studied him in silence, waiting for him to say something more. Locke knew it was a deliberate tactic to sweat him out, in the hopes that he would volunteer something. He felt uncomfortable. He had never been on the receiving end of an interrogation before—in 'Nam he had grilled the VC, not the other way around—and he realized how difficult it was to remain clearheaded and not blurt out something incriminating when under even mild duress.

Patton broke the silence. "Mr. Locke, we didn't tell you this before, but the button in question was found several inches to the right of three other buttons. Political campaign buttons, to be precise. Our criminal profiler thinks this may have been done deliberately to make a political point. Are there any outside groups that have threatened AMP? Anti-religious groups, that sort of thing?"

Be careful here. You don't want to seem vindictive or eager to blame. Still, it shouldn't be a problem to give up a few of the usual suspects.

"We are under constant attack by any number of left-wing groups, if that's what you mean. People for the American Way, Americans United for Separation of Church and State, the Freedom from Religion Foundation, the ACLU, and many others have been attacking us for years. There's even an Anti-American Patriots group. They have their own website and spin outrageous lies about our organization. Then, of course, there's the FEC and National Democratic Party. They'll stop at nothing to undermine *people of faith.* Personally, I can't imagine any one of these groups going so far as to assassinate a president-elect. But I suppose stranger things have happened."

There was a knock at the door. Locke frowned. He had left explicit instructions to Marlene "Suie" Tanner, his executive secretary, not to be disturbed.

The door opened. To Locke's surprise, it was not Marlene, but his son—an almost exact replica of him but three inches shorter and fifty pounds lighter—who poked his head in.

"Yes, what is it?" demanded Locke, unable to conceal his irritation.

"Sorry to interrupt," Benjamin Jr. said, "but it looks like some group has claimed responsibility for the assassination."

CHAPTER 22

PATTON'S CELL PHONE WAS OUT IN A FLASH. After politely asking Locke and his son to leave the room so he and Taylor could confirm the report in private, he dialed John Sawyer, the Domestic Terrorism desk supervisor, at the field office and was quickly filled in on the details.

The Green Freedom Brigade, a radical environmental cell Patton knew little about, had issued a statement claiming responsibility for the assassination. Cyber sleuths with the U.S. Computer Emergency Response Team had already determined that the statement had originated as a computer virus released "in the wild." The virus had spread to hundreds of thousands of personal computers across the country as one worker after another opened up the file from his email inbox. The virus had even been given its own name: Ares, the Greek god of war. Though the statement's authenticity had yet to be verified, it seemed to be the genuine article.

Patton recalled the Green Freedom Brigade from the Silver Springs Ski Area arson case a year earlier, but the Bureau's dossier on the group was thin at best. Based in Northern California, the group was made up of militant ex-members of EarthFirst!, the Earth and Animal Liberation Fronts, and the Ruckus Society, although the FBI had never actually been able to track down any of its members. The Brigade had claimed responsibility for several arsons across the West—in Colorado, Arizona, Utah, and California—but it had never resorted to killing before, to the best of Patton's knowledge. He recalled that two office cleaners had died during the bombing of an animal testing lab in Salt Lake City; however, the deaths were believed to be accidental.

The group hadn't made any demands; it had simply claimed responsibility for the assassination and rambled on about how evil assassinated President-elect Kieger had been because of his loathsome environmental record. The governor was to blame for California's clogged freeways, toxic air pollution, offshore drilling, endless housing tracts, deforestation, and other "ecocatastrophes." But what caught Patton's attention was the mention of the man who would continue to hold the White House for the next three months until the new president, Republican Katherine Fowler, was officially sworn in. The statement ended by giving thanks to "our comrade, current Democratic President Gregory Osborne, for exposing Kieger as an anti-environmentalist, for showing us the way to achieve real change, and for providing inspired leadership in environmental policy."

Patton pictured tomorrow's newspaper headline: PRESIDENT LINKED TO ECOTERRORISTS, ASSASSIN.

They finished up the call by going over the new assignments. The FBI Regional Computer Forensic Laboratory, Google, and two computer science professors from prestigious Colorado School of Mines were to get cracking ASAP. Their job would be to break down the source code line by line, looking for the key "fingerprints" of Ares's author, to pinpoint the source of the virus. Additionally, a special FBI team would be assembled to work exclusively on the virus angle and track down members of the Brigade; this would be handled largely by the San Francisco field office, which was more up to speed on the Brigade.

When Patton punched off, he and Taylor spent a few minutes discussing the ramifications of the shocking new development before summoning Locke and his son back into the room.

"We're finished here," Patton said to the Christian leader. "We appreciate your cooperation."

They shook hands. "Glad to be of service. Can you tell me though, what do you make of this new development? Is this radical Green Freedom Brigade behind the assassination?"

"We can't comment at this time," Taylor said. "All we can say is we are taking it very seriously."

"I see. Will you require any further assistance from me?"

"We might," Patton said. "We'll call you."

"Well, I guess that's it, then. I'll show you out."

Stepping from the room, they walked down a plush hallway toward the elevators. Halfway there, an older man in a blue blazer and another man who looked as though he had just stumbled in off the street came walking up to them. Patton saw Locke's face light up at the sight of the heavily-bearded, dirty-looking younger man.

"Mr. Brown, good to see you again today. May I ask how things are going?" asked Locke with a genuine note of affection in his voice.

"Great, Mr. Locke, things are going great. Mr. Johnson here has been a big help."

Johnson nodded. "Mr. Brown is catching on quickly."

Locke touched the man kindly on the shoulder. "Just take it one day at a time, Mr. Brown. We'll have you back on your feet in no time."

"Thank you, Mr. Locke, sir. You have been a godsend. And please call me Pedro. All my friends do."

The man reached out and hugged him, tears of gratitude in his eyes. Patton was surprised to see Locke's eyes water up too as he patted the man on the shoulder. After a moment they gently broke apart and Locke started down the hallway with Patton and Taylor in tow.

"Mind if I ask you something, Mr. Locke?" asked Patton. "Who was that man?"

"That was Peter Brown. Only yesterday afternoon he was a homeless thief—and today he is a gainfully employed member of our society, reaching out to others in need. I pray that he sticks with it and carves something out for himself. Unfortunately, not all of them do. But I have a good feeling about my new friend Pedro here."

Patton saw the tender look in Locke's eye and realized that there was far more to the man than what was reported in the media. True, the new millennium's second most important Christian power player—second only to the Pope—seemed at first glance to be more of an A-list celebrity than a humble servant of the Lord. But there was no doubt that he was a deeply caring person who held strong convictions about helping those suffering in the world.

They continued down the hallway in silence. Halfway to the elevator, Patton thought he saw a familiar face emerge from the restroom on the other side of the elevator.

He took a closer look. His heart rate suddenly went off scale. He couldn't believe his eyes.

No fucking way! That can't be her!

The woman glanced in his direction, but he was partially blocked by Agent Taylor, so she didn't recognize him. She smiled—a courteous work smile that seemed a tad contrived—and then turned and headed down the hallway. She wore a charcoal-gray business suit with black heels, a ridiculously conservative corporate ensemble that was the last thing he would have expected to see her wearing. And what the hell was she doing working here at American Patriots of all places? He studied her gait: gracefully smooth strides, perfectly coordinated yet sexy, like the prance of an exquisite racehorse. He wanted to say something, but his lips wouldn't move. It had been so long.

But just as she was about to pass out of sight behind a cubicle, he called out her name.

"Jennifer," he said, feeling his heart thump against his chest, the eyes of the others shifting to him. "Jennifer Odden."

The woman stopped in her tracks, and ever so slowly, turned around. He took two steps forward, the others looking at him curiously.

"You two know each other?" gulped Benjamin Locke.

Patton didn't answer at first. His focus was on Jennifer as she walked down the hallway toward him. When she recognized him, her face at first registered surprise. Then her eyes lit up with something closer to genuine affection and that brought Patton a feeling of warmth, but also longing. All the wonderful memories—and the last terrible one—came flooding back to him. She was older now, but the perfectly symmetrical face, the silky blonde hair, the easy stride, they were all still there. There was also a womanliness she had lacked twelve years ago—a maturity—and yet it seemed as if only a short time had passed since he had last seen her. He wanted to ask her what she had been doing with her life and especially what in the hell she was doing working at American Patriots of all places. But instead he merely answered Locke's question, keeping his tone neutral.

"We went to college together," he said, keeping his eyes on Jennifer. "Michigan."

Locke gave him an appraising look, as did Taylor. "A pair of Wolverines, eh," he declared good-naturedly. "Well, you'll be pleased to know that Jennifer is one of our rising stars here at AMP." He motioned her forward with an enthusiastic wave of his hand.

She came walking up wearing a polite smile though Patton could tell she was nervous. Inside he felt a jumble of emotions. The old amorous feelings came rushing back, but there were other things too: anger, pain, betrayal, and more than a little trepidation. In spite of his scrambled emotions, the sight of her was like a spell.

"Hello, Ken."

All he could muster in response was a muted "Jennifer" and he felt like an absolute idiot. They were only a few feet apart, but he was grateful for the distance between them because he wasn't sure what the hell to say or do next.

She extended her hand; to his surprise he took it. Her touch was light and tentative, and for some reason this bothered him. In fact, the entire handshaking business seemed wrong given how close they had once been, though he understood her reason for doing it. It made him sad to think that, after all the good times they had shared in college together, they were reduced to a silly professional handshake.

"You look well," she said.

"So do you."

There was an awkward silence. Why did she have to look so damn good? He struggled mightily to stem back the flood of memories and knew he had to get the hell out of here. He was ill-prepared for this right now.

"Well, the Lord certainly works in mysterious ways," said Locke cheerfully. "You and Special Agent Patton went to college together and now here you stand reunited. Hallelujah indeed."

Jennifer raised a brow. "Special Agent Patton?"

"I work for the FBI." For some reason he felt embarrassed saying it.

"He and Agent Taylor are investigating yesterday's unspeakable tragedy," said Locke by way of explanation. "It was a terrible, terrible day for us all."

Jennifer looked puzzled. "I didn't realize that AMP…"

"Oh, it has nothing to do with us," Locke put in quickly. "We're just doing our part to help the investigation."

"And we appreciate your assistance, Mr. Locke," said Taylor, all business. "I think we can show ourselves out."

"Very well, gentlemen. I pray that you catch those responsible swiftly and bring them to justice."

"Thank you, sir," said Patton. He looked at Jennifer, still feeling all jumbled up inside.

"Good luck, Ken. It's good to see you again," she said, and he could tell that she meant it.

"Nice to see you too," he replied, though all he wanted was to get the hell out of here.

"If I can be of further assistance, gentlemen," offered Locke, "please don't hesitate to call."

"Thank you, Mr. Locke. We won't," said Taylor.

Patton took one last look at Jennifer and then he and Taylor turned and walked away. When they reached the bank of elevators, the Senior Secret Service agent turned to him with a mischievous smile.

"So you two had a thing. Obviously it didn't end with 'Let's still be friends.'"

"I don't want to talk about it," said Patton, and he jabbed irritably at the elevator button.

CHAPTER 23

SKYLER DIDN'T CLIMB out of bed at her Venice Beach apartment until after eleven. She had tossed and turned until dawn and felt foggy-headed from lack of rest. Her field assignments often left her dissipated the next day from both lack of sleep and the strain on her nerves. All the rigorous planning and careful execution—of both the kill and escape—took a heavy toll on her, as did the inevitable guilt that came afterwards. Her body cried out for food and strong coffee, but these would have to wait. Checking her email was her top priority right now; she was expecting an important message from Xavier.

In fact, there were two messages from the control agent, both disappointing. He had made no headway in the negotiations with the contractors; they were still refusing to pay the balance. He said he would keep trying and that she would just have to stand by and wait. He warned her not to do anything rash, which pissed her off. She hated it when he treated her like an impetuous child.

Cursing to herself, she logged off the computer and took a long, soothing shower. Afterwards she wrapped a towel around herself, opened the bathroom window, and peered down at the street below. Outside, the weather was clear, bright, and windy. A Santa Ana was blowing in from the Mojave and the air smelled of a mixture of the sea and windblown dust. She put on a dash of makeup, tied her hair up, and put on a sundress and leather sandals. Then she went to a secret compartment in her closet, rummaged through her identification documents and credit cards, and selected the credit card and driver's license for Jeanne Olive, one of a half dozen false names at her disposal. Xavier had equipped her with false credit cards, passports, driver's licenses, and birth certificates to match each of her identities. After placing the false license and credit card in her purse, she went out.

Out of long habit, she discretely checked to see if she was being shadowed as she hit the street. To her relief she saw no signs of a tail or anyone suspicious. Even in daylight, there was no need for her to alter her physical appearance in Venice Beach. Though many locals knew her by face, and a few by her current alias, no one really *knew* her. It was easy for her to buy groceries and receive other basic services without uttering a word. On the rare occasions when someone asked her to a party, over for dinner, or out on a date, she politely declined.

She purchased a copy of the *Los Angeles Times* and took lunch at a casual bistro near the pier. The patio was buzzing with conversations about the assassination, but she said nothing to anyone except her waiter. She quietly read the paper and ate her lunch: a plate of fruit and a Swiss cheese, sun-dried tomato, and artichoke-heart sandwich. The bistro served a rich dark French roast and she drank two large cups.

There was an entire pullout section on the assassination in the *Times*. The paper showed colored-graphic illustrations of both the shooting and the Secret Service's response. There were several eyewitness accounts, a few uninformative quotes from federal agents and cops, and a terse description of the task force handling the case, no doubt the product of a press leak. The paper briefly presented the physical evidence, but gave few details. Twenty-eight people—all male—had been brought in for questioning in connection with the assassination. There was no mention of anyone matching her description, and no prime suspect.

She studied the pictures of the three men heading the case and read brief summaries of each man. Henry Sharp, assistant special agent in charge of the FBI's Denver field office, was in overall command. With his squinting eyes and dark mustache twisted at both ends, he looked intense, like an old-time gunfighter. Then there was Frederick Taylor, the man in charge from the Secret Service's end of the joint investigation. He had many years in both personal protection and investigation under his belt, and looked it. Here was the consummate veteran: smart, determined, but not cocky. The paper gushed on about how, as a young agent, he had knocked John Hinckley, Jr. down and saved President Reagan in 1981.

But the most intriguing of the three, from her perspective, was the thirty-three year old FBI special agent named Kenneth Patton. Skyler recognized him immediately as the man who had stopped her outside the Union Plaza Building. A slight grin crossed her face as she recounted how completely she'd fooled him; of course, there was no mention in the newspaper of any woman wheeling a baby in a stroller.

Finishing her lunch, Skyler paid her bill and picked up her Fiat at the garage. She loaded the stroller containing her long-range sniper's rifle and other paraphernalia into the car and drove to Marina Del Ray. She stored all of her ordnance and disguises at a locked safe room at the marina. After dropping everything off, she went to the bank and withdrew five hundred dollars in twenty-dollar denominations. Then she headed back to her apartment and put on a green jogging suit, sunglasses, and a two-hundred-dollar pair of Nikes. She wanted to clear her head with a good run and workout.

Ten minutes later, when she hit Ocean Front Walk, she turned right and headed off at a brisk pace toward Santa Monica to the north. The trees along the boardwalk strained in the wind, which had picked up in the last hour. As if prompted by the wind, Skyler increased her pace. She began to sweat and her legs found a pleasant rhythm. Off to her left, the azure blue sea sparkled in the sunlight and white-capped rollers chugged toward the sandy beach. A flock of seagulls fought stubbornly against the stiff breeze. Windsurfers and sailboats splashed through the waves offshore. To the south, more boats shot out from the marina's entrance, frothy white water spilling over the gunwales.

She ran north for a full half hour before retracing her footsteps back to Muscle Beach. A score of skimpily-clad fitness freaks, mostly men, were busily pumping iron on the weight-training pad. She joined them for a dozen sets, without speaking to anyone. Finishing up with two hundred pushups and three hundred sit-ups, she walked to the Windward Avenue pavilion, her body bathed in perspiration.

She was greeted by a cacophony of street noise: chattering voices, hack guitarists strumming three-cord rock anthems, grinding skateboards. Hippies in colorful tie-dyes peddled trinkets and other useless junk as smartly dressed businesspeople darted past. She bought a mineral water from a street vendor and drank it down in front of the graffiti-disfigured tribute to Botticelli's *The Birth of Venus*. Her mind was clear now. She watched the sea rush in to meet the sand as wave after wave broke over the beach. She thought back to those simple summers in Cinqua Terra and Stromboli, before Don Scarpello and Alberto, and wished she could start over again at the age of ten.

The crash of a huge wave brought her back to reality. It was foolish to daydream of turning back the clock. Of course she would live out her life as an assassin. Of course she would never change, never be able to divorce herself from the demons that haunted her. It was ludicrous to imagine an impossible utopia. She was a contract killer and would always be a contract killer, until she was put behind bars, killed, or built up a sufficient nest egg to retire in comfort. Regrettably, turning back the pages of her life was not an option.

Feeling a wave of melancholy, she headed back to her apartment. It would have been nice to bring her camera and take some pictures of the tempestuous sea, but that would have to wait for another day. When she turned on Mildred Avenue, her cream stucco apartment building came into view.

Her jaw dropped when she saw the man from last night at the entrance.

CHAPTER 24

"IF THOSE ARE FOR ME, you're wasting your time," Skyler said brusquely as she walked up, making sure to use the same generic California accent she had used the night before.

With feigned surprise, he looked at the colorful bouquet of flowers in his left hand then the bottle of Merlot in his right. "Actually, these are for your much nicer identical twin sister. She just moved in across the hall from you. But, of course, I'm not supposed to say anything."

Skyler was taken aback. She had hoped to discourage him straight off and send him away with his tail between his legs, but he had deftly parried her thrust.

She crossed her arms. "I thought I told you to stay away from me, Anthony Carmeli."

"Ah, so you remember my name. That's a start."

This is not a start—this is what's called an end. She moved past him wordlessly, a sultry expression on her face, and began punching in numbers on the entry keypad next to the door.

"This is great," he said, his tone turning more desperate. "You and I are really starting to communicate. My mother always said this is what it takes, give and take. This is a big step in our relationship."

Her fingers stopped moving; she turned and glared at him. "We don't have a relationship."

"I don't know, technically speaking..."

"I believe I made myself quite clear when I told you to stay away."

"What? Just because you chained me to the bed, treated me like a sex toy, tossed me out in the middle of the night, and told me you never wanted to see me again?"

She shook her head discouragingly. *Am I supposed to find this amusing?*

He held out his hands, palms out. "Okay, okay, I was just trying to make you laugh. And besides, sometimes when people say stay away, they really mean come by and see me sometime."

He smiled and his brown eyes lit up just a little. Skyler thought back to their lovemaking, if it could be called that, and had to admit it had been delicious. She tried to tell herself that he was just another evil man out to get laid, but somehow he didn't seem to fit the bill. He seemed genuinely decent, just as he had last night.

"Why are you here?" she asked him, her head tilted at a challenging angle.

"I'm not sure. At the moment I guess it's to be your punching bag."

"You want to fuck me again, don't you? That's why you brought me wine and flowers."

"You've got it all wrong—this isn't about sex. After last night's exertions, I'd rather be handed a court marshal than sent back to the front. Unless, of course, you have fully encapsulating body armor."

With difficulty she stifled a grin. She hated to admit it, but there was something endearing about him. He was trying awfully hard to be funny and she couldn't begrudge him that. Others had come back around, but their salacious motives were always transparent. But if it wasn't for sex, what was he doing here? It didn't make any sense. Men weren't friendly or romantic without ulterior motives. That's what Germaine Greer, Gloria Steinem, Susan Faludi, and all the other experts on male behavior said. That's what her whole life experience had revealed to her. Men were only nice when they wanted something, usually food, money, or sex. Men were evil liars, cheats, and ruffians who couldn't be trusted to treat women with decency unless they got something in return.

"Look, I came by because I wanted to talk to you. Last night had great moments, it really did, but there was something missing. And I feel bad about it because the best part of last night—for me—was when we talked at the bar."

Skyler didn't know what to say. No man had ever spoken to her so openly. She liked that he got a little angry; it suggested his professed motives were genuine. She found herself curious as to how far he would go to win her affections.

"I want you to know I have some issues with the world too. That's why I brought this seventy-dollar bottle of Merlot, so we could drink to our postmodernist angst together—in style."

"I have to go now," she said flatly. "I do not have time to drink Merlot."

"Okay. Maybe some other time."

Skyler kept her expression blank, neither rejecting or accepting him.

He looked at her with the most sincere brown eyes she had ever seen. "I just wanted to see you again. That's what this is about. Nothing more, nothing less."

She felt her resolve weakening before him. "What does a Hollywood producer want with me anyway? You need some new flesh for one of your X-rated films?"

He laughed, a mirthful bellow that carried across the street, and in that moment she knew she sort of liked him. *He's definitely not like the others.*

"I don't do X-rated movies. In fact, I don't do any kind of movies at the moment. I'm taking a kind of sabbatical. The truth is I'm working out some emotional problems. I guess it's what you'd call a work-related burnout. From one too many scripts written by adults with first-grade intellect and one too many tantrums by spoiled twenty-million-dollar actors. Not to mention that I've become totally marginalized by special-effects technicians."

"So why not go with a different studio and make good movies? If you have the talent, there must be work available."

"I wish it were that simple."

"I don't know what you want from me, Anthony Carmeli."

"Maybe I like you."

"I think you are confusing romance with lust."

"Somehow, cruelty doesn't suit you. I'd take a different direction if I were you. There are lots of avenues out there."

"And plenty of boulevards of broken dreams as well," she responded coyly.

"Been down them myself, more times than I'd care to admit." He held out the bouquet and bottle of wine. "Please take these as a gift. If you don't want to see me again, I can understand that. But you should know that I didn't come here to have sex with you. And I didn't go to that bar last night because I wanted to get laid. I went there to listen to some music and recharge my batteries. But in the process I met *you*."

Taking the flowers and wine from him, Skyler found a mixture of emotions vying for space inside her: guilt at being a contract killer and for treating him so badly last night; rapture that he was pursuing her as a person and not a sex object; fear at the idea of violating one of the cardinal rules of her profession, getting involved with someone who could blow her cover. The strange thing was she knew last night there was something special about him, something beyond his good looks and sense of humor. There was a world-weary charm about him and, though she hated to admit it, she had felt a connection.

"Tonight," he said, abruptly. "Tonight would you have dinner with me?"

"I'm busy tonight."

"How about tomorrow night?"

"I don't know...I..." She swiped a hand across her face in exasperation, like the host of a party scrambling around at the last minute to prepare for guests. *This is crazy—absolutely crazy!*

"I'll tell you what. I'll come by at six and we can go out for dinner. Not a date, just to talk. And no hanky-panky. Not unless you guarantee me medical clearance from a board-certified physician."

His grin widened, and a hint of a smile crossed Skyler's lips, vanishing quickly. "I wouldn't get your hopes up. I'm not looking for a relationship—with you or anyone else."

"I'm not either. But at least we're sort of connecting. When I was chained to the bed, I felt like we weren't connecting very well."

"You weren't chained, you were handcuffed."

"Yeah, but they felt more like chains."

He winked at her and started down the sidewalk. When he had gone about ten feet, he turned back and said, "I'll see you tomorrow night."

"Maybe," she said, and she watched him walk away.

CHAPTER 25

TURNING RIGHT ONTO NEVADA AVENUE, Benjamin Bradford Locke pressed down gently on the accelerator of his Cadillac Seville. His loyal assistant, Gregory Powers, sat next to him; they were on their way to their meeting with President-elect Fowler. The world around them was a portrait in urban anonymity: dingy motels, homogeneous fast-food chains, dilapidated auto shops. Locke preferred the I-25-to-Lake-Avenue route to the Broadmoor, but they were running a little late and this way was faster.

He made a quick inventory of the people on the street: the old hag pushing the shopping cart full of aluminum cans; the cheap shop owners in their shabby clothes; the nervous-looking man and raffish prostitute sneaking into the motel on the right; the vacuous young adults with the glowing-neon hair and obscene rings projecting from all regions of the face. He felt a deep, profound pity for them and hoped that one day they would be touched by the hand of God and go on to live productive, meaningful lives. He only wished that he could give every one of them the same fresh start that he had given Peter Brown, but he could not help everyone in the world. It was a pity because if only he had the resources, he would happily do it.

His thoughts turned to Katherine Fowler. For those poor people out on the street, she was truly the nation's best hope. It was the dawning of a new era. The Chosen One would step into the bully pulpit of the Oval Office and, over the next eight years assuming her reelection, enlighten the masses with a vision of hope. She would bolster the struggling economy, reduce the size and scope of government, and reclaim America's standing in the world just as the Great Communicator, Ronald Reagan, had done. With a charismatic, photogenic, articulate conservative president presiding over a Republican-tilted House and Senate and a 7-2 conservative advantage in the Supreme Court, there was as much chance for a successful paradigm shift and economic renaissance as there had been during the Reagan Revolution.

The Coalition was banking on it.

When Locke reached Lake Avenue, he took a right and headed into the famous Broadmoor area, one of Colorado Springs' oldest and finest neighborhoods. The towering spruce, oak, and elm trees along the road were set at regular intervals and threw their heavy limbs over the broad avenue, dappling the sunlight. The sprawling mansions and wide streets perfectly captured the idle elegance of early twentieth-century Colorado. Ahead soared the world-renowned Broadmoor resort, where the gold barons of Cripple Creek—today it was hard not to call them thieves—once came to relax in luxury. Visitors today came for the same reasons Gilded Age blue bloods did: the gentle climate, healthy mountain air, and easy access to the great outdoors.

Locke took a left onto Tanglewood and turned right on Broadmoor Avenue. After passing a dozen multimillionaire's homes, and several obligatory Jaguars and Mercedes, they came upon the former two-term senator's English country manor. The twenty-room dwelling looked like a castle with its steep-pitched roofs, creeping vines, and exquisite turrets, dormers, and gables.

A thronging pack of media hounds outfitted with the latest gadgets crowded the pavement outside the electric gate to the house. Inside the gate stood a veritable army of Secret Service agents, which Locke took as a good sign. It meant that Katherine Fowler was already being treated like a president.

This is the will of God, he thought. *She truly is the Chosen One.*

CHAPTER 26

AFTER AN EXASPERATINGLY LENGTHY and thorough security check, they were escorted by two Secret Service agents to the president-elect's home office. The hallway was cluttered with nattily clad aides scurrying about industriously. When Locke and Powers appeared at the open door, Katherine Fowler looked up from the phone and waved them in. She had returned an hour earlier from her press conference, where she had paid tribute to her running mate, expressed condolences to his family, and confidently reassured the American people that she would work tirelessly on their behalf, striving to overcome the many challenges facing the nation.

Locke was reminded, yet again, of what an excellent choice he had made in Katherine Fowler. Here, most assuredly, was the person to lead America's renaissance. Though she could not be described as beautiful, she was attractive in a wholesome ex-athlete kind of way and she had a natural leadership quality about her. Her eyes were aquamarine, her hair blond without a hint of artificial coloring, her figure vaguely muscular. With her All-American looks and affable smile, Fowler presented a pleasant package to voters. Even before her selection as Kieger's running-mate, she had been considered the new blood of the Republican Party. Though well right of political center, she nonetheless managed to convey, by her salubrious physical presence and articulate manner, an impression of moderation.

Peter Frautschi, Fowler's campaign manager during the primary and likely chief of staff, stepped forward to greet them. It was Frautschi who had secretly given Locke Kieger's campaign schedule weeks earlier, as well as informed the group last night of Fowler's swearing in as president-elect following her speech in Colorado Springs. The former director of a conservative Washington lobby and regular contributor to *The American Spectator* had a miser's eyes and a pugilist's nose, and was reported to be tough as nails in protecting his own turf and that of his boss. Locke considered Frautschi the operation's most critical insider; not only did he have ready access to Fowler, he was the new president-elect's most trusted political advisor.

While Fowler worked her way off the phone, they were served drinks by an aide and settled into the Southwestern-style lounge chairs set about an engraved Spanish table. Locke had given up alcohol years earlier, and opted for soda water with lime. Minutes later, Fowler hung up the phone and turned to face her guests.

It was time for the much-anticipated meeting with the Chosen One.

CHAPTER 27

"I'M PLEASED TO SEE YOU, GENTLEMEN," she began solemnly, "though I wish it were under better circumstances." She picked up her Perrier from the desk and stepped towards them. "Our nation lost a great man yesterday. We will be in a state of mourning for quite some time, I'm afraid."

Locke felt the familiar sting of shame and regret at the taking of poor Kieger's life, though he ultimately regarded it as a necessary evil in order to save his beleaguered nation. "Yes, it's terribly sad," he said with genuine contrition as they shook hands. "But as in every tragedy, there is a silver lining. We still have you, Mrs. President-elect. In two months' time, you will be the first female president in the nation's history. Despite the terrible sense of loss that our mournful nation feels, this is a truly historic occasion."

Though Fowler no doubt understood the deeper implication, she merely nodded as if she accepted the compliment at face value, and offered her hand to Powers. "Hello, Gregory."

"Mrs. President-elect."

Fowler motioned for everyone to sit down. Locke could feel the tension building inside him—there was so much at stake!

"Have you gentlemen heard anything more about this Green Freedom Brigade?"

"Nothing since this morning. The TV and radio stations are going full tilt, but no one seems to have any new information. The president is taking a beating. Do you think it's possible he's involved as reported?"

"All I know right now is that this will take some time to sort out. By the way, Benjamin, I had a little visit from two federal agents after my press conference. I understand they spoke with you this morning as well."

A flash of surprise crossed Locke's face, swiftly suppressed. "Yes, they came by. Apparently, the gunman left some promotional buttons in the office where the shot was fired. An AMP button and three other campaign buttons. I take it one of them was one of yours."

She nodded. "An old button from my first senate campaign. I told them I didn't have any idea where it came from, but I'd look into it."

"I told them the very same thing. You know, anything I could do to help."

Powers fidgeted uncomfortably in his seat. The involuntary gesture, while subtle, made Locke feel uneasy.

Fowler rose from her chair and began pacing in front of a large oil painting of the Battle of New Orleans. "What do you make of these buttons? What do they mean?"

"I'm not sure. Seems like the assassin's trying to leave behind a few false trails to confuse the authorities. But, of course, I'm no expert on such matters."

"The whole thing is troublesome. But I know you didn't come here to discuss criminal matters." She walked back to her chair and sat down. "What can I do for you, gentlemen?"

Locke took a moment to collect his thoughts. "We realize this is a time of sober reflection and mourning," he said with an unintentionally sententious air. "But we feel it is important for the party, and you in particular, to demonstrate to the country that the situation is under control."

"So you want assurances?"

He decided to play innocent, hoping to conceal the Coalition's true ambitions from her. "We *are* interested in how you might govern differently from your able colleague. You know we always like to have a little input on behalf of our constituents."

"What can we expect in return?" asked Frautschi bluntly.

Locke kept his gaze on Fowler. "We're prepared to donate twenty million into your reelection coffers."

The president-elect's eyebrows raised slightly. "Twenty million dollars?"

"It has a pleasant ring to it, doesn't it?"

"Why yes, as a matter of fact it does."

"That will pay for a lot of TV spots four years from now," Frautschi said.

The president-elect's expression brought to mind wheels in motion, as if she was already making plans on how to spend the money. "How soon can we have the...donation?"

My, aren't we greedy? "By the end of the week."

"And what, might I inquire, are you asking for in return?"

"The usual. Some assurances on the party platform and a *little* input into your minor cabinet appointments. Not secretary of state or defense— just attorney general and heads at Health, Interior, and Labor. Nothing binding, of course. We're just looking for a gesture of good faith on your part."

Fowler nodded, as if she had expected as much. "I can assure you, Benjamin, my stands on the key issues important to you two gentlemen are the same as during the primary. I still see no middle ground on fiscal austerity, taxes, job growth, abortion, gun control, anti-terrorism spending, or school vouchers."

"We were hoping for a little more than broad brush strokes." Locke kept his voice deferential yet forceful, recognizing that now that he had offered the money, he controlled the meeting. "We gave you tremendous patronage during the primary and general election and we need to reassure our members that you will govern as judiciously as we all have hoped."

Fowler considered this a moment. "You know where I stand, gentlemen. You know every bill I've voted for or against the last twelve years. But given the tremendous support you have given me, and continue to give me, I agree it's only fair I lay out my positions for you. As long as you promise not to quote me to the media." She followed with the same little wink and disarming smile that had won over the Midwestern heartland, Southern states, and Western interior during the Republican primary and general election.

"We promise." Locke returned the wink and leaned forward eagerly in his chair.

"Very well, here's where I stand. I am committed to appointing men and women to the Supreme Court and federal bench who interpret the constitution in the manner intended by our Founding Fathers, people who will put a halt to this judicial activism that is spreading like a disease. I am committed to shrinking the size and reach of the federal government, not expanding its powers. I hold zero-tolerance positions on homosexual marriage and adoption, flag burning, and public financing of the NEA. I back a constitutional amendment banning abortion, human cloning, and embryonic stem-cell research. I want to expand religious rights in public schools and roll back unnecessarily restrictive gun laws. I'm for across-the-board corporate tax cuts and unlimited soft money contributions. And finally, I would fill my domestic cabinet positions with people of unassailable character who believe, as I do, that 'conservatism' is not a dirty word. There, does that give you some feel for where I stand on the issues important to your constituency?"

Locke smiled. "Why yes, it most certainly does." That was Fowler's gift, he realized, her ability to make you support her, to make you literally hers, absolutely, without coming across as harsh or extreme in her views. Again, Locke congratulated himself for making such a fine choice. This really was going to work!

"I think we're set, then." The president-elect rose to her feet, signifying the meeting was over, and extended her hand. "Benjamin, I just want to tell you again how much I appreciate your tireless support. I can say, without equivocation, that I wouldn't have gotten this far without your help."

If you only knew, thought Locke, resisting the urge to glance at Frautschi for a reaction. "Thank you, Mrs. President-elect. And I can say, also without equivocation, that we have the greatest confidence in you."

She gave a winsome smile. "Well then, I just hope I don't let you down."

"Oh, you won't," he said. "I'm one-hundred-percent certain of that."

CHAPTER 28

AFTER THE MEETING, they were escorted to Locke's car by the Secret Service. Locke was ecstatic: the meeting had turned out even better than expected. Fowler was absolutely the perfect person for the job, a true American patriot. Phase Three was shaping up spectacularly. She didn't just agree with the party platform, she would be its most zealous promoter. In two months' time, she would take charge of the nation's highest office and unleash a whirlwind of political reform.

It was all going so perfectly.

Modern liberalism had brought America to her knees and made her doubt her own exceptionalism, but here was a bold opportunity to turn it all around. Fowler would be the new Reagan. Once again, a charismatic conservative—a new Great Communicator—would control the White House. Only this time the president would not be held in check by a Democratic Congress. She would be backed by a fiercely loyal cabinet, a conservative-leaning House and Senate, and the most conservative Supreme Court in the nation's history. It would be a political paradigm shift of epic proportions and, once again, the country was ripe for positive, groundbreaking change.

When they climbed into the Cadillac, Locke fired the engine and pulled forward to the electric gate. A flock of reporters stood restlessly beyond, while a wall of Secret Service agents stood implacably in front. When the gate opened, Locke turned left onto the street, feeling the euphoria coursing through his body like a mighty river.

It was truly the time of the *Chosen One.*

CHAPTER 29

THE FBI'S DENVER FIELD OFFICE, located in the Federal Building at 1961 Stout Street, wasn't particularly imposing, especially compared to the majestic State Capitol and other Corinthian-style government buildings a few blocks away. It looked somber, elephantine, and antiquated—a throwback to the bygone Hoover era. But what the office lacked in aesthetic grandeur, it more than made up for in the ability of its personnel. The playground of the Rockies appealed to many an FBI careerist, and the Denver office tended to attract a disproportionate share of the best and brightest from other field divisions and residencies around the country.

On the eighteenth floor, Special Agent Kenneth Patton was giving instructions to an FBI computer expert with an exquisite complexion and silver tongue ring named Lorrie Elert. There were now more than a hundred individuals in the Denver office working full-time to solve the triple homicide. The team—officially dubbed the Assassination Task Force—had set up shop in what was affectionately known as the "bullpen," the only conference room large enough to house the myriad of computers, wall boards, maps, phones, video machines, and working tables required for a fully operational command-and-control center. In addition to Patton and the three other supervisors, there were fifty-seven agents from Domestic Terrorism and thirty-five from the Reactive squad on the task force, as well as two dozen Secret Service agents working on the case in a supporting role. Another three hundred FBI agents had been assigned out of the Washington, New York, and San Francisco field offices to look into the Green Freedom Brigade and other terrorist cells.

Patton was disappointed that no viable suspect had been apprehended after the shooting and that the campaign buttons seemed to be a dead end lead. But there was plenty of other physical evidence, and, in the end, he felt it would be the key to the case. With physical evidence, he could establish an MO and build a profile. And once he did that, the assassin's days would be numbered. Even Carlos the Jackal hadn't stayed anonymous forever.

"What I need is a program that allows us to interface between two separate databases," he said to Lorrie. "One containing all assassinations of prominent figures in the last ten years. The other for all known or suspected professional assassins in the world."

"Okay, I'll start with NCIC," she said, referring to the FBI's National Crime Information Center in Washington, D.C., a massive computerized information system that constituted the world's largest collection of data on known criminals. "But NCIC won't have everything if the shooter's international so I'll also need access to Interpol and CIA records. By the way, who's going to access the electronic files?"

"Gillin and Pinkerton. You'll be working with them."

"Tweedledee and Tweedledum? They're complete losers, you know, but I suppose I can live with it." She glanced down at the three hand-painted lead miniatures on his desk. "Hello," she said, picking one up and looking it over with apparent amusement.

The military figure with the green uniform and helmet, brace of ivory-handled Colt .45 pistols, and loyal Bull Terrier at his feet named after William the Conqueror was a nearly exact reproduction of his great-grandfather: hard-fighting, controversial World War II tank commander General George S. Patton.

"You like playing with toy soldiers, Special Agent?"

"Sometimes. I like painting them more."

"You a World War II buff?"

"Let's just say I've always liked *The Great Escape, Von Ryan's Express*, and *The Big Red One* better than anything Martin Scorsese's ever done. And I've been to Sicily and Normandy in the exact spot where the Allied Forces landed and read over a thousand books on the war by authors not named Stephen Ambrose. Some people might call it an obsession. By the way, that little bugger you're holding is my great-grandfather, General Patton."

"*The* General Patton? Now I am impressed. How come you weren't named after him?"

"I don't know. My grandfather and father were. I guess that's enough George S. Pattons for one family. My grandfather was a two-star general and, believe it or not, was probably a better commander than my more famous great-grandfather. He died in 2004. I worshipped the old bastard and was lucky enough to reenact the D-Day Omaha Beach landing at the pond on his farm in Massachusetts every summer for a decade."

"That must have been something."

"It was. I loved that cantankerous son of a bitch."

"Aren't all Pattons cantankerous sons of bitches?"

"Why I believe they are."

"So let me get this straight. You were not only a blue chip quarterback at Michigan, but you are the direct descendent of two legendary American generals named George S. Patton. You're quite the All-American, Special Agent. I'll bet you were a Boy Scout too."

"Yup."

"I got kicked out of the Girl Scouts."

"For what?"

"For kissing another girl...on the lips."

"What, they don't give out merit badges for that?"

"No siree. The funny thing is Donna Lance and I were just fooling around—we wanted to see what it was like so we knew what to do when we kissed a boy—and our group leader just happened to catch us. We were both sent home that night."

"And here you are today a top analyst with the FBI."

"I'm a junior programmer, Special Agent. *Top* isn't exactly the word I would use."

"Well, you're smarter than anyone else in this office. That's tops in my book." He winked at her playfully. "Sorry, Lorrie, but we've got to stop flirting and get back to work now. We've got a political assassination case to solve, remember? Now where were we?"

"You were telling me about those two losers, Gillin and Pinkerton."

"Oh yeah. Your first order of business will be to have them pull together files on anyone who fits the profile of an assassin. Terrorists, independent contractors, government sharpshooters, especially deep-cover operatives who've had fallings-out with their governments. They'll also get you police and intelligence reports on every assassination of an important figure in the last ten years. Once they've pulled it all together for you, I want you to build the database."

"Once it's populated, what do you want to query for?"

"I want global flags for long-distance killings similar to the Kieger assassination. Cases involving military-style infiltration tactics, glass-cutting, heavy-caliber rifles, or explosive cartridges." He handed her a sheet of paper. "These are the keywords. Once you've flagged the data, I want you to sort it by date, beginning with the most recent record."

She was writing notes furiously, eager to perform the task. Most people thought building databases and analysis tools amounted to pointing and clicking a mouse, but it involved far more than that. To query a vast data set and perform a trends analysis, as Patton was having Lorrie do, required the system to be programmed to ask the right questions and to sort the data in an easily recognizable format. The custom-designed analysis tool Lorrie would build would help Patton sort through thousands of records and come up with something meaningful, a pattern, an MO used over and over again. With a recurring MO, he stood a much better chance of catching the killer.

"How soon can you have it done?" he asked.

She gave a mock salute. "Thursday, General Patton. I'll have it done by Thursday."

He saluted back. "That'll be just fine, Commander Elert," he said with a smile. "You are dismissed. Now get to work."

"Roger that, General."

She smiled and walked off. Looking back at his desk, he saw his computer screen blink. There was a report flagged as URGENT in his email inbox.

CHAPTER 30

IT WAS THE PRELIMINARY FORENSICS REPORT from the FBI Crime Lab he had been expecting. After decrypting the file, he launched it in Adobe Acrobat and scrolled to the first page until he came to the heading FORENSIC MICROSCOPY RESULTS. He began reading.

According to the report, the two hair samples he had found in Lee Wadsworth Brock's office, and a third strand recovered in the elevator by the ERT, belonged to a single individual. Based on the racial characteristics of the hair and the presence of fluorochrome staining in the follicular tissue, which was used to differentiate sex, the subject was a blond Caucasian male. The hairs contained no dyes and showed no evidence of having been cut, though it could not be ruled out whether they had been forcibly removed. Chemical and mitochondrial DNA analyses would also be performed on the samples, but the results wouldn't be available until later in the week.

Patton leaned back in his chair to ponder the significance of the findings. There were two main questions in his mind. First, who did the hair belong to, the shooter or an innocent party? And second, if the hair did belong to the shooter, how could the guy have been so careless?

Patton didn't think the samples belonged to anyone who worked at Front Range Investment Advisors. From the security people, he had learned that no one from the company had come in to work over the weekend and that the cleaning staff had vacuumed Friday night, two days before the assassination. Assuming the cleaning crews had vacuumed thoroughly, it was unlikely that three hair strands from the same person would remain behind. However, the cleaners were still being interviewed, so it was premature to draw any conclusions.

Because of the close proximity of the blond hair strands to the cut window, Patton had already assigned several agents to collect samples from all fair-haired male employees in the company, as well as from all maintenance, cleaning, and security staff matching the description. If no match was found with any of the individuals sampled, there was a decent chance the hairs belonged to the shooter. But Patton would just have to wait and see.

Returning to the report, he scrolled to the next section prepared by the forensic firearms examiners. The projectile that had killed the governor was identified as a .50-caliber HEIAP, or hi-explosive-incendiary-armor-piercing bullet. Because it had exploded into more than twenty fragments, the examiners had had a hell of a time analyzing the rifling impressions and other properties, though they were still confident they had a positive ID. Normally, they could obtain meaningful data on the bullet length, nose and base shape, and other rifling characteristics, including the number and width of land and groove impressions and direction of twist. These properties would, in turn, help determine the bullet manufacturer and caliber of the weapon that fired it. But in this case, because of the fragmentary nature of the bullet, they had been forced to rely as much on chemical composition and color banding as surficial striations.

Using the lab's Standard Ammunition File, the examiners had narrowed the list of candidates to four .50-caliber HEIAPs manufactured in Norway by Raufoss. From the small slivers of metal, they had identified a silver-and-green tip, a portion of a copper jacket, and two unique surface markings. They had also recovered particles of a tungsten carbide penetrator, some lead, and a trace residue of zirconium incendiary. With this information, they checked the general rifling characteristic (GRC) database for a listing of firearms that could have fired the bullet.

What they came up with told an interesting story.

There were numerous .50-caliber rifles on the commercial market, but when the GRCs on the bullet were compared to the database, only one firearm matched a specific manufacturer, model number, and type of weapon. Reading through the description of the rifle, Patton saw that the Barrett M82A1 semiautomatic rifle was a serious piece of hardware. Fully assembled, the rifle was five feet long, weighed in at almost thirty pounds, and discharged its lethal load at nearly 3,000 feet per second. It was one of the most accurate long-distance sniper rifles in existence, credited with upper body hits beyond a mile. The weapon was used primarily by elite outfits of the U.S. Military—Marine Corps, Army Rangers, Navy SEALs—but it was also the long-distance weapon of choice of both Israeli and Islamic-terrorist snipers in the Middle East.

That didn't guarantee the assassin was military or ex-military, Patton knew, but it did add weight to his working hypothesis that the guy came from at least a paramilitary background. If he wasn't military or former military, he was damn sure a professionally-trained terrorist or government sharpshooter with a sound knowledge of military-style weaponry and sophisticated infiltration tactics. Only a true pro had the balls and expertise to sneak a thirty pound rifle undetected to the fiftieth floor of a major commercial building, decommission two security cameras, take out the president-elect from a half mile away, and escape into thin air without a trace.

So who in the hell is this guy?

The question was still ping-ponging through Patton's mind when his phone rang.

He looked at the caller ID. It was Sharp. Feeling as though he had forgotten something, Patton looked at his watch.

Oh shit, the meeting!

A wave of anxiety shot through him and he cursed himself for his lapse. Picking up the phone, he braced himself for a severe scolding.

"My office now, Special Agent—you're two minutes late, goddamnit!" the ASAC barked without preamble. "And bring your 302s!"

Patton snapped to attention like a footsoldier. "I'm on my way, sir."

CHAPTER 31

WHEN PATTON ENTERED THE OFFICE, Sharp scowled at him like an Irish drill sergeant from behind his paperwork-filled desk. He felt himself involuntarily stiffen. Closing the door, he handed over his first batch of 302s to the ASAC and took his usual seat in front of the desk.

The 302 was the standard reporting form FBI field agents had to file to chronicle case developments and justify actions taken, which was of paramount importance to the U.S. Attorneys who might one day try the case if it went to trial. Without saying a word, Sharp looked over each form like an IRS auditor, as if checking them not for substance but completeness.

"This is all you've got?"

"At the moment. I realize we don't have a suspect, but we are narrowing down the list of possible shooters who could have pulled this off. I'm having Lorrie Elert build an analysis tool so we can query the database for common MOs and—"

"Wait a second," Sharp interrupted, glancing over the top 302 on his desk. "You're telling me you've gotten nothing from the eyewitnesses? No physical description? Nothing?"

"No one questioned so far saw or heard anything. Whoever our guy is, he was in and out without being seen. We don't have even a rough sketch."

"What about the videotapes?"

"We're still working on those. We're IDing everyone who came into the building over the weekend. We've been through Sunday, and now we're going through Friday and Saturday."

Sharp pulled out a handkerchief, blew his nose, and stuffed the snot-caked handkerchief back in his breast pocket. "What about the Kieger campaign tapes?"

"Still working on them too."

"What about the Brigade? We must have made *some* progress by now along that front."

Patton groaned inwardly at the prickly tone, but let the affront pass. "We haven't tracked down any members. But we have made some headway on Ares. One of our computer techs has found a name in the revision log of the source code. It's an obscure feature in Microsoft that reveals the name of a person modifying a file. Apparently the code has been used before by some hacker who likes to spread nasty viruses. The name embedded in the code is 'Rainbow Warrior.'"

"Is that supposed to mean something?"

"It's the name of the ship Greenpeace planned to use to protest nuclear tests in the South Pacific in 1985. But the French government blew it up in New Zealand, killing a Greenpeace photographer."

"So the virus's author could be connected to Greenpeace—where President Osborne used to work."

"We're not sure what it all means. What we have for sure is a name, albeit a code name, for the author of Ares. We also have the programmer's source code signature. We've posted the code on the Net, which means we've got a hundred cyber sleuths from the antivirus companies working on this thing."

"I suppose this all could lead to something," Sharp said, without much enthusiasm. He was old-style FBI, not very cyber savvy, and the vagaries of the Internet were still a mystery to him. "Tell me about the physical evidence. You must have *something* there."

Again, Patton didn't like the ASAC's tone, or the implication, which seemed to be that he was not handling the investigation properly or producing the desired results. But again, he kept his emotions in check. "We know how the guy was able to cut through the glass. Hydrofluoric acid, HF, fifteen percent dilution. Lethal stuff, highly corrosive. It was likely sprayed from a polyethylene bottle into the initial cut. We believe that once the rough edges were dissolved, the glass was pulled free with a suction gadget of some kind. Unfortunately, hydrofluoric acid's a standard lab product. Anyone can buy it in small quantities without any special requirements."

"That doesn't give us much, then."

"It shows our guy knows how to handle a dangerous substance as well as how to apply it. It fits our profile of a highly-trained pro, with expertise extending beyond firearms."

Sharp acknowledged this fine distinction with a slight dip of his chin. "What about the fingerprints? Anything on that?"

"We pulled seven usables, four from Brock's office and three from the elevator. But none of them match anyone with a criminal record."

"So no probables, then?"

"IAFIS kicked out two." He was referring to the FBI's Integrated Automated Fingerprint Identification System. "The reliability factor for both was in excess of ninety-five percent. But when the two probables were manually checked, it was determined there wasn't a match. Basically, the prints are useless until we find the perp."

Sharp groaned. "Why don't you have any fucking good news for me?"

Because this guy's smart as a whip and not making it easy on us. Who do you think we're dealing with here, an amateur? "We have several promising leads. We just need time to follow them up."

"The governor doesn't care about promising leads. We're meeting him tomorrow and he wants results. And he's not the only one on my back. Washington's on me like flies to shit, not to mention the goddamned media. I want to know what the connection is between the president and this Green Freedom Brigade."

"We haven't established one yet, except for the Greenpeace link. And even that's pretty shaky."

"So what are you saying?"

"That it's possible the Brigade's claim of responsibility might be a complete fabrication."

"Come on, they fall within the parameters of the profile. They have a well-documented history of arson and murder."

"The deaths at the animal testing lab were accidental. Personally, I think this thing is too big for them."

"Never underestimate fanatics. They're full of surprises."

"I'm not saying the Brigade couldn't be behind it. But we both know terrorist groups blame killings and bombings on other groups all the time to deflect suspicion from themselves. That's why I'm trying to figure out who Kieger's biggest enemies are, or were. For me, his environmental record in California doesn't seem bad enough that the Brigade would want to take him out. At the same time, we don't have anything that points to Islamic militants, right-wing militias, or hate groups."

"Okay, so who else would have reason to do it?"

"I don't know yet. But it's obvious who benefits most with Kieger out of the way."

"Fowler."

"That's right."

Sharp considered this a moment, stroking his cowboy mustache in the way that drove Patton nuts. "Too obvious and it just doesn't fit. Fowler's squeaky clean, and let's not forget she's only forty-eight. She can afford to serve as Veep for the next eight years and build up her creds."

"That may be. But she's about to become the first woman president in the history of the United States—all because of an assassin's bullet."

"Officially, I know you have to check into Fowler. But unofficially, I'm telling you I don't think she has anything to do with this. So don't waste too much time on it."

Patton wanted clarification. "Are you telling me to back off, Henry?"

Sharp's eyes narrowed. "No, but I am telling you to tread softly."

"We're the Federal Bureau of Intimidation. Discretion isn't our strong suit."

"It's going to have to be on this case."

"Okay, fair enough. But I think we've got to ask ourselves one important question. How powerful do you have to be to bring about regime change in the most powerful nation on earth?"

"We're not the most powerful anymore, remember? The fucking Chinese are. What the hell's your point?"

"Only this. Every radio blog, TV station, Twitter feed, and Internet chat line in the country is talking like the president of the United States is a bagman for ecoterrorism. Yet, no one's come up with a reasonable explanation as to why he would do such a thing. And then there's the matter of the Brigade. If they're the ones behind this, their plan sure backfired. Instead of getting an anticorporate tree hugger like Mason Schumacher, they just got themselves Dick Cheney in a dress."

Without responding, Sharp rose from his chair and went to the window. For a long moment, he stared out at the cobalt-blue mountains in the distance. When he looked back at Patton, his face was iron hard, his voice filled with warning.

"You just catch me the killer, Special Agent, and let *me* worry about the goddamned conspiracy theories."

CHAPTER 32

ANDERS HOUSER, code named Pep Boy, was so scared he thought he would shit his pants.

He sat in a room in Berkley, California, in front of a custom-designed, next-generation desktop supercomputer, eyes unblinking, sweat beads clinging to his brow. His left leg twitched as his nervous fingers worked the keyboard. This was never supposed to happen—his system was supposed to be impenetrable—yet all the evidence before him told him otherwise.

Someone had broken into his frigging computer!

When news of the Ares virus first broke, he had been in an upscale hotel room in Chatham, on the Cape, recuperating from a wicked hangover. He had flown back East for the wedding of his best friend from prep school. Between the pot, ecstasy, and prodigious quantities of Bass Ale, it was a killer party, not to mention a great nuptial. But by one o'clock East Coast time, a mere three hours before he was to fly back to the West Coast, it appeared he had been out of town at a very inopportune time.

Pep Boy wasn't sure exactly what had happened. The early reports said only that a radical ecoterrorist cell calling itself the Green Freedom Brigade was claiming responsibility for the assassination. This in itself was shocking news, considering he was an active member of the clandestine group. In fact, he was its sole cyber guru/saboteur, having hacked dozens of laboratory, government, and corporate networks during his three-year stint with the group. Later, he learned that the claim of responsibility was released as a computer virus. It was then that he really began to worry. As the Brigade's cyber lord, he would have been the one to release Ares. Yet he had been at a wedding, three thousand miles from his workstation, when the virus was turned loose.

Which meant something was monumentally wrong.

His first step was to verify the authenticity of the claim. He suspected it was a hoax, but wasn't sure, so he called Q-Tip and Gen-Mex, the leaders of the Brigade back in Berkeley. Their first reaction was to blame him for Ares, but he explained that he had been on the Cape over the weekend and had nothing to do with it. It quickly became obvious that some powerful unknown entity was trying to pin the assassination on the group.

Q-Tip and Gen-Mex were already in the process of preparing a vigorous denial. It was all bullshit, they told Pep Boy, and the Brigade wasn't about to take the rap for something it didn't do. As a precautionary measure, they were going to break up the fifteen-member group temporarily. Everyone was to lay low for a while until things quieted down.

Pep Boy was ordered back to Berkeley to check out his system ASAP. It was possible that whoever was behind the setup had used his computer to unleash the virus, to provide evidence the group was involved. If his computer had been used, the fact that he had not yet been tracked down by the authorities suggested the coding had been sophisticated enough to elude the feds, at least for awhile. He was to determine if his system had been physically tampered with once he'd verified that he wasn't under surveillance.

Now, sitting before his thirty-four-inch color monitor, he saw that both he and the Brigade were in serious trouble. There was no mistake. Someone had broken in and released the virus from his terminal—of that he was certain. And every terminal was traceable in time.

It was mind-boggling that, with the technology at his disposal, his system had been penetrated. Not only did his computer have a thumbprint ID system, but it was equipped with more antitampering protections than there were days in a week. Yet, despite all the built-in precautions, his very own computer had released Ares at precisely eight o'clock this morning Pacific Coast Time. There was no doubt about it—the virus had been sent out from his terminal.

Without his knowledge, without even his presence. And that was frigging creepy!

It took him over an hour to check through the source code. Every so often he rose from his squeaky chair and snuck a peak out the window, to see if anyone was watching him. He didn't see anyone, but that didn't lessen his anxiety.

By the time he had examined the entire code, line by line, he knew he had been taken by an ace programmer working with surgical precision. His very own cyber prints were cleverly embedded in the source code, mostly stylish programming devices he had used on other jobs, but also a few obvious things, like his code name and initials. His gut feeling was it was a spook job. Only those rogue elephants at Langley could come up with something like this. Whoever *they* were, they had obviously captured some of his prints illegally, in Orwellian fashion, and that pissed him off. The Net was at once both panacea and anathema. However, the coding was so good, it would take the fed code breakers several days to track Ares to him.

That was the only good news—he had enough time to make a

getaway.

Still, by the end of the week, Big Brother would be after him with a vengeance, expending vast sums of money and serious manpower to apprehend him. But at least he would have a head start. There was no way he was going to turn himself into the law and try and exonerate himself. That might be an option later if things got desperate, but not now. It was always possible that whoever had set up the Brigade would be identified, but he wasn't banking on it. He had a narrow window of opportunity and he planned to make the most of it.

He decided to pack a couple duffel bags and stay in a motel tonight. Tomorrow, he would clear out his checking account remotely and sell his remaining high-tech stocks. He would have the money wired to a numbered account in some dirty bank on Grand Cayman. That wouldn't be a problem; he had done it many times before for the Brigade.

When finished packing, he surveyed his apartment a final time. A dozen empty Four Loko and Red Bull cans sat on the coffee table that carried a hundred bumps and bruises. The rest of the furniture was scarcely distinguishable from the mélange of clothes, bicycle parts, and computer magazines cluttering the room and adjoining hallway that led to his bedroom. Sure, the room didn't look like much, but at least he had done good, meaningful work here. At least he had been fighting against the insanity that was the human condition in the new millennium.

And that alone had made it all worthwhile.

CHAPTER 33

THE APOSTLE pulled back deeper into the shadows, his crystalline eyes fixed on the apartment. *This one's going to be special,* he whispered under his breath, as he saw the nervous young man pull aside the curtain and peek out the window for the tenth time, searching vainly for signs of surveillance. The Apostle wondered what the kid's face would look like at the moment of truth. What he liked most was the look of surprise on his victims, the raw shock as they realized what was *really* happening in the final moments of their lives. It was *the look* that got him off. That was what made it all so—how else to say it?—titillating.

The Apostle liked being out on assignment. Years ago, when he was a U.S. Marine, life had been such a bore. He had loathed the sheer tedium of the daily routine, playing the silly war games when there was real fighting to be done. Though a highly decorated captain, he had always hated having to suck up to the senior commanders. Most of them had come away from West Point or VMI with a chip on their shoulder and misguided education. They talked endlessly about battles fought a half-century or even a millennium earlier. *Who gives a shit?* he had often wondered. War was now. Fighting was about the present—who could inflict the heaviest casualties, and win, today!

It was time to move. He had observed his prey long enough to know what to expect, what possible surprises the kid could have up his sleeve. Whether Pep Boy had a gun or not, he posed no threat. But the time spent watching him would prove beneficial for another reason. By now, the kid's fingerprints would be all over the keyboard. This was important, since it had been necessary to wipe the keyboard clean early this morning during the penetration of the system.

When the kid pulled away from the window, the Apostle slipped out of the shadows and began crossing the street. Instantly, a trickle of excitement played through his nervous system, like a melodious violin. His lightweight combat boots were surprisingly noiseless. Already he was feeling the inexorable rush of adrenaline—and something else. That something else was an almost orgasmic sensation, low in his gut, and it was growing stronger with every passing second.

Semper fi and praise the Lord Jesus Christ the Savior! This was what he liked to call *active duty.*

Reaching the sidewalk on the other side of the street, he took cover behind a large bush. He looked up at the window again to make sure the coast was clear. Check. He moved quickly to the front entrance of the apartment building. It was a nondescript, low-tech complex, with no keypad or intercom security system, so he was inside in a flash with his standard tools, a tension tool and feeler pick, a burglar's best friends.

He eschewed the elevator for the stairs, taking them swiftly but silently. The rush grew stronger and he began growing hard. He felt supremely confident; he had reconnoitered well and knew his prey. So adept was he at creeping into places unknown to him, performing his assignments, and getting out quickly without a trace that it was positively intoxicating. It was uncanny how easily he could blend into his surroundings and pull off a job.

Still, the Apostle was smart enough to know that caution was the better part of valor.

When he reached the third-floor fire door, he stood frozen a long moment studying the layout through the vertical window. He went over the series of maneuvers required to accomplish his objective. A TV droned in a nearby apartment, but that was the only sound. He waited a few seconds until he was certain the coast was clear.

Then he opened the fire door.

The resulting squeak from the rusty hinges was scarcely audible, but to the Apostle it sounded like a deafening screech. Every muscle froze.

He kept his eyes fixed on the hallway. To his relief, no one came out.

He pulled the door open all the way. It squeaked again, but this time he ignored the sound and slipped quickly into the hallway. Tiptoeing noiselessly across the carpeted floor, he felt his heart calling out to him in a turbulent rhythm.

When he reached the kid's room, he stopped and touched the doorknob.

Locked—too bad.

He moved from the door and withdrew a black Beretta 92F semiautomatic from the military-style shoulder holster beneath his camouflage jacket.

He felt his blood pumping and his breathing accelerated. The sweat seeped from his body. He could feel the warm dampness on his neck and beneath his arms. Inside, he felt ready to explode. This one was going to be special, he could tell. But he had to make sure to hold back at the end, like always, so he didn't cream his pants and leave behind any evidence.

He plucked the custom-designed suppressor from the pocket of his fatigues and threaded it into the nose of his specially adapted handpiece.

This is it—the moment of truth.

His heavy breathing turned to low panting. His mouth was partly open, his lips moist with desire.

Chest heaving, the Apostle lowered the barrel of his silenced Beretta and shot off the lock. Then, without a split-second's hesitation, he drove his shoulder into the door and charged into the room. He almost tripped over a pair of duffel bags at his feet as he hurtled through the door.

The kid was reaching to turn off the light at his desk. He jumped back, mouth open.

The Apostle smiled lustfully. His chest pumped as he raised the pistol to fire.

"W-Who are you?" Pep Boy asked in a faltering voice, his entire body quaking with fear.

The Apostle's smile deepened and his face became contorted in a rictus of pleasure. He could feel himself about to explode and knew he would have to summon all his self-discipline to withhold from climaxing. "I'm Ares," he gasped. "The god of war."

A look of disbelief crossed the kid's face, and his expression quickly turned to disgust. "Jesus Christ, you're not about to…?" he spluttered as he realized what was happening.

"You're right, I'm not—I'm holding back," the Apostle said.

And with that, he shot Pep Boy three times in the face.

CHAPTER 34

TURNING OFF THE TV, Jennifer Odden went into the kitchen to make herself a sandwich. She spread hummus inside a piece of pita bread and threw in a few pitted Greek olives, several slices of cucumber, and some crumbled feta cheese. After pouring herself a glass of soymilk, she sat down at the small kitchen table and ate her dinner.

Her thoughts turned to Ken, the tough but soft-spoken, blue-eyed ancestor of General George S. Patton, Old Blood and Guts. The young man she had loved in college—and that a part of her would forever love—was now an FBI agent investigating the murder of the man who had been poised to become the next president of the United States. It was strange the curious twists life took, the way the past came back to mingle with, or perhaps alter, the present. Though she had seen Ken once in the flesh and twice on TV being interviewed by reporters, it was still difficult to comprehend that he was a big-time federal agent, and that, because of fate or happenstance, their paths had crossed again.

The years had been kind to him. He was still lean and athletic, with a sparkle in his eye and the same quiet air of competence. She realized she had never really gotten over him. After the disaster twelve years ago, they had both moved on with their lives, but she had never forgotten how meaningful their relationship was. She had never wanted to end it; she had been strong-armed into doing so by her father, for whom she would always feel nothing but burning contempt.

Several times since the dark episode, she had contemplated contacting Ken. But she had never summoned the nerve, after what she'd done to him. By not telling him the truth about why she couldn't see him anymore, she had intended to protect him from her father. But in the end, all she'd accomplished was to hurt him. The hardest part had been lying to him when she loved him, hurting him when that was the last thing she wanted to do.

Finishing dinner, she went to the bookcase in her bedroom and picked out her college photo album. Though she and Ken had gone out together less than a year at Michigan, most of the pictures were of them together: strolling along the Sleeping Bear Dunes National Lakeshore tucked away in Michigan's Lower Peninsula; hugging after his fourth quarter comeback over Ohio State where he had thrown four TD passes; hiking in the rugged

Adirondacks of upstate New York; making funny faces in front of the Stanley Theater in Pittsburgh before a Dead concert; whitewater rafting and caving somewhere in Kentucky; tossing Frisbees and riding bikes on the Ann Arbor campus; and jumping in huge piles of autumn leaves. All great memories—all of them.

Jennifer's favorite photo was taken at Sleeping Bear Dunes. She and Patton stared out at the scenic lakeshore at sunset with their arms around one another and the ripple-marked sand dunes at their back. Their fall sweaters rustled in the breeze and their faces appeared rosy, ignited with youthful mirth. Jennifer pulled out the photograph from its plastic slot and examined it closely in the light. She felt a tide of emotion wash over her. This was how she wanted to remember their relationship.

She put away the photo album and headed into the living room, padding softly across the hand-woven Navaho rug she had brought from San Francisco. She loaded a live Dead tape, Atlanta 3/30/94, into the tape deck and adjusted the volume to a comfortable listening level. Picking up Amy Tan's most recent book from the pine coffee table, she sat down on the couch and started reading.

Before she'd finished a single paragraph, the phone rang. Reaching for the handset, she prayed it wasn't that pompous asshole Reid Farnsworth Lampert.

"Hello."

"Jennifer. It's Ken."

Oh, no. What do I say?

"I'd like to see you. I'm here in town."

"How did you get my number? It's unlisted." *That was stupid. Why did you say that?*

"Let's just say where I work we have access to certain privileged information."

"Oh, Ken," she said softly. "I want to see you too."

"Good. I'll be there in five minutes. And by the way, I've got a surprise for you."

CHAPTER 35

WHEN HE SAW HER on the front porch of the little Victorian, he felt the same jumble of emotions he had first felt when he had seen her this morning. Relieved of her stiff business suit, she looked more as he remembered her in college. She wore a simple *Steal-Your-Face* Dead T-shirt, faded jeans, and brown cowboy boots—a casual Western ensemble that he particularly liked. Her long blond hair was pulled up, her face and arms the color of honey from the summer sun, lending her the organic quality that had attracted him to her when they had first started going out.

He crossed the narrow street and climbed the stairs. When he reached the top step, she stepped forward to greet him.

"Hi, Ken," she said simply, her blue eyes lighting up with a gentle glow.

"Hey, Jenn," was all he could manage in reply. Suddenly, he felt presumptuous for the six pack of Detroit-brewed Stroh's, their beverage of choice in college, under his left arm.

"Been a long time," she said.

"Yes, it has." To conceal his discomfort, he held up the six pack. "This stuff's as rare as gold in these parts. I thought you might tip one back with me."

"I'd like that," she said. Her eyes lit up again for a moment, but then her expression changed to one of sadness. "Oh, Ken. I'm so sorry for...for everything."

He saw sincerity in her eyes, but the words still echoed painfully. He looked down, pensively, feeling twelve years of emotion welling up inside him. "Let's not go there just yet," he said, unsure if he was ready for all this.

She gave a little nod and gently touched his wrist.

He thought of how the relationship had ended. Though there might be a perfectly logical explanation why she had cast him adrift twelve years ago, he found it difficult to imagine one. He secretly hoped there had been important extenuating circumstances and their relationship hadn't fallen apart simply because of her goddamned father. Jesus Christ, there had to be more to it than that, right?

She broke through his thoughts. "It really *is* good to see you. Kind of surreal though, isn't it?"

"You could say that."

Neither of them seemed to know what to say next. Looking at her in the porch light, he realized how much he had cared for her.

"Let's go inside," she said softly.

He followed her up the stairs to her apartment. While she put the beer in the fridge, he took a moment to glance around the living room, smiling as he noticed her personality in the furnishings. Everything was tasteful, but inexpensive and organic. The couches and chairs were attractive, not garish or overly feminine, and he liked the Native American and Western touches. There were nice, simple wood-framed prints on the walls, one showing tall mountain peaks reaching up through gray clouds, another of a buckskin-clad frontiersman paddling a canoe.

"Like your apartment."

"Thanks." She walked up and handed him a beer. "By the way, do you still play a mean blues guitar?"

"You bet. They don't call me Kenny 'Guitar' Patton for nothing. But lately I've been playing mostly bluegrass. Got the hillbilly bug, I guess."

"Good for you, Panama Red," she said, and both laughed.

He smiled at her as she took a seat on the couch. When she smiled back, her eyes lit up like gemstones and took his breath away. He took a seat in the chair across from her and for a moment just watched her, thinking back to how things had once been.

CHAPTER 36

"IT'S HORRIBLE WHAT HAPPENED YESTERDAY," she said finally.

"Yes, it is," he said quietly.

"Of course I didn't vote for Kieger, but I'm still mad as hell. And sad."

"The whole country is."

They talked about it all for a few more minutes. But no words could adequately convey the sorrow and outrage they felt. It was a national tragedy that tugged at the soul of virtually every American, regardless of one's age, race, or political beliefs.

"Any new leads on the case?" she asked him.

"A few." He raised an eyebrow. "But nothing I can tell *you* about."

She grinned mischievously, and he remembered how much he had missed that grin. He felt himself relax; it was coming easier between them now.

"Want to hear my theory?"

"Sure. But first, why don't you tell me what you're doing working at American Patriots. That's the last place I'd expect to see you."

"Maybe I've changed."

"And maybe I'm Pat Robertson's long lost son. Come on—level with me. What's this all about?"

She broke into a guilty grin. "Okay, you've got me," she said, discarding all pretense. Over the next ten minutes, she described in detail her double life as a Christian activist and journalist, how she was putting together an unflattering exposé on AMP while at the same time posing as a loyal employee.

"I'm impressed," he said when she was finished. "I didn't think there were any true investigative journalists left anymore."

"Not all of us have gone the way of the Dodo."

Close to it though. "Okay, so tell me about this theory of yours."

When she leaned forward to speak, he felt as if time had warped and they were back in college again. "First of all, I don't think the Green Freedom Brigade has anything to do with the assassination. The only reason their name has come up is to implicate the president and cast suspicion upon the Democrats."

"Guilt by association."

"If Osborne and the Dems are damaged goods, that will ensure smooth sailing for Fowler. She already has a lot of goodwill from the American people—in essence, a mandate. And because we're definitely not talking about a lone gunman here and Fowler's an Establishment conservative, the group behind it is most likely hard-line too. I'm thinking a radical right-wing group like the Phineas Priesthood, Tea Party Militia, or Red State Confederacy—or maybe a small group of extremists who've splintered off from the main group. Whoever it is, they want Fowler in power instead of a progressive like Kieger. That's why they had him killed."

Patton was surprised at the breadth of her knowledge; then again, she was a journalist. But what struck him most of all was how quickly she had put together a working theory, even if he thought it was a major reach.

"I see the conspiracy theorist in you is alive and well," he said, poking fun at her.

"You don't buy it?"

"Not really. Why would right-wingers kill a Republican? Why kill one of their own? And if you're accusing the religious right, well, that's just not how they operate. They may whine like fussy children and engage in political blackmail to get what they want, but they don't kill people. That's just not their style."

"What if this group tried blackmail first and it backfired on them?"

"Then I'd say you were onto something." He took another swig of beer and decided to change the subject. "So how far along are you on this story of yours?"

"I've done all of the background research, but I'm still waiting on a few things. With this assassination, there may be a new wrinkle."

"Come on. You work with these evangelical types every day. They may be out there, but I hardly think they would kill a presidential candidate, especially a conservative one like Kieger."

"Maybe, but remember what Lyndon Johnson said. He said you don't have to worry about the left, because they rarely pick up the gun. It's the right you have to worry about. If they don't get what they want, they kill."

"I shouldn't even be discussing this with you. Not only is this an ongoing FBI investigation, but how can I possibly trust a journalist masquerading as a born-again Christian?"

"Come on, you can talk to me. I may be able to help you."

He sensed she was making a journalistic play. "You're serious, aren't you?"

"Look, I know how the system works. The FBI often uses confidential informants on cases like this. Let's just say, I too have access to certain *privileged* information."

He considered this while taking in her intense blue eyes. *Oh no, she has that look—like an insistent child.*

"Partners, Ken. Just like old times."

"This isn't why I came here tonight, to strike a deal with an informant."

"Then *why* did you come?"

"You know why."

Her face darkened with guilt. "It's been bothering you all this time, hasn't it?"

"Let's just say, I think about it now and again. The same way I think about the time I almost drowned when I was six years old."

She looked away and, for several seconds, they did not speak. Then she looked him straight in the eye and said, "I fucked up, Ken. I fucked up and now I owe you an explanation."

CHAPTER 37

IT TOOK HALF AN HOUR, but Jennifer recounted the entire story from start to finish: getting pregnant with Ken's child just before his graduation; her father coercing her into having the baby, giving it up for adoption, and ending her relationship with Ken; her banishment for eight miserable months to the unwed mother's home outside Gary, Indiana; giving birth to the baby boy she and Ken had created together; and, most anguishing, having to give the child away to the adoptive parents. She found the retelling painful, yet, at the same time, cathartic.

Patton moved onto the couch next to her. "I don't know what to say except that I'm sorry."

Jennifer's eyes were inky pools, sad and unblinking. "Kenneth Whitney—our son. I named him after you." She rattled off the vital statistics in her head, as if it had happened yesterday: *Twenty-one inches, seven pounds six ounces.*

"Where is the boy now?"

"San Francisco. Until my AMP assignment, I had been living in the Bay Area. That's where I've worked and lived the last eleven years. I had to postpone my senior year at Michigan. I transferred the following year to Berkeley, where I finished up."

"Was moving to San Francisco so you could be closer to the baby?"

"What do you think?"

"Have you seen him since...since giving him up for adoption?"

"I see him on occasion, or at least I did before I moved out here."

"Without the adoptive parents' permission?"

She detected a note of disapproval in his voice. "Every few months I just need to see him, that's all. Always from a distance. Sometimes I see him outside school, other times I go to one of his sports games."

He said nothing, just stared at her.

"I know it sounds like I'm some kind of stalker, but it isn't like that at all. He's *my* son, Ken. I don't invade his personal privacy, but that doesn't mean I can't live without him altogether. He doesn't even know I'm there. I'm like a guardian angel. I just like to watch over him, to make sure he's okay."

"My God, Jenn, how could this have happened? To you? To us?"

"I just told you how—my father." She felt the bitterness coagulate in her throat.

"I don't want to make this any harder on you than it already is. But why couldn't you have told me what was going on between you and your father? We could have found a way to work it out. After all, it was my baby too."

"What choice did I have? My father threatened to take away everything important to me unless I did what he wanted. Not only was he prepared to disown me, not only was he never going to allow me to see my mother, brothers, and sisters again, but he was going to tell your parents and force you to capitulate by embarrassing you. He was prepared to do all of these things, if I went through with an abortion, kept the child as my own, or didn't stop seeing you."

"But there must have been something we could have done. I couldn't even be there for you."

She shook her head ruefully. "It was either the unwed mother's home in Indiana—or hurting the people I loved. That was the dilemma I faced, and to this day I hate myself for buckling under my father's will. Because giving into him has cost me *more* in the long run. I didn't just lose the man I loved and my son, I lost my whole family, or at least everyone but my older brother."

She paused a moment, her mind laden with painful remembrance.

"The truth is the rift between my father and I could never heal, and it finally just tore the family apart. I'm the one they blame. I'm the selfish homewrecker who went out and got herself knocked up. I'm the one who turned dear old dad into a bitter old man. That's why I haven't seen either of my parents or siblings, except my older brother Jack, in seven years. There's just too much anger and resentment and it will never go away. Never."

His head bowed in reflection. Jennifer felt bleak, compromised. For her, the whole conversation underscored just how devastating having your path in life chosen by someone else could later turn out to be. How often had she wished she had the spring of her junior year back, that she had never gotten pregnant and trundled off to Europe with Ken as planned? She felt diminished, a hostage to the nightmare her father had forced upon her: an obsession over a son she could never hope to know.

"Was there a reason you told your parents about being pregnant and your decision to have an abortion? Instead of just keeping things between us?"

"I'd hoped they'd accept my decision. I was twenty years old—old enough to make my own choices in life—for better or worse. I wanted them to accept that, after careful soul-searching, I had made a mature, adult decision not to have the baby. I didn't want to go behind their back."

Now his tone carried a note of anger. "But what about me? You made the decision without me. You were going to have the abortion with or without my consent."

"That's not true. I was going to talk it over with you once I'd convinced my parents to support my decision. If you had felt strongly about us keeping the baby, if you'd been willing to commit to being a father, I would have agreed to it. But I didn't want to force you into anything. I didn't want us to have to elope, or to have some shotgun wedding. And I didn't want to quit school to raise a child. I was trying to be realistic. It was after my junior year of college. We were so...young."

"But you left me out of the decision. You let your crazy father determine both our fates and look where it's gotten us. We could have worked something out. You shouldn't have told your parents *anything*!"

Jennifer felt the words pierce her. It was painful to drudge up the bitter memories, to see his anger directed at her instead of her father. *But the truth is he's right,* she thought, sinking into the couch like a deflated balloon, tears welling in her eyes. In hindsight, it was obvious the decisions she had made were disastrous and far-reaching. But at the time, she had wanted to be forthcoming. She had always dealt with situations head-on instead of furtively going behind people's backs.

"Tell me, Jenn. Were you trying to get even with your father, to get him to bow to your will?"

"I don't know. Maybe," she hedged.

He took a long pull from his beer and set it down on the table. "This home for unwed mothers—what was it like?"

"It was called Christian Charities, outside Gary. It wouldn't have been so bad—if I had made the choice to have the baby on my own. But I was forced into it. I had no choice."

"What did you do there?"

"Basically, I spent eight months praying with corn-fed Midwestern girls and listening to pasty-faced nuns quoting Scripture. That, by the way, was the good part."

"And the bad part?"

"When I had to give little Kenny away. That was the worst day of my life."

The room fell silent. A tear trickled down her cheek and dropped onto her lap. Seeing Ken's numb, desolate expression, she wondered: *Why did this have to happen to us?*

"You want to know about the second worst?" she asked, wiping away the trace of the tear.

He gave a gentle nod, and took her hand.

"It's every time I see my own flesh and blood being raised by others.

It's my own private nightmare. Once that baby came out of my womb, I could never again think of him as anything other than my son. That's why I have to see him, Ken. That's why I have to see my child."

"What about the parents? Are they...are they good parents?"

"They're very good parents. It's just that..." Her voice fell away sadly.

For a moment, neither one could speak. Jennifer felt like shattered china and stared off at the painting of the storm clouds sweeping over the mountain, wondering if she would ever be able to move beyond the agony of the past.

"What happened to us, Jenn?" he whispered hoarsely, his forehead deeply creased.

"A nightmare, that's what happened. I gave up the man I loved and our child so that I wouldn't become an outcast. The truth is I was weak."

"You weren't weak. How could anyone be expected to risk never seeing their mother again, or their brothers and sisters, over a baby that hasn't even been born yet?"

"I didn't know that I would become so attached to little Ken. But then, after spending those first few days with him, I couldn't bring myself to give him up altogether."

He took her in his arms, letting her grief siphon into him. "I understand now," he said softly.

She drew closer. "Choosing between an abortion and bearing a child is not an easy choice for any woman. That's why calling an abortion a simple medical procedure is wrong, because it's *always* a heart-wrenching dilemma. If my father hadn't been involved and I'd decided to have an abortion, I'd still live every day with that loss. But it would have been my choice and the moral burden would rest solely with me. Instead, I had no real choice. And that was wrong. A woman should have the right to choose what to do with her own body."

He held her tighter, his voice turning to an anguished murmur. "Yesterday's gone, Jenn. No matter how hard we try, we can never get it back."

"I know," she said. "Instead we have to live with it for the rest of our lives."

TUESDAY

CHAPTER 38

THE OLD NORTH END—the upper-brackets neighborhood near the Colorado College campus where the illustrious Benjamin Bradford Locke lived—was only a few blocks from the heart of downtown Colorado Springs. It was here that early 20th Century Cripple Creek mineral barons built a sumptuous enclave of spectacular mansions and filled them with the finest furnishings Europe and the Orient had to offer. For several blocks in each direction, intricate wrought-iron fences enclosed soaring Victorians and Tudors. The streets were wide—General William Palmer, the city's founder, insisted on them being wide enough to make a U-turn in his carriage—and lined with towering spruce, elm, oak, and pine. The Old North End spoke of an idle grandeur of a bygone era, and contrasted sharply with the blandly homogeneous subdivisions and obscene trophy homes being thrown up around the state.

Locke's two-story Tudor manor was not as imposing as those from Millionaire's Row, the Old North End's most celebrated enclave of aristocracy, but it was impressive nonetheless. Erected in the Roaring Twenties, the house was fashioned of cream-painted stucco and dark brown timber trim. Serpentine ivy ran up to the windows on the second floor. A grand old maple stood resolutely near the center of the expansive front lawn, and a pair of towering oaks gently nudged the side of the house. The front walkway was an intricate pattern of Colorado Lyons Sandstone.

Setting down his mineral water, Benjamin Locke took a seat at his spacious desk, checked his watch, and mentally prepared himself for his important conference call in three minutes. To the casual eye, his private study looked like nothing more than the masculine retreat of a very wealthy man with a fussy fondness for Christian religious artifacts. One wall displayed original copper engravings by late fifteenth-century German master Martin Schongauer illustrating Holy Night and other spectacular motifs deeply rooted in the Northern European Protestant tradition. From another wall hung a popular painting by William Holman Hunt entitled "The Light of the World" in which Christ was portrayed knocking at the allegorical door of the heart, waiting to enlighten it with his lamp of truth. Beneath the picture's frame was a quote from Revelation 3:20: "Behold, I stand at the door and knock." The glass cases built into the walls were packed with Christian icons, images, bells, Eucharistic vestments, church ornaments, and three priceless illuminated manuscripts. To the right of his monstrous desk, the floor-to-ceiling bookcases were stuffed with the leather-bound writings of Martin Luther, John Calvin, Billy Graham, and other renowned Protestant religious leaders throughout world history.

But Locke's *sanctum sanctorum* actually contained so much more, things that had nothing to do with God Almighty and couldn't be seen. The walls were soundproofed and contained microlayers of copper and zinc to protect against directional microphones. The hidden speakers at the window and along the walls quietly hummed with background "white noise" to filter out the sound of voices, a built-in electronic surveillance jammer. His phone was equipped with a pre-programmed controller that automatically swept the line for wiretaps. Similar devices were embedded in the ceiling and scanned for eavesdropping equipment in the room twice daily. The small metal box next to his phone was equipped with a tonal modulator that electronically distorted voices and rendered them unrecognizable. And in the right hand drawer of his desk was a Beretta 9mm semiauto, stoked with seventeen rounds and equipped with custom noise- and flash-suppressors, not exactly the firearm of choice for the average home protector.

After again checking his watch, Locke dialed a number from memory in Chesapeake, Virginia. The call was received by a switching box and forwarded to an unlisted number and switching box, and from there to an untraceable number in Orange County, California. Ten seconds later, four ranking members of the Coalition's Executive Committee were patched in on secure lines from four different locations. Locke pressed a button on the small black box beside the telephone, activating the voice modulator.

"Good morning, gentlemen," he announced, his voice a full two octaves lower than normal, like a record played at slow speed.

"Good morning, Mr. Chairman," several voices chimed in unison, each and every one also electronically distorted so they couldn't be identified.

"There have been some new developments. First, I was paid a little visit yesterday." Locke quickly recounted his interview with Agents Patton and Taylor regarding the buttons.

Joseph Truscott, his main rival for the chairmanship of the Coalition, challenged him right off the bat. "And you're not concerned?" sniffed the retired CIA deputy director for operations, calling from his sprawling ranch in nearby Westcliffe.

Locke deftly parried Skull Eyes. "Not at all," he replied smoothly. "The souvenirs are a wild goose chase. There are millions of them. It will lead to nothing."

"I still don't understand the why of it," said Senator Dubois, Locke's most loyal ally on the Coalition's Executive Committee. The renowned Republican senator was plugged in from his antebellum mansion in Baton Rouge. "Why would the asset pull a stunt like that in the first place?"

"I believe it's to get our attention. Gomez is letting us know that he knows about us in case we refuse to pay him or send someone to pay him a visit. A thinly veiled threat, if you will."

"Then how do the other souvenirs fit in?" Skull Eyes pressed him.

"I'm not sure at this point," Locke admitted. "It's possible they were left behind simply as false clues. But I don't think the item in question can be included in that category."

"Is the asset's agent standing by his story?" posed A.W. Windholz, media and tobacco magnate, president of United Broadcasting, and head of the American Right-to-Life Foundation. He was patched in from Herndon, Virginia.

The response came from "Skull Eyes" Truscott, to whom the question was directed. "Xavier says he doesn't know why it happened but that it doesn't matter. He still wants the remainder of the compensation."

"Are we going to give it to him?" inquired Windholz.

"I don't see how after that damned stunt."

"Are you suggesting we take the produce off the shelf?" asked Colonel Caleb Heston, calling from his commodious, Southwestern-style adobe house just south of the Air Force Academy.

"I don't think we need to venture down that path at this time, gentlemen," interjected Locke before Skull Eyes could answer, asserting his control over the meeting. "True, the asset and his agent both pose a potential risk, but I believe the situation can be resolved peacefully."

"We definitely don't want to mess with Gomez," said Skull Eyes. "But we can't just let him get away with this either. We need to send both him and Xavier a message."

"I think the asset poses more of a threat than we are acknowledging," said the colonel. "Our friend the Apostle could handle the assignment quickly and efficiently. We could put this ugly business behind us once and for all."

"He would certainly get the job done—and for cheap," agreed Truscott.

"As I said, I don't think we need to resort to any precipitous action at this early stage," said Locke, feeling a touch of consternation, as he so often did, with Skull Eyes and the colonel. In his view, violence was only to be used as a last resort or to keep someone from talking, which was at odds with his two more bellicose counterparts. "My recommendation is to make Xavier sweat for a few days before paying up. I know none of us like surprises, but the buttons won't amount to anything."

"I concur with our humble chairman," said Dubois, coming to his defense. "Let Xavier sweat for a couple days then pay the balance."

"I second the motion," agreed A.W. Windholz.

"Very well, that settles it," said Locke, relieved to have outmaneuvered his two main rivals on a technicality. "Let's move on, gentlemen, to the next action item on the agenda, the progress on the California front. The Apostle has completed his assignment. Apparently everything went off smoothly. It should be days before the merchandise is even found."

"How long until the point of origin is tracked down?" asked Windholz, a cryptic reference to the source of the Ares virus.

"The best estimate is Wednesday or Thursday," the colonel replied.

"I had the opportunity to see the feds in action at my office yesterday afternoon," Locke said. "They fell for the deception like bees to honey. The word from our inside sources is they are devoting considerable manpower to tracking down the point of origin."

"Working out of Denver?" Dubois asked.

"No, San Francisco."

There was a momentary silence. "So everything is proceeding according to plan," said Truscott.

Am I mistaken or is there a trace of skepticism in his voice? "Yes," replied Locke. "Everything is proceeding according to plan. But we must keep in mind that it is still early."

"What about your meeting with the president-elect? Did that go *as planned*?"

Locke refused to allow himself to be goaded by Skull Eye's skeptical tone. "The meeting went very well. I laid out our offer and, as you might expect, she was quite pleased with it. She's on board with the platform in every respect and the Stealth PAC transfer will go through by the end of the week. We have chosen wisely, gentlemen."

There was a low rumble of approval on the other end, which Locke found gratifying.

"I know I speak for *everyone* when I say, you've done a masterful job, Mr. Chairman," said the colonel, taking him pleasantly by surprise.

Everyone except Skull Eyes that is, Locke wanted to say, knowing full well where he genuinely stood with the one man who would be more than happy to end his reign as chairman of the Executive Committee. "Thank you, Colonel. My compliments." He raised an imaginary glass in a toast. "To Phase Three, gentlemen."

"To Phase Three!" all but his chief rival chanted in unison. And with that, the conference call was brought to an inspired conclusion.

It was then Locke heard a knock on his office door.

It must be his wife, he realized. "Yes, just a moment, dear," he said.

He rose from his chair, went to the door, unlocked it, and slowly opened it. To his surprise, both his wife and daughter were standing there, looking tense and anxious, as if they had something important to tell him.

"We need to talk, Benjamin," said his wife. "And you're not going to like it."

CHAPTER 39

SEATED AGAIN AT HIS OFFICE DESK, Benjamin Bradford Locke took a deep breath to control his outrage. He couldn't believe what he had just heard. In fact, the widely-respected Christian leader, acting chieftain of the publically visible American Patriots organization, and elected chairman of the secret political society, the Coalition, could not remember having ever been blindsided like this before.

"What do you mean Susan's pregnant? There must be some mistake."

"It's no mistake," replied his wife, Mary. She was a healthily plump, ruddy-cheeked woman in her late-fifties. Normally she would have had a pleasant smile on her face, but not today.

Locke looked disapprovingly at his daughter. The girl's face was red with shame. He felt badly for her, but he was still in shock at the startling announcement.

"How far along are you, Susan?"

"Eight weeks," answered his wife.

He looked at her and shook his head. "Did you know before today?"

"No, of course not."

"But you suspected. For how long?"

She looked at him guiltily. "A week, maybe two."

Locke looked back at his daughter. "Susan, you know that we both love you dearly. But I don't understand how you could have possibly allowed this to happen. After everything we've done for you, how could you treat us like this?"

The seventeen-year-old's lips trembled and tears suddenly poured from her eyes.

Locke felt horrible for making her cry, but he was still mad as hell. He looked sternly at his wife. "I take it Todd's the father?"

She nodded ruefully.

Locke shook his head again, this time with disgust. The truth was he had never approved of Todd Somersby. It didn't make any difference that Susan was crazy about him or that he was co-captain of the Cheyenne Mountain football team or that he came from a prominent family from the Broadmoor. Locke had never quite trusted the kid, but he also couldn't stand his daughter dating a boy who wore an earring, only went to church at Christmas, and whose parents were fundraisers for Planned Parenthood.

But he put up with it because he truly loved his daughter more than anything else in the world and he wanted her to be happy. Now it was painfully obvious that his lack of trust in the boy had been well-founded. If only Susan had stayed away from Todd Somersby, this shameful indiscretion would never have happened.

"Todd and I love each other. That's why…that's why it happened." The girl's voice trailed away despondently.

Locke rose from his chair, went to the window, and stared out at the mountains as Susan quietly sobbed and his wife soothingly reassured her. Massive Pikes Peak seemed unusually cold and distant to him today.

"I never trusted that boy," he admitted to them both for the first time. "And now he's gone and gotten you pregnant. I always knew he would do something like this."

Suddenly, an unexpected voice at the open door interrupted them.

"What's this I hear? Dear little Sis has gotten herself knocked up?"

All eyes turned toward the doorway.

Benjamin Jr. strutted into the room like a game rooster. The nineteen-year-old was the spitting image of his father, but he lacked his father's charismatic personality, dignified sense of etiquette, and ability to command a room. He also had an egotistical, venomous quality that people found offensive. He had been expelled last spring from Bob Jones University, after he and two other boys were arrested for beating up a homosexual student in Columbia. Locke's high-powered attorney succeeded in getting the charges dropped in return for a $250,000 settlement, so Benjamin Jr. didn't do any prison time. But given his father's national prominence, the story received ample media coverage and the Bob Jones disciplinary committee, which normally would have dismissed such actions as mere fraternal "hazing," had no choice but to send the kid packing.

After the incident, Locke brought his son home with the proviso that he take a year off from college, undergo Christian counseling, and work at AMP. For the last few months, Benjamin Jr. had been helping with the voter scorecards and gathering research for religious rights newswatch stories, but he was harsh and arrogant and the employees resented him. Meantime, Locke was pulling strings to get him into lowly Grapevine Bible College in Texas. The task was proving difficult.

"Your mother and I are taking care of the situation, Benjamin. There's no reason for you to get involved."

"Really? Dear little Sis is behaving like Madonna and I have to keep my mouth shut, is that it?"

"My God, have you no feelings?" cried Mary, wrapping both arms around Susan protectively to comfort her. "Can't you see what she's going through?"

"I'm sorry, but she brought this upon herself."

Locke felt his temper rising. "That's enough, Benjamin," he bristled. "I said your mother and I are handling this."

"You've always been too soft on her. That's why she's gone and done this. Please tell me you're not going to actually let her see Mr. All-State Linebacker again. Not after this disgrace."

Susan appeared terrified. "What? Of course I'm going to see Todd again."

"I'm afraid that's out of the question," said Locke, and he instantly felt a stab of regret at the harsh finality in his voice. "At least for a while," he added to soften the blow.

"But he's the father of my child."

"One can only hope," snickered Benjamin Jr.

"That's enough, Benjamin," Locke said for the second time, stepping protectively between the boy and Susan, who started to cry again.

"Why are you protecting her like this when she's gone and performed the worst sin imaginable? What the little harlot needs is to be severely punished."

Locke couldn't believe what he was hearing. "How dare you talk to your sister like that! I've heard quite enough out of you, young man! Leave us at once before I kick you out of this house!"

He wagged his finger and stepped toward him aggressively to underscore his parental authority. The boy backed up. For the first time, a look of genuine fear—and the warranted respect—appeared on his beefy, pimply face.

"Leave us now," commanded Locke. "I'll be down in a minute. And never talk to your sister like that again. Do you understand me?"

The boy bowed his head submissively. "Yes, sir." He started to leave, but turned around when he reached the door. "You know, Dad, I'm just trying to help. You know that, right?"

Locke knew perfectly well it was a lie, but held his tongue. The boy was up to his usual trick: trying to make Susan look bad while at the same time win over Locke's affections. The ugly truth was that Benjamin Jr. didn't care a lick what happened to his sister, nor did he care for anyone but himself. Looking at him standing with fake contrition in the doorway, Locke felt nothing but fatherly disappointment. *Good Lord, will he ever amount to anything, or am I going to be bailing him out of trouble for the rest of his life?*

"Wait for me in the kitchen, Son."

The boy nodded obediently and walked from the room. Locke watched him disapprovingly for a moment before returning his gaze to his wife and daughter. They both looked at the bulky, receding figure with burning contempt. What was happening to his family? First his son had been kicked out of college, and now his daughter was pregnant out of wedlock at the precise moment that he was trying to rescue America from self-destruction. Could the timing possibly be any worse?

"That son of yours will be the death of us," grumbled his wife.

"He's your son too, Mary."

"Sometimes I wish he wasn't."

"Come now, you can't mean that. He's going through a tough time right now, just like Susan, and needs our support."

"He's nothing like Susan."

"It is not right to favor one child over another, regardless of their shortcomings."

"Well, I've given up on him. He's mean as a snake." She gave a weary sigh and looked worriedly at her daughter, whose eyes were bloodshot. "We need to leave Susan in peace. I'm keeping her home from school. She's been through enough for one day."

"That's fine." He looked at his daughter with a mixture of sympathy and disappointment. "Susan, I'm sorry for the way your brother treated you. And I'm also sorry if I upset you. But you must realize that you have let us all down. Your parents, your peers, and the Lord our God." He let his forceful gaze linger, making sure she understood the seriousness of the situation. "At the same time, we are going to give you the opportunity to make up for this."

"B-But how?"

"Your mother and I will decide. All you need to worry about is coming through this stronger and better than before."

She leaned over and hugged him, tears in her eyes. "Thank you, Daddy. Thank you for your understanding."

He smiled reassuringly. "Everyone deserves a second chance in this world. Especially my baby girl."

CHAPTER 40

AFTER THEY LEFT THE ROOM, he sat back down at his desk to make one last call before eating breakfast and heading off to work at American Patriots with his son. But as he reached for his daytimer, the secure phone on his desk rang, beating him to the punch. Only a select group of individuals had the unlisted number, so he knew it had to be important. He punched a button on the voice modulator next to the phone before speaking into the mouthpiece.

"Hello," he said, his voice electronically distorted.

"How are you today, Mr. Chairman?" It was a man's voice, undistorted, and Locke recognized it instantly as that of Fowler's right hand man, Peter Frautschi.

"Just fine, thank you, Pete," he replied, though he was still furious over his daughter's pregnancy and his son's cruel ways. "Congratulations on your being appointed chief of staff."

"Thanks. Things are moving quickly."

"Indeed they are. I know this can't be a simple courtesy call. You want your money, don't you?"

"I wouldn't have put it quite that bluntly. Let's just say I'm a big fan of twenty-million-dollar political contributions delivered at precisely the right moment in history."

"I'll make arrangements for the transfer today."

"Good. I want two people to have full discretionary authority on the accounts. The names are Chip Chapin and J.D. Wells."

Locke wrote the names down on a piece of paper. "I'll call you back with the account numbers later this afternoon."

"Pleasure doing business with you," Frautschi said, and he was gone.

CHAPTER 41

AFTER CHECKING UP on the troops in the bullpen, Patton returned to his desk, pulled out a stack of case files, and grabbed his iPod from his desk drawer. He didn't feel like fiddle music right now while he worked, so he scrolled from Vassar Clements to something a little jazzier and more wildly improvisational, Bela Fleck and the Flecktones. As he was about to place the headphones on, his desk phone rang. He quickly checked the caller ID.

Sharp—damn!

He lifted the phone after the second ring. "What's up, Henry?"

"I need to know what went down at the elevator on the fourteenth floor before we brief the governor."

"I'll be right—" But Sharp was already off the line.

Asshole! Patton muttered to himself as he hung up the phone. Reaching across his cluttered desk, he grabbed the autopsy report on Chris Clark and Kim Purky prepared by the Armed Forces Institute of Pathology and headed down the hallway to Sharp's office.

He gave a little rap on the half-open door and walked in.

"Take a seat," his boss commanded him, scratching a gold pen across his notepad.

Patton did as instructed, pondering the supreme irony of being handed the case of his career, but under the direction of Wyatt Fucking Earp!

As if on cue, the ASAC put his pen down, leaned back in his chair, and began twisting the tips of his gunfighter's mustache with his fingers in the way that Patton found irritating. "All right, tell me what you've got on the elevator killings, Special Agent—and don't leave anything out."

Suppressing a gulp, Patton quickly scanned the summary page of the autopsy report. "Both victims received gunshot wounds from a high-velocity, heavy-caliber firearm. The bullets were expanding, softnosed types. Three perforating wounds in each victim. Not penetrating wounds."

"So what you're telling me is the shooter used dum-dums."

Patton nodded. Dum-dums were the poor man's explosive cartridge. Their soft- or hollow-point tips ensured that a bullet flattened and expanded on impact, providing maximum knockdown power and causing massive damage. They were far deadlier than normal bullets, because they left a gaping hole upon exiting the body much larger than the entrance wound.

"But dum-dums are everywhere these days. And the slugs are probably useless for ballistics."

Patton conceded this point with a nod. "The projectile deformity was severe in both victims. The recovered slugs were flat as a pancake. No land or groove markings. The examiners couldn't even come up with a probable firearm, let alone a match."

"That doesn't leave us with much."

"We still have one thing."

"I'm listening."

"The examiners were able to reconstruct the trajectory of one of the bullets that struck Kim Purky. Based on the reconstruction, they found a descending firing line. They determined the shooter had to be over six feet tall, but no taller than six-three."

"That's assuming the victim was standing upright when shot. But we don't know that for sure."

Patton couldn't help a little smile. "Ah, but we do. The spatter patterns show that both victims fell straight back when they were shot. Had they been kneeling, their legs would have been trapped beneath them as they fell back and the mist portion of the spray wouldn't have been as dispersed. By all indications, Chris Clark and Kim Purky were standing upright, about to step into the elevator, when they were killed."

"Why didn't they just turn and run?"

"Chances are they were shot the instant the elevator doors opened and didn't have time to. Also, there were no powder burns or tattoos on the skin or in any of the wound tracks. So the shots had to have been fired from over two feet."

"Still, you'd think they would have tried to run or duck for cover."

"Not if they were paralyzed with fear. Or maybe the assassin didn't look threatening to them."

"What do you mean?"

"Maybe the guy didn't look like a killer. Maybe he was in disguise or something."

The phone rang, interrupting the conversation. Sharp leaned across the desk and picked it up before the second ring. "Yeah," he said impatiently.

Patton pretended to study the patterns of the perfectly vacuumed carpet as Sharp spoke into the mouthpiece. His boss was getting on his nerves. It was like he was playing some kind of psychological game, trying to score points with subtle putdowns and shallow contradictions. But why was he doing it? What could he possibly stand to gain?

Sharp hung up the phone and smiled.

"What is it?" Patton asked.

"Taylor's found something—something important."

CHAPTER 42

THEY DASHED down the hallway to the bullpen where the task force was busy at work. The room was as frenetic as a stock trading floor and smelled of stale pizza and bitter coffee. There were four standard DVD players with color monitors set up on a long table against the wall, and in front of each one sat a technician and a small crowd of agents. Senior Secret Service Agent Fred Taylor parted through the crowd and led them to the monitor where Agent Weiss was sitting. The screen was frozen with a grainy image of a fair-haired, medium-built man with a mustache and dark sunglasses. The man wore a brown UPS delivery uniform and matching cap and was pushing a package cart.

Taylor instructed Weiss to roll the disk. The man in the uniform began moving toward the camera with the cart, which was filled with long tubes, boxes, and letter-sized packs, all with UPS air bill stickers. Patton noted that the man's brown UPS cap was pulled down low over his eyes and he kept his head inclined downward toward the pavement. There was a shadow of facial hair along his chin and running up to his ears, and a tuft of light-colored, curly chest hair was visible in the V of his unbuttoned UPS shirt. Using the cart for scale, Patton estimated his height at around five foot eight.

"This is the southwest entrance to the Union Plaza Building," Taylor said, providing a narrative to the silent film. "The subject you see here entered the building at 3:57 P.M. on Friday afternoon, took the elevator to the fiftieth floor, and disappeared. We have no record of him coming back down or leaving the building."

As the man began pushing his way through the revolving door, Taylor motioned to the technician to the left of Weiss to begin rolling a second DVD, showing a different camera angle. "This is from the lobby," he said. The man in the uniform appeared again, pushing the cart through the door towards the bank of elevators on the right.

"Do we have any idea who he is?" Sharp asked.

"Not yet. But he's no UPS delivery man," Taylor said. "He's gone to great lengths to conceal his identity from the security cameras."

Patton had noticed that straight off. The guy hadn't looked up once. Even if he had, the cap was pulled so low it would be difficult to see his upper face. But Patton did manage to catch an important detail as the third screen was activated and the man was filmed from the rear. A blond ponytail dangled from the guy's UPS cap and down the back of his jacket.

To the fourth technician, Taylor said, "Let the last one run."

The view showed the man pushing the cart into an elevator. In the background, Patton could see a security guard pause a moment to check out the man and then look away, disinterested.

The elevator doors closed and the man disappeared. They all watched as the floor numbers lit up above the elevator, one after another. Taylor moved closer to the screen, his face filled with expectancy. "Here it comes." He pointed to the light for the fiftieth floor, which lit up. "Bingo."

They all looked at one another.

Sharp said, "You're sure none of the footage shows this guy coming back down to the lobby or leaving through any of the exits?"

"Positive," Taylor said. "He went to the fiftieth floor and there's no record of him after that. None of the ten or more security cameras still operating Sunday afternoon show him coming back down. My guess is this guy took out the two cameras in the parking garage so he wouldn't be seen leaving the building."

"Okay, so we know he's an accomplice at least. But is he our killer?"

"I don't know if we have enough to answer that question. His role may have been to get the shooter inside once he disabled the security cameras in the garage."

"But there's no record of entry in the garage on the day of the assassination," Patton pointed out. "So he couldn't have let someone in unless he disabled the card keypad. And the security company said it wasn't tampered with."

Sharp held up a hand. "Let's go through it one more time."

As Patton watched the sequence again, it dawned on him how perfectly suited the UPS delivery guy was for the job, if he was, in fact, the assassin. Anonymity was a contract killer's best friend, and with his bland uniform and air of quiet efficiency, this guy blended in like an everyday package handler. Here he was, pushing a cart into a building, past a security guard, and heading to the fiftieth floor without raising a single eyebrow. The guy was the very picture of anonymity.

"I think he's our shooter," Patton said when they were finished. "He doesn't care about being seen going in, but he definitely doesn't want to be ID'd going out. Why? Because he wore a disguise, something different than the UPS uniform he wore going in. What the package handler front gives him is the perfect way to sneak in all his gear: his disguise, sniper's rifle, and other equipment."

"If you're right," Taylor said, "he would have had to wait all weekend to make the hit. The speakers' platform wasn't set up until Saturday afternoon."

"But just by knowing the speech was going to be at the plaza, he could easily find out where the platform would be. It's always set up on the west end, closest to the City and County Building."

"You two can work the details out later," Sharp said impatiently. "Right now, we've got to move on what we know for sure." He looked at Patton. "I want you to talk to the receptionist again plus the security people, the guard, and UPS. See if anyone remembers this guy. Also, put together a photo-kit and send out a wanted pronto."

"I'm on it."

"I'll get started on the campaign footage," Taylor said. "Chances are this guy's been trailing Kieger for some time."

"Let's get busy then, people," snapped Sharp.

Suddenly, Patton thought of something. "Wait a second, Henry. We still have a problem."

"Yeah, what's that?"

"If this guy's the assassin, why is he not even close to six feet tall?"

CHAPTER 43

FIVE MINUTES LATER, with the unanswered question still ringing in his head, Patton went to Dr. Thomas Hamilton's office on the seventeenth floor. Hamilton was the sole criminal profiler in the Denver field office, which meant he had the responsibility of trying to get inside the mind of every violent wacko pursued by the FBI in the Rocky Mountain region. A Ph.D. in Criminology-Abnormal Psychology from Penn State and a decade with the Critical Incident Response Group in Quantico garnered him this unusual honor. Quantico was home base for the Bureau's foremost behavioral sciences sleuths, who grappled with the most twisted, horrifying, and intriguing aspects of the criminal mind. It was, needless to say, more than just a job.

Patton had given Hamilton all the case information so he could work up a profile on the assassin. That insight would, hopefully, produce promising leads on the perpetrator's identity. But having just seen the video, Patton wanted to hear what Hamilton's thoughts were on the assassin before the profiler had observed the video footage. That way, his profile would not be tainted by visual bias.

"Howdy, Doc. How's it going?"

The freckle-faced criminal profiler was hunched over a book as thick as Tolstoy's *War and Peace*. When he looked up and saw his new guest, he pulled off his John Lennon glasses, rubbed his eyes, and pushed the book to the side. "I've made some headway. The profile's still preliminary, but I think I have enough to give you some idea of who we're dealing with here."

Patton took a seat in the upholstered leather chair in front of his desk. "Music to my ears."

"Okay, we already know we're dealing with a pro, but now we can get into some specifics. I believe our man is a veteran freelance assassin backed by a well-organized, ideologically driven group. He himself is not an ideologue, but an intelligent, highly trained operative who kills for money. A great deal of money."

Patton began typing notes on his iPad. "You said *he*. Can we be certain it's a man?" he asked, playing devil's advocate even as the image of the UPS man on the tape floated through his mind.

"Not one hundred percent. But the preliminary results from the firearm analysis and the hair samples are most consistent with an adult male suspect. There are other considerations too—for example, the nature of the crime. Ninety-eight percent of violent crimes are committed by men. So from the start, without any evidence in the case, there's a ninety-eight percent statistical probability the assassination was committed by a man.

"Now why is this the case? Why is it that women don't kill in anywhere near the numbers men do? The answer is—you're going to love this—we don't know. Some researchers speculate it has to do with testosterone levels or other hormonal interactions. Others point out that women seem to internalize their stressors, punishing themselves instead of lashing out at others. They tend to turn to drugs, alcohol, suicide, things like that to take out their frustrations, whereas men simply take it out on the rest of the world."

"But you're talking about postal nutcases, petty murderers, and serial killers not professional assassins. There are women trained by the global terrorist groups who have no problem killing."

"Those women are unique. They perceive themselves as soldiers, freedom-fighters for their cause. They're pursuing dreams of a better life for their people, trying to change social and governmental policies. Many of these women come from brutal political regimes that subject dissenting citizens to extreme psychological or physical abuse. This helps them convince themselves they are soldiers fighting for a noble cause."

"Okay, so what you're saying is it's mainly men who are greedy enough to do it for money, and violent enough to make a career out of it."

"So much for our lofty position in the hierarchy of organic life."

"So based on what you've told me, I can probably eliminate women from my database search."

"I'm not sure I would do that, but I would keep any female suspects in a separate file. I can't say a woman couldn't have done it, mind you, just that it's highly unlikely."

"Seems that way to me too," Patton said, picturing the man in the video. "But I just wanted to cover my bases. So, now that we've done that, tell me more about our perp. We know he's an experienced pro, not some military wannabe loser like Oswald or Sirhan Sirhan. He blends into unfamiliar surroundings easily. He probably works on a recommendation basis and doesn't deal directly with strangers."

"Or has a control agent that handles these matters for him." The profiler smiled with amusement at his pupil. "Please continue, Special Agent."

"Okay, he comes from a military, paramilitary, or terrorist background. Which is why he's equipped with sophisticated military hardware and has the ability to move into an area unknown to him, perform his assignment, and get out quickly. He doesn't get any satisfaction when he kills, but he doesn't feel remorse either. He's not like a crime-of-passion murderer, a serial killer, or sexual predator. He has no psychological motivation for killing. For him, it's all about the money. How am I doing?"

"Not bad. But I would add a few things to our laundry list. First, he kills only when the money from the last job is close to spent. Judging by the importance of the figure he just killed, I would say he takes in a small fortune for every successful hit. Which means he doesn't work very often, because he doesn't have to.

"Second, our man is a student of the game. He learns a great deal about his victims beforehand to ensure the cleanest hit possible. He will follow his target for weeks, maybe even months, amassing photographs, memorizing daily routines, perhaps even finding ways to coerce or bribe members of the target's inner circle."

"We're looking into all the Kieger campaign tapes to see if we can pick this guy out."

"Good. Third, we're dealing with one clever and experienced S.O.B. He's a master at complex problem-solving and has many years of practice at this sort of thing. But that presents a problem for him. As brilliant as he is, he must feel enormous stress in his life. A shooter of his caliber is, no doubt, being pursued by many of the world's law enforcement agencies and perhaps rival assassins. Slowly but surely, they are closing in on him. How he deals with this constant stress and tension in his everyday life is critical."

"So the probability of the killer being an ideologue is remote?"

Hamilton nodded. "What we have is a cool, calm, and collected professional killer. One clever and anonymous enough to steal his way into a high-rise building undetected despite a state-of-the-art security system and an army of law enforcement people. Someone with the training necessary to assassinate the president-elect at long-range with a rare American-made military-style rifle. Someone capable of taking out two unsuspecting innocents without blinking an eye and then disappearing into thin air, perhaps with the assistance of others, perhaps not. This guy shows the classic profile of the highly organized violent criminal: military-style planning and execution, preselected weapons, and nonrandom victim selection."

Patton held up his hand, signaling he needed a moment to catch up with his iPad notes. He was excited by what he had learned thus far; Hamilton seemed to have pieced together a plausible conceptual model of the killer, one untainted by preconceptions since he had not viewed the video footage. It was time now to allow him the opportunity to see how his theory gibed with celluloid reality.

"You should know, though, there is a problem with this type of criminal," added Hamilton.

"Yeah, what's that?"

"He's, by far, the most difficult to catch."

Patton gave him a knowing look. "Oh, I don't know about that, Doc. Let's see how you feel after you've seen my little video."

"Is it X-rated?"

"Not exactly. But I think you'll find it titillating just the same."

CHAPTER 44

JENNIFER ODDEN ATE LUNCH at her desk while listening to a killer Dead tape on her iPod. The show was Vegas 5/31/92 with a heart-stirring *Help is on the Way→Slipknot→Franklin's Tower* opener that brought down the house. At half past noon, she took a last bite of her lunch and put the plastic container back in her Arctic Zone mini-cooler. The angel hair pasta with marinated tofu, snow peas, and carrots was delicious, but it failed to satisfy her. She decided to grab some tortilla chips from the lunchroom vending machine.

As she started down the hallway, she saw Marlene "Suie" Tanner stepping into the elevator with an orange, accordion-style folder under her arm. Marlene was no ordinary employee. As Locke's executive secretary, she had unique insight into his daily schedule and what went on at the highest levels of American Patriots. She was also one of only four people with access to Fileroom E, the others being Locke, Archibald Roberts, director of communications/PR, and Chuck Valentine, director of human resources. Unlike Filerooms A, B, C, and D, which were also in the basement, Fileroom E was the only fileroom with restricted access. The room supposedly housed HR records, but Jennifer suspected far more revealing documents could be found there. As a journalist, she knew that records kept behind locked doors usually contained secrets worth knowing about.

Jennifer had never seen the contents of a file from Fileroom E, but she knew everything stored there, including CDs and DVDs, was put into an orange folder like the one Marlene now carried. If the room did contain sensitive documents, she *had* to get her hands on them. She had promised one Reid Farnsworth Lampert that she would, and the last thing she wanted was to fail in her mission and allow the sniveling bastard the satisfaction of yanking her off the story. She only had until Thursday to turn up something big—or that was the end of it.

But Marlene could help her solve her problem.

Without drawing attention to herself, she made her way quickly to the fire stairs. If she was going to get to the basement before Marlene, she had to scramble down ten flights of stairs and beat the elevator. When she reached the stairs, she moved at breakneck speed, her low pumps clattering against the concrete, making stabbing echo sounds in the stairwell.

Reaching the basement, she peered through the narrow window that looked out into the hallway and the door to Fileroom E. To her relief, Marlene had not yet arrived, though Jennifer could hear the click-clack of her high-heeled shoes on the linoleum floor. The stairwell was directly across from the room, giving Jennifer a good angled view to the door and, more critically, to the cyber keypad that unlocked Fileroom E.

This was Jennifer's fourth attempt at identifying the six numbers of the keypad's digital code. From the three prior occasions, she'd discovered the first three numbers and the last number. This time, she hoped to catch the fourth and fifth numbers, giving her the complete code.

Marlene materialized from the left and scanned the hallway. She was tubby and pug-faced, with blood red fingernail polish, matching lipstick, and the kind of polyester stretch-pant business outfit worn by seriously overweight women. Jennifer stepped to the edge of the window and peeked through cautiously, keeping her head out of view.

Be careful—don't let her see you.

Marlene raised a stubby index finger to the digital keypad. The numbers were arranged in two vertical columns, numbers one through five in descending order on the left, six through nine plus zero on the right. Jennifer had no problem confirming the first three numbers. The two, three, and six were all high up on the keypad and easily observed. But then Marlene's hand slid down to touch the two lower keys Jennifer had been unable to catch the last two times. She saw the first number punched— five—but the next number was obscured by Marlene's pudgy knuckles. *Was that a zero, or another five?* Then Marlene pushed the last number— six—which Jennifer already knew.

There was an audible *click* as the door unlocked.

Marlene pulled back the handle and stepped inside the room, the door swinging closed behind her.

Jennifer waited a few seconds, making sure the coast was clear, before opening the stairwell door and creeping into the hallway. While it was still fresh on her mind, she wanted to recreate the way Marlene had held her hand when she had punched in the second-to-last number. Jennifer felt fairly sure it had been a zero, but she wanted to be certain. It would take Marlene a few minutes to file away the contents of the thick orange folder, so the risk was acceptable, as long as she was quiet and didn't actually touch the keypad.

She pretended to punch in the numbers, just as Marlene had done. Two, three, six, five, zero, six. *No, that's not right.* She tried it again, this time substituting a five for the zero. *That's it—two fives after all. Marlene must have punched twice with her middle finger.*

There was a sudden shuffle of feet inside the room. What was going on? How could Marlene have possibly finished her filing already?

Jennifer darted across the hall, reached for the door to the stairwell, slipped through the door, and closed it quickly behind her.

Her heart thumped against her chest.

As the door clicked shut, she turned and peered through the window looking out into the hallway. The door to Fileroom E opened and Marlene stepped out, scanning the hallway with the suspicious scowl of a prison guard.

Oh no!

Jennifer ducked down. Then she crept to the stairs and ascended them quickly but quietly, too scared even to breathe.

When she reached the first landing, the door to the stairwell flung open. She lunged for the wall and crouched down, hoping the staircase and steel railing concealed her from below.

In the metallic echo of the stairwell, Marlene's voice came across as brittle as cracking ice. "Who's there?"

Jennifer held her breath.

"Who's there I said? Show yourself this instant!"

But again Jennifer didn't heed the command. Instead she quietly crept up the stairs, praying that she hadn't been seen.

CHAPTER 45

FIVE MINUTES LATER, Jennifer was in her office when her desk phone rang. She nearly jumped out of her seat. She looked anxiously at the caller ID: it was Benjamin Locke. The phone rang again. Her hand started to move towards it, as if by a will of its own, before stopping like a car at the edge of a cliff. Did she dare answer it? Before she could tell herself "No!" her hand crawled forward the last inch and carefully lifted the receiver.

The gruff voice on the other end launched in without preamble. "Jennifer, come to my office immediately—I need to have a word with you." He hung up.

As she set the phone back down, the breath seemed to leave her all at once. She felt a momentary paralysis. Marlene must have seen her after all and told Locke, and now he would demand to know what she had been doing down in the basement snooping around Fileroom E. She would lie, of course, as she had been doing for the past several months. But would it be enough? Wouldn't he just see through her and fire her? If that happened, that would be the end of her story. All the hard work and risks she'd taken up to this point would amount to nothing.

Which meant that obnoxious prick Reid Farnsworth Lampert would win after all.

She took a few deep breaths to steel her jangled nerves. There was no alternative but to meet with Locke. There was still a remote chance his call had nothing to do with Marlene or Fileroom E, though by the sharpness of his tone, she must have fallen into his disfavor in some way. Maybe he wanted to talk to her about a work-related problem. In any case, she couldn't just run away from the situation; it had to be dealt with. Before she had a chance to talk herself out of it, she rose from her chair and headed out the door.

When she reached Marlene's desk, she tried to present herself in a calm and professional manner. "Good afternoon, Marlene," she said in a pleasant business-like tone.

Marlene's pug face seemed to darken with suspicion, and Jennifer's flesh turned cold. *You saw me, didn't you? You caught me red-handed, didn't you, you corpulent toad?*

"Mr. Locke will see you now," Marlene chirped like an automaton.

Jennifer was puzzled as she knocked on Locke's door. *I can't tell—*

did she see me or not?

"Come in."

The voice was like a booming cannon and Jennifer took an involuntary step back. Then, summoning her courage, she turned the knob and opened the door.

Locke sat behind his desk, shuffling through paperwork. When he looked up at her, he seemed gargantuan, even seated, and she had the uncanny feeling he could read her thoughts. Though she was completely opposed to American Patriots as an entity, she found herself utterly captivated by Benjamin Locke, but in a fearful way, as one might feel viewing a physically awesome but terrifying great white shark from an underwater cage or a massive Kodiac bear in its native habitat. The man was, quite simply, larger-than-life. But there was something else about him that was captivating: his altruism. The word had spread all around the office that he had plucked a homeless robber off the street on Sunday and already set him up with a good job and housing. The man—Peter Brown— had cut his fire-hazard beard and cleaned himself up and was said to be showing up regularly at 8 a.m. sharp and striving hard to turn his life around. All thanks to Locke.

"Jennifer, please come in and sit down."

She licked her lips, closed the door, and walked to the chair in front of his desk. As she sat down, her eyes passed over three of the hardcover titles in the bookcase: *"Slouching Toward Gomorrah: Modern Liberalism and American Decline"* by Robert Bork, *"Blinded by Might: Can the Religious Right Save America?"* by Cal Thomas, and *"Foundations of God's City: Christians in a Crumbling Culture"* by James Boice. *What garbage,* she thought.

"Is there something wrong?" he asked her.

Looking back at him, she involuntarily shrank back in her seat. "Um...no. Everything's fine."

"You find me intimidating, don't you?"

"No," she said, but she felt transparent. "Well maybe sometimes. But you're my boss—it's supposed to be that way, isn't it?"

Locke gave her a reassuring smile. "My wife is always telling me I come across too strong. Too much of the lion, she says. I apologize if I intimidate you, Jennifer. I can say this to you now that you're part of our heralded A-team." His face took on a gentle glow like a distant star.

Jennifer was wary. *Is this a set-up?*

He leaned forward, placing his elbows on his huge mahogany desk. On the corner of the desk, Jennifer saw the most recent copy of *The American Spectator*—"a feisty little right-wing magazine" in the words of the late editorialist William Safire. "You thought you were being called into the principal's office, didn't you?" he said with a chuckle.

"Something like that," she replied, still unsure of his motives.

"Then let me be frank, Jennifer. You have been doing a commendable job for us here at AMP. Though you've only been here less than a year, you're as sharp as someone with five years' experience. Your writing abilities have dramatically improved the quality of our press releases and voter materials. In short, I'm promoting you to second-in-charge of our communications/PR group. The actual title is senior communications specialist. You'll report directly to Archie Roberts."

"That's...that's great," she said without conviction. *Did I just hear that right? I was paranoid over nothing and he's actually offering me a promotion?*

"Your first assignment will be to fill in for my speech on Thursday."

"This Thursday—the day after tomorrow?"

"It's on a subject quite familiar to you—American exceptionalism. I thought to myself, who better to give the speech before the Colorado Springs Family Focus Group than you? With all the hard work you've put in, 'American Exceptionalism and the Power of the Christian Spirit' is sure to have a big impact. We owe a large part of that to you."

Now Jennifer felt a combination of nausea and panic. Not only did she not have time for this when she had Reid Farnsworth Lampert's deadline to meet, but she couldn't possibly give a speech to a group of people explaining how Americans were better than everyone else in the world because of their Christian spirituality and democratic ideals. Every country in the world thought it was exceptional, so why should the U.S. think that it was special? Especially when it had a history of slavery, genocide towards Native Americans, imprisoning its own countrymen during war, illegally torturing international suspects, wiretapping its own citizens, and lining the pockets of Big Business and Wall Street fat cats while its own middle class died a slow, painful death? Could a country truly be the most exceptional country in the world when it did stuff like that? she wondered.

You have to find a way out of this!

"I'm sorry, Mr. Locke, but I don't know if I can make it on Thursday. I still have a lot to do on the press release."

"Archie can handle that. This presentation is very important. Several of our co-supporters in the exceptionalism movement will be there. The presentation is already prepared—it's actually the standard one—and you shouldn't have any problem fielding the questions from the audience."

"With all due respect, I'm not much of a public speaker. I wouldn't want to say something wrong that might cast AMP in an unfavorable light."

"Come now, Jennifer, show some confidence in yourself. You'll do a great job. The presentation covers the same materials you've been preparing for the press release. The main thing is to explain to people exactly why we here in America are a 'shining city on a hill' through our fervent commitment to Christ our Lord and democratic principles. I believe the great French writer and philosopher Alexis de Tocqueville summed it up best: 'The position of the Americans is quite exceptional,' he said when he visited our fledgling nation, 'and it may be believed that no democratic people will ever be placed in a similar one.'"

"I know about de Tocqueville, sir. But is it that simple? I know that American hegemony is part of our PR program here at AMP, but I'm—"

"Jennifer," he cut her off, a tiny spasm of irritation crossing his broad face. "As second-in-command of the PR group, you're going to have to learn to take orders better. All that's required is a twenty-minute speech. Remind our supporters how lucky we are to live and work in the greatest nation in the history of the world."

"I agree that America is the greatest nation on earth, sir. I just don't know if I'm the best person to wave the flag and—"

"I've heard quite enough, Jennifer," he cut her off, brooking no further opposition. "Just tell it like it is and have some fun with it because I need you to do this."

It took great effort for her to clamp back her rising consternation. Locke may have been an altruistic human being and important national figurehead who was going to make extremely good copy for her exposé, but he was still maddeningly right-wing and the whole business of her working here made her feel physically ill. *Is the story worth all this?*

"We need to educate these people on the facts, Jennifer. Only then can we touch their lives in a positive way."

"I understand that, Mr. Locke. It's just that I don't feel like I'm qualified to be a public spokesperson on this issue. It's too complicated."

"I know it's a complicated subject and that many of us here don't agree on every aspect of the program. But at the end of the day, Jennifer, we have to get the job done. This is all part of God's plan not just for you and me, but for our supporters and America as well. So I need you to get with the program."

She struggled to find some other excuse to get out of the speaking engagement, but nothing came to her.

He looked at his watch, then, with an air of finality, said, "So we're in agreement—you'll do the presentation."

As painful as it was, Jennifer knew she had to go through with it. If she refused, Locke would be suspicious and she couldn't have that when she was so close to getting into Fileroom E. "All right, sir, if you think it's the right thing, I'll do my best."

"That's the spirit. I know you'll do a fine job. You're one of our rising stars."

"Thank you, sir," she said, but she wanted to fall off the face of the earth.

CHAPTER 46

WHEN HIS DESK PHONE RANG, Kenneth Patton was daydreaming about his son.

He was throwing long looping spirals to the kid, who hauled in the pigskin like Randy Moss and Demaryius Thomas rolled into one. One-handed catches, diving catches, over-the-shoulder catches. The kid grabbed everything thrown his way, and Patton was proud to be his father. It dawned on him—in that instant before his thoughts were interrupted—how badly he wanted a son. The weird thing was he already had a child, but it didn't belong to him. Because of events that had taken place without his knowledge twelve years ago, his very own son belonged to someone else.

It made him sad. And angry. And a dozen other things he couldn't put into words.

He picked up after the third ring. "Special Agent Patton."

"It's me."

He felt himself relax as he recognized the voice. "Lois Lane? I thought you'd never call."

"Flattery will get you everywhere," said Jennifer Odden.

Patton took a moment to pull the phone cord around a pile of paperwork. "How's your day going? I've been getting kicked around like an old hound dog."

"My day hasn't been much better. I just found out I have to give a talk on Thursday to a Christian community group on why America is the greatest country on earth while every other country is populated with backwards, drooling idiots. But that's not why I called. I got the cyber lock code to Fileroom E."

"Fileroom E?"

"That's where they keep the confidential records. The X-Files stuff in the orange folders."

"And of course you're planning on sneaking in to have a look at them."

"Damn straight."

"I don't mean to pop your bubble, but what you're doing sounds more like espionage than journalism."

"There are secrets in that room and I plan to get my hands on them. I've already penetrated the computer files as far as I can go. They keep

Fileroom E under tight security for a reason—and I'm going to find out why."

Patton was impressed with her determination, but wondered if she wasn't taking unnecessary risks. "Just don't get caught," he said.

"I'll try my best." They settled into a silence. "You sound a little quiet," she said after a moment. "What's up? Any new leads on the case?"

"Actually, I was just thinking about something else."

"What?"

"Our son."

Another silence. "It's not easy putting him out of your mind when you know he's out there, is it?" she said finally.

"No, it's not. Like when you said you've seen him playing sports, I was dying to ask you what he played."

"But you were embarrassed, right? Because you felt like you were spying?"

"Yeah," he admitted. He picked up the painted lead miniature of his great-great-great grandfather—a blue-jacketed U.S. Civil War cavalry commander with a fire-hazard beard and quarter-inch tall sword—from his desk and idly looked him over.

"You shouldn't think of it as spying, Ken. He's your son. And to answer your question, he plays football, basketball, and lacrosse. I think football's his best sport though."

He couldn't help a little smile as he thought back to his quarterbacking days with the Wolverines. "Football, huh. What position does he play?"

"Quarterback."

"No way! You're pulling my leg!"

"I'm afraid it's in his blood—he was born to play QB just like a certain field general I once knew who had a penchant for throwing interceptions at the worst possible times."

"Okay, now I know you're fucking with me."

"No, I'm not. Even at tender age of eleven I have to say he's got a great arm. Plus he reads coverages really well. If he keeps progressing like he has been, I figure he'll probably get drafted in the first round. Unlike his father."

"Ouch!"

They laughed. Listening to her describe the boy filled Patton with longing, and he knew that she was only half-joking. How much would he give up to catch a single glimpse of his son winging a tight spiral over the top or running a naked bootleg to score the game-winning touchdown?

He posed a question. "Doesn't it make it hard on you to see him when you know he belongs to someone else?"

"He'll always be our son, Ken. All you have to do is take one look at him to *know* that."

"But what you're doing, doesn't it just make it harder to let go?"

"Maybe. But even if I wanted to, I can't change my wanting to see him. Why do you think there are so many mothers out there who've given up a child years ago and now want to be a part of their lives again? Why, after so many years, they want to spend time with a child that has been a stranger to them? They can't control their emotions, the sense of something lost, any more than an artist can control the urge to paint."

Her tone turned thoughtful, a little dreamy.

"It's the not knowing that gnaws at you. You wonder is my child like me? Does he have the same mannerisms, the same interests? How will his life turn out? Will he become president, save the environment, help the poor, quarterback the 49ers to a championship? I thought the *wondering* would go away. But it hasn't."

"When you see him how do you know where he'll be? You must know his daily routine."

"Early on, I hired a private investigator, a woman from San Jose. I was completely up front with her about what I wanted to do and why. Every few months, she puts together a rough schedule of Little Ken's current activities and a list of the places he'll be. That way I can see him discretely, from a safe distance, and not be detected or impose on the family."

"When was the last time you saw him?"

"Last spring. All I've ever wanted to do was make sure he's okay, that he's being treated well. A part of me feels responsible for him."

"Why haven't you just gone to court and obtained visitation rights?"

"I would never do that to the parents. That would be unfair to them."

"You call him 'Little Ken.' But what's his real name?"

"Thomas Steele."

"What do his parents do?"

"His father's a trial lawyer and his mother is a part-time social worker."

"Are they well off...financially."

"Very. They live in Pacific Heights."

"Is he an only child? Or did they adopt other children?"

"He's an only child. Look, I know all this must come as a shock for you. Maybe we should take things slower. This is probably not the best time for you to be hearing all this with the case and all."

Patton considered this a moment and decided she was right.

"I'm sorry," she said. "I'm sorry things have turned out this way."

He said nothing, feeling overwhelmingly conflicted inside. For a fleeting instant, he wondered what it would take for him to begin a new life, one that included Jennifer and their son. He wished with all his heart that it wasn't just a fantasy, but deep down he knew he couldn't undo the past. The wheels had been set in motion too long ago, and his son was gone and would never be a part of his life.

But perhaps Jennifer could.

Suddenly, he blurted out, "I want to be with you, Jenn. I want to try and..."

"I do too," she finished for him, her voice resonating with feeling.

The words brought him solace. After all these years, after the secret that only yesterday had emerged, he still felt deep emotions for her, and she obviously felt the same about him. He couldn't escape the feeling that somehow, in some ineffable way, their coming back together was destiny and that they truly were soul mates. But what united them this time around was something different than before. They were now linked not so much by friendship, or love, but by the terrible tragedy of how their relationship had ended and the reality that, together, they had produced a life. He felt the same tingle of electricity between them, the same spark, but there was an underlying poignancy and sadness too. He realized that he needed a woman that wasn't just like Jennifer, but *was* Jennifer. He needed her in the way an Irishman needs his daily dose of Guinness or Bushmills.

She was his elixir.

"I'd like to see you," she said, as if reading his thoughts. "Can we get together tonight?"

He longed to see her, but with the case his foremost priority right now, he wasn't sure he could get away. "Tonight's going to be tough."

"How about tomorrow night?"

He took a moment to ponder, not wanting to make a promise he couldn't keep. Over the next two days, the forensics results would be pouring in and there were bound to be some hot new leads. He couldn't very well duck out of the office when he was making the task force work late each night. Somehow, though, he would have to find a way.

"Can you meet me halfway?" he asked.

"You name the place and I'll be there."

"How about scenic Castle Rock? Let's say nine o'clock at the Castle Café?"

"I'll be there. Is this like a date, Special Agent?"

"I think we're a little beyond that. I'll see you tomorrow night," he said, and he smiled as he hung up the phone.

CHAPTER 47

AS THE CAB pulled up to her apartment building, Skyler saw Anthony Carmeli sitting out front on the edge of the planter. All day she had wondered if he would show up. On the one hand, the last thing she could afford was to take unnecessary risks with a man she didn't even know. But on the other, she had secretly been rooting for him to make an appearance and try to win over her affections.

Looking at him sitting there, she knew that the smart thing would be to send him away without causing a scene—and make sure he wouldn't come back.

When she stepped from the cab, he smiled at her in a carefree way, clutching a bottle of red wine in one hand and a beautiful bouquet of flowers in the other. He wore a blue polo shirt, tan chinos, and spanking new Nikes. She pulled a pair of twenties from her purse and handed them to the driver. The cab pulled from the curb and Skyler walked toward the front door of her apartment, keeping her expression neutral.

He stood to greet her, squinting into the fading sunlight. When he smiled again, Skyler's breath quickened and a chill of excitement crept up her back, turning her skin to gooseflesh. There was just something likeable about him and she felt as anxious and giddy as a schoolgirl on a first date.

Don't even think about it, Angela. There's too much risk. Be firm yet polite and he will go away.

"How are you?" he asked in a friendly voice.

"You are a persistent fellow," she said, ignoring the question. "You said you would be here, and here you are."

"How can you expect me to resist a woman of such impeccable intellect and beauty?"

Though she tried not to show any reaction, the compliment brought a hint of a smile to the edges of her mouth. "I don't know what you want from me, Anthony Carmeli."

"First, I'd like you to have these," he said, and he held out the bouquet of flowers.

Taking the flowers from him, she instantly scolded herself for giving him even the slightest bit of encouragement. *What the hell are you doing, Angela?* She had to put an end to this now. "I'm sorry, Anthony, but this isn't going to work. I just got out of a bad relationship, and I'm not anxious to jump back into another."

"I thought you might say that. That's why I brought this fine bottle of Chateau St. Michelle Cabernet Sauvignon. The wine-seller guaranteed me that a single glass would make *the* most beautiful woman on the planet putty in my hands."

She couldn't help but smile. "You're not going to go away, are you?"

"Not a chance. So you'd better give me a fair shot."

He politely offered her an arm. Shaking her head with amusement, she locked her arm in his and they started up the stairs.

"Are you *really* sure you want to try to win over my affections? I will definitely test your mettle."

"Yes, I'm sure," he said. "As sure as I've ever been about anything."

CHAPTER 48

AFTER THEY polished off the bottle of Cabernet Sauvignon, Skyler loosened up considerably and, against her better judgment, she agreed to accompany Anthony to Ambrosia for dinner. Located in Santa Monica, the trendy restaurant was owned by a Greek chef named Stryka Papadopulos, who had perfected his culinary art under the tutelage of Wolfgang Puck. The dining room was done in nouveau art deco-style with sweeping track lights, pastel colors, and a central skylight. Informed by the maître'd that there would be a half-hour wait, they put their name in and went to the bar. Skyler ordered Cabernet for herself and Anthony from the bartender. They stood next to the bar, sipping their wine, chatting, people-watching.

After a moment, President-elect Fowler appeared on the TV screens at each end of the bar. The volume was turned up and the crowd at the bar stopped chattering as Fowler stepped to the podium to give a speech with the backdrop of the Washington Monument lit up behind her.

Reading from a prepared script, Fowler began by praising William Kieger and expressing sorrow and outrage over his death. He had been a good family man, a mentor to her, a fine leader, a steady voice of reason in an uncertain world. Fowler's words were predictably uplifting, but Skyler sensed her sincerity was not faked. She went on to say that, while Kieger would be hugely missed, it was critical that the country come together in this time of crisis. William Kieger would not want the American constitutional process halted because of a lowly assassin's bullet; and that's why she would be busy in the coming weeks working with President Osborne to effect a smooth transition and to build her cabinet. It was up to both political parties and the American people to put the ugly business behind them and move on. Fowler concluded her speech by saying that, as president, she would do her best to make the nation proud, and hoped to continue in the footsteps of William Kieger, for whom she had the greatest admiration.

When the speech was finished, a buzz quickly circulated through the bar. "Wow," exclaimed Anthony. "Lady Luck changes hands mighty quickly."

She took a sip of Cabernet, letting it trickle down her throat. *If you only knew that I'm the one who brought it all about.*

He said, "I think it was planned all along. Someone wanted regime change in the worst possible way."

"Kieger out, Fowler in, is that it?"

"Exactly. What do you think? Could it be a massive conspiracy extending to the highest levels of government?"

"You've been watching too many movies."

"And making too many bad ones."

They shared a laugh. She leaned forward in her seat, wanting to draw him out further with his little conspiracy theory, to see how closely it matched the actual truth. "Okay, suppose it is a conspiracy, who do you think is behind it? The Green Freedom Brigade?"

"I don't know. They're definitely a radical group and they've killed people before."

"What about Fowler? Do you think she could be involved?"

"I don't think so. She looked sincere when she paid tribute to Kieger. I think he really was something of a mentor to her. I guess that's what surprises me most about her. I thought she was a rabid right-winger, and here she goes praising Kieger. Still, at this early stage, she's clearly the one who has gained the most from the assassination. As things stand, she's the next president of the United States and leader of the free world. So she has to be a prime suspect."

Skyler decided not to press the discussion further, lest the Cabernet make her blurt out something she shouldn't. "I guess we'll have to wait and see how it all plays out. Perhaps there will be a few surprises in store for us."

"I'm sure there will be," he said with a smile. "I'm sure there will be."

CHAPTER 49

THEY WERE SEATED at a table overlooking Santa Monica Bay. For a few minutes, they quietly looked over the four-star menu. Skyler felt deep hunger pangs as she perused the selections: Shanghai lobster risotto, scallops on watercress purée, grilled Szechwan beef, barbequed quail, wok-charred salmon, and other ultra-deluxe California cuisine dishes meant to be savored one bite at a time.

In the back of her mind, she knew she was taking a grave risk getting involved with Anthony. At the same time, she couldn't deny her feelings for him. She liked that he was trying to win her over. She enjoyed being with him and the little tingle she felt when their bodies touched.

A waiter with slicked-back hair done in a ponytail arrived to take their order. Skyler opted for the lobster risotto, Anthony the wok-charred salmon. They both went for a house salad with vinaigrette and Skyler ordered a bottle of Patz & Hall Mount Veeder Carr, a choice the waiter enthusiastically commended.

As the waiter walked off, Skyler placed her napkin in her lap and said, "Now tell me about some of your films. Perhaps I've seen one of them."

"Well, my last one was *Rhino Man*. The story of a genetically engineered half-human, half-rhinoceros that escapes from a laboratory in Oxnard and wreaks carnage on L.A."

She threw him a bemused smile. "I don't believe I saw that one."

"How about *The Artful Hunter*?"

"No, I don't think so."

"Well, it's about a transvestite serial killer who flies his victims to remote wilderness locations and then hunts them down like wild animals. Monumental film. It grossed over two hundred million. And of course we all know that movie grosses and quality are directly proportional."

Skyler was amused by his self-deprecating humor. "I'm afraid I missed that one too."

He clutched his chest and gave a look of mock hurt. "I'm appalled. I hope you at least saw *The Jetsons 3-D*. I think it's my most stunning achievement. It grossed over a quarter billion in the U.S. alone. I still can't believe it didn't win a single Oscar or Golden Globe nomination."

He gave a wry smile, but Skyler sensed an underlying seriousness to his self-inflicted gibes. She looked at him thoughtfully. "I take it you're not very proud of some of your films."

"Oh, no, they're great—if you enjoy a hundred million dollars' worth of gadgets, hype, and flagrant product plugs."

Now she understood why he'd gotten burnt out on the motion picture industry and was taking time off to regroup. That's why she rarely went to see American films; most of them were just too damned moronic, pandering to the lowest possible denominator.

"Why do you think there are so few good films today?" she asked him.

"The answer's simple. Hollywood's steeped in corporate greed, like a farmer ankle deep in manure. Everything—and I mean, everything—revolves around breaking box office records on opening weekend. To do that, you have to have either sophomoric humor or special-effects overkill."

Skyler sipped her wine. *I'm liking you more and more, Anthony. I hope I never have to kill you.*

"A friend of mine at Universal told me that what Hollywood creates is mostly product, rarely entertainment, and never art. He told me to get used to it, because it wasn't going to change any time soon. That was twenty years ago and I didn't believe him. Until it was too late."

"As a consumer," Skyler said, "I have two possible reactions to American movies. I either hate them, or I really hate them. That's why I usually see foreign films."

"Me too, and I'm an American film producer!"

They shared a good laugh at the irony. In that blissful moment, she realized how much she missed such a simple pleasure as laughing with someone else. She hadn't done it very often in recent years.

"It all begins with formulaic scripts," he said. "Most of what's out there is no better than a pilot for a sitcom. Half the time they're dusting off a 1960's TV corpse and throwing in the latest special effects for good measure. The directors are just as bad. These days the only necessary qualification is to have a hit music video on your list of credits."

"So is that why you left Inverness Entertainment?"

"I grew weary of it all. I began to lose my mind. I made tons of money, but the downside of Hollywood is that it leaves its victims prone to nervous breakdowns, heart attacks, and suicide. I was one of the lucky ones. I only suffered from the first affliction."

They looked up as their salads arrived. The waiter ground fresh pepper onto the crispy Romaine lettuce, refilled their wine glasses, and disappeared.

"Have you considered getting back in with a more artistically inclined company?" she asked as they began eating.

"Thought about it. Some of the established indies are doing some interesting, edgy projects. Hooking on with one of them is a possibility, but even they're becoming predictable."

"Maybe you just need a new direction. If your heart is in putting quality films together, you can't give it up entirely."

He considered this a moment. "I know you're right. I'm just not ready yet."

"You know what I think? I think Hollywood needs to rediscover how to make films that are both commercial and intelligent. Get back to quality storytelling and move away from flashy special effects. When it's all said and done, interesting characters and deep emotions are what people remember most, not fancy gadgets and effects. You could help lead that revolution, Anthony, if you put your mind to it. Leave the terrific stunts and stunted scripts to someone else."

"Wow," he exclaimed. "Sounds like you have it all figured out."

"Of course I do," she said with a self-assured grin. "I'm a woman."

CHAPTER 50

AFTER DINNER, they went for a walk on the beach. Skyler liked the feel of the cool ocean breeze on the back of her neck. Every once in a while, they stopped and stared out at the dark, mysterious sea. The waves rolled lazily toward the sandy beach, but the occasional big one broke through with a rhythmic roar, a thunderous echo that served as a reminder of nature's indisputable power.

As they came upon one of the lifeguard towers, Anthony said, "I can't believe I spent the whole dinner talking about myself. And I know almost nothing about you."

Skyler felt a prickle of anxiety. Though she knew how to navigate through minefields like these, she always got a little anxious. She had been fabricating her personal history for so long now that it was second nature, but it was still hard to lie face-to-face.

"What do you want to know?" she asked him.

"How about where you're from?"

"Los Angeles originally," she said, giving the standard prevarication. "But I moved to Barcelona when I was very young and spent most of my childhood there."

"And your parents?"

"They're both dead. Car accident."

"I'm sorry."

"They were wonderful people. My father was American and my mother Spanish. He was a venture capitalist and my mother was an art consultant."

"Any brothers or sisters?"

"No, I'm an only child."

They took off their shoes and walked on in silence, occasionally slowing down to stare out at the flickering boat lights far offshore. Though still nervous about saying the wrong thing and blowing her cover, Skyler liked the feeling of the wet sand between her toes, the sensation of the cool ocean surf as it swept past her ankles. They heard the bright beat of Jimmy Cliff's *The Harder They Come* coming from the north.

He said, "I've told you what I do for a living. But you still haven't told me what you do."

She went with her standard lie. "Actually, I work for the CIA."

He came to a halt and looked at her with stupefaction. "What?"

"I'm not joking—I work for the CIA."

"So you're like a spy?"

"Actually, what I do isn't found in any Daniel Silva or John Le Carré novel. I'm in the Domestic Resources Division. Not one of the country's most closely guarded secrets and certainly not the most glamorous posting at the agency. Still, I have to be a little careful about what I say and who I spend time with. That's why I didn't tell you at first."

"Are you and I *spending time* together?"

"For the time being. After the bombshell I just dropped, I'm surprised you're not scrambling to make a getaway. That's the usual reaction I get."

"Actually, I find the whole government spook thing intriguing."

"I wouldn't get your hopes up. Domestic Resources is about as James Bond as the IRS."

He laughed and they started off again.

"So what do you do in the Domestic Resources division? Or is it like off-limits to tell me?"

She decided it would be best to tell the whole lie. Then, at the end, she could make it clear that that's all she could say. Real CIA operatives had to do the same thing with their friends, lovers, and spouses so it would be believable. She would throw in the usual technical jargon she gave her few female acquaintances, to make it sound official.

"We gather information," she replied. "Domestic Resources is a branch within the National Clandestine Services, which used to be known as the Directorate of Operations."

"So what does your job involve? Tracking down spy rings inside the country, that sort of thing?"

"No, we gather information on foreign countries using domestic resources. Which is a fancy way of saying that we ask Americans living or traveling overseas to report on what they know or see abroad."

"And all of this is done in secret?"

"Actually, we operate overtly for the most part. We do have a commercial cover, for protective reasons, but our activities are more open than other branches of the Company. Our staff members are allowed to identify themselves as CIA officers."

"Is that what you are, an officer, not an agent?"

"Agents are foreigners recruited by our Foreign Resources branch to become spies. Officers are actual employees. That's what I am. I'm what's known as a 'nonofficial cover officer.' Which means that when I'm outside the country, I'm not officially attached to any U.S. government agency. I'm NOC."

"So that way it's harder to trace you to the CIA."

"It allows the Company to deny all knowledge of my activities. Being an NOC is far riskier than working under official government cover since an NOC has no diplomatic immunity and can be arrested and imprisoned for spying. Or consorting with spies."

"Sounds scary."

"Not really. Most of my interviews are in the U.S., questioning American businesspeople and university professors about the information they pick up on their travels. I use the NOC cover only when the interview needs to be done outside the country. Important cases usually. Sometimes we try and obtain plans on military targets from workers who have built the facilities, but usually we're after technological and business secrets. Basically to keep us competitive."

"Interesting."

You've been convincing but it's time for the final pitch.

"I'd tell you more, but I could get into trouble," she said. "You know, national security and all."

"I understand."

She rewarded him with a smile and breathed a sigh of relief that the elaborate lying was over. But she also felt guilty. At dinner he had spilled his life to her, and all she could offer him in return were clever lies. But what else could she do? There was no way she could tell him the truth. How would she even begin? *"I just wanted you to know, Anthony, I'm a professional assassin. I just killed the next president of the United States. It's my job so I'm sure you understand."*

They strolled onto the pier. Skyler liked the quiet rhythm of the waves lapping lazily against the heavy timber bollards. Green phosphorescent bundles of seaweed slid gently past the dock. The sliver of moon lit up the water just enough to see the mackerel wriggling at the surface.

After a half hour of pleasant conversation thankfully not involving any lying, they retraced their footsteps, went to Anthony's car parked on Main, and drove back to her apartment. As they got out, Skyler wished the night didn't have to end. Anthony was almost too good to be true. He was funny, he was smart, and he was considerate. But what she related to most was his vulnerability. Somehow Hollywood had broken his spirit and he was taking time off to regroup. She could sympathize with what he was going through and saw his soul-searching not as a sign of weakness, but something admirable. It made him seem more human.

She knew she was falling for him.

Which made it all so confusing. She wasn't supposed to fall for anyone. Things like this weren't supposed to happen to her.

When they reached the doorstep to her apartment, Anthony politely asked, "May I kiss you goodnight?"

"If you don't I shall be disappointed."

He leaned forward and their lips softly touched. As she kissed him back, she wanted desperately to pull him inside and make love to him. She didn't want to handcuff him and mount him like she did the lapdogs she used for her immediate gratification. She wanted to make love as lovers did, to feel the emotions they felt. Then afterwards, she wanted to lie around lazily, talking and caressing.

"Do you want to come upstairs?" she asked him hopefully.

"It's been such a wonderful night. Let's just end it like this."

"Of course, you're right," she said, though she was a little disappointed.

He kissed her again and she felt warm all over. "Can we get together tomorrow?" he asked.

"I'd like that. I might even be able to get the day off. I've logged a lot of overtime recently."

"That sounds great. I'll call you." He kissed her softly on the lips once more.

"Goodnight, Anthony."

"Goodnight."

When she went upstairs, she opened the curtain to see if she could catch a glimpse of him. To her delight, he was still waiting for her beneath the street lamp, making sure she reached the apartment safely. He waved up at her, giving a winsome smile. At first, she hesitated to respond because she felt ridiculous. But then, as if under the force of a spell, she returned a smile and her hand passed back and forth across the window. She couldn't believe it, but the sensation was delightful.

Watching him move off, she thought to herself, *How could I possibly feel this wonderful? I must be dreaming.*

CHAPTER 51

BENJAMIN BRADFORD LOCKE saw the stubborn look he had been hoping not to see take root on his teenage daughter's face—and he knew instantly that he was in trouble.

"But I don't think I can do it, Daddy. I don't want to give my baby up for adoption. I want to raise the child myself."

"I don't see how that's going to be possible." He looked to his wife for help. "Tell her, Mary."

"Your father's right. You are too young to have a baby. That is why, when the time comes, you're going to have to give it to the adoptive parents. That's what your father and I have decided."

"But I don't think I can do it."

Locke couldn't believe what he was hearing, but held his tongue. Why was she being so stubborn? She had already agreed to go to Sacred Heart, the home for unwed Christian mothers in the fresh mountain air of Summit County. Yet she was clinging steadfastly to the ludicrous notion that, upon the successful completion of the seven-month program, she would keep her baby.

Of course she can't keep the damned baby! She's only seventeen!

"I don't want to give my baby away. What if the adoptive parents turned out to be cruel or incompetent? I can't bear the thought of someone hurting my child. Or not loving it as it should be loved. Or neglecting it in some way."

"You can't keep a child out of wedlock," said Mary. "It isn't Christian."

"But it is my baby and I'll be eighteen when it's born."

Locke shook his head with irritation. "Haven't you embarrassed your parents enough, Susan?"

The girl started crying.

"I'm sorry, I didn't mean to make you cry," he said quickly, reaching out and touching her reassuringly. "But you have to understand—we are extremely disappointed."

"Here, let me handle this," said Mary.

Grabbing a tissue and wiping the tears from her eyes, Susan tried to put forward a stoic front. "I know you're just going to lecture me, Mother. And I don't want to hear it right now."

"I'm not going to lecture you. But I am going to give you the cold, hard facts because that's my job as your mother."

"No, you're not. You're just going to lecture me like you always do."

He didn't like his daughter's insolent tone. "Please, Susan. Just give your mother a chance and listen to what she has to say."

The girl's eyes narrowed and it appeared as though she would dig her heels in. But after a moment's reflection, she changed her mind and bowed her head in reluctant acquiescence. Locke quietly nodded for his wife to proceed.

"Susan, I know you feel strongly about keeping the child inside you. But you should know the difficulties you would face. First, it would break my heart, as well as your father's, if you chose to keep this baby. Having a child out of wedlock is not the proper Christian way. But even more important is how other people will view you. I'm afraid they will not perceive you in a sympathetic manner and fear that this might place an enormous strain on you at a very fragile time in your life."

"I know all that, Mother. But I'm still not comfortable giving my baby to complete strangers."

"I understand how you feel," she continued in her soft Georgia inflection. "But you have to realize that there are practical considerations when it comes to a baby, especially at your young age. Your college counselor, Ann Reid, is confident you will be accepted at Stanford or one of the other top schools you've applied to for next fall. It is not reasonable to try to look after a baby and go to college at the same time."

"But, Mother, they have day-care centers right on campus."

"A day-care center is no place for a baby, honey. Your scholastic load at Stanford, or wherever you end up, is going to be difficult enough. You will have to devote an extraordinary amount of time to studying, and looking after a baby will place a severe burden on you. Then there's the question of dating. It will be very difficult to meet nice young men in college when you have a baby. It is very tough for women in that position, I can assure you."

Locke's expression turned sour as he thought of Todd. He definitely didn't want his daughter dating boys like Todd in college. Picturing the beefy linebacker climbing on top of his poor, innocent daughter and performing acts of lechery made his blood boil.

"But the most important thing," continued Mary, "is that raising the baby on your own is unfair to the child. A baby needs a mother and father. These days people treat conception like a science project—as if you can create a child in a test tube and let it develop on its own. But it's so much more, Susan. Raising a child is a gift, but it's also a major responsibility that takes a lot of sacrifice. It takes both a mother and father to do the job properly. Even then, it's a lifelong challenge."

After a reflective silence, Susan nodded. "I don't know, Mother. I'm still afraid of giving my baby away to someone else."

"It will be hard, honey, but it's the responsible thing to do."

"But I don't know if I can do it. I've heard bad things about Sacred Heart."

"What…what are you talking about? Sacred Heart is a wonderful place."

"That's not what I heard."

"Stop this, Susan. Your father and I are not going to argue about this any further with you. If you want to go on to live the life you have always dreamed about then you will do this. It's that simple. Single motherhood is terribly difficult. You have your whole life ahead of you. You will have a family some day when you are properly married, just not right now."

"But how can you be so sure, Mother? How can you know the future?"

"I don't. But God does. Everything is part of His plan, as you well know."

Locke saw that his daughter was filled with self-doubt. But then his wife leaned in close, took Susan in an embrace, and whispered something in her ear. A moment later, they pulled gently apart and his wife looked at Susan firmly yet compassionately.

"Now have we reached an understanding in this matter?"

The girl still looked unsure.

"Susan, have we reached an understanding?"

"Yes, Mother."

"Are you sure?"

"Yes, I'll go to Sacred Heart."

"It really is for the best, dear. One day you'll understand that."

"Your mother and I will always be here for you," said Locke, and he leaned in and hugged them both tightly. "Don't you worry, my child—everything will work out in the end. I promise you."

"I want to believe you, Daddy, honestly I do. I'm just scared."

"Don't be scared, for it is the will of God. And remember, we're here for you. We both love you so much."

"I know you do. And I love you too."

He kissed her on the forehead and hugged her and she hugged him back and he felt a wave of relief wash over him. Thankfully the matter was settled: Susan would leave school starting next week, go to Sacred Heart, and give her baby up to the adoptive parents in seven months' time. It was all settled.

A moment later, they pulled apart and he headed for the door. Just before reaching it, he turned around and looked at Susan. There was kindness in his eyes, a hint of humility.

"I know this a difficult time for you. But you have made the right decision for you and your baby. I also want you to know that, despite our differences on this matter, your mother and I respect your opinion."

"I know you do. And I know you both love me."

"You will always be our sweet baby girl. Never forget that."

"I won't, Daddy. I won't."

CHAPTER 52

AS HE MADE HIS WAY DOWNSTAIRS, he heard his secure phone ring inside his open study. He quickly shuffled into the room, closed the sound-proofed door behind him, punched a button on the small black box beside the telephone to activate the voice modulator, and spoke into the mouthpiece.

"Hello?" his electronically distorted voice queried.

A low voice, also filtered, came back with, "Have you heard from Frautschi?"

Locke stiffened. It was unlike Senator Dubois to be so urgent, so he knew the news had to be very grave indeed.

"No. What is it? What's happened?"

"He and Fowler are up to something. They've brought in Dick Potter."

Dick Potter! As in the sleaziest political consultant in all of Washington, so vile he would sell his own mother for a better poll number! Why the cretin had indulged in several well-publicized trysts and had worked with the loathsome Democrats over the years as well as several moderate Republicans. Even worse, he was known for corrupting the ideology of his clients, getting them to flip-flop their positions and move towards the slippery center in the name of political expediency.

All Locke could say in response was, "You can't be serious."

"Apparently it's a done deal. When you spoke to our little filly yesterday, did she mention anything about this? Or, for that matter, did Frautschi?"

"No."

"Then I think we have a problem." He paused, and Locke shifted uneasily in his seat, knowing he was about to hear more disturbing news. "I'm afraid, Mr. Chairman, that whatever they've got going with Dick Potter is just the tip of the iceberg."

The warning, rife with implied danger, hung there for a moment.

Locke swallowed against the knot in his throat.

"It seems our handpicked successor had a closed-door meeting today with the late president-elect's wife," Dubois continued, the voice box distortion only adding to the excruciating tension of the moment.

"Hana Kieger. But why?"

"That's what we have to find out. It couldn't have been just to pay her respects. They reportedly spent two full hours alone together right before Fowler's press conference."

"How'd you find out about all this, if it wasn't Frautschi?"

"I'm afraid that's need-to-know, Mr. Chairman. Let's just say I have my own sources. To make sure we don't get caught with our pants down."

Once again, Locke was glad he had the Prince of Darkness—as Senator Dubois was known in Washington power circles—on his side as well as in his confidence. Skull Eyes and the colonel would definitely not be so diplomatic if they were in the senator's position.

"It's still early. How do we know what she's really up to?" asked Locke.

"We don't, but I got a bad feeling. Did you see her little speech?"

"In its entirety. The glowing tribute to Kieger did seem a bit over the top. As did the part where she said she hoped to 'follow in the footsteps of her predecessor.' Until proven otherwise, though, I'm still inclined to write off Fowler's mawkish display as political posturing. If her goal was to win over skeptical Independents and RINOs"—*Republicans in Name Only*—"to strengthen her bully pulpit, I'd say she accomplished that hands down."

"Or she may be tipping her hand. In either case, we've got to make sure she's on track with the program before it's too late."

"You really think she and Frautschi could go rogue on us?"

"Lord, I hope not. But we have to face an unthinkable possibility: by taking out Kieger, all we may have done is opened up a barrel of snakes. At a minimum, they're doing things behind our back."

Locke felt his anger, and resolve, picking up. "You leave this to me—I'll take care of it."

"What are you going to do?"

"Put together a little face-to-face meeting. Remind Fowler who just filled her war chest and clarify our expectations in no uncertain terms."

"Sounds like a wise approach. But be careful. Ain't no place in heaven, no place in hell if Skull Eyes or the colonel find out about this."

"I'm very much aware of that. Thanks for the heads up—I'll keep you posted."

"You do that, Mr. Chairman. Because if this dog won't hunt, you and I are going to have to come up with an alternative, if you catch my meaning."

"Oh, I catch your meaning all right," said Locke, and he hung up the phone.

CHAPTER 53

HE QUICKLY DIALED a number embedded in his memory. Two rings later, the man he wanted to talk to answered.

"Frautschi."

"I saw President-elect Fowler's little speech," Locke launched in without preamble, his voice still distorted. "Interesting word choices throughout. Did you write that piece, Pete?"

There was a pause on the other end, a moment of uncertainty, and Locke knew he had caught him off guard. "What are you talking about?" Frautschi said with transparently fake innocence.

"Answering a question with a question. Are we to that point in our professional relationship, after I just transferred twenty million grade-A American dollars into that special account of yours?"

Another silence.

Locke imagined him on the other end, trying to decide how to respond, how much to reveal. He decided to make the decision for him. "I know about Dick Potter and the meeting with the bereaved widow, Pete. What I want to know is why you haven't called to tell me."

"I was going to. It's just that it's...been so hectic."

Locke could tell he was lying. "I can understand that because I'm an understanding man. But I have to confess to you that I'm feeling less than warm and fuzzy about our little arrangement. I'm concerned that, despite my more than generous campaign contribution, the president-elect may not be quite on board with the program. You follow?"

"I can assure you there's nothing to worry about. We're on board with the Christian platform."

"That's good because we both know my associates and I are the ones who've made Little Miss Muffet here a national hero. She's going to be the first female president in the history of the United States and the leader of the free world because we—that's me and my patriotic associates, Pete—made it all possible. Have you seen today's papers?"

"Of course."

"Nearly eighty percent of Americans think current President Gregory Osborne is a liar and a murderer. He's bringing the Dems numbers down across the board."

"Okay, what do you want?"

"I want a closed-door meeting with Fowler to reach a formal agreement on her platform, pick for Veep, and cabinet selections."

Frautschi groaned. "You've got to be kidding me."

"I am dead serious, Pete. And if you want to be the next George Stephanopoulos when this is all over, making seven figures a year blathering your opinions, you'll do as I say."

"All right, I'll see what I can do. But it won't be until next week. We're flying out to California for Kieger's funeral tomorrow morning and will be busy putting together the cabinet until Friday."

"Listen up because I'm only going to say this once. Without me and my generous associates, you're just another Beltway wannabe with an ego the size of Texas instead of chief of staff. The same goes for that boss of yours. We made her what she is and what she'll soon be. You'd better keep that in mind. I said I want a meeting—and I want it this week."

"I honestly don't know why you're making such a big deal out of this. She's on board with the program. And so am I. We're on your team and we always have been."

"Then prove it to me and take a strong vocal stand on the platform. We wrote it for a reason. Unfortunately, Kieger didn't take the platform, or its authors, seriously enough—and look what happened to him."

An ominous silence settled over the phone; not a word was spoken.

"We are sticking to the platform," Frautschi said finally, "but we have to be sensitive to the voters. You have to give us a little latitude on this. Laying out Contract with America Part Two at this early stage is only going to jeopardize us for the next election."

"You're not listening. We own you, Pete. Your debt to us is to make sure that Katherine Fowler puts forward *our vision* for the country over the next eight years. And you're going to keep me informed every step of the way. Until you regain my trust, you are to report to me on a daily basis. Is that understood?"

It was several seconds before grudging acquiescence came. "Yes, sir."

"That's good news, Pete. I'm glad we see eye to eye on this."

CHAPTER 54

AT 6:42 P.M. THAT SAME TUESDAY EVENING, Jennifer made her move. She had reconnoitered the entire building and found it deserted. The last employee on her floor had left fifteen minutes earlier. There were no security guards on the company payroll—that she knew of anyway—and the cleaning crew didn't arrive until eight or nine.

Fileroom E beckoned like a dinner bell sent out to toll the hungry!

Rising from her chair, she picked up her backpack from the credenza, went to the door, and peered out her office. Confirming that no one unaccounted for was lurking in the shadows, she turned off her light and stepped into the hallway with the alert air of a spy. When she reached the elevator, she pushed the *Down* button and waited, scanning the corridor anxiously for any hint of movement, the slightest whisper of sound.

There was nothing.

She took the elevator to the basement and, when the doors opened, she scanned the corridor. All clear. Stepping from the elevator, she headed to Fileroom E, moving swiftly but stealthily. As she neared the door, her nervousness multiplied exponentially.

Maybe an alarm goes off if the room's unlocked after hours. Or what if someone comes when I'm inside? I'd be trapped.

Pushing aside her fears, she carefully punched in the six numbers on the keypad next to the door.

Two, three, six, five, five, six. Click.

No alarm sounded.

But what if the alarm was silent? There was nothing she could do about that; she would just have to chance it.

She flipped on the light switch and closed the door behind her. It was a small fileroom, rather ordinary, with file cabinets arranged in rows, a photocopier, a shredder, and a desk with a PC. The photocopier was a bonus; if the records she was after were, in fact, stored in the room, she could copy the files here instead of hauling them upstairs. There was also an audiovisual set-up, a desk in the corner with a double DVD machine and large video monitor. To her relief, she saw no security cameras.

She set down her backpack and checked the cabinets to see if any were unlocked. None were.

She withdrew a set of keys from her pants pocket. The file cabinets for Filerooms A through D were keyed alike, and she hoped that the master key would unlock Fileroom E's cabinets. The last thing she wanted to do was use the crowbar in her backpack. She shoved the key into the lock on each cabinet, but it didn't fit any of them.

Damn. How am I going to get inside?

She tried picking one of the locks with her Swiss army knife, but again she had no luck.

She looked at her pack. *Am I going to have to use the crowbar after all?*

And then it dawned on her that there might be a key hidden somewhere in the room, like the keys people stashed outside their homes. She searched the desk drawers first. Nothing. She crouched down and checked under the desks and tables, hoping to find a magnetic hide-a-key. Still nothing. Finally, she reached behind several of the file cabinets stacked close to the walls.

On the last cabinet, the one in the corner, she felt something. A small hook and a key.

Bingo!

She quickly unlocked all the cabinets. Each one was identified by either a single letter or a range of letters. She took a few minutes to pull out a few of the drawers and flip through several of the project files, CDs, and DVDs. The files were arranged alphabetically by the names of individuals, groups, or AMP pet issues. The individuals included hard-line politicians, lobbyists, and donors with whom AMP worked, and also moderate Republican, Independent, and Democratic enemies. The groups included political action committees, lobbying firms, and special legislative committees. The issues included local, state, and national legislative issues and court cases in which AMP had a particular interest.

It was almost frightening how perfectly organized the file system was. All the files were arranged with Germanic efficiency, though she wished there wasn't so many cumbersome paper files to sift through. She also managed to locate three special cabinets filled exclusively with DVDs from important meetings between AMP and prominent legislators and other closed-door events. The DVDs were affixed with neatly typed labels, listing dates and attendees.

She quickly made up her mind on how to conduct the search. She would not try to copy everything, but would focus on records most critical to her story. There were at least twenty cabinets, a lot of material to cover, but it was not quite 7 p.m. so she would have essentially twelve hours at her disposal. Her goal was to finish before 7 a.m., which was when the early birds started arriving for work.

For a veteran journalist who knew what to look for, twelve hours was enough time to topple a government.

CHAPTER 55

AT 6:52 A.M. it was time leave. The early birds would arrive any minute, and Jennifer didn't want to risk being caught. By any measure it had been a successful night. She had copied over six hundred pages of documents in the high-speed copier as well as downloaded the contents of several CDs onto her 50-gigabyte flash drive. She had a veritable gold mine of material, exceeding even her wildest expectations.

She had five DVDs of closed-door meetings between Locke and major GOP legislators, including Kieger and Fowler.

She had political blackmail letters from Locke to the Republican National Committee and several moderate GOP candidates for federal office, threatening to keep AMP's huge voting bloc away on election day if the demands of Christian conservatives weren't met.

She had copies of checks made out to prominent Republicans, including Kieger and Fowler, from secret Stealth Political Action Committees and shady 527s set up by AMP.

She had a copy of AMP's comprehensive plan to influence the Republican presidential nomination during the last election.

She had the complete AMP donor list for the last five years as well as the lists of the other Stealth PACs and 527s to which AMP funneled money to direct the outcome of local and state ballot initiatives.

And she had copies of correspondence between Governor Stoddart and AMP. Colorado's own governor, in bed with the religious right, and the public scarcely knew about it.

All the dark secrets were there just as she had hoped.

Just give me the damn Pulitzer!

She now had conclusive proof that AMP was not only a political beast masquerading as a religious organization, but was also engaged in questionable campaign financing practices and misrepresenting itself to its members. Its primary purpose was not to promote Christian goodwill, or even to give its members a political voice, but to elect rabid conservatives to public office.

All her hard work was going to pay off—all her clever deception.

But now the story had a new twist: the connection between Locke, Kieger, Dubois, and Fowler. The Locke-Fowler relationship was, on its own, no surprise since AMP had courted the senator since her election to

Congress. What was surprising, however, was the degree to which they were intertwined. Likewise, Jennifer had known that AMP had approached Kieger on at least two occasions before the primary, to secure his support of the Christian agenda. But now she knew the relationship had run far deeper. Then there was the matter of the Prince of Darkness, Senator Dubois. AMP had funneled significant sums of soft money into his failed primary campaign. This, in itself, wasn't surprising since campaign donors often backed several candidates at once, until a frontrunner emerged from the pack. What made it newsworthy was the secretive nature of the transactions.

Based on everything, a disturbing pattern was beginning to emerge. AMP had at one time supported Kieger, concurrently with Dubois. It had secretly funneled substantial money Kieger's way six months before the Iowa straw poll, via AMP's largest anonymous Stealth PAC contributors. But by the New Hampshire primary all funding had ceased. From what she had seen on one of the DVDs, Kieger had been lukewarm, at best, on AMP's public policy proposals. In fact, during the last closed-door meeting in early February, just before the kick-off of the primary, Locke and Kieger had actually gotten into a shouting match over the governor's pro-choice stance on abortion.

It was around then that AMP's Stealth PACs began feeding money to Fowler, while continuing its support of Dubois. Huge sums began pumping into her war chest. And with the new inflow of unregulated soft money, Fowler had damn near won the primary, coming on particularly strong at the end. Meanwhile, by mid-March, when it was obvious Dubois couldn't win, AMP had withdrawn its financial support for the Louisiana senator altogether.

True, the questionable campaign financing practices weren't particularly troublesome in their own right. And being unfamiliar with the intricacies of federal election laws, Jennifer couldn't be certain that actual laws had been broken. But the records did establish solid connections between the key players of what was currently the nation's biggest melodrama. The connections raised intriguing questions.

How deep was the rift between Locke and Kieger? Did AMP stop backing him and switch to Fowler because of ideological differences, or because it believed she had a legitimate shot at winning the primary? Did Locke know who was behind Kieger's assassination? Could he have something to do with it? Could Fowler be involved in the scheme? Or Dubois? It had to be considered a possibility in light of what Jennifer now knew.

Turning these unsettling questions in her mind, she shut off the copier and put the last file away. For some reason, she felt like she was being watched.

She went to the door, opened it, and checked the hallway.

There was no one.

But something didn't feel right.

She closed the door, suddenly very aware of her own breathing.

She looked around the room. It seemed terribly small, as if the walls were closing in. She felt a wave of claustrophobia, a sepulchral quiet that seemed to portend doom. The confined space, the white sterility of the walls, the harsh overhead lights—all of these conspired against her, making her feel like she was being hunted.

I have to get out of here!

She made a quick pass-through, making certain she had closed all the cabinets and hadn't left any paperwork behind. With nervous hands, she stuffed the pages she had copied into her backpack, along with her flash drive and the five DVDs she had pilfered, which she would return once she'd made copies. Completing her pass-through, she surveyed the room one last time. There was no trace of her incursion here tonight.

She went to the door, opened it, and checked the corridor. Again, it was empty. Feeling emboldened, she turned off the light and went out, closing the door behind her.

Now all she had to do was make it to her car.

CHAPTER 56

THE TENSION played through her like an electrical storm as she rode the grinding elevator to the first floor. She glanced at her watch. *Damn, it's already two minutes to seven!*

When the doors opened, she peered out cautiously. Muted pink light filtered through the lobby windows. Outside, beyond the glass, loomed safety. Jennifer stepped out of the elevator and headed straight for the front door, trying to look as nonchalant as possible.

I'm going to make it!

She pushed open the door and started for the parking lot on the south side of the building.

Her heart lurched in her chest as she turned the corner.

There, a mere ten feet away, was beefy Benjamin Jr. And he was walking straight towards her!

Shit, how am I going to get out of this?

Their eyes met. For a moment, he was as surprised as she, but then his expression narrowed with suspicion.

"What are *you* doing here?"

She felt her whole face flush with guilt. "Nothing," she said, and she instantly regretted the defensiveness in her voice.

He stepped towards her, crowding her with his bulk, and pointed to the huge backpack on her shoulder. "Doesn't look like nothing from where I'm standing."

She decided to play dumb. "Oh, you mean my pack. I'm going rock climbing this morning—Garden of the Gods. I left some of my equipment here and had to pick it up."

"Rock climbing," he said, disapprovingly. "Why would you want to do that?"

"Because it's fun." She decided to turn the tables on him. "I should ask you what you're doing here so early, Benjamin. Normally you don't come in until nine."

"I have to get some papers for my dad," he said, with an air of importance. "He's driving to Denver to give a speech this morning."

She started for her Subaru Outback. "I'll let you go then."

"Oh, I expect *we* have a little time," he said, taking hold of her arm as she tried to slide past him. His eyes took on a pernicious glint and his thin, moist lips parted. "Why don't we sit in my car and...you know...talk?"

This wasn't the first time he had tried to hit on her, but she still felt a tremble of fear as he grinned at her suggestively. She quickly decided against making a scene, unless he persisted. She was too close to the biggest story of her life to risk blowing it now. There might be more records in Fileroom E that she wanted to copy and she still had to return the DVDs. She decided to be firm but nonthreatening. He was likely to explode if sharply rebuked or outright rejected.

"I don't think that's a good idea, Benjamin. Your mother and father wouldn't approve."

"They wouldn't know about it. It would be our little secret."

Jennifer pulled her arm away, firmly but without anger. "I think you should go upstairs and get what your father needs. You don't want to get in trouble with him now, do you?"

"I don't care about him. I care about you."

"This is not Christian behavior," she said, and she pushed her way past him.

"Christianity has its time and place," he sneered, tromping after her aggressively. "And this isn't the time *or* the place."

"You must stop this. Your parents wouldn't approve," she said as she reached her Outback.

He closed in on her, pressing her against the cool metal door. "I've got desires like everybody else," he said. "That doesn't make me sinful."

"If you don't back away from me right now, I'm going to report this incident to your father. And the police."

For the first time he showed a flash of fear. Then his face relaxed, as if it was all a simple misunderstanding. "Why'd you have to go and say that? I was just horsing around."

Oh no you weren't, you twisted little shit. "I certainly hope so," she said, pretending to give him the benefit of the doubt.

"You're just so beautiful, I can't control myself."

"You must learn to." Pulling her car keys from her pocket, she unlocked the car door, slid the backpack off her shoulder, and was about to place it inside the back seat when he slipped his hands underneath and started to grab it from her.

"Here, let me help you with that."

"That's okay, I've got it."

"I said let me help you."

She jerked it back from him, but his plump hands held on stubbornly. She felt a wave of panic, but then forced herself to give a calm smile. "It's okay, Benjamin, I've got it."

"All right, suit yourself." He released his grip and she took the pack, quickly stuffed it in the back seat, shut the door, and started for the driver's seat.

But he had blocked her path and was peering suspiciously inside the rear car window at the backpack. "Awfully heavy bag. What do you have in there anyway?"

She felt momentary panic.

"I asked you a question, Jennifer. Why is your bag so damned heavy?"

"I already told you, Benjamin. It's got all my climbing equipment: ropes, clips, climbing shoes, the works. I do more than sport climb. That's why the bag is so heavy."

His beefy, pimply face bore a skeptical smirk. "I don't believe you."

"Y-You don't believe me?"

"No, I don't. You must think I'm dumb or something? I know what you're up to."

Her muscles froze.

"You're taking office supplies—photocopier paper, pens, notepads, that sort of thing. That's why your bag is so heavy." He gave her a conspiratorial grin, like this was just between friends. "Hey, I don't have a problem with that. Hell, I do it too."

She felt a wave of relief. Thank God Locke's son was a complete idiot unlike his powerful, clever father.

"Look, Benjamin, I hate to disappoint you, but it really is my climbing gear in that pack," she said to him sternly.

"It is? Really?"

"Yes, really. And now I suggest you go inside and get what your father needs before you get yourself into trouble. I don't want to have to tell your parents about this little incident. But I will if you ever come on to me inappropriately like that again."

And with that, she hopped in her car and drove off, wiping away the beads of perspiration from her forehead when she reached Cascade Avenue.

WEDNESDAY

CHAPTER 57

PATTON DIDN'T WAKE UP UNTIL THE FOURTH RING. With a half-conscious groan, he picked up the phone from the bedside table, his eyes struggling to adjust to the dirty light filtering through the bedroom curtains.

"Yeah," he mumbled, his voice laced with sleep.

"Boy, do I have a story for you," he heard Jennifer Odden blurt excitedly, too excitedly in his view, considering he had managed only a few hours' sleep.

"Give me a second here. I'm still on the deserted isle with Ginger and Mary Ann."

"Both of them at the same time? I wonder what Freud would say about that?"

"He'd probably say I was a boringly normal heterosexual male. What's up?"

"You need to get your butt out of bed, come down here, and interrogate Benjamin Locke."

Patton rubbed the slumber from his tired eyes. "You broke into the fileroom, didn't you?"

"I didn't break in anywhere. I work there for Christ's sake."

"Pulitzer fever. That's what you've got, Pulitzer fever."

"This thing is even bigger than I thought, Ken. I'm not sure, but I think Locke could be involved in the assassination. He tried to strong-arm Kieger into taking hard-right positions during the primary, but Kieger refused. There's conflict there—and conflict leads to motive."

"I suppose you have actual proof of this?"

"I have DVDs of their meetings. They had a shouting match during the last one around the time of the New Hampshire primary. Over abortion."

"So that proves Locke killed him," he said skeptically, turning on the light on the side table. "Kind of a leap of logic, isn't it?"

"I've just handed you motive on a silver platter. Don't tell me you don't see it?"

"You haven't handed me anything. AMP, or someone associated with the group, has always been one of our prime suspects, Jenn. Not just because of the button, but because Locke has close ties to both Kieger and Fowler. Of course we're looking into all of AMP's activities and public documents, but we're doing it in a methodical manner. I'm just not sure a shouting match between Locke and Kieger proves anything. When you put two powerful egos like that into a room, quite frankly I would expect discord. When was it again, nine months ago?"

"Jesus, can you really not see this?"

He said nothing. It felt weird arguing with her for the first time in twelve years. He reached for the lead miniature next to the clock: a Berdan's Green Coat 1st U.S. sharpshooter. He had painted the figure two weeks ago and thought he might touch up the tunic. During the Civil War, Union Green Coat snipers had targeted high-ranking Confederate officers during engagements to disrupt the command structure—precisely, he reflected, what Kieger's conspirators had accomplished last Sunday.

"Come on, Ken, you know a right-wing group's behind it. The Brigade's just a ruse."

"I don't know that. That's your theory—I have to deal with facts."

"Oh, so that's it. You're the G-man expert and I'm just an overzealous journalist with an *agenda*."

"I didn't mean it like that. Look, it's too damned early in the morning for this—I need java."

She chuckled. "You're still not a morning person, are you?"

"You remember," he said softly.

"Of course I remember. I was in love with you in case you forgot. But that was before you turned into a poster boy for J. Edgar Hoover. Just listen to what I have to say—the facts speak for themselves."

She quickly told him what she'd found in Fileroom E. While he still thought she was jumping to premature conclusions based on inadequate facts and seemed to have it out for Benjamin Locke and AMP, he had to admit there was sufficient justification to again question Locke. And Fowler and Dubois, for that matter. Unfortunately, it would be impossible to talk to the president-elect or the senator; they were just too damned powerful and they wouldn't tell him anything voluntarily anyway. The starting point, then, was Locke. Patton would have to question him carefully, without disclosing his source. He would be treading in murky legal waters since, at present, the DVDs were stolen property and there was some question as to whether the files were legally obtained. Jennifer had copied the files without AMP approval, and although she hadn't signed a nondisclosure agreement, how records were obtained was a critical factor in federal cases. As an FBI agent, Patton spent more than half his time preparing cases and assisting federal prosecutors in trying them. In many ways, he was as much an attorney as a detective. But before he could request a subpoena or refer a case to the U.S. Attorney's Office for indictment, he had to have all his ducks lined up. He damned well had better get Sharp's approval before he made a move.

"Okay," he said, setting the miniature sharpshooter back on the table next to a triumvirate of World War II era U.S. Marines he had painstakingly painted by hand. They were storming a Japanese machine gun nest, their M-1 Garand semiautomatic rifles fixed with gleaming bayonets. "I'll try and set something up for this afternoon."

"He's giving a talk in Denver later this morning. Why don't you just interrogate him then?"

"Who's running this investigation, you or me?" he said, feeling like a horse being led to water. At the same time, he had to admit the possibility that Jennifer might be onto something big. It seemed far-fetched for a prominent Christian leader like Locke to be involved in something flagrantly and violently illegal, but stranger things had happened. "Okay, I'll call him. But just so you know, we don't interrogate people unless they're suspects. And I'm telling you right now, Locke isn't a suspect."

"He will be after you give him the third degree. Good luck, Mr. G-man."

"Why do I feel like I'm Eliot Ness when I talk to you? By the way, we're still on for tonight, right?"

"Are you kidding? I've waited twelve years for this date."

CHAPTER 58

HANGING UP THE PHONE, Jennifer headed to her bedroom to undress. After the long sleepless night, she wanted to revive herself with a shower—not to mention several cups of coffee—before she pitched into the files she'd copied. But before she had taken three steps her telephone rang. Her first thought was that it was Ken calling her back.

She picked up before the second ring. "Okay, what did you forget?"

"Why isn't your first draft in my email inbox?"

Jennifer instantly regretted answering. The voice on the other end wasn't Ken at all, but the insufferable Reid Farnsworth Lampert. She felt blindsided. *Shit, what should I say?*

"I'm waiting, Ms. Odden."

"You sure are an early riser, Reid. It's not even six thirty out there in California."

"The name is *Mister Lampert*, as I've told you before, and this isn't early for me. I've already completed my five-mile run and Vitamin E facial scrub."

Jennifer wanted to gag.

"Where's the first draft of your story? How come you haven't emailed it to me yet?"

"You said I had until Thursday."

"I did? Well, I've changed my mind."

"Well, old boy, you're about to change it again because I managed to get inside the secret room last night—Fileroom E."

To her delight, she reeled him in hook, line, and sinker. "You did? What did you find?" he inquired breathlessly.

Jennifer told him. But to her surprise, he said nothing. The line went absolutely quiet.

Finally, she could stand it no longer. "What do you think?"

"I like it, but you can forget about all this AMP political hardball stuff. What our readers are going to want to know about is the Locke-Kieger-Fowler connection. I can picture the headline now: THE FATAL TRIAD: THE TRUE STORY BEHIND THE ROLLINS ASSASSINATION."

"I don't think we can print that, Mr. Lampert, not yet anyway. Most of what I've told you is speculation. It's going to take me some more time to thoroughly review all these files and the DVDs."

"I have the solution to that. I'll send a team out there to help you sort through everything."

"That won't be necessary—I'll take care of it."

"Nonsense. I'll have a senior editor and two assistants out there on the next flight."

She felt a stab of resentment that he would even suggest sending others. Didn't he have any idea how hard she had worked for this story, the sacrifices she'd made? "I appreciate the offer, but think it best if I handle it myself. It would take too long to bring them up to speed."

"Then you'd better get plugging away, young lady. I'm wondering how Senator Dubois fits into the puzzle. You do know what the Democrats and his own staffers call him behind closed doors."

"The Prince of Darkness."

"Funny how no one seems to know much about him. He's a staunch right-winger, but he's still something of a mystery. Though he finished third in last spring's primary, there's very little in print about his private life. He strikes me as a very secretive man. And one day he could be president."

That's a scary thought. "I'll look into it. But I'm going to need more time to put this thing together. The story's grown into something much bigger than I anticipated. I'm not going to be able to get you the story by tomorrow. The best I can do is Monday morning."

"That late?"

"This is a huge story."

"All right, if that's the best you can do. But in the meantime, have a PDF of the documents made and email them to me today. I'm also going to want a copy of that disk—the one where Locke and Kieger are arguing."

"I'll take care of it."

"There's another thing. I'm going to have to run this by Legal, especially the DVD issue. I realize you didn't sign a confidentiality agreement, but there could be some legal ramifications to this."

"Everything you need to know is in those documents and on the disks. There's no sourcing issue here because print and audio don't lie."

"My sentiments exactly, but we have to be thorough. What do you think about returning to the fileroom? There's got to be more there."

Jennifer felt uneasy thinking about how closely she had come to being caught this morning. "Are you suggesting I dig deeper?"

"You might be able to fill in some important information gaps."

"I'm just not sure when I can do it," she said, thinking aloud. "It's too risky in the daytime."

"Then do it tonight. Think of the treasures you could unearth from those file cabinets, the dirty little secrets."

She rolled her eyes. If Reid Farnsworth Lampert was the kind of editor she would have to work for from here on out in the brave new world of modern journalism, maybe she should search for a new career.

"I'll take care of it," she said, hoping to appease him.

"Ms. Odden, I must admit you have surprised me. This is exactly the kind of can-do spirit that Mr. Stavros is looking for."

She wanted to throw up. "Thanks."

"You've got to get into that fileroom again. There's got to be more there, I just know it."

"If there is, *Mister Lampert*, I guarantee I'll find it."

CHAPTER 59

THE CATHEDRAL WAS GOTHIC, but with classical Renaissance motifs, as one would find in Italy, not France. The heavy oak doors were open. Skyler walked inside, her leather sandals tapping lightly on the laminated, dark-blue slate stones. The floor turned to wood as she parted her way through a second set of doors, which gave way to an immense nave. There were a dozen or so people in the church, kneeling in prayer or sitting gazing into space. Skyler walked the length of the nave and took a seat in the fifth-row pew on the right.

Built at the turn of the twentieth century, St. Johns was one of Los Angeles's oldest churches, a tribute to a bygone era when stone was as valued as glass and steel. Skyler attended Sunday masses regularly when she was in town, but rarely did she venture here on a weekday. Today, her visit was for quiet reflection for there was something—something important—on her mind.

It was impossible not to be inspired here. The vast interior seemed to dwarf all humanity that found its way inside. The lofty ceiling was vaulted in stone, the cross-ribs covered in shimmering gold paint. The columns separating the nave from the side aisles were exquisitely decorated, and the tracery of the pews was lithe and graceful. While many cathedrals were condemned to a state of perpetual twilight, St. Johns carried no such gloom. Thanks to the endless Southern California sunshine, the stained glass windows along the walls and behind the altar shone like precious gems, throwing pools of brilliance into the church. Electrified candle bra and the bank of guttering candles in the nave provided additional illumination. All in all, the faithful who came here to surrender themselves before God, or to contemplate the beauty of the church, could feel closer, at least for a moment, to understanding the mystical power of the universe.

She pulled out her rosary, knelt down, and began to pray.

Hail Mary full of grace, the Lord is with thee...

It was a simple prayer, as much a vestige of her Roman Catholic upbringing as a supplication to a higher authority. But Skyler truly believed in the words as she recited them from long memory. She accepted Jesus as Lord and Savior and sought, in quiet moments like these, to draw closer to Him. She knew that all true believers endured to the end, that only through faith could a person, even someone who had committed terrible sins like her, remain in a state of grace. She also knew that she needed to turn away from sin toward God, to show genuine repentance, if she was ever to be accepted into His kingdom upon her death.

But it wasn't a quest for God's acceptance that brought her here today. It had to do with the new feelings in her heart. She couldn't remember feeling this euphoric in a long while, not since she was a little girl bounding across the Tuscan countryside on her favorite pony. Years ago, she had resigned herself to a life of loneliness instead of love, family, and intimacy. But now, for reasons she was only beginning to comprehend, she wanted something more out of life.

The last two days she had begun to consider quitting the game. She knew her change of heart was largely because of Anthony. He made her feel special and loved in a way she hadn't known since she was young. The intimacy they shared made the killing seem dirty, reprehensible. She was also growing tired of it all. After a decade and a half, being an assassin was taking a physical toll on her. Then there was the ever-present danger of being caught. The longer she stayed in the game, the tighter the net became as the world's intelligence forces and her enemies closed in around her. At the moment, Xavier was doing a good job keeping the bloodhounds away, mostly through clever misinformation, but how much longer could he cover her tracks?

Wasn't it time to get out, while there was still a good chance she could lead a somewhat normal life, perhaps even atone for her sins?

The question wouldn't leave her mind as she began reciting *Our Father*.

For years now, since she had become an assassin, she thought of herself as simply an extension of her gun and the men who hired her as the real killers. It had been easy to rationalize what she did, and she had considered herself no different from the sharpshooters under the employ of the CIA, Mossad, or Russian intelligence. In fact, she had believed herself superior for she was far better paid, took on only those assignments she wanted, and took orders from no one. In her field, no man was her equal or left investigators in a greater state of confusion. But now all the old arguments seemed feeble and she wanted out.

She thought of how she felt when she was with Anthony. When he kissed her, she got goosebumps. When he looked her way, she lost her concentration. When she was alone with him, she felt a sense of inner peace. And when she lied to him about her job, her life, her past, she felt miserable. The excitement on the one hand and the guilt on the other were but different sides of the same coin, she knew. She had strong feelings for him, feelings she could not deny. If not love, it was something equally as intoxicating.

Rising from her kneeling position and sitting back down on the solid oak pew, she felt a powerful sense of irony. On the one hand, she felt inordinately blessed to have found Anthony; on the other, she felt unworthy of such good fortune. What had she done to deserve God's blessing when she had spent half her life as a killer? Was He giving her a second chance? If so, why had she been chosen? Surely, there were many others more deserving of a second chance than her.

Knowing she might never find the answers to such questions, she again let her eyes drift around the church. With childlike wonderment, she took in the sheer vastness and graceful artistry of the sanctuary; the pained, otherworldly expression of the savior nailed to the holy cross in humble surrender; the multicolored brilliance of the stained-glass windows. Gradually, as the holiness of the place took hold inside her, as the sense of God's design and majesty permeated her soul, she felt at peace with herself.

CHAPTER 60

TWO HOURS LATER that same afternoon, Jennifer Odden was staring out the window of her office at American Patriots, watching the branches of the cottonwoods and box elders along Fountain Creek swaying melodically in the breeze, when she heard a knock on her door. She turned from the window to see Susan Locke standing meekly in the open doorway. Though she had spent a lot of time with Susan at the company picnic last summer—they had been on the same softball team—and had spoken with her on a number of occasions during the girl's frequent visits to the office, she didn't know her that well and was surprised to see her here.

"Come in, Susan," Jennifer said with a sympathetic smile, sensing the girl's discomfort. She rose from her chair and stepped forward to greet her.

"I don't mean to bother you, but I was hoping we could talk," the girl said timorously.

"Sure." Jennifer closed the door and showed her to a chair in front of the desk. "How can I help?"

The girl's lower lip trembled and Jennifer saw how deeply troubled she was. "Something's happened."

"What is it?"

"It's all so crazy, I'm not even sure where to begin."

Jennifer reached out and touched her hand. "Take your time. I'm here to help."

"Can you promise not to tell my parents?"

"It'll be our secret. I promise."

"I'm pregnant, Jennifer. I'm pregnant and my father and mother are angry and disappointed in me."

Jennifer was stunned. "You're…you're pregnant?"

"That's not the worst of it. My boyfriend Todd and I went to the Family Planning Group clinic in Widefield last week. We went to see the doctor about my appointment for…for *an abortion*."

Jennifer felt something very close to shock pass across her face. *An abortion? My God, her parents and the media will crucify her!*

"Todd wants me to have one but I…I don't know. We set up the appointment for this Friday, but I'm still having second thoughts."

Jennifer reached out and touched Susan's hand again. The girl acknowledged the gesture of support with a gentle dip of her head.

"When we first found out, neither of us wanted to go through with an abortion. But we were so scared of what my parents might do to us that we couldn't think of what else to do. Todd's really frightened of my father, so much so that he won't even come over to my house anymore."

"Have your parents said anything about what they want you to do?"

"They've already arranged for me to go to a home for unwed mothers in the mountains. Sacred Heart—it's somewhere in Summit County. But I don't know if I can go through with it."

The room went silent. Jennifer felt sadness, a loss of innocence around every word, and felt a deep sympathy for Susan. It was almost exactly the same predicament she had faced twelve years earlier. She hoped Susan wouldn't have to suffer the same fate she had, but it looked as though that was precisely where things were heading.

"So what are you thinking?" asked Jennifer.

Susan's grave countenance turned to one of perplexity. "I don't know...I'm torn. I don't want to have an abortion. But at the same time, I don't want to be forced to give birth to a baby and give it away to complete strangers. To people who might not love the child as I would."

Looking at Susan, Jennifer saw a haunting image of herself a dozen years earlier. And along with the image came all the old memories, the pangs of guilt and remorse. What her father had forced upon her was a cruelty undimmed by the passage of time.

"I just don't know what to do," Susan said. "I'm supposed to leave for Sacred Heart next week. But I don't know if I can go through with it." A teardrop spilled down her cheek and she took a moment to methodically wipe it away before continuing. "If I had an abortion, I don't think my parents would ever forgive me." She tried to say something else, but couldn't bring herself to finish.

Jennifer could see another wave of tears climbing steadfastly toward the surface.

"I'm scared, Jennifer. I'm scared that whatever decision I make will be the wrong one."

Jennifer rubbed her hands together. Her thoughts turned darkly to her past, to her father, to the big mistake, to the nightmare that to this day continued to torment her. Susan's crisis was a disturbing reenactment of her own personal trauma, although Locke and his wife appeared to be far more sympathetic and reasonable than her crazy father. For a moment, she considered telling Susan what had happened to her, but decided against it. She didn't want to sway the girl's decision. She would lend a sympathetic ear, but the choice had to be Susan's alone.

"Do you know the reason I came to you?"

Jennifer shook her head.

"It's because of the time we spent together at the AMP picnic last summer. I knew then that you were different."

Jennifer raised a brow. "Different?"

"Different from my parents. Different from most of the people who work here at AMP."

Jennifer saw a look on the girl's face that was wise beyond her years; then her expression changed and she seemed to lighten with a touch of humor.

"Todd and I were walking through the parking lot when you drove up. When you opened your car door, we caught a whiff."

"A whiff?"

"Of the pot." Susan smiled. "I may be a devout Christian, but I don't live in another century like my parents. What you do is your business."

Jennifer gave a guilty, knowing grin. Clearly, she had misjudged Susan Locke, thinking her more prudish than she was.

Susan looked at her watch. "I have to get back to school—I'm in between classes."

"How did you get here?"

"I borrowed Todd's car." She stood up from her chair. "Thanks for talking with me."

"I wish I could be of more help."

"Oh no, you helped me out a lot. I feel better already."

Jennifer looked at the girl. She felt jangled and restless, full of unresolved feelings. But one thing was clear: Susan Locke was a good kid and a kindred spirit. Life, with all its random twists and turns, with all its unforeseen zeniths and nadirs, had dealt them both the same unenviable hand. And right now, Jennifer found herself wanting, more than anything else, to help Susan through her crisis.

She reached out and touched Susan's hand again. "I'm here for you, anytime," she said softly.

Susan's face took on a gentle glow. "Somehow I knew you'd say that. And if you ever need me, I'll be there for you too."

CHAPTER 61

JUST BEFORE NOON, Patton got a call from Taylor requesting his presence in the bullpen. He grabbed his iPad, scurried down the hallway, and stepped into the crowded room, which overnight had turned into a frenzied command-and-control center. Added to the existing high-tech gadgetry were five 36-inch color monitors, a stack of supercomputer towers, and an array of sophisticated equipment for video enhancement and color printing. A technician sat in front of each screen and there was a new face talking to Taylor. Patton realized, belatedly, that he must be the specialist from the CIA Directorate for Science and Technology, Office of Technical Service, Sharp had requested. All of the new equipment must have arrived with him last night from Langley.

Taylor gave a professional smile as Patton came up. "This is Charlie Fial from OTS."

Patton shook the man's hand. "Welcome to the Wild Wild West. Bet you're glad to get a break from the backstabbing bureaucracy of Langley and get a little taste of ours, huh?"

The pale young techie nodded bashfully and pushed up his half-frame glasses. He looked like he had spent every day of the last ten years gazing at a video monitor, and every night solving partial differential equations in his sleep. Which meant he was perfect for the job at hand.

"With Charlie's help we've identified John Doe at three different campaign rallies," Taylor said, sweeping his hand across the color monitors in front of them. He pointed to the screen in front of Weiss, the one furthest to the right. "This footage is from last Friday—Kieger's speech in Sacramento. You can see John Doe five rows back from the stage."

The senior Secret Service agent then handed off to Fial, who pointed out the differences in John Doe's physical appearance compared to the Union Plaza Building footage shown on the far left monitor. The guy had the same sharp jawline, mustache, and dark sunglasses as before, but this time he was dressed like a businessman. He wore a light-blue button-down shirt, a conservative red-and-blue-striped tie, and a ROLLINS FOR PRESIDENT cap, pulled down low over his forehead just like the UPS cap at Union Plaza. The ponytail was gone, or at least hidden from view, and the mustache and hair were darker in color. His face was also more closely shaven, but it was still the same guy.

"Where'd you get this?" Patton asked Taylor.

"Media pool." He pointed to the next screen, to the left. "Okay, here we've got him at the Oakland rally the day before. This is one of ours, from a security camera to stage left. A little different disguise, but still our man."

Again Fial stepped up and pointed out the differences in the man's disguises, his physical presence, the way he interacted with those around him. This time John Doe had a blue-collar look and stood further from the podium, perhaps ten rows back. A factory worker's uniform encased his slender but strong frame, and his face was smudged with oil or dirt. He had black hair this time, and Patton could see a forest of chest hair in the V in the man's uniform. The same ROLLINS FOR PRESIDENT cap was pulled low over his brow, and he peered out impassively from behind his impenetrable sunglasses. As in the Sacramento footage, his air of focused concentration and lack of emotion separated him from the rest of the crowd.

They went through the remaining two tapes from a rally in Bakersfield. When they were finished, Taylor said, "We haven't found him yet in the footage from San Diego, San Bernadino, or any of the other venues. But hopefully we'll track him down. We could even get a better shot of him. We've been getting a good response over the Net."

Fial picked up a copy of the wanted poster from the table and began looking it over.

"Every law enforcement agency in the country has that by now," Patton said to him. "Plus we've issued an alert to Interpol and our friendlies overseas."

Without responding, Fial continued to look over the grainy photograph and artist's sketch on the poster, comparing them to the images frozen on the screens. Studying his expression, Patton sensed there was a problem.

"Something wrong?" he asked.

"I'm not sure."

Everyone looked at him with puzzlement.

"What is it?" Patton persisted.

"Okay, let me see if I can explain this. What we see, in each frame, is a person who looks like a man, right?" Fial pointed to the five images on the screen, from right to left. "We've got a mustache, chest hair, two day beard growth, et cetera. We've got male clothing—the business suit and worker's uniform. And finally, we've got the male physical presence, the posture, the gestures, the way he moves. Did you see in the Bakersfield tape where he scratched his crotch? Or the Union Plaza tape when he rubbed his hand across his beard? Now the images are somewhat grainy, but in every case the picture we see says, *Man!* Except there's a problem with this picture."

"I'm not sure I follow," Patton said, brows knitting together.

"There's too many woman-like discrepancies. The smooth shape of the nose, the curved hips, the slender wrists, the soft lips and jaw line. Now these features are, for the most part, swamped out by the masculine features, but they're not completely lost. There's something feminine there. You can see it in some of the body movements and gestures too."

"Wait a second. Are you saying John Doe's a goddamned woman?"

"I'm not sure. Could be a transsexual. All I can say is something's not right. I've observed thousands of criminals, male and female, from surveillance tapes over the years. So I know what I'm talking about. Something about this character doesn't gel."

"Am I supposed to go to my boss and tell him the assassin's some kind of cross-dresser or cold-blooded La Femme Nikita? He'll demote me to GS-5 on the spot."

Fial laughed nervously. "I was hoping we could keep this between ourselves until I've had a chance to test my theory further. You know, go over the tapes in detail, try and find this guy at other rallies. Maybe somewhere along the line he—or quite possibly she—slipped up."

Patton's head swam with vexation. *Is this asshole wasting my time or does he know what the fuck he's talking about?* "Can't you give us something more concrete?"

Fial scratched his chin thoughtfully. "I can tell you one thing."

"What's that?"

"Things are not what they seem."

CHAPTER 62

LOOKING FOR ANSWERS, Patton went down to the seventeenth floor to see Dr. Hamilton. The door was open, so he walked right in. "Howdy, Doc. I'm baaack!"

The freckle-faced criminal profiler was putting away a book in the shelf and he nearly jumped out of his skin at the sound of Ken's voice. "Jesus, you scared the shit out of me!"

"Sorry, Doc, but I need to know about female assassins."

"I don't recall mentioning that particular breed of criminal in my profile."

"I realize that. But Charlie Fial—"

"Who the hell is Charlie Fial?"

"He's the audiovisual nerd from Langley. He thinks John Doe could be a woman disguised as a man. He's looking into it further, but in the meantime I'd like to hear what you think."

"Sounds interesting, but I think he's got a fanciful imagination. I saw the video."

"Just suppose for a moment we are dealing with a woman. In your expert opinion what kind of background would she have?"

"Women generally become assassins or terrorists for two reasons: one, the equality of opportunity available; and two, because they're convinced violence can bring a better life to their oppressed people. Unlike the men in the male-dominated American terrorist groups you're used to dealing with, women rarely do it in the name of religion, to destroy the opposition, or for the sheer thrill of violence. They are driven by deeper passions and a desire for the egalitarian. Men are driven by this too, but not as intensely as women."

Patton turned on his iPad. "So it would be unlikely for a woman to be a freelancer. She would be attached to some sort of group."

"The female terrorist is motivated by a desire to help people in need or to change societal and governmental policies. It would be difficult to accomplish such lofty goals on her own, so she would probably be part of a larger terrorist cell."

"Like the Green Freedom Brigade?"

"You're the one knowledgeable in terrorist cell dynamics. You tell me."

"Its members have limited paramilitary experience—basic infiltration tactics and explosives. They don't kill people, at least not intentionally. And their motive's questionable. I just don't see them taking out Kieger because of his lackluster environmental record in California."

"What about a right-wing group?"

"We're looking into a dozen of them, including fairly innocuous Christian organizations like American Patriots and Families First. But we haven't turned up anything definite yet linking any of these groups to the assassination. All the evidence we have is circumstantial."

"You'll get a breakthrough soon. But let's return, for the moment, to our female assassin or terrorist. The interesting thing is she usually performs a dual role. On one hand, she sees herself as a soldier for her cause. On the other, she fulfills the role as nurturer to the other group members, who are like extended family to her."

"That's what I've seen in some of the militias," Patton said, typing on his iPad. "But the men still dominate and the women are invariably in secondary roles."

"In America, that may be true, but not in other parts of the world, especially Europe and the Middle East. For years now, criminologists have been pushing the ridiculous notion that female terrorists are followers, not leaders. These women have supposedly fallen into bad ways because of misguided loyalty to their lovers, who are attached to terrorist cells. But this is hogwash. Today, around seventy percent of the leaders in the German, French, Spanish, and Italian cells are women. So we know women are capable of both killing and giving orders to do so without any qualms. But they must feel as though they are fighting for a noble cause. They need to see themselves as freedom fighters."

"So the problem you have with a woman in the Kieger case is that you envision the assassin as a loner, a professional sniper whose sole motivation is money?"

"I think the physical evidence supports my contention. But there's another reason: statistical probability."

"I'm not sure I follow."

"Let me explain. Suppose this Charlie Fial fellow is correct, and we are dealing with a woman. How does that gibe with the fact that the world's leading snipers, the known ones at least, are men? I did some checking with a friend of mine at Interpol after we talked last. There is not a single woman among them, and most are either ex-military or ex-intelligence, male-dominated fields."

"So that's where it becomes a question of statistical probability?"

"There are plenty of female terrorists, but no known long-distance snipers. It's like astrophysics. Where are the women? For the most part, they're simply not there. They're doing other things."

Patton was typing furiously. The good doctor gave him a moment to catch up before continuing.

"When I consider the three most distinctive aspects of the case—the sophisticated penetration, the military-style weaponry, and the world-class marksmanship—I call to mind a specific type of criminal. An ex-military, alpha-male loner who considers what he does an exciting job with great benefits. A soldier of fortune who can rationalize away his guilt rather easily. A woman would never be satisfied with such a mundane existence. She would need a *passionate* reason to kill."

"But you still believe this lone assassin is backed by a group," Patton said.

"A very well-financed and well-connected group."

Patton stopped typing, closed his iPad, and rose to his feet. "Thanks, Doc. I'll keep my mind open on this one."

"That's why they put you in charge of the case, you know," Hamilton said, like a teacher to a star pupil. "Because of your open mind. Quite different than most of the agents around here."

"Thanks, Doc. I just hope I can live up to everybody's expectations—including my own."

CHAPTER 63

WHEN SKYLER RETURNED to her apartment, she found Anthony waiting outside. He wore casual shorts, a polo shirt, and Birkenstocks and greeted her with a soft kiss. They stepped inside and sipped some wine, a robust Chianti Anthony had brought with him. Then they went out.

They strolled happily through the streets of Venice Beach. The city's crown and glory had once been its Venetian-style canals, with wonderful vaulted arches and rococo-style hotels. Such was the vision of tobacco magnate Abbot Kinney, whose goal was to bring the romance and refinement of Venice, Italy, to sunny Southern California shores by dredging the wetlands along Santa Monica Bay and creating a vast network of interconnected waterways. In 1905, his dream was complete, but within a generation the canals became dirty and oily. The renaissance town began to change in other ways too, no longer attracting society's upper crust, rather gamblers, prostitutes, bootleggers, and other assorted rogues. By the time local hero Jim Morrison and the Doors were ripping out *Break On Through* in the mid-sixties, Kinney's once grand vision was long forgotten. Most of the canals were completely filled in and buried, and those that weren't were nothing more than cryptic vestiges of their former glory.

After walking past a few abandoned canals on their right, Skyler and Anthony headed in the direction of the beach. Funky wooden houses sprouted up next to them as they made their way through the narrow, Venetian-style streets and alleyways. At one point, they slipped into an art gallery to browse. While Anthony looked over the modern art, Skyler examined prints of famous paintings by Fra Angelico, Botticelli, Ghirlandajo, and Raphael of winged angels and sweet-faced Madonnas. Her favorite art would always be that of her native Italy, and her favorite artists would always be the Renaissance Old Masters.

From the gallery, they headed to the pavilion on Windward Avenue. The street circus artists were out in full force and she and Anthony took a moment to watch a talented juggler on a unicycle. With ridiculous ease, he tossed five burning torches in the air and peddled about with a young girl from the audience on his shoulders. Skyler confessed to Anthony that, as a little girl, she had wanted to run off and join the circus as her favorite film director, Federico Fellini, had done as a child. Life in a circus had always seemed so full of risk and freedom to her.

They walked on unhurriedly, browsing through several shops along the way. There was a Mediterranean feel, with the sidewalk cafés and small shops lining the avenues. This was one of the things that had attracted Skyler to the region originally. It was like a home away from home. Occasionally, they held hands as they took in the ocean views in the distance, the warm breeze blowing on their faces. There wasn't much need for conversation, but when they talked, it was about art and films, mostly.

After the pavilion, they walked to the beach. The late afternoon sunlight sparkled off the water. Foamy white rollers slammed into the sand. Squadrons of seagulls soared overhead. In the distance, sailboats slid across the ocean, airbrushed with sporadic splashes of white.

They walked the beach for more than an hour then took a late lunch in a cozy restaurant a short distance from the pavilion. A full bottle of Chianti rounded out the meal of California-style thin crust pizza nicely. Then they were off to the beach again, walking and talking. To Skyler's relief, Anthony didn't ask her any questions about the CIA or her past, nor did he broach the subject of the assassination. They talked about light and pleasant subjects.

While she wasn't sure if she loved him, she did know that she had never felt this way before. It made her feel a sense of loss for all the years she had missed out on emotions like these. She had known almost no intimacy in her adult life. She loved her parents and siblings, but she rarely saw them. When she was young, there was Alberto, but that was so long ago it was nothing more than a distant memory of tainted intimacy. He had only wanted a beautiful young lover in his bed and a loyal freedom fighter at his side. When she had posed the slightest risk, he had ordered her execution.

But this—whatever was going on between her and Anthony—meant something. This was different. She felt a throbbing pulse of excitement whenever she was with him and her confidence, her sense of self-worth, ran high. Her heart brimmed over with emotions—deep emotions, connected emotions, visceral emotions she hadn't felt in eons. She could almost slap herself, she felt so lucky, and she hoped it would never end.

That was what she wanted most of all: to feel like she did now forever.

CHAPTER 64

"SO WHAT HAPPENED TODAY?"

She and Ken were sitting in a booth at the Castle Café, beneath a huge painting of an 1870's wrangler knocking back a bottle of Taos Lightning, while the trusty stead beneath him gulped greedily from a clear mountain creek.

"I'll tell you what happened," Patton growled, his irascible tone taking Jennifer by surprise. "Nothing good—not a single damned thing."

"Did you interrogate Locke?"

"No, my boss wouldn't let me. He said there wasn't enough evidence."

"But I thought you—"

"Sharp shut it down, all right?"

"My aren't we grumpy?"

"This case is fucking killing me. I don't know what happened exactly, but somehow Governor Stoddart caught wind that we're looking into American Patriots and flipped his lid. I told Sharp what you told me, and he told me point blank to back off the AMP angle. He must be getting pressure from the governor's office and maybe even Washington. I don't know what's going on, but for some reason everyone thinks I've been overzealous—and they just might be right."

Jennifer knew what he really meant: she was the overzealous one and now he was in trouble because of her. But she had established a perfectly viable connection between AMP and both Kieger and Fowler. While it didn't prove a conspiracy, it did provide a plausible motive for the assassination.

A waiter in a chambray shirt with a Castle Café logo, blue jeans, and pointy-toed boots swung by the table. They both ordered Coors drafts to drink, and for dinner, Jennifer opted for roast duck enchiladas in a tomatillo-chipotle pepper sauce with black beans and rice, while Patton went for buffalo meatloaf and garlic mashed potatoes smothered in brown onion gravy.

When the waiter moved off, Patton said, "Let's face it, neither of us has any hard proof that Benjamin Locke or anyone else at AMP has anything to do with the assassination. That's why my primary focus has to be on tracking down the shooter. That's what's going to give me the best chance to solve the case."

"Sounds to me like your boss and the governor are trying to pull you off the scent. I think you have to ask yourself if they could be involved."

"You're serious?"

"Damn right I'm serious. I'm a journalist, Ken. These are questions that have to be asked and answered."

"Okay then, I don't see how Sharp could be involved. He's a twenty-five-year vet, a born and bred G-man. He thinks the law is Super Glue holding the world together. But Governor Stoddart, now there's a horse of a different color. He'd put his kids up for auction if he thought it would bring him a thousand votes. But in this case he's probably just worried that I'll dig up some campaign financing stuff on him. That would explain why he's on my back."

He sighed before continuing.

"Look, Jenn, I realize AMP practices hardball politics and that many of its members are right-wing Christian windbags, but don't you think you might be overreaching here? Trying to make them the ones responsible for the assassination and this big conspiracy of yours?"

The words stung her, but she said nothing.

"You might be right about some of this," he went on. "But I question your motive. Is all this because of your father? Is that why you're trying to bring AMP to its knees, to get back at him?"

She didn't answer, but deep down she knew that he was right. What drove her *was* revenge against her father. She hated him for forcing her down a path that would always gnaw at her soul. As head of the most powerful Christian political organization in the country, Locke was simply the most prominent symbol with which to direct her anger, like Custer to Native Americans or Hitler to Jews. He and his organization were the embodiment of the narrow-minded evil she saw in her own father.

She leaned forward, putting her elbows on the wood table. "Ken, regardless of my personal feelings, you have to admit I could be onto something big here."

"I don't deny that. But we're going to need more—a hell of a lot more—if we're going to be able to prove it."

CHAPTER 65

AFTER DINNER, as they were heading out the door, President-elect Fowler appeared on the television screen at the bar. Several people had gathered around to watch, and Patton and Jennifer joined them. Fowler stood behind a podium, a dozen microphones pointing up at her. Despite her youth, she looked august, presidential. Behind her, slightly to her right, stood the wife of the slain leader, Hana Kieger, bereaved yet stalwart in her knee-length, charcoal-black dress. The president-elect cleared her throat, then, as the air of expectation around the bar thickened, she read from a prepared script.

"My fellow Americans, as you know last Sunday we lost a great leader and friend. Today the body of President-elect William Ambrose Kieger was laid to rest in his hometown of Santa Barbara. There is nothing we can say or do that will make up for his loss. But we can pay our respects to him—indeed we must pay our respects to him. I ask you now to join me in a moment of silence."

The crowd at the bar quieted, heads bowed, as thoughts and prayers went out to Kieger and his family. Patton felt the same curious mixture of despair and anger that had haunted him all week. It defied all logic that a man so full of promise had been gunned down by a lowly assassin.

After the moment of silence, Fowler's expression changed and she took on a puissant gleam. "There is a terrorist out there, still at large, who has left behind a trail of blood, murder, and suffering. This man has left behind a widow and fatherless children. He has killed our innocence and despoiled our nation with his hateful act. But this coward shall not remain beyond the reach of the law for long. Nor shall those who supported him, who nurtured him in his cruel enterprise, if such persons exist."

Patton gave a sidelong glance at Jennifer. While the other faces around the bar were entranced or expressed shared outrage, she appeared more skeptical.

She doesn't believe Fowler. She thinks she could be part of this.

"In his barbaric act, the assassin makes us all feel guilty, as if we are a party to his conspiracy. Like the devil, he misleads us into thinking that our nation, our state, our laws are ineffectual. He plunges us into a world of emptiness. But in truth, this is a mirage, for in our hearts we know he's wrong, that in the end, he is bound to fail in his treacherous mission.

"We will not—indeed we cannot—let such evil make a mockery of our deepest aspirations. We Americans, we who feel the milk of human kindness, will not live in fear. We will find this man and prosecute him to the full extent of the law, and in doing so we will keep the inspiration of William Kieger alive. The assassin has violated the sacred gift of life, and for this, he will be punished. Make no mistake, his judgment day will come—and soon."

Fowler paused and stared out from the podium. The camera panned over to Hana Kieger, who looked no less stolid than Jackie Kennedy. *This is heady stuff,* Patton realized: the wife of a slain president-elect endorsing, by her solemn presence, the woman taking her husband's place. Around the bar, knowing glances were exchanged as this historic fact was assimilated.

"The greatest refutation of this evil force is to continue with William Kieger's legacy. In this respect, the assassin has underestimated us. He has reinforced in our own minds how truly monumental the president-elect's mission was.

"Fellow Americans, we cannot let William Kieger's legacy die. We cannot, in good conscience, allow ourselves to forsake virtue and righteousness at the hands of this assassin, this living icon of failure. No, the dream that the president-elect strove to realize must continue on, in the wells of congress and in the Oval Office. So I am telling you all here and now today that it is my solemn oath to follow through with William Kieger's vision. A vision of prosperity for all Americans, a vision of tolerance and inclusion, a vision without bitter division and partisanship, a vision of reaching across the aisle and building consensus on every major issue confronting this great nation."

There was another pause. Again, Patton noticed Jennifer's dubious expression. *Does she still think it's all an act?*

"In memory of President-elect Kieger, I will be giving a tribute this Saturday afternoon. With the consent of Hana Kieger, Governor Stoddart, and Mayor Richardson, it will be held at the Civic Center Plaza in Denver, Colorado, where William Kieger lost his life. I do this to pay homage to this great man and his family. But I also do this to protest the assassin, who has stripped us of a great leader. This is our moment. All who admired William Kieger, all who want to show the world America's strength in a time of national crisis, can peacefully demonstrate against the atrocity that took place last Sunday."

Now Fowler's voice turned commanding, a war trumpet of a voice. "In conclusion, my fellow Americans, I have a message for the assassin and his accomplices. We now stand as one against you, undaunted by your threats, more resolved than ever to carry on the historic work that William

Ambrose Kieger began. To you I say, WE—SHALL—MARCH—ON!"

With that, Hana Kieger stepped forward to the podium, head and shoulders held in a dignified, resolute pose. When she reached Fowler, she took the president-elect by the hand and they raised their hands together in triumph. There they stood, the two remarkable women, gazing out at the audience with absolute determination, united as one, for several seconds.

It was history in the making.

The on-air audience and the one gathered around Patton and Jennifer at the bar were both cloaked in silence. A stunned, intensely patriotic silence. Then, up on the screen, the media pool gave a light, respectful applause that lasted a full minute. As the sound slowly faded away, President-elect Fowler and Hana Kieger quietly exited the stage, leaving behind an empty lectern smothered in microphones as they entered the sacrosanct realm of America's history books.

Patton knew exactly what it all meant: With Hana Kieger's powerful endorsement, Katherine Fowler—soon to become the first woman president in the nation's history—had just won a mandate never seen before in the history of the grand republic.

THURSDAY

CHAPTER 66

"YOUR CONCERNS ARE UNFOUNDED, GENTLEMEN. Phase Three is proceeding precisely according to plan."

Even as the final word left his mouth, Locke could feel the liar's phlegm seeping into his esophagus. But he had to lie; there was no alternative. Talking on his secure coded phone in his home office, he couldn't allow the four Coalition Executive Committee members patched in on the conference call to think he'd lost control of Fowler. That would be admitting failure—and the Coalition had little tolerance for failure.

"We feel it's a little more complicated than that, Mr. Chairman," countered Skull Eyes, the former CIA man's electronically distorted voice carrying the usual threatening undercurrent that sent shivers down Locke's spine.

"On the contrary, the situation is well in hand. Our very generous contribution has been wired to the appropriate accounts and, in return, I have secured verbal assurances on the platform and cabinet selections. Nothing's changed. Fowler's kinder, gentler image is nothing but an act. She is trying to reassure the American people in a time of crisis and gain some goodwill beyond her base, so she can hit the ground running and have a clear mandate when she takes office."

The phone fell silent as the men scrutinized his explanation. "So let me get this straight," said Colonel Caleb Heston. "This new public image is merely a front? This glorification of Kieger and reaching out to the grieving widow are part of an act?"

"That's why the speech in Denver on Saturday is so important. It allows Fowler to come across as a sympathetic mourner and representative of the people in a time of crisis."

A.W. Windholz, head of United Broadcasting and the American Right-to-Life Foundation, posed the next question. "Can you tell us what specific commitments you've received from the president-elect?"

Locke knew he had to respond quickly or it would appear as though he was hiding something. "There are several. She plans to slash government spending, reduce taxes, and reemphasize our hegemony and exceptionalism in the world so that we're no longer playing second fiddle to the Godless Mandarin. She holds zero-tolerance positions on homosexual parent adoption, flag burning, and public financing of the

NEA. She backs a constitutional amendment banning abortion and embryonic stem-cell research. She wants to expand religious rights in public schools and plans to roll back restrictive gun laws. Most importantly, she's committed to appointing federal justices and filling the vice-presidency and her cabinet with party loyalists who share our views. In short, she sees things our way on every major issue, just as she did during the primary."

"What about the hiring of Dick Potter as a consultant?" the colonel asked.

"I don't approve, but I'm not worried about it."

"You're not concerned that this might undermine the platform?" Windholz pressed him.

"Not particularly. I may disapprove of Dick Potter's cavalier morality, but he's a proven winner."

"He's also a damned liberal," groused Skull Eyes.

"A more apt description would be chameleon. His politics change depending on the candidate and the situation."

For the first time, Senator Dubois chimed in. The only Committee member whose loyalty Locke didn't question, he was already aware of the Fowler situation and could be counted on as a critical ally. "Personally, I don't give a hoot in hell's hollow if our gal's brought Dick Potter on as chief advisor," the senator said, rising subtly to Locke's defense. "We just gave her twenty million big ones. She knows who brung her to the dance."

Locke was relieved to have Dubois in his corner, but he was still worried. He took a moment to methodically wipe his damp brow with his handkerchief. He was not used to being on the wrong side of an interrogation. "Despite Fowler's public posturing, gentlemen, she's agreed to the platform. And we still have Frautschi on the inside."

"*My* sources paint a different picture," Skull Eyes said, his tone filled with cool challenge. "They say you had a heated argument during your conference call late last night."

Sweet Jesus, how did he find out? The Service? Frautschi? "It was a small misunderstanding," Locke said, downplaying the contentious telephone call with Fowler and Frautschi. "I tried to convince the president-elect to commit publically to the platform, but she's insisting on waiting until after she takes office. As I said, she's intent on coming across as a moderate and getting her mandate."

"Did she seem at all suspicious?" the colonel asked.

"No, not at all. She doesn't care how she got her golden opportunity. She's just anxious to take office and implement the platform."

"I doubt our gal knows B from bull's foot about what's really going on," Dubois said, again coming to Locke's aid in an indirect way.

"That may be," Truscott allowed. "But what concerns me is that we may have misjudged her—you in particular, Mr. Chairman."

Locke bristled at the accusation. "If you think you can do a better job," he spat back without circumlocution or apology, "then why don't you handle it."

"Gentlemen, there's no need to argue," A.W. Windholz said. "We are all Christians here, with the country's best interests at heart."

Another brief silence, signaling a momentary truce, then Dubois' logical voice reappeared. "Maybe we need to back off a bit. Our gal's under tremendous pressure right now. We may be aggravating the situation by placing demands on her at this early stage."

"I agree," Windholz was quick to put in. "There'll be plenty of time to get her to sing to our tune when she takes office."

"By then it might be too late," warned the colonel. "We all know how short politicians' memories are once elected. Just look at all the supposed loyalists caving in to public pressure on stem-cell research, gun control, and campaign finance reform."

"The contribution has produced the desired result," Locke said. "We have unlimited access and Fowler has given us the assurances we requested. All she's doing is getting all her ducks lined up for the day she takes office. By pretending to reach out to the center, she's maximizing her ability to control both sides of the aisle three months from now. It's actually a very clever ploy on her part, and one, if you'll remember, we anticipated."

"What we should be trying to do is get someone else we can trust on her transition team," said Dubois. "Someone besides Frautschi."

"I agree. We should have more than one egg in the basket," said the colonel.

Skull Eyes was still skeptical. "Do we know for sure Frautschi's the one behind this...*shift* in Fowler's public image?"

"I think we have to consider the possibility that his priorities might no longer be the same as ours," Dubois said. "He wouldn't be the first chief of staff to have his own agenda."

"Maybe we should have a talk with him," the colonel suggested.

"I have been talking to him," Locke said, a touch defensively. "All week long."

"Maybe someone else should have a talk with him," Truscott said icily.

"Someone else?" Locke asked innocently, though he knew where Skull Eyes was heading.

"Someone with unusual skill in the art of persuasion—like the Apostle."

Locke didn't like this one bit, nor did he appreciate Truscott questioning his judgment. "There's no reason to go to that extreme. In fact, I can guarantee I will veto such a measure should you attempt to put it to a floor vote." He paused to make sure they felt the full weight of his words and to demonstrate his conviction in the matter. "I'm only going to say this one more time: Fowler and Frautschi are on our side. That doesn't mean they aren't working their own agendas to some extent to make themselves look good. But the bottom line is they are in our court and completely on board with the program."

"So what you're saying is the situation's under control," the colonel said.

"Yes, gentlemen, the situation is totally under control."

CHAPTER 67

HANGING UP, Locke felt a wave of relief. He had been convincing, and, if nothing else, had managed to buy himself some time. True, the situation with Fowler was a disaster, but perhaps he could turn it around, especially with Dubois' help. All the same, he still felt deeply uneasy and disappointed. He had devised a bold plan to install the perfect president, but the lead actor of the melodrama was refusing to play the part scripted for her. Rather than the Chosen One, Katherine Fowler was proving to be the reincarnation of the unpredictable, independent-minded William Kieger.

With these troubling thoughts on his mind, Locke trudged outside, grabbed the *Gazette-Telegraph* from the drive, and went into the kitchen.

That was funny, his wife wasn't there. She always made breakfast for the family before he and Benjamin Jr. drove to work and Susan headed off to school. Where could she be?

As if on cue, a semicatatonic Benjamin Jr. materialized, dumbly scanned the empty table, and looked at his father with the same look of incredulity. "Where's breakfast?"

Locke set his paper on the kitchen table. "I'm not sure. I'm going to check on your mother. I hope she's okay."

"Hurry up, I'm hungry."

Locke felt a jolt of anger at his son's rude manner, but at the moment he was more concerned about his wife. He hoped that everything was all right. He walked out of the kitchen and started up the stairs. Halfway up, he heard her and Susan talking in hushed tones down the hallway in Susan's room. Curiosity swiftly overtook him. As quietly as possible, he tiptoed up the last few steps and crept down the hallway, stopping near the entrance to Susan's room. The door was half-open. Listening carefully, he could hear every word now.

"...else I need to tell you. But you can't tell Daddy. You have to promise me."

There was a tense silence, and then Locke heard his wife say, "Your father and I have always agreed we should both be involved in family matters."

The bed squeaked, and he heard the sound of feet padding across the floor. "Not this time, Mother. Whatever I say to you now will have to be kept between us. I want you to swear on this Holy Bible."

"You're scaring me with this talk."

"I'm not going to confide in you if I can't trust you. Now do you swear or not?"

There was a moment's hesitation, and Locke heard his wife say, "If you feel this strongly about it, then yes, I swear on the Bible."

He felt a stab of resentment knowing that his wife and daughter were conspiring to keep things from him. But he was also anxious to hear what Susan was going to say. He leaned closer, tilting his ear toward the half-open door.

"Todd and I spoke to a doctor about having an abortion. We wanted to find out how it works, just in case."

A twitch of shock passed across Locke's face, and he heard his wife give an audible gasp. "My God, Susan. Where...where did you go?"

"The Family Planning Center in Widefield. We've had two visits with Dr. Sivy."

Locke could hardly believe what he was hearing. It was an outrage, a repudiation of everything good, moral, and righteous. It was bad enough that she had engaged in intercourse with Todd and gotten pregnant. But now she had visited one of those murdering clinics where they snuffed out helpless unborn babies. He felt as though a stake had been driven through his heart!

He heard his wife's voice again. "Why didn't you tell me things had gone this far?" she asked Susan. "That you had actually met with a doctor?"

"I was afraid you wouldn't understand, Mother. And that you wouldn't love me anymore."

"How could you think such a thing? I love you—and I will always love you. Always."

The room went quiet again, and Locke heard his wife and daughter embrace. He appreciated the fact that his wife was providing emotional support, but he still found himself incensed that his daughter would do such a thing. Getting pregnant was one thing, but inquiring about an abortion—now that was sacrilege!

"There's something else I didn't tell you, Mother."

There was another pause, charged with emotion. Locke edged closer, desperate to hear what would come next.

"Mother, I know this is going to be hard for you to accept. But after talking with Dr. Sivy and looking into it on my own, I've learned there are a lot of psychological problems for women who have an unplanned child and are forced to give it away. Low self-esteem, severe depression, sometimes they even become suicidal. In some cases, these things affect them their whole lives. That's why so many mothers try to track down the children they've given up later in life, because they can't handle the guilt. I don't want to be torn apart like these other women. That's why I refuse to go to some home for unwed mothers up in the mountains or anywhere else. I'm either going to have the baby and raise it on my own—or have an abortion. But I will not give my—"

"But I thought we agreed you would go to Sacred Heart!"

"I didn't agree to anything. You backed me into a corner and I told you what you wanted to hear. But I'm telling you now that I'm not going to go through with it. I'll get an abortion before I give my baby away to complete strangers and have to live with that the rest of my life."

"You can't mean—"

"Mother, please. This is my decision, not yours. This is my body we're talking about. I know I would hate myself if I went through with an abortion. But I would hate myself a thousand times worse—and second-guess myself for the rest of my life—if I gave my child away to complete strangers."

Locke felt the anger rising inside him like water behind a dam. *I can't believe this. What's happened to her? Where has the daughter I have loved all these years gone?*

"I could never live my life feeling like I'd failed my child. Wondering if she was being taken care of properly. Worrying whether I could have handled it differently. What kind of mother gives her baby away to others? A lousy mother, that's who!"

Locke gritted his teeth at this last assault. His own daughter—a full-fledged casualty of the Culture War. But how? A year ago she had been a good, obedient Christian girl; now she was stubbornly challenging her own parents and discussing abortion as if it were not murder, but a God-given right to choose. *Who has planted these subversive thoughts in her fragile mind?*

"I don't want to hurt you and Daddy. But I have to make my own decision on this."

"But this goes against everything we stand for. Your father and I believe life is sacred, whether a week in the womb or six months. We've always hoped that you felt as strongly about it as we."

"But it's not that simple, Mother. It's not a question of pro-life versus anti-life, it's a question of choice. In my heart, I know if I had an abortion, I'd be going against God's will. But a decision like this has to be weighed against the harm it does to the woman carrying the child too. It's my body, my choice, and the ultimate decision must be with me."

Compounded with the strain of the Fowler situation, this was too much for Locke to bear. The love he felt for his daughter was momentarily pushed aside by these last defiant words. His own flesh and blood was talking about abortion as if it were not a sin, but a simple choice from life's daily menu. And his wife was no better. Though she wasn't condoning abortion, she was doing little to stop Susan from spouting these murderous ideas. She had handled the matter so perfectly the other day—why in the Lord's name was she caving in now? Abortion was murder, pure and simple, and his wife understood this implicitly. Suddenly, he was filled with volcanic rage.

He burst into the room, fists clenched. *I'll show them both what choice is all about!*

Susan screamed.

"No!" Mary shrieked as she scrambled to protect her daughter.

But she was too late.

CHAPTER 68

TWO MINUTES LATER, as Locke puffed his way back downstairs, he felt terrible. He had shoved his wife to the side, taken Susan over his knee like an intractable toddler, and spanked the hell out of her. He was utterly ashamed at what he'd done and realized that he had lost all self-control. The expressions of horror on his wife and daughter's faces when he had stormed into the room and meted out his punishment crushed him inside. They looked at him like he was some sort of a monster when he was merely a father who cared deeply about his family.

He tried to convince himself that he was simply obeying the will of God, that he was the instrument of discipline, not the judge or jury, but he still felt terrible. All the same, abortion was wrong, pure and simple. There was no middle ground when it came to respecting the rights of the unborn. Under no circumstances would he allow his own flesh and blood to murder the innocent. Though he felt badly for savagely spanking Susan, he was confident that the desired effect had been achieved and she would no longer even consider getting an abortion.

He passed his son at the foot of the stairs and, presenting a face flush with mixed anger and guilt, sent him scurrying back into the kitchen. Tromping into his office, he reached for the secure phone on his desk.

To his surprise, it rang just as he was about to press the voice modulator. He jumped back like a frightened rabbit. *Good heavens am I skittish? I wonder who it is?*

He hit the voice modulator. "Hello?"

"I've got some bad news for you." It was voice of a very dangerous man—a voice that he had not heard for over a week.

His heart was still racing from his encounter upstairs, so he took a deep breath to collect himself. "Yes, go on."

"You told me to call if Truscott or the colonel ever went behind your back."

"You're telling me that time has arrived?"

"I'm afraid so, Mr. Chairman."

"What is it? What are they up to?"

"You recall the Family Planning Group in Widefield? They want me to hit it."

Good heavens, the same clinic Susan visited? "What, the doctors?"

"No, everyone in the building. They want me to leave no witnesses. There's eight full-time staff: two doctors, four nurses, an intern receptionist, and a security guard. They sent me the complete dossier and architectural plans yesterday. But that's not all."

Locke held his breath, bracing himself for the worst.

"I think their plan is to blame it on you."

"Blame it on me?"

"Yes, sir. They said that you had approved the sanction up front, but I know that's not true. Is it, Mr. Chairman?"

"No, it's most emphatically not!"

"Just as I thought. It's always been my understanding that you are the only one who can authorize discretionary spending and official termination contracts."

"That is correct."

"Well then, I think they're setting you up, sir. I think they're finally making their move. They're trying to make you look bad so Mr. Truscott can step into your place as chairman of the Executive Committee. That's why I called to warn you."

"How much are they paying you?"

"A lot. It's a spanking new clinic with a state-of-the-art video security system and armed guard, and multiple engineered safe spaces. The staff have undergone extensive safety training on the three-step, run-hide-fight strategy. They know how to get quickly to the safe spaces and stay quiet until the danger has passed. This particular clinic is a fortress, sir, and that's why they're paying me triple my usual fee."

Locke shook his head in dismay. The room seemed to spin around him. With everything that was happening with Fowler, the Coalition, and his family, was it possible that his life was spinning out of control too? Was it possible God was abandoning him in his time of greatest need?

"It was my understanding, Mr. Chairman, that we were no longer hitting abortion and fertility clinics."

"I shut down all such sanctions over four years ago when I took over as chairman." He pondered a moment. "Why the hell are they doing this now?"

"They think you're vulnerable. That's why they're making their move. You're distracted with Fowler and Phase Three—and they know it. They planned it this way. That's why they also paid me an extra twenty thousand not to talk to anyone, not even you or the other Committee members. They said it had all been voted on and approved, but I knew right off they were lying. I told you I would keep an eye out for you, sir."

"Did they tell you why this particular clinic?"

"It's a shock-and-awe campaign all the way. They told me they wanted that clinic shut down once and for all since it's in our own backyard."

Locke thought for a moment. So Skull Eyes and the colonel had finally mustered the courage to attempt their devious little coup. Scarcely did they know they were in for the surprise of their lives.

"What are you going to do, Mr. Chairman?"

"I don't know yet."

"Do you want me to call it off?"

"If we do that, they'll know we've spoken. The last thing we want to do is raise suspicion. When did they say they wanted the clinic hit?"

"Next Tuesday."

"So we have some time then." He considered a moment. "Just stand by until you hear from me. I need some time to look into this."

"Okay, I can do that."

"Don't contact me—I'll be in touch with you. Our two friends may be keeping tabs on us at this very moment. You've already gone out on a limb in telling me and I don't want to put you in further jeopardy."

"I copy, Mr. Chairman. And sir, you know my loyalty is to you."

"I know, Captain. May you walk with the Lord."

"Amen, I always do," replied the Apostle, and he hung up.

CHAPTER 69

PATTON ANSWERED THE PHONE AFTER THE SECOND RING.

"Ken, it's Don Shea. Did you get my email with the DNA results?"

"When did you send it?"

"A half hour ago."

"I haven't had a chance to check my email yet." Patton glanced at his watch. "Hey, wait a second, you're early. You said noon."

"The wheels of a massive bureaucracy grind along slowly, but sometimes we surprise ourselves and actually beat a deadline."

Finally, the break I've been waiting for!

"Once we verified the DNA match with the other lab, the NCIC people put together a little care package to go with our report. The offender's name is Franz Schmidt. Just one prior, for firearms violations."

"Last known address?"

"Somewhere in Oakland. It's all in the file."

"Thanks, Don. If I need anything else, I'll give you a buzz."

"Happy hunting."

"I'm banking on it." He hung up.

With a few clicks of his mouse, he brought up the encrypted email, quickly unscrambled the two attached files into English, saved them to the appropriate folder, and then read them over. The first file summarized the DNA results. The second from the NCIC provided background information on Schmidt. He examined the CODIS material on the lab specimens, QA/QC procedures, and DNA profiles first, before going over Schmidt's records.

Franz Dieter Schmidt was no run-of-the-mill convicted offender. Born in West Berlin in 1984, he emigrated to the U.S. in 1994 when his father, a German research chemist, was hired by Lawrence Livermore National Laboratory in California. He graduated U.C. Santa Barbara in 2006 with academic honors, majoring in oceanography, and was hired by Woods Hole Oceanographic Institute, where he published a number of articles on deep sea current patterns and submarine fans. After three years, he was fired for insubordination during research at sea, and in 2011, he was arrested for statutory rape. The case was settled out of court for $20,000. That same year, he was granted a federal license to purchase and sell firearms. In 2013, he was convicted of firearms violations, including the sale of banned 9mm Israeli-made Uzi semiautomatics, 10-plus capacity magazines, and flash suppressors. He served a year and a half in the joint, minimum security, time off for good behavior. He applied for federal firearms license reinstatement in 2015, but was rejected. His IQ was a superior 134. His last known address was 2150 Webster Avenue, Oakland, California. Phone: (510) 286-1267. There was no known work address.

After looking over Schmidt's social security and motor vehicle records, Patton took a look at the two color mug shots of the guy. He did an immediate double take.

It wasn't John Doe!

Just to be sure, he pulled out the wanted poster and compared it to the mug shots of Schmidt. The differences were striking. Though both subjects had blond hair, Schmidt's forehead was higher, his chin longer, his features more angular. He was also much taller than John Doe. The height-scale backdrop to Schmidt's mug shots showed he was six foot two, while the upper estimate for John Doe based on the video analysis was five nine.

So who is this fucking clown?

He reread the dossier a second time, trying to figure out how Schmidt fit into the case. With the assault weapons' rap, he obviously knew his way around firearms, so it would make sense for him to be the shooter and John Doe simply an accomplice. If that were the case, then John Doe would have probably smuggled Schmidt in through the parking garage when the security cameras were down. But how could he have done that without triggering the alarm? He would have to have had someone else inside, someone from the security company or maintenance outfit. And what if Schmidt wasn't the shooter? Then what was his hair doing at the two crime scenes?

Who the hell is this guy?

Patton was determined to find out. He had Travel book a reservation for him on the next available flight to Oakland. United flight 407 departed DIA at eleven-fifteen, which gave him two hours to make assignments and brief Sharp. It also gave him time to make arrangements with the San Francisco field office, which would need to participate in the arrest.

As he was about to head down to Sharp's office, Lorrie Elert walked into his cube. "You're gonna shoot me, General Patton," she said without preamble.

"What happened?"

"D-base, smee-base. It'll kick some serious booty when it's done, but it's not done, and it's Thursday."

"How far along are you?"

"The programming's done. I just need to configure the spook files."

"How long?"

"Tomorrow morning."

"How many records are we talking about here?"

"At least three hundred."

"Okay, here's what we're going to do. I've got to fly to Oakland today. I'll call you this afternoon and tell you where to email the query printout, case files, and other stuff. How's that sound?"

"Sounds peachy, General," she said, giving a mock salute. "Have a pleasant flight."

"Thanks, Commander Elert. I'll call you from California."

CHAPTER 70

WHEN SHE WALKED OFF, Patton called Wedge and told him to get Schmidt's mug shots to Charlie Fial. The CIA dweeb might be able to identify Schmidt in the security or campaign tapes, as he had John Doe. Finishing the call, Patton headed down to Sharp's office. The door was open. The ASAC looked up from a pile of paperwork with a dyspeptic expression on his face.

Patton quickly told him about the latest lead and that he was leaving on the next flight out.

Sharp blew his nose into a crusty handkerchief. "I'm going with you," he said.

Patton's heart sank. "Why? I can handle it."

"Like you handled Benjamin Locke and Governor Stoddart? Have Travel book me on your flight. And Taylor too. Then make your team assignments and contact San Francisco for support."

Patton nodded reluctantly. It was unusual for an ASAC to go in the field, and he most certainly didn't want Sharp looking over his shoulder, scrutinizing his every decision like an anal-retentive IRS auditor. *But what can I do? I can't tell him not to come.*

Sharp twirled the tapered ends of his cowboy mustache in the way that drove Patton crazy. Then he rose from his seat and went to the window. "Franz Dieter Schmidt," he said with a wolfish smile, "it's time the Effin BI had a little talk with you."

A sense of anticlimax washed over Patton as he returned to his desk. When he had walked into Sharp's office, he had a hot lead and full freedom to pursue it as he saw fit. Now, with his boss clinging to him like a barnacle, he would inevitably be reduced to a subordinate role. That's not how the system was supposed to work. Special agents were supposed to be given substantial latitude in making inquiries in the field and running cases. But now, for reasons that eluded him, standard operating procedures were being discarded.

He wanted to know why. For a brief moment, he allowed himself the fantasy that Sharp was in on the assassination. But what would be his motive? Why would a career FBI agent, a lifer, get mixed up in something like that? What would he stand to gain? And what did that fucking snake

Governor Stoddart have to do with the case?

Unable to come up with any answers, he decided to call Jennifer. They were supposed to get together tonight, but that wasn't going to happen now that he was flying to California. His thoughts turned to last night: to the fragrant smell of her hair, the warmth of her body when they kissed goodnight. He felt more than just a spark between them. Twelve years had come and gone, but it didn't dampen his affection. If anything, he felt a deeper bond to her now because of their son, even though the boy belonged to other parents.

He dialed her at AMP and told her that he was sorry he wouldn't be able to see her tonight because of his unexpected trip to California.

"That's a bummer—I was looking forward to seeing you," she said.

"Yeah, me too," he said. "But the case beckons."

"Sounds like it's really heating up. By the way, have you seen the papers today?"

"Not yet—haven't had time. What's up?"

"With Hana Kieger's endorsement, Fowler's favorability ratings have risen to over eighty-five percent."

"Jesus. What about Osborne?"

"The president's rating has dipped below ten percent. That's the lowest for any president ever. Whoever's behind this thing has ensured that the Democrats are toast for the next generation."

"That's unbelievable. Thank God I don't have to worry about all that. My job is simple: catch the killer."

"When will you return from your trip?"

"Tomorrow afternoon, most likely. I'll call you."

"I'd like that."

Suddenly, he felt a wellspring of emotion, as if he were embarking on a distant voyage and might not see her again. "Jenn, there's something I want to tell you—something important."

The phone went quiet, as if she was holding her breath on the other end.

"I know it sounds crazy after all this time, but I...I still feel the same about you. Am I off base here, or do you feel the same way?"

"Oh Ken," she said after a moment's silence. "Those are the words I most wanted to hear."

He felt a surge of joy and, again, thought back to last night: walking under the vast canopy of stars, holding her close and kissing her, talking about things that had nothing to do with the case. He wondered if he was falling in love with her again or clinging to a romanticized notion of her from college, a long-vanished ideal.

"Will you promise me one thing?" she asked him, pulling him from his thoughts. "When you go after this Schmidt guy, promise me you'll be careful."

"I will," he said. "I definitely will."

CHAPTER 71

HANGING UP THE PHONE, Jennifer realized that she needed to return the DVD tapes she had copied yesterday before they were noticed missing. She had planned to do it early this morning before work, but had forgotten. It would be a little risky during normal working hours, but she would slip in and out so quickly she thought it worth the risk.

She took the disks from her daypack, placed them in an accordion-style folder along with some papers, and walked out her office, heading straight for the elevator. She didn't bump into anyone along the way and didn't see anyone watching her, so she took the elevator straight to the basement. When the doors opened, she checked the hallway.

The coast was clear.

She went to the door to Fileroom E, looking nervously over her shoulder, and punched in the keypad code.

Hearing the click, she turned the handle, slipped inside, and closed the door behind her. Darkness enveloped her. Sliding her hand along the wall, she found the light switch and flipped it on. Squinting against the harsh light, she took off her small daypack and surveyed the orderly fileroom.

She had taken the DVDs from the three file cabinets on the right. She opened them one by one, stuffed the disks into their labeled plastic cases, and closed the cabinets. Then she turned to leave.

But curiosity got the better of her.

She wanted to search the files some more. She had planned to do it later tonight after work, when no one was around, but why not take a look now? As long as she didn't take too long no one upstairs would miss her. The fileroom was seldom used and it was unlikely someone would come down to the basement. Plus she would be able to work quickly now that she knew the file system.

She set down her empty pack and went to work.

Forty minutes later, she decided she had better photocopy what she'd pulled so far. She hadn't managed to track down anything new on Kieger, Dubois, or Fowler, but she did have some interesting correspondence between Colorado Governor Stoddart and AMP, as well as related financial records. Substantial sums of money had been funneled from AMP's publically-anonymous donors to the governor's reelection campaign via what looked like secret Stealth PACs. The governor was obviously going to great lengths to conceal his campaign contribution sources and cover up his ties to the religious right. But how did it relate to Kieger, Dubois, and Fowler? Jennifer felt there had to be a connection somewhere. She decided to come back tonight to go through the records more thoroughly. But for now, she would just copy what she had.

She fired up the photocopier and started making copies.

Two minutes in, she heard a faint click-clack sound coming from outside the door in the hallway.

She hit the *Clear* button and listened intently.

The sound was unmistakable: someone was walking down the hallway toward her. The feet stopped in front of the door.

Then she heard another noise: the code being entered on the keypad.

She was seized with panic. *Shit, what should I do!* The cabinet drawers were open, and a stack of files lay on the table next to the copier. There wasn't enough time to put everything away, and there was no place to hide. Her only chance was to bluff her way out of this, to say she was handling a special task for her supervisor, Archie Roberts.

But what if he's the one at the door? If that's the case, I'm in deep—

There was a click. The door started to inch open.

Jennifer reached for the handle. Somehow she had to take the offensive—and put the intruder on the defensive.

She jerked the door open all the way.

Suddenly, she was face to face with Benjamin Locke!

Summoning her deepest reserves of sangfroid, Jennifer put her hand to her chest and faked a sigh of relief. "Oh, it's only you, Mr. Locke. I was scared there for a moment. I thought it might be a—"

"Jennifer, what are you doing here?" he cut her off.

He towered above her like Goliath and she felt the air leave her lungs all at once, rendering her speechless.

"Please answer the question, Jennifer. What are you doing here?"

"I-I'm putting together a piece for our contributors and the governor. For the…for the fundraiser."

He squinted down at her skeptically. "The fundraiser? What fundraiser?"

"For the soldiers' families at Fort Carson."

He stared at her. His clever mind seemed to be calculating the odds of her telling the truth. She felt her heart sink at her own fumbling. *Get a grip on yourself—you've got to be more convincing than that!* She smiled pleasantly, trying to bluff her way through the situation, but it didn't seem to have any effect. He tried to look over her shoulder, to see inside the room, but she stood implacably in the doorway, blocking his view. It had quickly turned into a battle of wills.

"Mr. Roberts gave me the assignment, Mr. Locke. He said I wasn't supposed to be disturbed. That's why I'm surprised to see you. It's so lonely and quiet down here in the basement—I think you just scared the heck out of me. I hope you're not angry with me."

For an instant, it looked as if Locke might actually buy her explanation. But then his eyes contracted into pinpoints. Benjamin Bradford Locke was not a man easily fooled. "Archie didn't tell me anything about your working in here. And he didn't say anything about a fundraiser either."

Jennifer feigned surprise. "That's odd, he said he had mentioned it to you."

"How did you get access to this room? The only personnel allowed in here are myself, Archie, Marlene, and Dick Valentine."

"And now me. Mr. Roberts gave me the code when I was recently promoted."

"Oh, he did, did he?"

"Yes, sir. Wait a second. Was he not supposed to?"

"No, it just surprises me that Archie would do that—without my authorization."

Jennifer softened her expression, pretending as though it was all a simple misunderstanding. "Mr. Locke, there's no reason to get worked up about this. I've explained what I'm doing here."

"You were here the other day, weren't you?"

Jennifer pretended to be affronted. "What are you talking about? This is the first time I've been in this room. I was only given the code yesterday when my promotion came through."

To her dismay, Locke was not fooled by her feigned innocence. "Marlene said someone was snooping around down here. It was you, wasn't it?"

She was too stunned to answer. *Jesus, it's as though he can read my mind.* She felt her heart suddenly racing uncontrollably in her chest.

His eyes narrowed on her like lasers. "I should have listened to Marlene."

"L-Listened to her? About what?"

"About you. She's never trusted you. She says you don't belong here at American Patriots. Do you belong here, Jennifer? Are you one of *us*?"

Suddenly, Jennifer felt as though she was in *Invasion of the Body Snatchers.* She wasn't one of *them* and *they* were onto her. A palpable fear took hold of her. "I don't know why you're putting me through the third degree, Mr. Locke, when you just promoted me. It isn't fair."

"So you're telling the truth then. This has all been a simple misunderstanding, is that it?"

"Yes, sir. And I'll tell you another thing, I don't appreciate being called a liar. Now please leave me be, I have work to do."

He stood there a moment, thinking things through. With her adamant self-defense, she seemed to have planted a seed of doubt in his mind and at the same time put him on the defensive. "All right, Jennifer, I'm going to give you the benefit of the doubt."

"You don't need to give me the benefit of anything. I am a loyal employee and that's exactly why you just promoted me."

"Well, we'll just see about that, won't we? I'm going to go have a little chat with Archie—but I'll be back," he said softly, so softly that it brought a chill to the nape of her neck.

She tried not to appear intimidated, though she felt as if she was about to faint. "I'll be here, Mr. Locke. I'll be here working."

"I guess we'll see about that too." He scrutinized her closely again— she could swear he saw right through her—before turning on a heel and walking off.

She felt a wave of relief followed quickly by panic. Her bluff would buy her five minutes tops. There was only one alternative now: it was time to make the best of the situation and escape. Her clandestine career as an AMP employee had come to a premature end; she had no choice now but to get the hell out.

The adrenaline surged through her like spring runoff as she closed the door and darted back to the photocopier. With trembling fingers, she flicked off the copier and threw the files back in their proper drawers, not wanting Locke and his lieutenants knowing what she'd copied. Luckily, she had left the drawers open, so the task only took her a couple minutes. It would take Locke at least that long to make it to Archie Roberts' office on the tenth floor.

When finished, Jennifer grabbed her folder, turned off the light, ran down the hallway, and rushed up the stairs. There was no need to stop at her office. She had copies of all of her files at her apartment and she wouldn't be leaving behind anything she couldn't do without.

All the same, she knew she had entered treacherous waters. For the first time in her life, she had been discovered to be a fraud and had no idea what her future would hold.

CHAPTER 72

HER CAR fired up on the first try. She swung the wheel hard left before turning right onto Cascade, the rubber radials screeching as she zoomed in front of the traffic barreling down from the south. Her mind awash with fear and worry, she missed the turn onto Platte, which would have taken her home. Instead she continued north on Cascade, coming quickly upon the picturesque Colorado College campus. Rolling down her window to get some air, she realized, belatedly, that she would have to drive past the school and take a right on Uintah to get back home.

Damn! She pulled out her cellphone and dialed Reid Lampert in San Francisco.

"Mr. Lampert speaking."

"It's Jennifer Odden. I've been found out."

"Found out? What do you mean found out?"

"In Fileroom E. Locke came upon me when I was copying files."

"Did he actually catch you in the act?"

"No, I blocked the door. But he knows I was up to something."

"Where are you now?"

"On my way home. I can't go back to American Patriots now."

"Did you manage to copy any more records?"

"Some fundraising documents on Governor Stoddart. He's an AMP puppet. They've been funneling money to him for years via secret Stealth PACs with misleading names like Coloradans for Tax Relief and the Western Slope Agrarian Society. It's all a front."

"Did you return the DVDs?"

"Yeah, and I put all the files back in their proper drawers so Locke won't know what I copied."

"Have you read through the other files, the ones from your first visit to the fileroom?"

"Most of them."

There was a silence and Jennifer had a feeling of impending trouble. She wasn't sure where this was heading.

"I want you to listen very carefully to me, Ms. Odden. I'm going to send someone out there to go through those records with you. I've read over what you sent me and this thing is even bigger than I thought. You're going to need some help on this."

Jennifer was stunned, but quickly regrouped for a counteroffensive. "That won't be necessary. I'll take care—"

"I'm going to send J.R. Welch. We've got to have our top political writer on this."

"No way! This is my story!"

"Come now, Ms. Odden, don't you want to be a team player? You'll still be the second author. It's just that J.R. brings twenty years of experience to the table."

"I know how J.R. Welch operates. He lets everyone else do all the legwork then throws in a few lines of flowery prose and takes all the credit. No way I'm working with J.R. or anyone else on this."

"But you're not even with the magazine—you're a freelancer. We've got to have one of our regular journalists on this. It's too damned big and we have the magazine's reputation to think about."

Jennifer was so enraged she wanted to scream. Who did this jerk think he was trying to steal her story and hand it to someone else?

"J.R. Welch has won a Pulitzer. He can help you whip this material into shape in no time. And time is of the essence."

"I have a written contract for this piece."

"You have a contract to do a series on Benjamin Locke and American Patriots. It says nothing about digging into the political lives of Kieger, Dubois, or Fowler. Face it, this thing has turned into something much bigger than what was in your original scope of work. I have the contract right here in front of me. Do you want me to read it to you?"

"I'm finishing this story on my own, and when it goes to print, there's going to be one name on it and that's mine."

The phone went silent, and for a fleeting moment, she felt triumph. But then she pictured him scheming on the other end, trying to come up with yet another way to outmaneuver her, and she felt a tremor of fear.

"There's a legal component to this too," he said at length. "You may not have signed a nondisclosure or confidentiality agreement, but removing those DVDs from the building could classify as stealing. The paper could be held liable. However, if you send us all your materials anonymously and we use you as a confidential source, those legal issues would go away."

Stunned at his audacity, she said nothing.

"You have to face it—this is simply too big for you. I can have a Pulitzer Prize winner on the next flight out there. Having J.R. Welch on board will give the magazine unprecedented name recognition. And you would have been the team player that made it all happen. You are a team player, aren't you, Ms. Odden?"

"How can you even be saying this? This is my story. I've done all the work and taken all the risks. Do you have any idea what it's like to be a spy for ten months just for a damned story?"

"A story that is the rightful property of Mr. Stavros and *The New Constitution*. You don't want to cross Mr. Stavros, do you? If you do, you'll be lucky to be writing obituaries in the *Tuscaloosa Quarterly*."

"I've earned the right to see this thing through to the end."

Again, the phone went silent; the line was thick with tension.

"Okay, I'll give you one last shot at your fifteen minutes of fame," Lampert relented. "But I'm getting in touch with Legal. We'll see what they think about these disks you pilfered. And since you're getting all self-righteous on me, I'm giving you a new deadline. You have until noon tomorrow to get me your first draft. Otherwise, I send in Mr. Welch."

"That's fine by me—Friday at noon it is," and she punched off.

CHAPTER 73

SOMETHING FLASHED in front of her windshield.

She slammed on the breaks and screeched to a halt, missing two college kids crossing the pedestrian crosswalk by a fraction of an inch.

Through the open window, Jennifer heard one of them yell, "What are you doing, lady! Keep your damned eyes on the road!"

"I'm sorry," she apologized, feeling her heart pounding in her chest.

They scowled at her long and hard before finishing crossing the street. Feeling emboldened, the other three coeds waiting at the crosswalk began to cross the street, keeping a wary eye on her. Jennifer watched them walk past in guilty silence, scolding herself for her lapse of concentration.

She couldn't believe she had almost plowed over two innocent people!

Finally, all the students made it safely across the crosswalk. Expelling a sigh of relief, Jennifer checked to make sure no one else wanted to cross and moved her foot cautiously to the gas pedal.

There was a blur of movement to her right and suddenly someone was banging on the passenger window. Nearly jumping from her seat, she quickly realized it was Susan Locke.

What's she doing here! Shouldn't she be at school?

Jennifer hit the button to lower the passenger side window.

Susan thrust her head in the car. "Please, Jennifer, I have to talk to you!"

A car horn blared. Jennifer looked in her rear view mirror and saw she was backing up traffic. Looking back at Susan, she pointed to a parking lot a short distance up the road.

"I'll meet you over there!"

Susan gave a nod and darted back to her mountain bike lying on the grass next to the road. Jennifer pulled forward slowly through the crosswalk, drove the fifty yards to the freshly painted blacktop lot, and cut the engine. As she got out of the car, Susan pedaled up on her bike.

"What's going on, Susan? Are you okay?"

The girl jumped off her bike and set it down on the grass. Her voice was desperate. "I was on my way to see you at the office. My father's gone crazy. I was talking to my mother about my pregnancy before school this morning. He must have overheard us because all of a sudden—"

"Where did this happen?"

"In my bedroom. He must have been listening outside in the hallway. I was telling my mother that I didn't want to give my baby away, that I would rather have an abortion. He busted in and started hitting me."

"Your father hit you?"

"Actually, he spanked me. But it was brutal and really hurt. He was so angry. My mother tried to hold him back, but he knocked her down. We screamed for him to stop. But he wouldn't...he wouldn't stop!"

Jennifer reached out and took her in her arms. There was nothing she could say that wouldn't be better expressed with a reassuring hug. But thank God it was just a spanking. At the same time, did she dare tell the girl about her own terrifying experience with Susan's father at American Patriots ten minutes ago? She decided that this wasn't the time.

Within a minute she had calmed Susan down. But now the girl's voice took on an edge of defiance. "I've made up my mind, Jennifer. I'm going to have the abortion. It's still scheduled for tomorrow morning with Dr. Sivy. I never canceled it."

"An abortion? But, Susan, are you sure you—?"

"It's the only choice I have that makes sense. I'm not going to give my baby away, and my father won't allow me to keep it. That leaves me with one option."

"But your father will crucify you."

"He's already crucifying me. This way I'm in charge of my own body and peace of mind. I'm almost eighteen, old enough to vote and die for my country. It's time for me to take responsibility for my own actions. I've made my decision."

Jennifer's gaze fell to the ground. What could she possibly say? Though she admired Susan's tenacity and fortitude in standing up to her father, she felt that, to some extent, she was acting rashly. Was Susan using the abortion to lash back at her father? Jennifer's mind spun back to the dark period with her own father. It came back to her as a Gothic horror story and she felt all the old, bitter feelings, the sense of desolation, resurfacing.

Susan gave a heavy sigh. "I'm sorry to involve you in all this. But I didn't know who else to turn to."

"You did the right thing." They went over the incident and its ramifications some more. At the end, Jennifer asked, "Are you sure you want to go through with this? I mean, we're talking about abortion, Susan."

"I've made up my mind," the girl said firmly. "I have to do this my way."

"You're sure?"

"One hundred percent."

"Well then, you'd better call your mother and tell her you're all right. Then you and I, we have to put together a plan."

CHAPTER 74

"HOW COULD YOU HAVE LET THIS HAPPEN?" Benjamin Locke bristled, glaring at Marlene "Suie" Tanner and Archibald Roberts. Locke had just finished recounting his run-in with Jennifer Odden in Fileroom E.

Roberts shot Marlene an accusing look. "She didn't get the code from me."

"Well, she said she was working for you on the project," Marlene countered, pointing a stubby finger at him.

"She was, but I never gave her the code."

"It must have been Chuck then. It's his fault."

"Shut up, both of you." Locke stood up and went to the window behind his desk. "I've heard enough excuses. We need to rectify this situation pronto, not quibble over whose responsible. Obviously Jennifer Odden, if that is in fact her real name, is working for some political or media group. We must find out who that group is and seize the documents before she makes contact."

Marlene and Roberts stood obediently still in front of the desk. Not a sound escaped their lips; not a single muscle twitched. The stumpy executive secretary provided an almost comical contrast to the tall, cadaverously thin director of communications/PR. Standing side by side, they looked like circus freaks or something out of a house of mirrors.

"Do we know what she was after?" asked Roberts.

"Marlene and I went back into the fileroom, but by that time Jennifer was gone," said Locke. "But she must have cleaned up after I left the first time because the documents I saw next to the copier were all put back."

"But who could she be working for?" inquired Roberts.

"That's your job to find out, Archie—she worked in your department. It's probably one of those liberal organizations like People for the American Way. They're always making mischief. She could even be a journalist, undercover reporter, something like that. In any case, you must get to work on this immediately. This assignment is to receive top priority."

"What should I do?" Marlene asked.

"Go back down to Fileroom E and conduct a more thorough search to find out what she was after. Figure out which files she may have pulled."

"I'm still not clear what I'm supposed to do," Roberts said, timorously.

Locke took a deep breath to keep from exploding. *What are you, a complete imbecile?* "I just told you, Archie. I want you to find out who this Jennifer Odden really is and who she's working for. Benjamin will assist you, but no one else."

"Benjamin, sir? You mean your...your son?"

"He'll do a bang-up job for you—a bang-up job."

"I'm sure he will," Roberts said, though his expression revealed serious doubt.

"Then get to it," Locke commanded, and the two subordinates fumbled towards the door.

"Oh, there's one more thing," he added, as Marlene "Suie" Tanner's porky hand gripped the doorknob.

The pair of lackeys turned around in unison and looked at him sheepishly.

"Make sure to complete your assignments discretely—and to my total satisfaction—or that will be the end of your employment here at American Patriots."

CHAPTER 75

AFTER TOUCHING DOWN at Oakland International Airport, Patton, Sharp, and Taylor walked to the passenger pickup outside the baggage claim, where a midnight blue Dodge Grand Caravan was waiting for them. Standing in front of the van was a crisply dressed man and woman, both in their midthirties. The man extended a stiff hand to Sharp.

"Special Agent Smith, San Francisco field office. And this is Agent Donatello."

"What's the situation?"

"Schmidt's still at his apartment. We have a team in position."

Sharp smiled harshly. "Well, what are we waiting for? Let's go get the son of a bitch."

They climbed in the van and were off, heading north on Hegenberger Road with the windows rolled down. The sky was gray and overcast, the air leaden with moisture. Though they were right on the bay, the air smelled of exhaust, petroleum products, and chlorinated industrial pollutants instead of the sea.

They went over the plan.

It was actually more of a standard operating procedure. In the FBI lexicon, it was officially a "raid." The objective was to take Schmidt by surprise with overwhelming numbers and arrest him without loss of life. It was a technique that usually worked for the heavily scrutinized—and often beleaguered—agency, but not always. And there was the rub: Franz Dieter Schmidt had to be taken alive. Whether he was the shooter, an accessory, or merely a material witness in the case, it was absolutely essential that he be interrogated.

They struck the Nimitz Freeway, 880, and headed northwest through the urban sprawl. To the west, the mercury-colored water of San Francisco Bay was as smooth as glass beneath the haze. Patton stared out at a steely cargo ship. Across the salty water body was the son he had never seen, a boy who called other people Mommy and Daddy. It made him ache to think about it.

A few minutes later, they exited the freeway and slogged down Webster Street, past Chinese restaurants and shoddy hotels. Donatello spoke into her crackling Saber hand-held radio, preparing the strike force for their arrival. A light drizzle began to fall. Eventually the van pulled into an underground parking structure and took a space next to a Crown Victoria and three other vans.

Supervising Agent Morrison J. Shafroth and another senior agent emerged from the Crown Victoria and, after a ten minute briefing and review of building blueprints, the strike force was ready to move. Four plainclothed agents had already infiltrated the building, and the three vans bore another thirty field agents. They were dressed in standard raid gear: navy-blue jackets and caps with FBI printed in bold gold lettering; Kevlar bullet-proof vests; and black belts with magazine pouches and two-way radios. In addition, they were armed to the teeth with standard FBI-issue 9mm Glock 17 pistols and Remington 870 shotguns. As was so often the case, they would have the element of surprise, and the sheer weight of numbers, on their side.

Patton wondered what advantages Franz Dieter Schmidt would have, if any.

On radio command, the five vehicles crept out of the parking structure into the drumming rain. The caravan came to a crisp halt a block up the street in front of a drab stucco apartment building. A second command was given and the van doors slid open simultaneously. One by one, bodies spilled out, and within seconds, they had coalesced into a cohesive tactical force, moving stealthily toward the front entrance, like Washington sneaking up on the unsuspecting Hessians at Trenton. The whole affair was handled with quiet competence; no shouting voices, screeching tires, or shrieking sirens like in the movies. Patton, Sharp, and Taylor followed behind Shafroth and the lead element.

Two minutes later, the raid team had sealed off all the exits and assembled in front of Schmidt's apartment, 201. Clutching his Glock, Patton felt a ripple of nervous energy. *This is it.* In a matter of seconds, he would have his man in custody. There was no way Schmidt was going to get away. Not a single escape route remained unless, of course, the fucking asshole could fly.

Shafroth gave a hand signal and knocked hard on the door.

"FBI—we have a search warrant—open up!"

It was merely a formality, for less than three seconds passed before Shafroth commanded two brawny agents forward with a shoulder-rigged battery ram. They bashed through the door, ripping off both chain and lock, and the raid team poured into the room like a pack of ravenous velociraptors.

"FBI, don't move!" Patton heard Shafroth shout up ahead, over the thunder of feet.

"What the hell?" a surprised voice cried out.

"Put your hands above your head and get down on the floor!"

Now Patton could see Schmidt standing open-mouthed in the living room next to a threadbare couch. He was unarmed and had no choice but to comply. He dropped to his knees and his hands flew up in surrender as ten Glocks trained on him. The penetration had been swift, the surprise total.

But there was still a trace of defiance on his face. "What the fuck is going on?"

Four grim-faced agents knocked Schmidt facedown onto the hard floor and jerked his hands behind his back. A second later, cuffs were slapped on him and he was searched. In a tone of measured government neutrality, Shafroth informed Schmidt that he was being taken into custody in connection with the Kieger assassination and read him his Miranda. Meanwhile, agents began searching the other rooms for evidence.

Patton took a moment to study Schmidt as he was pulled to his feet. The big German was fit, chiseled, roguishly handsome, and flaxen-haired. Most importantly, at six feet two inches tall, he was definitely the right height to be the killer of the two people at the elevator.

As Patton examined his face for clues, Sharp circled the prisoner, eyeing him as if he had just captured the great Desert Fox, Erwin Rommel, himself. "Franz Dieter Schmidt," he declared gloatingly. "It's time we had a little chat."

CHAPTER 76

THE INTERROGATION was held on the thirteenth floor of the Federal Building at 450 Golden Gate Avenue in San Francisco. Along with Patton, the key players from the arrest were there, jackets off, shirtsleeves rolled up. Patton sat directly across from Schmidt, eyeing him closely. The guy had been booked, photographed, and fingerprinted without uttering a single word.

Patton wondered why.

The recorder on the highly polished conference table was turned on and, for the second time, Shafroth read the subject his Miranda warning. The Bureau was notorious for doing things by the book when it so desired, and from the moment the warrant was obtained from the federal judge to the current interrogation, there hadn't been a single procedural oversight. When Shafroth finished the Miranda, he asked the suspect if he understood everything said to him.

"Yes," Schmidt replied.

"So you understand you've been arrested in connection with the assassination of President-elect Kieger?"

"Yes, and I am completely innocent. That is why I do not need a lawyer." His Berlin accent was softened by more than two decades of American living.

"So you're waiving your right to have an attorney present during questioning?"

"That's right. I also understand that I do not have to answer any questions if I don't want to. And that whatever statements I make may be used in evidence against me in a court of law."

"You seem to know your rights, Franz," Patton said. Using the first-name was a calculated move, as was the complimentary tone. He hoped both would pay dividends later in the interrogation.

The team was also allowing Schmidt to smoke, which though unusual, was also part of Patton's calculated plan to get him to open up and talk. The big German pulled a Camel from the half-empty pack on the table; Shafroth lit it for him with a silver Zippo lighter.

"I did some time once," said Schmidt. "You learn a lot about the law inside."

"Especially on how to break them," said Sharp, who wasn't too keen on the kid-gloves approach that Patton, Taylor, and Shafroth had recommended. His eyes lingered on Schmidt before landing on Special Agent Shafroth. "Let's get on with this," he said impatiently.

Shafroth gave the time, day, month, year, and names and titles of those present. Then he had Schmidt state his full name and give a brief synopsis of his background and occupation, which at present was video store clerk. Patton could see the fall from grace in every line of the guy's face. On the rap sheet, it showed that Schmidt had gone from college whiz kid to oceanographer to gun runner to convicted felon to video store clerk, and now to suspected assassin. What was next, mass murderer?

When Shafroth completed the formalities, Patton said, "All right, Franz, I'm going to give it to you straight. Last Sunday, we found specimens of your hair in the Union Plaza Building in Denver. We know they belong to you because we ran them for DNA and cross-referenced the results against your profile on our Convicted Offender Index. The hair was found at two different locations in the building: the room where President-elect Kieger was shot from and the route the shooter used to escape. When we put it all together, Franz, the picture's clear: either you pulled the trigger, or you have a connection to the guy who did. What we want to know is which is it? We'll figure it out one way or another, but we're hoping you'll clear it up for us right now."

He paused, hoping Schmidt would feel compelled to volunteer something rather than sit there in silence, but he said nothing. Patton continued to study him for the usual signs of lying and unusual tension: contracted pupils, arms clasped around the chest, uneasy hand movements, facial blushing, stiffened shoulders. So far, he hadn't seen anything suspicious.

"Okay, Franz, why don't you start out by telling us where you were this past Sunday?"

"I wasn't even in Denver. I was on a wine-tasting excursion up north."

Sharp squinted skeptically. "A wine tasting excursion? You expect us to believe that?"

Patton watched Schmidt's reaction closely. There was a subtle twitch to his eye, but that was all.

"We're not here to make your life miserable," said Taylor, who, like Patton, was playing the good cop role to Sharp's bad. "We just want the truth."

"Look, I did my time," Schmidt said, looking at Patton. "I made some mistakes, sold some weapons. But that was a long time ago. These days I'm clean. What I'm telling you is the truth."

"Personally, I'd like to believe you, Franz," Patton said. "But you're going to have to tell us *exactly* where you were, what you did, and who you saw."

Schmidt nodded and took a pull from his cigarette. "Sunday was my day off," he said, thinking back, smoke draining from his nose in a bluish wisp. "I work six nights a week at Sal's Videos. On Sunday, I went up to the wine country. Napa and Sonoma Valley."

His swift and candid delivery suggested he was telling the truth, but Patton had observed many clever liars in his day that appeared credible under interrogation. "Did you go by yourself?"

"Yes."

"Can anyone verify your whereabouts?"

"At least one person. John Avery, the owner of Caruso Vineyards in Napa. He'll remember."

"Anyone else?"

Schmidt considered a moment. "I went to three other wineries—St. Francis, Rombauer, and Truchard. I don't know anyone at these places personally, but someone should remember."

"How long were you gone?" Taylor asked.

"I'd say from about eleven to six."

"And this John Avery," inquired Sharp skeptically, "he wouldn't be a friend of yours?"

Schmidt saw at once that he was being played. "I'd say he's more of an acquaintance."

The ASAC looked at him harshly. "As far as I'm concerned, you could have Mother Teresa vouch for you and it wouldn't change a damned thing. We have your hair at the two crime scenes, which means we've got you there too. It makes no difference what anyone says. You were there, pal."

Now Schmidt looked flustered. "I was not there! My hair must have been planted!"

"Oh, so now it's a conspiracy." Sharp gave a disdainful roll of his eyes.

Patton pulled out the wanted poster of John Doe. He leaned across the table and pushed it toward Schmidt. "Have you ever seen this person before?"

The prisoner squinted as he studied the two pictures, one a grainy freeze-frame video print, the other a police artist's sketch. For a moment, there seemed to be a glimmer of recognition, but it was gone in a flash. "No," he said, shaking his head and handing the poster back to Patton.

"I think you're lying," Sharp said. "You know this guy and you were with him in Denver."

Schmidt's look narrowed defiantly. "That's not true."

"Okay, then you sold him firearms. That's how you know him."

"No."

Sharp's hand crashed down onto the table. "I've had about enough of this crap. You'd better start telling us the truth and you'd better start right fucking now!"

There was a strained silence. Patton didn't like Sharp's combative style, though it was sometimes advantageous to have at least one pit bull during an interrogation to shake things up. He preferred to slowly build up a rapport with suspects while at the same time garnering useful information. Under the right circumstances, it wasn't unusual for even hardened criminals to come clean. And in this case, Patton had the feeling Schmidt was more valuable for what he knew than what he'd done. In spite of the physical evidence, he seemed to be telling the truth, though Patton was convinced he had some personal connection to the assassin.

The silence was broken by Patton's ringing cell phone. He quickly checked the caller ID and signaled the others to continue without him.

CHAPTER 77

"WHAT'VE YOU GOT FOR ME, WEDGE?"

"Good news. We've tracked down the source of Ares."

"Holy shit, that is good news. Hold on." Patton snatched up his iPad from the conference table and went to the corner of the room so he wouldn't disrupt the interrogation. "Okay, give it to me."

"The computer forensic lab has traced the source terminal to a guy named Pep Boy. That's his cyber alias. Believed to belong to one Anders Houser, a former Microsoft programmer. According to what we've got, he lives at Graystoke Apartments, 1651 Clayton Street in Berkeley. Apartment 308."

Patton had him go through it again so he could type it all down. "Any criminal history?"

"Negatory."

"Do we have a photo?"

"Yep. I've just emailed it to you out there—it's with the DT desk head. Along with the little background we've got on him, mostly on his programming. Apparently this guy's a freelancer. A little work for the Green Freedom folks, a little for ELF and ALF. We managed to track down someone who used to work with him at Microsoft. He was a top programmer there, but he got fed up and dropped out. The only trail this guy's left behind is the one he's left in code."

Patton felt as if he had just turned a corner on the case, and gave a little smile. "You're the man, Wedge. I owe you a six pack."

"Make it Guinness."

"Fuck that—I don't do imports. You get Fat Tire or you don't get anything."

"I can deal with that, boss. I'll call you if I get anything else."

"That'll work. Over and out, Wedge."

When Patton punched off, Sharp was looking at him curiously. Patton pulled him aside and quietly told him the news.

"Well, what are you waiting for? Take Agent Taylor and go get the son of a bitch!"

"What about the interrogation?"

"I'll take care of it."

Patton didn't like that idea because if Sharp was too combative,

Schmidt might feel threatened and request a lawyer. If that happened, they would get nothing more out of him until he was subpoenaed before a federal grand jury, which could take days, even weeks. Patton felt he was beginning to understand Schmidt, and that through a sympathetic approach, he might be able to extract the information he sought. At the same time, tracking down the author of Ares was a huge lead that needed to be followed up. He would just have to trust Sharp not to fuck up.

"All right, Henry, good luck to you then," he said. Then to Agent Shafroth: "It looks like I'm going to need your team again. How does a trip to Berkeley to pick up a guy named Pep Boy sound?"

CHAPTER 78

THE LONG, NARROW HALLWAY was poorly lit and smelled of cigarettes, cheap disinfectant, and something Patton couldn't put a finger on. He withdrew his Glock; the first round was already chambered. The raid team was still assembling on the far end of the corridor, in front of Apartment 308 where the illumination was weakest. The overhead light covering this section of the hallway was out. As Shafroth moved forward to give the order, a woman stepped out of a nearby apartment carrying a bundle of dirty laundry. An agent quietly whisked her away.

Once the team was in position, the agent closest to the door motioned vigorously to Shafroth. *What's he found?* Patton wondered. Shafroth stepped forward; Patton and Taylor followed to see what was happening.

"Someone's broken in," the agent whispered. He shined a small pen light on the door. Patton saw at once that the wood was splintered around the battered doorknob. Because the hallway was so dark, apparently no resident had noticed the damage and called it in.

Patton pushed the door halfway open with the barrel of his pistol. The doorknob, jury-rigged to appear intact, fell to the floor with a thud.

He entered the room slowly and cautiously, trailed by Shafroth and Taylor. It was dark inside, but he quickly spotted the body sprawled on the floor, open eyes gazing upward blankly. Now he smelled the unmistakable odor of death and decay, but the odor wasn't overpowering.

Putting away his piece, he said, "Agent Shafroth, would you be good enough to call an ERT and assign a group to control the crime scene. No one gets in or out but you, me, and Agent Taylor."

"You got it." Shafroth turned around and addressed his team. Several agents had already crowded forward to take a look, but Shafroth prodded them back like an Irish drill sergeant. "All right, all right, this isn't a goddamned peep show. I want everyone out on the double. You, Jackson, get me an ERT. Ganier, track down the property manager of this shithole. Rourke, get a team together and start interviewing the tenants..."

Patton stepped over a pair of nylon duffel bags, navigated his way around the body, and pulled back the cheap Venetian blind. The window was open. With the cool late-fall weather and open window, no wonder the smell wasn't so bad. Patton pulled open the blind, allowing diffused yellow light to trickle into the room. He and Taylor took a moment to allow their eyes to adjust before bending over the corpse for a closer look. The cause of death was unmistakable: multiple gunshot wounds to the face. The senior Secret Service agent removed the wallet from the guy's pants. They were about to check the picture on the driver's license against the photograph from Weiss when Shafroth walked back in.

"Is it Houser?" he asked.

"Looks like it," replied Patton, comparing the pictures. There were three entrance wounds—one through the eye, another between the eyes, and a third through the center of the forehead—but the face was intact enough for a visual ID. The entrance wounds showed perfect clustering and there were no powder burns, so the bullets were fired quickly and with exceptional accuracy from beyond two feet.

"Hell, he's just a kid," Shafroth said.

"Twenty-five. Too young to die, that's for sure."

"Looks like heavy caliber," Taylor said, pointing to the spatter marks on the desk and computer screen behind the victim.

Forty-five? Patton wondered before fixing his eyes on the bloody screen. "Our friends at the forensic lab will need to go through that hard drive," he said to Shafroth. "No problem with me bringing it back to Colorado, is there?"

"Fine by me."

"Good. We'll have you guys handle all the evidence except the computer."

"We'll take care of it. Say, you see any brass? I don't see any."

"You won't find any here," Taylor said. "Our killer's a house cleaner. Professional hit with a semiauto then he tidies up afterwards. Not just the casings, but the rigged doorknob."

Shafroth gave a nod and went back out to speak to his team. Patton and Taylor took a minute to chart out a rough trajectory path of the shots.

"I think the killer busted in and took our friend Pep Boy completely by surprise," said the veteran Secret Service agent. "Maybe his associates in the Brigade thought he'd give them up. Or the kill order could have come from someone outside the cell, someone who found out about the Brigade's involvement in the assassination and wasn't too pleased."

"There's also a third possibility," Patton said.

Taylor squinted at him. "Yeah, what's that?"

"Both Pep Boy and the Brigade have been set up."

CHAPTER 79

AN HOUR LATER, they drove back to the field office with Shafroth, leaving an army of agents behind to canvas witnesses. The Bay Bridge wasn't too congested since most of the traffic was heading east toward Oakland. By the time they crossed the bridge, a light rain began to fall again and Patton received more news from Weiss. Everyone identified in the Union Plaza videotapes had been accounted for except John Doe, which made it highly unlikely Schmidt had been in the building the day of the assassination. Weiss had also tracked down more background information on Schmidt. After his release from prison, he had dutifully performed his job as a clerk at Sal's Videos, had met the conditions of his parole, and hadn't received so much as a traffic ticket. The guy was clean as a whistle, unusual for a convicted felon.

Taken together, these facts reinforced the view crystallizing in Patton's mind that Schmidt was nothing more than an unwitting pawn in this high-stakes game. The same with Anders Houser and the Brigade. But that still didn't get him any closer to catching the bad guys. What he needed was some real evidence that tied one or more persons directly to the assassination. And he had to resist the temptation to get caught up in Jennifer's conspiracy theories involving Locke, Kieger, Fowler, Dubois, and Governor Stoddart. His foremost priority was to track down the goddamned shooter. That was his best chance to solve the case and apprehend the responsible parties.

When they reached the field office, they rode the elevator to the thirteenth floor and headed toward the interrogation room where they had left Schmidt and Sharp. As they rounded the corner, a field agent nearly bumped into them.

Shafroth's eyes bulged with surprise. "What's happening, Dave?"

"His boss"—he nodded towards Patton—"is about to strangle Schmidt."

"Are they still in the interrogation room?"

"Yeah. He hasn't done him bodily harm yet, but I think he's about to blow a gasket. And now Schmidt's demanding a lawyer."

"Let me handle this," Patton said, and he was off and running.

Reaching the glass observation window of the interrogation room, Patton saw Sharp standing behind the seated Schmidt, yelling in his ear.

Patton had considered the possibility Sharp would be overbearing during the interrogation, but hadn't dreamed he would have a complete meltdown. Subtle mind games and clever trickery were fair game during an interrogation, but it was crossing the line to employ physical abuse or cruel verbal harassment. The Hooverian mantra drilled into every raw recruit at Quantico was DON'T EMBARRASS THE BUREAU. Unfortunately, that's exactly what Sharp appeared to be doing.

Why is Henry doing this? Is Washington pressing him too hard? Or is there another reason?

Patton made eye contact with the two befuddled agents manning the door to the interrogation room. "Stand by, you two. If my boss won't come peaceably, we may have to drag his ass out of there." He stepped past them, opened the door, and slammed it shut behind him.

Sharp wheeled around and shot him a glare.

"What's going on, Henry?" Patton asked innocently, giving a look that was more puzzled than judgmental. He was hoping to quickly diffuse the situation without having to involve Shafroth or Taylor, if possible.

"Get out of here, Special Agent. He's mine and I'll interrogate him as I see fit."

"Why don't you let me take it from here? You look like you could use a breather."

"No fucking way. He's lying and I'm not leaving 'til I get the truth."

"I want a lawyer," Schmidt said, looking frazzled.

"We'll get you one, Franz," Patton said. To Sharp: "I know you're upset, Henry, but you've got to stand down. This won't look good on our 302s. Besides, I have new information. I think it'll help clear things up, but I'm going to have to talk to Franz alone for a few minutes."

To Patton's surprise and relief, Sharp took the bait. "What? What new information?"

Patton glanced at the tape recorder on the table; thank God it was off. "I'll tell you about it after you give me ten minutes alone with Franz here. That's all I'm asking for: ten minutes."

For a several seconds, Sharp stood there implacably, his lips set in a stubborn line, squinting like Wyatt Earp. Then the hard edge to his face seemed to soften, as if he had reached the conclusion it might be in his best interest to back down on this one.

"All right, Special Agent, you've got ten fucking minutes. You'd better make the most of it."

CHAPTER 80

WHEN THE DOOR CLOSED, Patton took a seat next to Schmidt. He reached across the table for the pack of Camels, grabbed two smokes, lit them up, and handed one to Schmidt. "I believe you're innocent, Franz," he said after taking a drag. "But you're going to have to help me."

Schmidt still looked distrustful. "I want a lawyer."

"I know you do, but first we have to talk. It has to do with why you're innocent."

"And suppose I say no."

Patton took another deep pull and blew perfect smoke rings. "Jesus, I haven't lit up since ninth grade. It's a good thing I quit smoking then 'cause this tastes pretty fucking good right now."

Schmidt gave a weary smile and their eyes met. *You're not evil, Franz. You're just another lost soul who's drifted astray. Like three-quarters of the people in this crazy world. I'm lost too. Sometimes I don't know what the hell I'm doing or why I'm even fucking here.*

When their eyes moved off one another, Schmidt seemed more trusting. "All right," he said, "I'll talk to you if you promise to keep that gorilla away from me."

Patton blew another perfect smoke ring. "The big boss man gives me the willies too. We got ourselves a deal."

Schmidt gave a little nod. "I wanted to cooperate from the beginning, but I just don't know how this could have happened. I have never even been to Colorado though I hear it is beautiful."

"You'd be right about that." Patton took another drag. "Look, Franz, I'm going to be honest with you. I think your hair was planted. For one, we haven't identified you in any of the building security tapes. For another, I've been checking up on what you've been doing the last couple of years."

A flicker of hope crossed the accused man's face. "And?"

"Looks like you've been keeping your hand out of the cookie jar, your nose to the grindstone."

"Any other clichés."

"Not at the moment. Now for the bad news. Our DNA experts in Washington tell me the odds are one in a gazillion that the hair found at the two separate crime scenes doesn't belong to you. So one of two things had to have happened. Either you were in the Union Plaza Building in Denver last Sunday and you're lying to us. Or—and this is what I think—your hair was collected at another location, preserved, and later transported to the crime scenes. Either way, you've got some serious explaining to do."

Schmidt sucked hard on his cigarette, his cheeks turning to shallow craters. He blew the smoke out in a rush and gave a heavy sigh.

"There's more, Franz. Ballistics indicate our shooter is somewhere between six foot and six foot three in height. That's you—you're six two. Then there's your criminal history as a weapons dealer."

"I wasn't a weapons dealer. I was a federally licensed firearms seller."

"You broke the law, Franz. You sold California-banned Uzis and high-capacity magazines. To a jury, not only are you knowledgeable in firearms, as a professional assassin would be expected to be, you're a lawbreaker. When you throw in the statutory rape thing, it looks pretty bad."

"I didn't rape anyone. It was consensual. She said she was nineteen."

"Try telling that to a jury."

All at once, the blood left Schmidt's face. "I want a lawyer," he croaked.

"You don't need a lawyer, Franz. You need me and I'll tell you why. You're innocent. That hair was planted at the crime scenes by someone else, and if you think real hard I believe you'll remember who it was. I want you to think back—let's say, to the last few months—and see if you can remember anyone who had the opportunity to collect samples of your hair. Especially criminals. Are you hanging out with any these days?"

"No. My friends are mostly artists and musicians."

"Well, who's been to your apartment?"

"Just friends. Some of them may have been busted for drugs, but none of them are involved in any criminal activity that I'm aware of."

"What about cleaning people? Do you have anyone clean your apartment?"

"No, I do it myself."

"Anybody angry at you? Someone who might want to get back at you? Someone with ties to a subversive group?" When the answers were no, no, and no, Patton stamped out his cigarette irritably in the ashtray. "You're going to have to try harder, Franz. Somehow, someone intentionally collected perfect strands of your hair. To do that, this clever asshole either had to recover them intact from some surface or article of clothing—or he had to distract you somehow and then rip them out."

A light seemed to go off in Schmidt's brain. "Wait, what was that last part?"

"I said the hair may have been pulled out forcibly."

Schmidt's mouth opened wide. "Oh, my God. It was...it was her."

"Who?"

"That woman?"

"What woman?"

"The woman that night. My God, I should have known."

Schmidt fumbled through his pocket for a cigarette, but the pack lay on the table. Seeing his desperation, Patton grabbed the pack, lit up two cigarettes, and passed one to Schmidt.

Okay, now we're getting somewhere. Talk to me, Franz.

"It happened about three months ago in L.A. I was there visiting a friend, but he left the bar and I stayed behind with this woman. We talked and danced for a while then went to her apartment. She was...crazy."

"What do you mean crazy?"

"She handcuffed me to the bed and fucked my brains out. At first, I thought it was all in fun, a sex game. But then I saw the hate in her eyes. She was on top and she was trying to hurt me. It was like she was reliving some kind of twisted fantasy."

"Okay, I understand you had sex with this woman. But what about the hair?"

"She pulled it out when I…"

"When you what?"

"When I came."

Patton's lower jaw dropped. "She what?"

"There's no other way to describe it. She tore a clump of my hair out during my climax. I thought it was some weird sadomasochistic thing in the heat of it all."

"What happened after you were finished having sex? Did you see her put the hair in a baggie, envelope, or something?"

"No, she just went to the bathroom. But I saw the little clump in her hand. I thought she was keeping a trophy or something. She scared the hell out of me. I tried to put her out of my mind. She kept me cuffed to the bed, like an animal. Like I said, at first it was exciting, then it was like I was being raped."

"You'd better not be messing with me, Franz. This sounds pretty far out there."

"How could I possibly make this shit up? You know what she said to me beforehand. She said, 'I'm going to hurt you, but you will like it.' Like she had the line memorized or something. It was fucking weird."

"Where did this happen?"

"Her apartment was somewhere in Venice Beach. We drove there in her car."

"Where in Venice Beach?"

"I don't know. It was the only time I had ever been there."

"Do you think you could find it?"

Schmidt considered this a moment, his mind reaching back. "I don't know—maybe."

"Did she ask where you were from? There must be a reason she chose you."

"I might have told her I was visiting from the Bay Area, just down for a few days. But I don't remember for sure."

Suddenly, Patton hit on an idea. He pulled out the wanted poster from his pocket. "Franz, I want you to take another look at this. When I showed it to you before, I believe I told you it was a man. But suppose I said it was actually a woman. What would you say then?"

Schmidt stared at the picture for several seconds.

"Well?"

The big German shook his head and shrugged. He wasn't sure.

"Come on, Franz. You're telling me you haven't seen that goddamned woman before?"

Patton pushed it closer to his face. Schmidt looked at the poster again, harder this time.

"Talk to me, Franz. We need a break in this damned case."

"Okay, okay, it could be her," he said finally. "It could be that crazy bitch from Venice Beach."

CHAPTER 81

"NO ONE PROMISED the road to America's rebirth would be easy," declared Benjamin Bradford Locke, staring out the window of his *sanctum sanctorum* at Cheyenne Mountain and massive Pikes Peak beyond. Under the current dire circumstances, the mountains looked cold and uninviting, an omen of bad things to come.

"You have failed to do your job and to keep Fowler in line," Truscott responded harshly, his cavernous eyes as black as a starless night. He sat in front of Locke's desk. The other chair was occupied by Colonel Caleb Heston, who, like Skull Eyes, wore a conservative, charcoal-gray, double-breasted Brooks Brothers suit.

You think you can do better? thought Locke acidly as he turned away from the window. His gaze fixed momentarily on the stuffed buffalo head on the wall before landing back on Truscott.

"We are a high-level organization, and as such, we have strict rules that must be followed and exacting performance standards that must be met. Mr. Chairman, you have failed to meet those standards."

Locke dismissed the accusation with a wave of his hand. But he knew that Skull Eyes was right. Failing to secure Fowler's loyalty was an onerous dereliction of duty. But if he admitted the president-elect was a lost cause, he would be acknowledging complete failure.

That he could not do.

"As I told you this morning, Fowler's on board with the program," Locke stated firmly. "Her new public persona is just an act. She's behind all our core issues."

Skull Eyes pounded his fist into his armrest. "I've heard enough of your lies!" He fixed Locke with a livid stare. "We're holding an emergency meeting of the Committee to discuss the Fowler situation, and to decide whether you're fit to continue as chairman. Frankly, the colonel and I are extremely skeptical. We know you withdrew a half-million dollars from the master account without authorization to pay off Gomez." His jaw tightened, as though to underscore his most important point. "That money's not for you to do as you please. It belongs to the Coalition!"

"You were dragging your feet with Xavier. I decided to go ahead and pay the balance. I'm not about to have Gomez out for my blood."

"That wasn't your decision to make."

"I am the chairman and have full authorization to disburse payments for services rendered on behalf of the organization." *You and the colonel, on the other hand, have no such authority and yet you engaged the services of the Apostle without my knowledge!* he wanted to add.

"But I am the contact with Xavier," Skull Eyes persisted.

"You *were* the contact. From here on out, I will be in direct communication with him. After all, it was his prized assassin who placed one of my organization's buttons at the scene of the crime. The second that happened that made Xavier and Gomez my problem, not yours."

"You've become too volatile, Benjamin," the colonel said. "At this critical juncture, we need more discrete and focused leadership."

Locke felt his whole body fill with indignation. He wished Dubois were here to run interference and divert some of the attention away from him, but he was on his own. "Listen here, Cassius and Brutus, because I'm only going to say this once. I am the chairman and there can be no successor without my approval."

"We'll see about that," hissed Truscott, standing up from his seat.

The colonel rose too. "You have let us all down, Mr. Chairman. The time has come for you to pass the torch to more capable leadership."

"You can't do this to me—I am the chairman."

"That will be the Committee's decision," Skull Eyes said harshly. "And whichever way the vote goes, you'd better goddamn live with it."

CHAPTER 82

WHEN THEY LEFT, Locke rose from his chair and stared out the window. How could everything have gone so wrong? His family was falling apart, he was under investigation by the FBI, a traitorous AMP employee had made off with secret records, Phase Three was an unmitigated disaster, and now, to top it all off, it looked as though he would lose his Coalition chairmanship. A mere week ago, he had been the gatekeeper to America's social and economic renewal. But now...now his whole world was crumbling around him.

How could God allow such a thing to happen?

It was all too much to be a test of his faith. It seemed as if the Almighty was picking on him, singling him out for cruel and unusual punishment. With a heavy sigh, he turned from the window and sat down at his desk. He listened for the voice of righteousness that always spoke to him in times of trial and tribulation, but he heard only silence.

A deafening silence.

After a time, he reached into his drawer and pulled out a leatherbound volume of the Old Testament. He felt utterly alone, an island of purity among a sea of unrepentant sinners. Scanning the contents, he debated reading Malachi for a moment before settling on Psalms. He went to Psalm 12, and though he knew it by heart, he read the words aloud.

Help, Lord, for there is no longer any that is godly
For the faithful have vanished from among the sons of men
Everyone utters lies to his neighbor
With flattering lips and a double heart they speak

Do thou, O Lord, protect us
Guard us ever from this generation
On every side the wicked prowl
As vileness is exalted among the sons of men

He closed the Good Book and prayed for his once great nation. Until its citizenry reclaimed the values of personal responsibility, hard work, honesty, and love of the family, there was little reason for hope and America would continue its downward spiral and allow China, India, and other emerging nations to rule the world. And until a popular conservative leader arose, one who rallied the masses like the Great Communicator, his once-great nation would be a veritable wasteland devoid of economic opportunity and moral enlightenment.

Something had to be done about it. He could not abandon the fight, not when he was so obviously on the side of righteousness.

But what should I do? What in the world should I do?

CHAPTER 83

HE STEPPED OUT the rear door of the study, leaving it cracked part way. After relieving himself in the bathroom, he walked down the hallway to the kitchen. The mingled aroma of pot roast and freshly baked bread rose to his nostrils, beckoning him forward.

When he stepped into the kitchen, his wife glanced up from the small television she occasionally watched while preparing dinner. This morning, he had gotten down on his knees and begged for her forgiveness for shoving her to the floor and violently spanking Susan, but she still hadn't forgiven him. It was unholy and reprehensible to use physical force on a woman and he knew he had been gravely wrong. As he expected, she gave him a chilly glance before returning to her A&E special and vegetable cutting.

"Where's Susan?" he asked, hoping not to get drawn into a verbal sparring match.

"She's spending the night at Jeanette's. She doesn't want to see you."

"I don't blame her. I feel terrible for what I've done."

"You can tell her that when she comes back tomorrow."

"I will, I promise," he said, and he meant it.

At that moment, they were interrupted by Benjamin Jr., who tromped into the kitchen carrying a can of Mountain Dew.

"You two have to see this," he snorted. "Fowler's lost her mind. Quick, turn to channel four," he barked to his mother.

She scowled at him. "Do it yourself."

He gave a wounded look and stared at them both. "What's gotten into you two?" He shook his head dismissively, reached for the remote on the kitchen table, and flipped the channel.

President-elect Fowler appeared on the screen behind a podium smothered with microphones. She was speaking without a prepared script to a large crowd gathered in front of a municipal building. A small caption that read SAN JOSE, CALIFORNIA flashed at the bottom of the screen.

"...like the great Theodore Roosevelt, I believe in a government limited in size, but not in what it can accomplish for its citizens. A streamlined, but active, government that addresses your concerns about the economy, education, the environment, and family planning. I want to increase the power of the Departments of Labor, Education and Interior, not shrink them. Jobs, the education of our children, and the preservation of our natural resources are three of the most vital responsibilities we have before us, whether we are Republican or Democrat."

The crowd applauded and Locke stood there openmouthed.

"Some have said there isn't room for reform in the Republican Party. My response is we *must* make room. That's why I support national licensing of handguns. That's why I support using surplus revenues to pay down our national debt and rescue Social Security. That's why I believe in continuing to maintain health care coverage for all Americans and in campaign finance reform..."

Locke's nose wrinkled. *How could I have misjudged her so badly?*

"...will not call for a constitutional amendment banning abortion. As far as I'm concerned, Roe versus Wade is established law. It is for the Supreme Court to decide whether it should be overturned, and no other body. After careful soul-searching, my belief is that it should not be overturned, that every woman deserves the legal right to decide what to do with her own body..."

Locke recoiled in anger. *How can she possibly rescue America's soul when she is no longer anything like the woman we groomed to assume the mantle of leadership?*

"...separation of church and state is fundamental to our way of life. We don't need prayer in public school and we don't need the Ten Commandments posted in every classroom. In 1980, the U.S. Supreme Court ruled that posting the Ten Commandments was unconstitutional, and I stand by that ruling. We need to teach our children the time-honored secular values of hard work, respect, and tolerance without invoking specific religious doctrines in school. We need to spend more time with our children, be more intimately involved in their lives, not look to our churches and schools as our babysitters..."

Again, the crowd cheered. Locke gawked in disbelief, thunderstruck at this brazen assault on everything he and American Patriots stood for. But Fowler wasn't just distancing herself from religious conservatives, she was taking on the entire Republican Establishment!

Has she no idea the powerful people she's defying? Or does she not care?

"...time for us to recognize that the GOP is no longer *God's Only Party*. The new Republican Party is a truly big tent, with room for everyone, including homosexuals and pro-choice advocates. That's why I met with the Log Cabin Republicans and Republicans for Choice earlier today, to try and find common ground..."

The breath came raw in Locke's throat. He felt the blood drain from his face. These were fighting words. In the past, conservative candidates like Fowler could be expected to take a few principled slaps at the Republican Establishment, to project a centrist image to the voters. But this was an overt attack on the very fabric of American society!

"There are many challenges ahead. The isolationists in my party must realize our nation isn't Fortress America. We must set an example to the rest of the world and embrace our global responsibilities beyond fighting terrorism. We cannot ask our allies around the globe to do something we ourselves refuse to do. And as far as domestic affairs go, we must use our conservative principles to help the poor and middle class as well as the rich. To implement policies based on limited, efficient government, but not a hatred of government itself. To focus on addressing the problems of all the people, not just on the economy and wellbeing of the richest Americans. With the shining example the late William Kieger has set, I plan to be the one leading the charge. God bless you all, and God bless America."

As the crowd burst into applause, Fowler held her hands up in a symbol of victory. Then, with the roar of the crowd swelling to a crescendo, she tilted her head down and beamed fondly at her audience. The camera turned and panned slowly on the faces, revealing a collective adoration that to Locke was nauseating. Even the normally irreverent media representatives appeared delirious with hope for this unconventional, reach-across-the-aisle conservative. Then the camera returned to Fowler. Her expression was resolute, proud, but what came through most was her idealism. It shone through like a full moon on a cloudless night.

Locke felt the bile rise in his throat. If a liberal Democrat had just uttered these words, she would not have been perceived as bold or extraordinary. But for a Republican, and a supposedly conservative one at that, it was dangerous talk. Anti-American and, worse yet, un-Christian.

Something has to be done.

There was no longer a scintilla of doubt Fowler had gone over to the dark side. This was no burst of political passion—it was a declaration of war. The woman had undergone a complete turnaround since the primary. She was on a mission. She genuinely admired Kieger and wanted to carry on his ideals. Already polls showed that most social conservatives were so smitten by her photogenic presence and ability to salve the nation's wounds that they didn't even care about her policies. Hell, even a large number of Democrats and Independents were getting excited about her; her favorability rating among these two groups combined was nearly sixty percent!

How can America ever reclaim her glory with this woman at the helm? Is American exceptionalism going to die here and now or live on for all eternity? Something has to be done. No, something drastic has to be done!

The crowd gushed forth with adulation, clapping and whistling thunderously. Fulminating inside, Locke stepped quietly from the kitchen and ducked into his office.

CHAPTER 84

LOCKE SAT DOWN AT HIS DESK, the anger roiling inside him like a tempest. What could he do to keep this horrible, horrible mistake from taking up residence in the Oval Office?

The answer came to him not from above, as he had expected, but from the steamy alligator swamps of Baton Rouge, Louisiana.

When Locke answered the phone, the voice on the other end spoke without introduction, and even through the distortion, there was a musical Dixie undertone that could belong to no other man except Senator Jackson Beauregard Dubois.

"Did you just see that?"

"Most of it," Locke said, and he punched his own voice modulator. "It was a crime against humanity. But what can we do about it?"

A stone-cold silence.

An answer unto itself, Locke realized. He had half-expected it to come to this, but he was still surprised. All the same, he had to be sure. "Are you suggesting what I think you're suggesting?"

"This dog can no longer hunt, Mr. Chairman. We misjudged her and now she's outgrown her usefulness."

"I know. In fact, I've known since yesterday."

"It's time to change our strategy. We'll never get another chance like this. We just placed the bet on the wrong racehorse. I will do the country proud, Mr. Chairman."

Lord knows, I don't want to kill again. But what else can be done? America cannot be allowed to die! "Will the party back you for vice-president?"

"The way I figure it, it's between me and Jamison," said Dubois, referring to popular Louisiana Governor Floyd Jamison. "But I own the tiebreaker since I finished third in the primary."

Are you really going to go through with this? "It's going to take a full court press. And you'll have to at least pretend to move to the center."

"If political expediency calls for it, I can talk the moderate talk and walk the moderate walk."

"What about Judiciary? Without you there to control the nomination process, our plans in that regard could be in jeopardy."

"Our plans are already in jeopardy. We have to take the chance now while there's still time. My successor will be McFarland. He's the next ranking member on the committee. He's not quite the firebrand I'd like to see stepping into my shoes, but he'll have to do. His party loyalty hovers at around eighty-seven percent. We could do much worse."

Tell me now, Lord, is this truly part of your Plan? "What about the Committee? I take it you want all this to happen without its consent."

"I don't see an alternative. Truscott and the colonel are out to get you like a South Texas wind. Have you heard from them?"

"They left a few minutes ago."

"So you know they've contacted the other Committee members and want you to resign as chairman?"

"Yes. By the way, I appreciate your standing by me. It has been a difficult time for us all."

"We can set things right, Mr. Chairman. If I can get the party's backing, the only way we can lose is if I get caught in bed with a dead girl or a naked boy. And trust me, the Committee will come around once they have one of their own as commander in chief."

Locke stroked his chin, appraising the situation, the inherent risks. The Prince of Darkness in the White House. The thought was appealing and yet somewhat terrifying. Beneath the senator's antebellum charm and professional calm lurked the icy fire of a true zealot, a man who knew no boundaries. But there was no denying his commitment to the cause.

"Are we in agreement then?" Dubois asked. "You'll back me. Not just financially, but with your constituency."

Forgive me God for what I am about to do. "There's no decision to make. You are our best hope."

"I'm pleased to hear you say that. Now we have to move quickly. Fowler has begun the vice-presidential vetting process and is expected to make her decision by early next week. Don't worry, I'll call in a whole passel of favors and get the party's backing, but we still have to get Frautschi to delay as long as he can."

"I don't think we can count on him anymore."

"We have no choice—he's all we've got. There's also the contract to consider. What are your thoughts?"

Too late, there's no turning back now. "It will be difficult, but not impossible."

"Can you get in touch with Gomez without the others finding out?"

Locke opened his desk. He withdrew the business card given secretly to him by Xavier in return for approving the outstanding payment for the Kieger contract. The name on the card read "Jane Halifax," no doubt an alias. Halifax was only a middlewoman, but Xavier had said she could put Locke in contact with Gomez. Xavier had said he didn't mind Locke negotiating with Gomez through Jane Halifax as long as he got his standard twenty percent cut.

"I can take care of the arrangements," Locke said. "Of course, it won't be cheap. But he is the best. If he'll agree to it, I'd say we have a very good chance of success—especially with the inside assets."

"You're referring to our government friends? The ones used only in a secondary role during Phase One?"

"Their services would prove invaluable this time around to keep risks to a minimum."

"Personally, I'd prefer the matter be settled during the speech in Denver on Saturday, but that might be too ambitious."

"I think it might be doable. The inside support will reduce the risks to a considerable degree."

"So you'll take care of it?"

"Consider it done."

"Then we should have a toast." Dubois paused, heightening the intensity of the moment. "To Phase Four, Mr. Chairman."

My God, what have I done? "To Phase Four," toasted Locke, and he hung up.

He reached down and picked up the fake business card on his desk, rubbing it between his thumb and forefinger, feeling the tension tearing him up inside. At the same time, it was amazing the awesome power he held. With one phone call, Katherine Fowler would cease to be a problem any longer.

One phone call.

And in Fowler's place would rise one of the Coalition's very own, a true patriot, a man so overflowing with red, white, and blue that the nation's glorious rebirth was a *fait accompli*.

Locke's mind was made up: the Chosen One would now give way to the Prince of Darkness. God had willed it so.

He dialed the number on the card.

CHAPTER 85

THIS IS THE WAY IT'S SUPPOSED TO BE.

Skyler lay next to Anthony on the bed, tingling as their naked bodies touched. There were no handcuffs, no ropes, not a single tool of human bondage. There were no feelings of anger, hate, or sadistic revenge. This time there was a powerful connection, a sense of profound intimacy; the kind of passion she remembered vaguely from long ago when she was hopelessly enraptured with Alberto.

She felt like a young adolescent experimenting with sexuality for the first time, swept up in the adventure of pure discovery.

Outside the window of her apartment, a light rain fell. Puffy gray cumulus clouds shrouded the Los Angeles Basin. The rainfall coming off the moisture-laden nebula was slowly picking up in intensity.

Skyler moved her body so that she was astride Anthony. Their lips touched softly. She felt desire flowing through her veins, but it was different than before. Her head swam with euphoria.

"Oh, Anthony," she whispered in his ear.

He rolled her over so that he was on top, and though it had been years since she had been beneath a man, she liked it. His tongue reached inside her mouth, softly, and she kissed him back. He began stroking her hair and rubbing against her moist area. She felt a delightful shudder of excitement take hold of her entire body, but it was the emotional connection that truly gripped her. She knew she was tapping into something sacrosanct, something only true lovers felt.

She kissed his mouth, nibbling his lips gently. A moment later, when he entered her, it was like a perfect dream. Everything about it felt right, natural.

As they began to move together in a gentle rhythm, she took more and more pleasure in his body, in his kisses and caresses and thrusts.

Her body was responding with a passion she thought she no longer possessed. All the usual selfishness—and violence—had vanished. Before the thrill of conquering the brutal male animal was what got her off. Now, she was resurrecting glorious emotions that had long ago atrophied.

I want you to feel what I'm feeling, Anthony.

She thrust back and forth knowingly, in a gentle rhythm. His hands squeezed her swelling nipples, and she gasped with delight.

She wondered if it were possible to go insane with pleasure.

He kissed her on the lips tenderly and she slid her tongue deep into his mouth, clasping his tight buttocks and pulling him deeper inside her. She moaned softly between kisses; she could tell the sound of her voice excited him all the more.

As the pace quickened, the air filled with desperation. She felt herself letting loose with excitement, coming as never before. She sensed that he too was about to let go of his seed.

"Look into my eyes," she gasped, pulling him still deeper.

He pulled his head up and his eyes locked onto hers. "I'm looking, I'm looking!"

She stared at him mesmerically, her eyes as wide as pebbles as the climax came. They held each other's gaze as their bodies shook fitfully and she felt his warmth flowing inside her. Then suddenly tears streamed from her eyes.

"Are you all right?" he asked, worriedly. "Did I hurt you?"

"No," she cried.

"Are you upset? What...what happened?"

"I'm overwhelmed, Anthony. I'm overwhelmed with joy."

CHAPTER 86

AFTERWARDS, THEY LAY IN BED for fifteen minutes—idly hugging, kissing, nibbling, stroking—before her coded mobile rang. Skyler debated whether to get up and answer the call, but it might be Xavier with another message so she decided to grab it. By working directly with Benjamin Locke, her control agent had managed to recover the outstanding payment for the Kieger contract. Her cut had been wired into her numbered Swiss account only this morning, which was yet another reason she was so happy.

Anthony gave a look of mock hurt and held onto her hand as she slipped from the bed. She threw him a playful smile, then gently pulled herself from his grasp and picked up the mobile from the side table. She said nothing into the mouthpiece, letting the voice on the other end speak first.

"Hello?" The voice was electronically distorted. "I...I'd like to speak to Ms. Halifax. Ms. Jane Halifax."

She wedged the phone in the crook of her shoulder and reached for the terrycloth bathrobe hanging from the chair next to the bed. "Who is calling, please?" she asked quietly.

"This is Benjamin Locke. Mr. Xavier gave me your number, as a courtesy. I take it today's financial settlement worked out to your associate Mr. Gomez's satisfaction?"

How is he changing his voice? A distortion box? "Please hold on a moment."

Anthony looked up at her expectantly. "I can go in the other room if you'd like."

She covered the mouthpiece and threw him a playful smile. "No, stay here and keep the bed warm. I'm not finished with you yet."

"That's what I like, an offer I can't refuse," he said with a smile before reaching for the *Los Angeles Times* on the side table, like a man without a worry in the world.

Skyler fastened the belt of her terrycloth robe about her waist. Then she went to the door, closed it behind her, and walked into the kitchen. "Is this line secure?" she asked.

"Yes," Locke replied.

She leaned against the refrigerator. "What is your business, then?"

"I have another proposition for your Mr. Gomez. It's a delicate assignment, which is why I'm not going through the normal channels."

"Why should he trust you?"

"Because I'm willing to make a substantial non-refundable down payment to secure his services. All Mr. Xavier insists upon is that he gets his standard cut."

"How substantial a down payment?"

"Two million even."

Skyler felt a shudder of raw fear. Two million dollars meant the mark was very important and, therefore, heavily guarded. But what an opportunity! The past few days she had given serious thought to quitting the game altogether and now perhaps this was her chance. When added to her current savings, the amount Locke was offering her—even minus Xavier's twenty percent cut—would certainly allow her to retire in comfort.

"Keep talking," she said. She hated to admit it, but the prospective assignment excited her. It dawned on her how much more difficult it would be to quit than she had anticipated. She would miss the meticulous planning, the adrenaline rush of the hunt, the thrill of outsmarting the authorities.

"I'll need to go over the contractual details with Mr. Gomez directly."

"That won't be possible. You talk to me or you don't talk to anyone."

She listened to the sound of his distorted breathing over the phone as he considered her conditions.

"Very well," Locke acceded. "The target is the *current* president-elect. The price is three million. Two million in advance, as I've alluded to."

Fowler! I should have known. Then the harsh reality of the crazy scheme came crashing down on her. It would be a suicide mission. The protection detail for the new president-elect would be several times what it had been a week ago for Kieger. And Fowler was a woman and Skyler didn't kill women.

"You can't be serious," she countered. "The chances of even getting into position are a thousand to one."

"Not if the assignment is handled in Denver on Saturday."

"You're referring to the planned speech in the plaza."

"Precisely. The same personnel made available to Mr. Gomez last Sunday will be available on Saturday. Now I realize he chose to handle the assignment in his own way last time, but it seems to me the available assets could prove quite useful this time around. To reduce the risks to, shall we say, an acceptable level. Wouldn't you agree?"

Skyler didn't answer. Already she was thinking back to last Sunday afternoon. From the beginning, there had been two plans. The first plan, what Skyler referred to as Plan A, had been put together by the men who had hired her and had been available for her to follow at her discretion. The plan had called for using an inside government team and taking the shot from the *Denver Tribune* Tower, roughly 500 yards from the speakers' platform. As the fictional Mr. Gomez's representative, Skyler had received a detailed package on the plan from a discrete field contact. But she had opted not to follow the script for Plan A.

Instead, she had followed the plan she had devised herself, Plan B, the details of which she had not disclosed to the men who had hired her. Plan B had involved taking the kill shot from the Union Plaza Building, where the distance to target was 800 yards. Though the odds of taking out the target and escaping had been better under Plan A because of the shorter distance and inside support, she chose Plan B for one simple reason: to keep her true identity concealed.

If she worked closely with others, they would know Diego Gomez didn't exist and that she was the real assassin. Her great secret would be compromised, and if any of the inside team members were caught, they might give her identity up in a plea bargain. The international law enforcement community and her enemies would have all the details they would need to hunt her down and it would be impossible for her to move around. Her days as an assassin would be numbered.

But if she wanted the big career-ending payoff, the golden parachute, she had no other choice but to follow Plan A, or something like it. With the additional security—on high alert no less—she would have to rely on the help of others if she was to complete the assignment. There was simply no way around it. Last time she had caught the Secret Service flat-footed; that would not happen again.

As they talked on, she imagined the field of fire from the twenty-two story *Denver Tribune* Tower. Clean line of sight over the tree line, 500 yards to target, three excellent escape options. Plan A had been a good plan, a damned good plan. And since its overall details had been worked out, only minor modifications would have to be made. However, it would mean blowing her Gomez cover, possibly even exposing her true identity, and even with the inside help, the risks were grave. The Secret Service and law enforcement detail would be substantially increased for the event, making it a dicey assignment even with the additional manpower.

"Well, will Mr. Gomez take the assignment?" asked Locke.

"I don't know. But I will contact him immediately and put your proposal to him. Call me in an hour and you shall have your decision."

CHAPTER 87

JENNIFER STARED ANXIOUSLY out the window of the Marriot Hotel at the cars and trucks speeding along I-25. The room felt oppressively claustrophobic. With every vehicle racing past, she had the uneasy feeling Benjamin Locke was closing in on them. In her febrile imagination, she pictured him as the creepy preacher–serial killer in *The Night of the Hunter.* He was dressed all in black and his face was cold and hard and he spoke in a calmly threatening voice and the words LOVE and HATE were scrawled on his knuckles and no matter how fast she and Susan ran, he was always just one step behind, the serrated knife in his hand glinting hideously in the...

Enough, Jennifer! You're going to drive yourself crazy!

But the image wouldn't go away.

A cold chill ran up her spine and she shuddered involuntarily. She felt like a hunted animal and hated having to hide out in a hotel room, waiting, praying she and Susan wouldn't be found. Unfortunately, it seemed to be the only option available since Locke had caught her red-handed in Fileroom E. She and Susan couldn't very well stay at her house, the first place anyone pursuing her would look. It had been risky enough swinging by to pick up her laptop and the AMP files, as well as some clothes.

To ensure that Susan's parents wouldn't come looking for her, Susan had told her mother that she was staying over at her friend Jeanette's house tonight. This was, at the very least, believable, considering the beating she had sustained from her father. But to make certain, Susan had explained her situation to Jeanette, and her loyal friend had agreed to cover for her tonight if anyone called.

Turning from the window, Jennifer looked at Susan. She was sitting on the bed, staring blankly at the TV. Jennifer walked over and sat down next to her.

"Penny for your thoughts."

Susan gave a sad but appreciative smile. "I was just thinking how much worse this would be without you here. I don't know what I'd do without you."

"We Yankee Chicks have to stick together," Jennifer said, giving her a gentle squeeze.

"Well, it means a lot to me. I've been trying to convince myself I know what I'm doing. But the truth is I don't and I'm scared."

Jennifer gave a sympathetic nod.

"I'm not worried so much about the...the procedure. Dr. Sivy's a good doctor. I'm more worried about my baby. I just hope it doesn't feel any pain. Do you think it will...feel anything?"

Jennifer had no idea what an eight-week-old fetus felt. She didn't even know if it could be considered viable life. After all, it was not fully formed, could not live outside a mother's body, and was not yet capable of self-conscious thought. *Still, it has to feel something—some degree of pain.* "I think it all happens pretty quickly," she replied, without answering the question.

"I hope so. It would make me even sadder, knowing my baby suffered."

Jenifer looked at the poor girl. "I know you've given this serious thought, but are you sure you want to go through with this?"

"I can't see any alternative. I'm not about to drop out of school, be shipped off to some special teenage pregnancy home, and be forced to give my baby away to complete strangers. And I'm too young to raise the baby on my own. So what's left? The way I see it there's only one option."

"Are you sure?"

"Yes, I've made my decision. I'm going to have the abortion."

In the silence that followed, Jennifer tried to imagine what that would entail. A plastic tube would be stuffed between Susan's legs and the fetus would be sucked from her by a high-powered vacuum. It was a terrifying process, and whether one was pro-life or pro-choice, the moral implications were far-reaching and perplexing. It was not a simple medical procedure, not a minor inconvenience, like having a broken leg set or a cyst removed.

She thought of what it must be like to be a doctor who routinely performed such operations, like Dr. Sivy. *How does he do it, day in and day out? Does he have to rationalize his actions to himself? Or has he performed so many abortions he no longer thinks twice about it?*

Jennifer touched Susan's arm. "Are you sure you're not doing this to spite your father? Because if you are, that's not a good reason to go through with it."

"What makes you think I'm doing this to get back at my father?"

"After what he did to you today, I know you're angry at him. I just don't want your decision to be motivated by anger. That's not a good reason. I know because I've been down that road myself."

"You have?"

Jennifer was hesitant to share her painful experience with Susan. But at the same time, she wanted to be honest with the girl. After all, Susan had confided in her and was looking for guidance in what was definitely the biggest decision of her life.

She told her the story. When she was finished, Susan quietly intoned, "History has a strange way of repeating itself."

"But the difference is you have an opportunity to make your *own* choice. And whatever choice you make, it should not be made out of anger or revenge."

Susan's face turned thoughtful as she considered this. "Maybe I am doing this partly to spite my father," she admitted. "But it's not the main reason. I'm doing it mostly because, for a young girl in my situation, it's the right thing to do."

"That may be, but you need the support of someone in your family. Is it possible your parents might come to accept your decision and help you through this?"

"My mother will be there for me. She believes the rights of the unborn should be protected, but she also understands it's a complex issue. She can see the grays my father sometimes is incapable of seeing."

Jennifer gave an understanding nod as the room slipped into silence.

"It just makes me so sad," Susan said, her youthful eyes haunted by an inner pain that made her look old beyond her years. "My family's falling apart." She started to say something else, but her voice quavered with grief and she dissolved into tears.

For several minutes Jennifer comforted Susan. Then they ordered room service and ate dinner while watching a Seinfeld rerun. The program made them both laugh and soon the atmosphere in the room lightened, as if a pleasant summer breeze had swept through the window and pushed aside the foul air.

During a commercial break, Susan looked over at Jennifer and said, "Look at us. We're supposed to be hiding out and yet here we are eating grilled cheese sandwiches, watching television, and laughing our heads off."

Jennifer's mouth creased into a weary smile. "Last time I checked having fun's not illegal."

"Somehow though I feel like a fugitive. Maybe they should call us Thelma and Louise."

"Maybe they should," said Jennifer. "Maybe they should at that."

CHAPTER 88

AFTER NEARLY TWO HOURS of streaking through thunderclouds, Delta flight 369 touched down bumpily on the tarmac at LAX and began its long crawl to the terminal. Five minutes later, the four turbofan engines ebbed to a low drone and the giant mass of aeronautic machinery came to a halt. Patton quickly deboarded the plane ahead of the other passengers with Sharp, Taylor, Schmidt, and two agents from the San Francisco office.

Schmidt's alibi had checked out. His signature had been confirmed on the guest registries at two of the wineries, and three credible eyewitnesses had remembered seeing him Sunday afternoon. Now he was cooperating, albeit reluctantly, as a material witness. It was his unenviable task to locate the apartment where months ago an unknown woman the FBI was calling Jane Doe had lured him, handcuffed him to a bed, and ripped hair from his head while having a shrieking orgasm.

They stepped outside the baggage claim and quickly located the L.A. office field support team: four agents in FBI raid jackets standing languidly in front of a pair of sparkling Dodge Grand Caravans. The agent on the left, a hollow-cheeked guy with a cigarette dangling insolently from his mouth like James Dean, stepped forward and introduced himself as Supervising Agent Roberts. With quick greetings exchanged, Roberts, Patton, Sharp, and the others climbed into the first van while the three remaining L.A. agents hopped in the second vehicle. They drove out of the airport to Sepulveda, then linked up with the Pacific Coast Highway and headed northwest.

Before hitting Culver Boulevard, a burst of lightning flashed through the sky, illuminating swollen Ballona Creek below the overpass. Patton saw a raging torrent, muddy and foaming. When they crossed into Marina Del Ray, the rain picked up and the visibility worsened. The windshield wipers slapped futilely at the slashing rain and the headlights weren't much help. Several times they ran into pools of water beneath the underpasses and were forced to an interminable crawl. It wasn't until nearly 9 p.m. when they reached the heart of Venice Beach.

They began the search for the apartment around the pier. Schmidt couldn't remember a street address or the exact location of Jane Doe's apartment, but believed he could find it based on a few salient landmarks. He recalled an arcade with a series of Italian-style colonnades not far from the beach and a short distance from the apartment. Once they found the colonnades, they set up a search grid running from Brooks Avenue to the north, Washington Boulevard to the east, South Venice Boulevard Avenue to the south, and Ocean Front Walk to the west. They put Schmidt up front of the lead van where the visibility was best and started along Brooks Avenue, moving slowly south.

Forty-five minutes later, after three false alarms, Schmidt tapped his hand on the dashboard. "Pull over—I think this might be it." He pointed to the apartment building on the left. It was upscale but not too fancy, done in a Spanish stucco style with palm trees in the grass planters.

The vans came to a halt next to the curb behind several parked cars.

"It looks like the right place, but I'm not positive," Schmidt said, studying the apartment complex through the flapping windshield wipers.

Sharp had no patience for such equivocation. "Jesus Christ, we've been driving around for an hour," he said, exaggerating how long it had been. "Is this the joint or not?"

"I think so, but with all the rain it's hard to tell."

"Let's take a closer look," Patton said. "Schmidt, come with me." He yanked off his raid jacket, threw open the door, and jumped out into the slashing rain. Before closing the door, he said to Roberts, "We'll be back in a minute."

Actually it took five.

When they returned to the van, Sharp snarled, "Well, is that it?"

"Jackpot. A woman on the first floor buzzed us in. Schmidt's certain it's Apartment 330, on the west side. I think she's there now too." He pointed up to the window. "Look."

All eyes cast toward the apartment. Indeed, the outline of a person was just barely visible through the drawn blind. The figure moved across the window then disappeared. By the silhouette, it looked like a woman, but with the blind drawn shut and in the downpour, it was impossible to be certain.

Sharp's eyes narrowed on Schmidt. "You're sure about this."

"Positive of the place. Not sure if Jane Doe's the one up there."

Sharp turned to the driver. "All right, Agent Roberts, call in the cavalry."

"Yes, sir. They're standing by at the Federal Center. They'll be here in twenty minutes."

"Hell, that's enough time for a cup of coffee. Pull into that 7-Eleven we just passed on Venice. They'll fix us up real fast. You can make the call from there."

"I don't think that's a good idea," Patton warned. "She may try and flee. We need to keep the apartment under surveillance."

"Oh, it *will be*. Because you and Schmidt are staying behind."

CHAPTER 89

SITTING IN THE SHOTGUN SEAT of the second van, Patton stared up at the apartment window. Roberts, Sharp, and Taylor had gone on to the 7-Eleven in the other van. The interior lights were off, and the rain drummed on the roof in a steady rhythm. Patton watched as the silhouetted figure passed in front of the window again before disappearing. He wondered if it really was Jane Doe.

Suddenly, his cell phone chirped to life.

"Patton here."

"Ken, it's me." The reception was poor from storm static.

"Jennifer?"

"How's it going out there?"

"Hopefully, I'll have a definitive answer to that question in the next ten minutes."

"Are you going after Schmidt?"

With the drumming rain and static, Patton was having trouble hearing her. He covered his right ear with the palm of his hand to cut off the outside noise. "What?"

"Are you going after Schmidt?"

"No, a different suspect—a woman."

"Who is she?"

He looked up at the apartment window again. The figure reappeared and stood there. "We don't know yet. But we're about to make the arrest."

"When are you flying back to Denver?"

"It depends on what happens here. My best guess is late tomorrow afternoon."

"Ken, the reason…called. It's…Benjamin…"

"Hold on, Jenn. I'm losing you."

"Here with…daughter…Susan. Could…imagination…but she says…father…involved…"

"Involved in what? Jenn, Jenn, I'm losing you."

"…not sure…group…assassination…"

"What?"

"…Locke…"

The line crackled a final time and went dead. He hit *Call Back* once, twice, a third time, but got nothing.

"Damnit!"

He looked up at the window. But the silhouette was gone.

CHAPTER 90

SKYLER ANSWERED HER CODED MOBILE AFTER THE SECOND RING.

"Get the fuck out of there now!"

For some reason, the warning was slow to register, though she recognized the voice instantly. It belonged to her field contact for the Kieger hit in Denver. But she had never given the man her number and had always contacted him.

"You have to get out now!" the man repeated, louder this time. "Your cover's blown—and Gomez could be in jeopardy. Is he there with you?"

"How did you get this number?"

"There's no time to explain. Get out while you still have a chance. Fifty federal agents will be breaking down your door any second!"

"How much time do I have, really?"

"Five minutes, tops."

Damn! The sense of urgency struck home. But before she hung up, she needed one important question answered. "Will your support team be there on Saturday?"

"The arrangements are being made as we speak. Someone will contact you. But get the hell out of there and make sure Gomez is not compromised. The assignment must go on as planned!"

"Don't worry, it will," Skyler said, and she punched off. She went briskly to the window and carefully pulled back the blind so there was a small crack. She didn't see any action on the street, no sign of a raid team, but that didn't mean one wasn't assembling out of view or waiting in the cars parked on the street. She wiped the fog from the window to get a better look. But the visibility was still poor with the heavy rain and water droplets on the glass.

Events were now moving at a dizzying pace. She had agreed to take on the Fowler contract, after wrestling with the dilemma for an hour. Of course, before agreeing, she had ensured the terms were favorable: $2 million up front and another deuce upon fulfillment of the contract. She knew it would be extremely dangerous, even with the inside support, but another chance like this would not come again. This was the golden parachute that would allow her to get out of the killing game and live in comfort the rest of her natural days.

The bottom line was her heart wasn't in it anymore. Since meeting Anthony, she no longer felt fierce hatred toward men or loathed the world at large for all the pain it had caused her. Without hate, there was little left to drive her except the money and rush of carrying out a contract, and these were no longer enough to justify the killings. What she needed most now was to share love and intimacy. For years, she had believed good men like Anthony didn't exist, but now she understood that wasn't true. Love was the strongest reason to quit the game and start a real life.

The irony was that in order to fulfill her objectives, in order to put aside her old life and start anew, she would have to kill one last time. Or die trying, since she would never let herself be taken alive if she was caught. She would not rot in some prison like Carlos the Jackal. She would either accomplish her assignment and go on to live a full and happy life, or die by her own hand, on her own terms. One way or another, she would die knowing that she had triumphed over her hate, that she was capable of giving and receiving love.

At the moment, however, all thoughts of the planned assignment and a happy future were removed from her mind as she peered out the window for signs of surveillance. Now she was confronted with a new problem: federal agents would be smashing down her door any moment. But how did they find her? Who tipped them off? And how was she going to get out of here?

With these unanswered questions racing through her head, she heard a sound behind her and turned to see Anthony stepping out of the bathroom.

CHAPTER 91

"IS SOMETHING WRONG?"

"We have to get out of here."

"Why? What's going on?"

The lie came to her instantly. "One of my former informants has sent someone after me. He's already supposed to be in L.A. There was a bad scene, a few years ago and this guy, this informant, wants revenge. I have to fly to Langley and give a briefing. The Company wants them both badly, the informant and the man he's sent after me. I can't tell you any more than that. I have to get you out of here."

He stepped toward her and took her hand, his face a mixed study in confusion and desperation. "What about you?"

"I'll be right behind you. I have to take care of one thing first."

He looked torn. "But I can't just leave you here."

"You must." She set down the mobile and started prodding him toward the door, feeling invisible walls closing in around them both.

"But why? I'm not going to let some wacko—"

"Please, Anthony! If you care about me, you'll do this for me!" She thrust her body at him and kissed him fiercely. The thought of never seeing him again made her dizzy with dread.

He pulled away, reluctantly, and grabbed his rain jacket from the coat hook and his umbrella. "Jesus, why do I feel like I'm in a goddamned movie?"

"This is no movie, believe me, Anthony. Here's what I need you to do. Take the fire stairs to the basement and head to the south end where the laundry room is. Go to the rear door. At night it's locked, but you can unlock it from the inside. Proceed quickly but quietly out that door. It opens onto a narrow covered parking lot. Just head for the trees on the other side of the lot—from the laundry room, it's only about thirty feet. Don't stop for anything. Once you've made it there, go straight to the pier. I want you to hang out at a bar or restaurant for a couple of hours, then take a cab home."

"Where will I meet you?"

"I'll call you from Langley."

"This isn't right. I should stay with you."

"No, you have to go." She pushed him toward the door. "I love you,

Anthony." She felt the emotion welling up inside her, swirling around with the unbearable tension.

"I love you too," he said, and he pulled her toward him and kissed her. For an instant, they were Bogie and Bergman in *Casablanca*. Then he was off and running down the hallway.

She closed the door and quickly went through what she had to do. Though she had always planned for this eventuality, she was still taken off guard. She had planted multiple sets of fingerprints and hair fibers all around the apartment, so at least the authorities would have to sift through a lot of misleading detail, but they would still get forensics on her since there wasn't enough time for a sweep through the apartment. The most important thing was to gather her critical belongings. All her long-distance firearms, disguises, and false passports were stored in her safe room in Marina Del Ray, but she still kept her SIG-Sauer and three sets of false identity papers, driver's licenses, and credit cards here with her. She would also need to get her laptop and the hard drive from her desktop computer.

She went first to the desktop in her office. She pulled off the monitor and set it down on the table, then popped the metal side to the processing unit. She reached in and withdrew the small hard drive. It contained the magnetic-coated disks, tape heads, and selector mechanisms used to store and access the programs and data inside the computer. She took the hard drive and stuffed it in the soft nylon carrying case with her laptop. Walking into her bedroom closet, she grabbed the daypack containing her SIG, holster, and ammo magazines. On the way out, she snatched her purse and her coded mobile, stuffing them in the pack. Zipped within a special compartment was a nine-inch stiletto and the false identifications. She went to the coat rack, put on her raincoat, and slung the pack over her shoulder. Though her blood was pumping and she was frightened, there was no evidence of panic in her movements. She worked with calm mechanical efficiency, like a well-trained spy.

She looked at her watch. Less than four minutes had passed since the warning call, and it had taken her less than two to gather up the critical items she could not leave behind. But she had to check one last thing. She went to the window, pulled back the blind, and peered down at the street below.

A cold hand closed over her heart. She was trapped!

CHAPTER 92

WITH THE STEALTH of a wolf pack, the FBI raid team crept into final position. Anticipation gripped the hallway, the face of each and every agent one of focused concentration. There was no sound, not even a creaking floorboard or squeaking shoe, as the team edged forward, sidearms cocked and unlocked.

Reaching the door to apartment 330, Patton cast a glance at Supervising Special Agent Roberts and his L.A. squad.

They were ready to move.

Patton smiled inwardly. The apartment building was surrounded, all possible escape routes sealed off. And beyond the door lay the unsuspecting quarry.

We've got you, Jane Fucking Doe—there's no way out.

Roberts gave a hand signal and rapped on the door, hard. "FBI—open up!"

Three seconds, two, one...battering ram forward, door smashed open.

Patton stormed into the apartment with the frontal wave, the adrenaline flowing through him like a mighty river.

He ran into the living room, but was shocked to find no one there. The team members fanned out to check each room. Patton and Taylor led a group into the bedroom. They checked the closets, behind the curtains, under the bed, but found nothing. An agent went to the window, opened it, and looked up and down the exterior of the building. Again nothing.

Jesus Christ. Where the hell has she gone?

Sharp poked his head in the room. "Anything?"

"Zip."

"Shit!" and Sharp was gone.

Finishing the search, Patton bolted back out into the main hallway where Schmidt was being held by the two escorts from San Francisco. The apartment was overflowing with field agents, checking and rechecking every conceivable hiding place with pistols drawn.

Patton led Schmidt to the bedroom. "Are you sure this is the goddamned place?"

"One hundred percent. The bed, the furniture, everything's the same."

"You're sure?"

"Look, I'll never forget what went down here. That woman is one twisted bitch."

Patton wondered: *Could the assassin really be a woman?*

They went into the kitchen. The search was wrapping up. No space small enough to hide a cat was left unexamined, but there was still no sign of anyone. Not more than five minutes ago, Patton had a prime suspect in his mitts. Now he didn't have jack shit.

He wanted to strangle Sharp, the goddamned idiot! Instead of driving off for a cup of coffee and waiting for the L.A. raid team to arrive, the ASAC should have ordered the subject's apartment raided right off the bat with the agents they had! Why it was almost as if he had deliberately allowed the suspect to get away!

"The bird has flown! I repeat, the bird has flown!" Agent Roberts barked into his two-way radio to the teams staked outside. "Perimeter One, any sign of anyone?"

"Negative."

"P-Two, Marvin?"

"That's a negative, sir. But we've got the rear covered. If anyone came this way, we would have seen 'em."

"P-Three, anything?"

"Negatory."

"Shit! Keep your eyes peeled. She may still be in the building. Over and out." Roberts turned and shook his head, severe disappointment evident on his features.

Sharp came walking up, red-faced. "Agent Roberts, have your team search the building and rooftop. Round up every tenant and get the property manager. We also need a ground search. Make it a twenty-block radius around the apartment complex. Set up checkpoints along Venice Boulevard, PCH, and wherever else you think we need them. And mobilize an ERT on the double..."

As Sharp rattled on, Taylor walked over to Patton. "If we're down to checkpoints, she's gone baby gone."

"Yeah, I know. We're fucked."

CHAPTER 93

IT WAS TWO HOURS LATER before Patton got to do his walk-through of Jane Doe's apartment. The building and ground searches had been completed. The LAPD had established checkpoints at all major arteries linking Venice Beach with the rest of the city. Interviews had been conducted with the landlord and tenants, thirty-eight people in all. Despite this exhaustive effort, Jane Doe was still at large and Patton had no idea where she was headed. She had been within his grasp, but now, to his dismay, he might never find her.

He logged in at the door to the apartment: flashed his creds, signed in, and slipped on a pair of latex gloves. As he stepped inside, he saw the evidence response team still busy dusting for prints and bagging and tagging. He was careful not to disrupt the process as he strode into the living room. After the ground search and interviews, he felt ragged. But mostly he was pissed off that they had let the subject get away.

He stopped and looked around the room, hoping to find some clue, however minute, that would shed light on Jane Doe. The room was tastefully furnished, a little arty, which revealed a certain cosmopolitan quality. The furniture was for the most part antique, spare but luxurious, dominated by classical styles. There was some photographic equipment lying about and the walls were covered with pictures showing dramatic scenes of people and landscapes. Patton could tell that photography was more than just a hobby for Jane Doe; in all the pictures, the lighting and scenery were exquisite, *National Geographic* caliber. The works showed a skilled artist, meticulous yet sensual, which seemed at odds with a criminal.

He walked to the large bookcase and examined the books. Most were modern male action-adventure and suspense novels by Barry Eisler, Clive Cussler, Lee Child, and Stephen Hunter, male self-help books, and bland non-fiction works on military history. But there were also female literary works by Jane Hamilton, Annie Proulx, and Amy Tan, feminist manifestos by Germaine Greer, Gloria Steinem, and Susan Faludi, a smattering of romance novels, and collections of woman's poetry. It was if two people lived in the apartment, one unabashedly male, the other female.

He walked into the bedroom and looked through Jane Doe's closets and drawers. They were filled with not just women's clothing, but similar-sized men's apparel. The male clothing was neatly separated from the female and ran the full gamut, from casual jeans and T-shirts to chinos and polo shirts to supremely costly Armani suits. Stepping into the bathroom, he opened the medicine chest and looked in the cabinet below the sink. He quickly found that the toiletry articles in the bathroom were for both sexes as well. There were men's electric shavers, combs, condoms, underarm deodorants, foot powders, and the like, adjacent to but separate from feminine hygiene and makeup products, like Tampax, perfume, and lipstick.

Based on the clothing alone, Patton would have concluded that either Jane Doe was sharing the apartment with a man or she had a male lover who stayed over regularly. But earlier, when he had interviewed Barr Hogen, the art-dealer living next door in Apartment 326, she had said Jane Doe lived alone, spent little time at her apartment, and didn't have a steady boyfriend who stayed over on a regular basis. Patton supposed the articles could belong to an ex-lover, but if that were true, they almost certainly would have been boxed up and not spread all over the apartment as if regularly used. It didn't make any sense.

Perplexed, Patton summoned Hogen, whom he regarded as the most credible witness, to the bedroom. Looking over the clothing and toiletries with him, she admitted to being as puzzled as he. But then she pointed out that she had been in New York all week on business and perhaps the woman had taken in a lover during her absence. She considered the prospect unlikely, however. Jane Doe, she said, was, despite her ravishing beauty, a loner and recluse.

Sending Hogen on her way, Patton continued to poke around, careful not to disrupt anything. He talked a few minutes with Charlie Fisher, the ERT supervisor. Slowly, it began to dawn on him that the apartment was as conspicuous for what was missing as what was actually present.

There were no personal documents, no bills, letters or postcards of any kind; no photographs of Jane Doe, a spouse, siblings, relatives, children or lovers; no diplomas, awards or certificates; no obvious objects of sentimentality or nostalgia. There was no phone, and though there was a computer, Fisher pointed out that the hard drive was gone, which meant she must have known they were coming and removed it before her escape. There was nothing to indicate the presence of a profession or hobbies beyond photography and an apparent fondness for California wines.

A woman with no name, no past, changing physical appearances, maybe even a split personality.

All in all, it was an unusual evidence scene, raising as many questions as it answered. There was nothing of great importance, nothing that couldn't be abandoned, nothing that revealed a past or future. If this woman was indeed Kieger's assassin that would explain why all personal records had been carefully cleaned out. There should have been some bank statements, bills or personal photographs, but there were none. She had left virtually no trace of her identity, as if she knew, one day, the authorities would come for her.

Patton went over how all this fit with what the landlord had said. According to the landlord's records, the apartment had been rented since July to one Dominique Rousseau. A background check by the L.A. team revealed that the social security and driver's license numbers on the rental application were falsified. When shown the police artist's sketch of Jane Doe, the landlord said it was definitely not Rousseau, which meant that for the past few months he had been renting to an imposter. He admitted he didn't make a habit out of keeping tabs on his tenants, unless they didn't pay their rent on time. In this regard, the fictitious Ms. Rousseau had been a model tenant, paying five days early each month at the discounted rental rate. Obviously, Jane Doe was doing everything in her power to maintain a low profile and keep her true identity concealed.

But where was she from? Barr Hogen and two of the other tenants had shed some light on this. They believed Jane Doe was from somewhere in California. Her tone was flat and generic, they said. But there was another tenant who had overheard her on the street speaking Spanish—impeccably fluent Spanish. Patton thought this might be an important clue and underlined it in his iPad notation.

He walked to the window and stared out at the slashing rain. The male clothing and other personal belongings vexed him. If Jane Doe lived alone and didn't have a steady boyfriend who stayed over nights, as Barr Hogen claimed, then what were these articles doing here? It was as if Jane Doe had a split personality: one-half distinctly male, the other half female.

But why? What was the cause of this schism?

He knew it might be the key to the case. Somehow he had to fit this piece to the puzzle.

Now at least he would have a high-quality computer sketch of Jane Doe based on the tenants' and Schmidt's descriptions. The fingerprints and forensics would help too; they would shed additional light on this bizarre woman. And hopefully Dr. Hamilton would be able to make sense of all the physical evidence and put together a meaningful profile of her.

But Patton was still gravely worried. He had the sense he was dealing with an extremely clever adversary, a person far more intelligent than the militia nutcases and terrorist extremists with whom he customarily dealt.

And there was the rub: catching Jane Doe, dead or alive, was going to be tough as hell.

FRIDAY

CHAPTER 94

THE FIFTEENTH OF NOVEMBER seemed like it would be no different than any ordinary fall day— certainly not one that would go down as one of the bloodiest in Colorado history along with Sand Creek, the Ludlow Massacre, Columbine, and Aurora. The sky was razor-blue with wisps of white, the sun a subdued peach orb above the vast Great Plains to the east. The temperature was cool in a hearty autumn way and a brisk wind stirred the fallen leaves, swirling them about. On the mountains to the west lay a fresh veneer of snow, like a shawl on the shoulders of a handsome elderly woman, Georgia O'Keeffe perhaps. The clear skies, chilly morning air, and spectacular backdrop of mountains seemed to reinforce the idea that this was truly God's country, as many native Coloradoans claimed, without reference to an actual deity, but to a natural physiographic majesty greater than humankind.

But today it was all just an illusion.

As if they understood this in some ineffable way, Jennifer and Susan Locke were preoccupied with their thoughts as they pulled into the parking lot of the Family Planning Group clinic in Widefield, a suburban enclave a few miles south of the Springs.

Today Susan was getting an abortion.

Jennifer parked her Outback in one of the many open spots and turned off the ignition.

Suddenly, the group of anti-abortion demonstrators near the front entrance stopped milling about and swooped toward them like vultures, quickly encircling the car.

"Fucking baby killers go home!"

Jennifer looked over at Susan and saw the panic on her face. "Don't worry—we'll get through this." She forced her way out of the car, fought her way around to the passenger side, and helped Susan from the car.

But the mob completely engulfed them.

Jennifer threw out a stiff arm to protect Susan as they started for the front door, cutting a path through the hostile crowd. There was supposed to be a "bubble zone" to shield family planning patients and workers from verbal and physical abuse, but as always with a controversial law, enforcement was severely lacking.

A crinkle-faced woman shoved a right-to-life pamphlet in Susan's face, but Jennifer pushed the woman's hand aside and kept Susan moving forward.

"Murderer!" a young, vulpine man with a crucifix about his neck shrieked, stepping forward to block them along with two other men.

Off to the left, a woman held up a placard that read: RESCUE THOSE WHO ARE BEING TAKEN AWAY TO DEATH; HOLD BACK THOSE WHO ARE STUMBLING TO THE SLAUGHTER. PROVERBS 24:11.

Jennifer looked at Susan and saw the tears in her eyes. The girl was ashamed, which was precisely the reaction sought by the protesters. This was their last chance to dissuade her from her mission and they were giving it all they had.

"No more selling baby body parts! No more selling baby body parts!"

Feeling a new wave of anger, Jennifer pushed her way through the men blocking their path. Susan followed in her wake, shaking with trepidation. Their progress was slow and difficult, but finally they were able to press through the gauntlet and make it to the clinic's front door. A young, physically fit, yet frightened-looking security guard opened the door for them and stepped outside to stem back the protesters.

Jennifer threw him a glare. *Where the hell were you when we needed you?*

The security guard gave a guilty look and, with an exaggerated pretense of authority, warned the crowd to move back to the parking lot. Undaunted, the protesters blared on like a lynch mob. Shaking her head at the insanity of it all, Jennifer closed the door and helped Susan inside. The noise died away to a low rumble.

Seeing how visibly shaken Susan was, Jennifer went to the front desk and told the female receptionist that they needed a moment before signing in. They sat down in the waiting area, which looked no different than an orthodontist's office. Susan wiped the tears from her eyes. A young woman in a Colorado College sweatshirt stole a nervous glance at them and ducked back behind her *Vanity Fair* magazine.

Once they had taken a deep breath and steeled their jangled nerves, they gathered the necessary forms from the receptionist and filled them out. Jennifer watched Susan closely and could see that the poor girl was having second thoughts. This was not just a routine medical procedure to her, but a time of great moral uncertainty, and the presence of the protesters only amplified the situation. Wracked with guilt and self-doubt, she was struggling to come to grips with her decision.

When the protesters returned to the parking lot, the guard came back in and grabbed a cup of coffee behind the receptionist's desk. Though he had managed to turn back the crowd, he was clearly on edge and looked too young and inexperienced for such a demanding job, a job in which he and every one of his co-workers were under constant threat from a fanatical right-wing fringe of antediluvian protestors who saw no middle ground in the abortion debate. He and the receptionist spoke, and though Jennifer couldn't make out what they were saying, she could tell from the security guard's body language that he was uneasy about the protesters.

She brought Susan's paperwork to the front desk. "Will Doctor Sivy be ready soon?"

The receptionist smiled efficiently. "Yes, he'll be with you shortly. We're sorry about the protesters."

"Thanks. Can you tell me where the women's restroom is?"

She pointed to her left. "Oh, it's down the hall and to the right."

Jennifer thanked her and went back to Susan. "I need to use the restroom. Will you be all right?"

"Yes, I'm fine," Susan said, wiping the dampness from her eyes. "You go ahead."

Jennifer felt the need to reassure her. "It's going to work out for the best, Susan. It will take time, but you will heal from this. You've got a great future ahead of you. I know that sounds corny, but it's the truth."

"Thanks for being here for me. I don't know what I'd do without you."

"It's going to be okay," Jennifer said. "Everything's going to be okay."

CHAPTER 95

THE MIDNIGHT BLUE PONTIAC with the unlit siren on top, ostensibly signifying an unmarked police car, passed quietly like a cruising Tiger shark through the drive leading to the rear of the clinic. Turning right, it disappeared behind the single-story building. A few seconds later a man emerged. He closed the car door, leaving it unlocked, and strode briskly along a narrow walkway on the east side of the building.

From a safe distance, Joseph "Skull Eyes" Truscott watched the Apostle move toward the front entrance. The strides were confident, authoritative. Beneath the commanding and seemingly legitimate physical presence lurked a man who was, quite simply, a killing machine. The former CIA deputy director of operations and current consultant to a host of security firms had seen many a covert act unfold from behind a pair of high-powered binoculars, but he had never known anyone who killed as efficiently as the Apostle.

The man never fails to rise to the occasion. If we'd only had a thousand more like him during Tet, we would have won that damned war.

Yes, the Apostle would show these abortionists, nurses, and misguided women a thing or two about violating the sanctity of human life. The same merciless fate that had claimed millions of unborn children now awaited them. In his mind, Benjamin Locke, acting in his role as Chairman of the Executive Committee of the Coalition, had unjustifiably put an end to attacks on national abortion and fertility clinics four years ago when he had taken over as chairman. But now there was a new sheriff in town. Truscott would teach these unholy monsters, who murdered the unborn and sold their body parts, a lesson that they and their misguided supporters would never forget.

He sat in his silver Mercedes on a small hill overlooking the clinic. Arriving only moments ago to bear witness to what was about to occur, he had the heat on low to take away the chill of the morning air. He adjusted the focus of his binoculars as the Apostle neared the front door. A crowd of picketers milled about in the parking lot outside the clinic, but the Apostle rounded the corner so quickly no one seemed to notice him.

He looked like the quintessential cop in his Colorado Springs Police sergeants' uniform: barrel-chest, broad shoulders, Rocky Marciano nose, square chin. He wore Ray Ban sunglasses and a stiff officer's hat so no one could get a good look at his face. He was outfitted with a Colt semiautomatic, baton, pepper spray, and handcuffs that conferred upon him the requisite law enforcement look. Later, when the interviews of the protesters were conducted, few would remember him, and those that did would have virtually no recall of what he looked like.

They would remember only a man in a police uniform.

This was not the first time Skull Eyes had watched secretly while one of his clandestine operations was carried out. What he liked most was the military precision, the mechanical swiftness. It was exhilarating, a war game in miniature.

But, most of all, operations like this were absolutely necessary.

Until the Supreme Court overturned Roe vs. Wade, these Sodomites needed to be taught that abortion was the unjustified killing of unborn children. Life didn't conveniently begin after the second trimester like the abortion-on-demand activists proclaimed; it began the instant a man's seed met a woman's egg. To abort an innocent child was murder, pure and simple, and the purveyors of this unholy commerce, the abortionists and their ilk, needed to be taught a lesson.

Murdering God's helpless children would not be tolerated!

Truscott watched with breathless anticipation as the Apostle opened the front door and stepped inside. A thin smile took root on his face, and his eyes shone harshly.

Let the lesson begin.

CHAPTER 96

BENJAMIN LOCKE sat in his office at American Patriots headquarters, feeling a tide of desperation washing over him. What was he doing ordering the political assassination of yet another human being, even if it was in a patriotic cause to make the country he loved better and stronger? What right did he have to play judge, jury, executioner, and final arbiter of the nation's fate? The guilt tore him up inside: he couldn't help but feel like a tragic figure from the Old Testament. Would he be banished to fiery hell and damnation in the afterlife for what he had done? And for what he was about to do?

And yet, there was really no way out. He had committed himself to America's return to glory, to her unquestioned exceptionalism in the world—no matter what the cost.

His cell phone rang. Jerking reflexively in his high-backed leather chair, he quickly scanned the caller ID. He was surprised to see that it was his wife.

Knowing that she was still angry at him, he was careful to speak to her in a soft, respectful voice. "Hello, dear. I am truly sorry for what happened yesterday."

"That's not why I'm calling, Benjamin."

Benjamin? Whenever she called him that he was in serious trouble.

"It's about Susan."

"Has something happened to her?"

"She didn't go to school today. The front desk just called me."

"Do you have any idea where she could be?"

"No, and I haven't been able to reach her on her cell phone. I'm worried, Benjamin."

He thought for a moment. "With everything that's happened, perhaps she just needed some time to think about things."

"No, it's more than that. She's not just playing hooky from school."

"How do you know?"

"Because I just found out she lied to us about staying at Jeanette's last night."

"What?"

"I called Jeanette's mother after the school called me and she told me that Susan wasn't there last night. Our daughter lied to us, Benjamin. I'm worried about her, especially with this whole thing about the abortion."

His cell phone vibrated. He quickly looked at the number, recognizing it instantly.

"What are we going to do, Benjamin? Do you think she's run away?"

He continued to study the phone: it was the Apostle on the other end. He had told him not to call—in fact, he had said that he would contact the assassin if and when he found out more information on what Truscott was up to—so Locke knew it had to be important. The ever-loyal Apostle would not violate a direct order without a very good reason.

Should I answer it or stay on the line with my wife?

"Benjamin, are you listening to me? I said I'm worried sick about Susan and afraid she may have run away."

"Yes, dear, I'm worried sick too." *Quick, should I answer or not?*

Her tone was urgent: "Well, what are we going to do?"

The phone was still vibrating. "I don't know yet. I'm trying to think."

"My God, she could have been kidnapped. Anything could have happened to her."

His cell phone stopped vibrating. He had missed the call and the Apostle was now leaving a message on his voice mail. That settled it: he would first finish up with his wife and then listen to the message and call the Apostle back in a few minutes.

"I have a bad feeling about this, Benjamin. She's never done anything like this before."

"Don't worry, dear, I'll take care of it. I'll make some calls."

"I'm worried sick. What if she's run away?"

"I'm sure she just wanted some time to herself."

"I'm going to call Todd's parents. Maybe she's with Todd."

He felt a jolt of anger at the mention of the irresponsible boy who had gotten his daughter in this predicament in the first place. "Please don't do that. Todd's parents don't need to get involved."

"Then I'm at least going to call the school and find out if Todd's missing too."

He considered this a moment. If his wife contacted the school, at least they would know for certain whether or not Susan was with Todd. "Okay go ahead and call the school then call me right back. And Mary."

"Yes."

"I'm sorry about losing my temper yesterday."

"I know you are, dear. I know you are."

"Wait, there's one more thing."

"Yes, dear?"

He could hear her sniffling now and felt badly for her. "Everything's going to be all right. I promise."

"I love you," she said.

"I love you too."

When she hung up, he quickly brought up the voicemail message from the Apostle. The modulated voice in the recording came across in a low, robotic tone.

"It's me. I know you said not to contact you, but the situation has changed. Skull Eyes and the colonel moved up the timetable and I'm here at the clinic in Widefield. I know you wanted to handle this matter personally, but I thought you should know what's happened. I'm turning off my cell now so this is the last you're going to hear from me until it's over. It's going to be bloody, Mr. Chairman, and it's going to be all over the national news. I just wanted to brief you before I go in. Over and out."

Punching off, Locke blew out a heavy sigh. What a disaster? Skull Eyes and the colonel had gone rogue after all and now innocent people were to be slaughtered! Locke may have been deeply opposed to abortion, but he would never sanction the murder of innocent people unless it was to make America great and strong, as was the case with Kieger and now Fowler. It seemed unthinkable that the greedy bastards would try to seize the leadership of the Coalition from him, but now he knew that they were actually going through with it. They had moved up the timetable and were executing the contract—and in the process they were hoping to oust him from his seat as chairman of the Committee!

But he would stop them. All he had to do was call off the Apostle.

But there was no way to get in touch with him. The Apostle had turned off his cell. *Dear Lord!*

Then he thought of something even worse.

The Family Planning Center in Widefield was the very same clinic where Susan and Todd had met with Dr. Sivy. What if by chance that's where Susan was now? What if that was why she hadn't gone to school today?

He had a sudden sick feeling inside.

Could his beloved daughter actually be getting an abortion? He had never thought that Susan would go through with it, but now he had the sinking premonition that that's precisely what she was doing.

Feeling his heart fill with desperation, he dialed his daughter's cell phone. No answer. He tried again. Still no answer. Then he called the Apostle to call him off, hoping he hadn't turned off his cell quite yet. But as expected there was no answer—he was sent straight into voicemail.

With panicky fingers, he dialed his wife at home, but the line was busy. He then tried her cell, but still no luck. *Good Lord!* She was either not answering or didn't have her cellphone with her.

He tried all three numbers again. Still no answer from any of them.

He snatched up his computer mouse and quickly performed an Internet search, pulling up the address and phone number of the Family Planning Center in Widefield, south of Colorado Springs. When he found the phone number, he quickly dialed it to warn everyone to leave the clinic at once.

But there was no answer there either.

The breath left him all at once and he thought he would faint. He had a sudden cruel, heartless certainty in his gut that his daughter's life was in imminent danger. It was as if God was delivering him a clear, unambiguous revelation of Himself and His will.

He felt his throat go dry as a cement kiln. *Dear Lord, please, not my baby girl!*

He grabbed his car keys from his top desk drawer, jumped up from his seat, and flew out the room.

CHAPTER 97

THE APOSTLE'S FIRST TASK WAS TO TAKE A QUICK INVENTORY.

He counted two young women in the waiting area, a security guard, and a receptionist. That left two doctors and four nurses down the hall in the rooms of slaughter, plus however many patients were at this very moment sacrificing the innocent to a cruel and grisly death. Outwardly, he was calm and commanding as he walked toward the reception desk, but inside he throbbed with sexual excitement.

There were so many victims to choose from. *But who will be the one? The receptionist? No. One of the Jezebels in the waiting area? No. How about one of the nurses? Yes, a nurse would do nicely.* He would take the most terrified-looking one and throw her onto the abortionist's table, the sacrificial altar where these unholy women set aside their morality for the quick fix. Then he would spread her legs just like a doctor and watch the fear on her face turn to pure horror as he performed his little routine, careful to hold back at the very end. He could feel himself growing hard at the very thought.

It was all choreographed in his mind.

The security guard stepped forward from the edge of the receptionist's desk and gave the Apostle a once-over. The Apostle took the opportunity to scrutinize his lone adversary, the only person with a remote chance of preventing what was about to happen. He saw nothing to change his initial impression. In his early twenties, pimples still on his face, the guard was too young and inexperienced to be the first and last line of defense for what was about to turn into a bloody war zone. He was armed with a .38, but probably hadn't fired the weapon since his training, and he had most certainly never pointed it another human being. In watching the young guard make his rounds around the building earlier in the morning, before the clinic had opened, the Apostle had noted that he seemed not only green but a touch skittish. He suspected that the kid was filling in for a regular, more experienced guard.

The young man was about to pay dearly for his lack of experience. And then the priority would be to kill all the clinic personnel and visitors as quickly as possible, before they had a chance to hide out and achieve full lock down in the engineered safe spaces. But with his police uniform, he already had inside access and would likely gain maximum penetration into the various rooms of the clinic once the opening salvo was fired.

The Apostle gave his patented I'm-a-cop-so-everything's-okay smile.

"Good morning, I'm Sergeant Wilson," he said politely to both the security guard and receptionist.

"Are you here about the security cameras?" the guard asked worriedly.

The Apostle suppressed the urge to gloat. The electrical short he had arranged to strike at precisely quarter to nine, fifteen minutes before the clinic opened for business, had come off perfectly. All of the security cameras were inoperable, which meant there would be no visual record of his presence here. The sabotage would, of course, be identified by the crime scene team, but he could live with that.

"No, I'm here about an email message intercepted by the FBI regarding this facility. I hate to call it a *threat*, but that's the word the FBI used. I'm here to follow up."

The guard's eyes showed genuine animal fear. "Our security cameras are down. Do you think it's related to the threat?" the kid asked.

"I doubt it," the Apostle replied, smiling reassuringly at him and the receptionist. "Usually these emails turn out to be false alarms. And your cameras...it's probably just an electrical glitch. We have the same problem downtown all the time."

That seemed to make the guard and the receptionist both feel better. But the guard still looked tense as he glanced out the front door at the protesters. Did the kid have a sixth sense about what was about to happen, or was he always on edge like this with the protesters outside? *Whatever the case*, thought the Apostle, *I have to take him out first.*

The Apostle smiled at him, like a kindly uncle. "Just to be safe, why don't I take a look around? But first, can you please show me the control panel for the security cameras. That's the best place to start."

The guard nodded. "Yeah, sure."

They turned to walk down the hallway just as a nurse walked up. "Kay," she announced to the girl in the Colorado College sweatshirt. "Dr. Murray will see you now."

At that instant, the receptionist's telephone rang and two more nurses appeared.

The Apostle felt a sudden rush of urgency. If he made his move now, he could take out seven of them right here in the lobby and still have surprise on his side for the others down the hallway in the examination rooms.

Take them, a voice called out inside. *Take them now!*

The Apostle's hand was a blur as he jerked out his noise-suppressed sidearm and shot the young guard two times in the face at point-blank range.

The kid didn't even have time to have time to reach for his gun.

The two young women in the waiting area screamed.

The three nurses and the receptionist were next. The Apostle delivered an instantly fatal, point-blank head shot to each of them. Then he twirled around to take a bead on the young woman in the Colorado College sweatshirt, who had stood up and taken a few steps toward him prior to the first shot.

The telephone at the front desk continued to ring.

"No, please," whimpered the college girl. "I-I only came here for a diaphragm."

"Liar!" He pumped two bullets into her chest. She fell down hard, shuddering convulsively. He'd seen this type of wound many times before during Desert Storm; she would be dead in less than two minutes as her lungs filled with blood.

The Apostle quickly locked onto the other young woman, a teenager. He saw a look of fear, but there was something else, something that bothered him. There was disgust, loathing. He had the feeling he had seen her somewhere before, but he couldn't remember where. Something about the way the girl looked at him, her familiarity, made him hesitate.

The moment of hesitation proved costly.

With surprising quickness, she bolted from the couch and darted for the front door. He squeezed the trigger, a split second too late, and the shot struck her in the shoulder. She lurched forward from the impact, jerked open the door handle, and collapsed in the open doorway in full view of the protesters and any passersby outside.

"Help!" Susan Locke called out to the people in the parking lot. "Somebody help me!"

Several protesters looked over with astonishment. "She's bleeding!" one cried.

"My God!" another exclaimed. "Look what those butchers have done to her!"

The Apostle grabbed the girl by the hair, dragged her back inside, and shot her again.

Her body went limp.

But the damage was done. Now the protesters realized what was going on and were sending an alarm through their ranks. Hearing the commotion, the Apostle knew he had to hurry if he was to complete the most important part of his mission: killing the doctors. Unfortunately, he would not have time for his little sexual escapade. That would have to wait for another time and place.

Leaving the girl prostrate in her own blood, he charged down the hallway, muttering a prayer for all the unborn children whose lives had been taken at the hands of the evil abortionist.

He opened the first door on his left and found the first doctor, Dr. Murray, bent over a washbasin scrubbing his hands. With the water running, the silenced weapon, and the meticulous soundproofing of the rooms, the doctor apparently hadn't even heard the gunshots. The Apostle shot him twice in the back of the head at close range, splattering grayish-pink brain matter against the mirror above the basin. As the doctor fell, he smashed against a tray of surgical instruments, sending them clattering to the floor.

Too damned loud!

Wasting no time, the Apostle bolted from the room. As he turned the corner, he saw the second doctor emerge from the examination room next door.

The Apostle gave a mirthless smile as he read the nameplate. "Dr. Sivy, I presume."

"What's going on here, Officer..." The words were left hanging, as the doctor, initially taken in by the uniform, realized the Apostle was no ordinary policeman.

"I'm just doing a little housecleaning—and you're next on my list."

The Apostle fired twice; a pair of red blots appeared on the doctor's chest.

The man staggered back and the Apostle finished him off with a kill shot to the temple. Then he crept into the examination room. A black nurse was struggling frantically to open the window to escape, begging for God's help.

His face hardened. *You shouldn't be praying for your own life, but for the hundreds, maybe even thousands, you have helped kill!*

She looked back over her shoulder, her face filled with terror, and for an instant he held her gaze, raping her with his eyes. He fired two rapid bursts at her back and she fell to the floor.

It was then he heard the sounds.

A squeaking hinge, followed by a gasp of shock. It had definitely come from somewhere nearby—and it meant only one thing.

There was someone else in the abortion clinic. Someone he hadn't accounted for.

CHAPTER 98

JENNIFER SLIPPED QUIETLY back into the bathroom, hoping feverishly she hadn't been discovered. When she had first heard the commotion, she had no idea what it was about; but now, after seeing the bloody bodies splayed on the floor, she realized what was happening. If she could remain hidden, she might live through this murderous rampage.

She heard footsteps.

They were coming closer, tapping lightly against the floor like a quietly ticking time bomb. The methodical footfall of a killer—a vicious holy warrior who thought that doctors and nurses who performed legitimate medical services were the enemy. It was so very American, a coward with a gun, going berserk. And he was heading her way.

Damn, you're trapped! There's no way out of here!

She felt like a cornered animal and wondered what had happened to Susan. Had the killer gone after only the doctors and support staff? Maybe he had told Susan and the other girl to lie down, remain silent, and he would spare their lives. Jennifer could only hope so because there was nothing she could do to help Susan now.

The footsteps grew louder.

You have to do something, Jennifer. Don't be a victim. Think!

Her best—hell her *only*—chance was to bash the killer over the head as he came into the bathroom. But she needed something big, something solid, something...she ran into the stall and yanked the lid off the toilet's water tank. The slab of porcelain was heavy enough to serve as a weapon. Tiptoeing back to the door, she choreographed the next few moments in her mind.

The footsteps stopped in front of the door.

She tried not to make a sound as she waited there poised with the slab of porcelain, her heart racing in her chest, the tense seconds ticking off. She had never felt so terrified before in her life.

The door flew open and Jennifer was smashed against the wall, the air leaving her lungs. Momentarily paralyzed, gasping at an atmosphere suddenly devoid of oxygen, her mind flashed an epitaph of hopelessness.

Goodbye Ken, goodbye Pulitzer, goodbye Scarlet-Fire, goodbye life.

Then the anger ignited within her like a flash fire.

I refuse to die like this! I will not be a helpless victim!

Willing herself to life, she drove into the door with her shoulder before the killer could enter the bathroom. She heard a heavy grunt and a shot ring out. She lunged forward and drove into the door again, then moved instinctively from behind the door as it swung forward and slammed against the wall. The man rebounded off the door as it struck the wall and turned toward her. But before he could fire his gun, she swung the slab of porcelain at him like a Louisville Slugger.

The stroke would have made the Great Bambino proud.

She caught him squarely in the jaw. His head jerked back like a prizefighter struck by a savage roundhouse right.

Stunned by the blow, he staggered against the door and looked at her dazedly. For the first time, she got a good look at him: a cop, or more likely, a psycho dressed like a cop. Though he was momentarily disabled, she could see the alpha-male-killer lurking beneath the policeman's cap and dark shades. This was a man who knew only too well how to dispatch people quickly and efficiently, without any sense of guilt or remorse. This was a man who deserved to die.

She hit him again, this time in the arm, thrusting downward like a guillotine. The blow dislodged the semiautomatic in his right hand and it skidded across the floor of the bathroom. She struck him again in the jaw for good measure, dropped the lid, and scrambled to scoop up the gun.

She still had not taken a breath.

When she turned around clutching the gun, the killer was gone. She thought about chasing after him, but there was no air in her lungs. She doubled over struggling to catch her breath. The sound of choppy footsteps receded down the hallway and then faded out altogether.

She collapsed against the wall, feeling as weak as a baby. *Where did all my strength go?*

A moment later, tires squealed behind the clinic. She continued to suck in air, greedily, like a resurfacing pearl diver. Finally, she willed herself to her feet and stepped out into the hallway, gripping the gun.

The clinic had turned into a combat zone.

There were bodies strewn about, smears and pools of blood, glossy and deep vermillion against the aseptic white floor. By the time she reached the receptionist's desk, she felt nauseated. It was unthinkable that such carnage could have taken place in the time it took her to go to the bathroom. She looked around for Susan, but couldn't see her anywhere.

Where has she gone? Did she get away?

She heard a commotion outside now, urgent voices and the distant drone of sirens. Her mind was numb with shock and grief; she was physically drained. Like a sleepwalker, she opened the door and stepped into the brisk morning air, unaware that she still clutched the pistol in her right hand.

CHAPTER 99

THE CADILLAC SCREAMED DOWN THE HILL.

Behind the wheel, Benjamin Bradford Locke slapped his foot down on the accelerator and the luxury car shot forward like a thoroughbred. He was muttering Scripture to himself—something from Amos about women with child being ripped up in Gilead—but the fierce determination on his face revealed every shred of concentration was on reaching his beloved daughter.

Seconds earlier, from a distance, he had witnessed Susan pushing open the front door and starting to crawl along the walkway leading to the parking lot. She was covered in blood, clawing at the concrete, and all he could think was, *How in God's name could I have allowed this to happen?*

The breath was hot in his throat. He was fueled by unbearable thoughts of a life without his beloved daughter.

I must save her!

He took a sharp right into a vacant lot for a more direct route to the clinic. A narrow bike path cut through the field, and as the tires gripped its loamy surface, a long brown cloud of dust rose up behind the racing vehicle like a jet plume. The front tire hit a bump. The Cad bounded in the air, coming down hard and jerking right. Locke struggled to keep the vehicle on the trail and away from the concrete blocks rising like small islands in the deep grass. The tires churned and pebbles ricocheted noisily against the grill of the Cadillac.

Eventually the trail leveled off, joining with a road that wrapped around the lot and led to the clinic. Locke jerked the wheel left and went flying into the street, sparks flying as the front bumper caught asphalt. He prayed desperately that Susan would live. At least she was moving under her own power. He forced himself to dam back the torrent of guilt flooding through him.

What have Skull Eyes and the colonel done? What have I done?

He nearly sideswiped a silver Mercedes as he screamed towards the parking lot entrance. To his surprise, behind the wheel he saw Joseph Truscott. Both of their mouths opened in astonishment, and then Skull Eyes gunned the engine and blasted down the road in the opposite direction.

Locke gritted his teeth. *You bastard, I'm going to draw and quarter you myself once I save my daughter!*

He flew into the parking lot and screeched to a halt. Scrambling from the running Cadillac, he dashed like a guided missile toward Susan. There was pandemonium everywhere, people running, screaming, sirens shrieking nearby. Most of the people were protesters bolting for their vehicles, but others were passersby that had stopped to see what all the commotion was about. He bulled his way through the frenzied crowd to the grassy lawn where his daughter lay. Two women and a man knelt around her prostrate body.

"Susan, darling, I am here!" he cried, kneeling next to her and taking her hand.

She looked up at him through foggy, half-lidded eyes. Her breaths came in ragged gasps and her yellow Cardigan sweater was soaked with blood. He gripped her hand harder, hoping to transfer his bodily strength to her. But she was limp, cool to the touch.

"Jesus is with you now. His strength will carry you through."

He placed his suit coat under her head and she looked up at him like she wanted to say something. But no words came out. He gripped her hand tighter. Her skin was clammy, her face anemic from loss of blood. The sirens were loud now, shrieking from the north.

"Just hang on, Susan—the ambulance is coming."

Her eyes rolled in the back of her head and she took on a glazed look.

And then a strange thing happened.

Her body shuddered and the glazed look disappeared. There was a look of intense focus, followed by an expression that was accusatory, betrayed.

"How could you do this, Daddy? How could you?"

Locke was taken aback. "What? What are you talking about?"

"How could you do this to me, Daddy?"

His face flushed with guilt. "My God, no...I had nothing to do with this, I promise!" *But you didn't stop it until it was too late either,* his inner voice reminded him.

He looked at the three faces gathered around him and saw the darkening hue of suspicion. From the doorway of the clinic stepped Jennifer Odden, looking dazed and carrying a gun. At first, he was surprised to see her, but then he understood why she was here: to give moral support to Susan while she committed her murderous act. Somehow Susan must have befriended the woman—Marlene had informed him that the two had spoken at the office two days ago—and they had come here together to snuff out the life that grew inside his daughter. Jennifer must have somehow managed to wrestle the Apostle's gun away from him and forced him to flee.

She is one tough woman all right, but she will pay for her treachery! I'll make certain of that!

Suddenly, in that tense moment, every shred of anger he felt at the unfairness and tragedy of his daughter's horrible fate he directed at Jennifer Odden. He rose to his feet and pointed accusingly at her.

"There she is! There's the killer!"

CHAPTER 100

JENNIFER FROZE.

In a state of shock, she couldn't bring herself to put down the gun or utter a single word in her self-defense. She was too shaken—not only by the grisly death scene inside the clinic but by Locke's accusation—to move or speak.

She stood there, stunned, like a deer trapped in headlights.

In the parking lot, engines revved, cars bolted. Nearly all of the protesters were driving away in panic. They wanted nothing to do with what had just happened.

Jennifer stared blankly at Locke and the three people kneeling next to Susan's motionless body. All but the Christian leader watched her fearfully, as if she might unleash a storm of lead at the slightest twitch. The moment seemed suspended in time, like a slowly unfolding nightmare. Though she had done nothing wrong, she felt as if she were a cold-blooded murderer, a pariah. It sickened her to think anyone could believe her responsible for this disaster. It went against everything she stood for.

She saw the blood on Susan's clothes, and her legs began to move forward down the walkway, slowly, tentatively.

Before she had made it ten steps, a pair of police cruisers screeched to a halt in the parking lot. Four guns quickly locked onto her.

"Drop your weapon—now!"

For the second time of the day, Jennifer felt her life flash before her eyes. Her head began to spin and her knees threatened to buckle beneath her. It was the same sickening sensation she had felt when her father had triumphed over her.

"Put the gun down now—or we *will* fire!"

Jennifer dropped the gun to the pavement.

The next thing she knew she was knocked viciously to the concrete and handcuffed. As she was being roughly handled, she felt as though the rest of the world had gone stark raving mad and she was the only sane person left on the planet.

This is unreal. How can they think I'm the killer? Don't they know they have the wrong person?

Finally, her mouth moved by a will of its own. "I didn't do it," she protested. "There was a man, a policeman. He did it. He killed everyone. I hit him and he dropped his gun and ran."

Without responding, the cops jerked her to her feet and forced her toward a police car. An ambulance pulled to the curb as three more police cruisers raced toward the scene.

When Jennifer saw Susan's body up close, she shook her head. "I am so sorry, Susan," she said tearfully.

The cops tightened their grip and shoved her toward the cruiser as a pair of paramedics rushed forward with a stretcher.

"Susan!" Jennifer cried, but she could see the girl was dead.

And then Benjamin Locke was right there in front of her. He looked violently angry and tragically sad at the same time, with big fat tears in his eyes and his huge chest pumping like a piston, as only a parent can look who has lost a beloved child and desperately needs someone to blame.

"You murdered my daughter in cold blood," he snarled.

"I didn't do it. I was here for Susan, not to hurt anyone."

"No, you killed her all right. You brought her here and you killed her just as Cain slayed his own brother Abel."

"No, that's not true!" she pleaded. "That's not how it happened!"

A Channel Nine news truck screeched into the parking lot. A Hispanic female reporter and pony-tailed cameraman scrambled from the vehicle and sprinted towards them.

When Jennifer reached the police car, she turned to look back at Susan one last time, but Locke and the paramedics blocked her view of the body. The illustrious Christian leader—a giant, hulking, tragic figure in the amber morning light—was appealing to Almighty God and openly weeping now.

Then she was shoved into the cruiser with the Channel Nine news camera rolling.

CHAPTER 101

AT PRECISELY ELEVEN A.M., a metallic green Buick LeSabre with U.S. government tags pulled to the curb at the corner of Seventeenth and Welton in downtown Denver. An attractive woman, who looked ten years younger than her actual age, climbed into the back seat before the light changed. She wore a conservative gray business suit with a black tie. Dark stockings plunged down to a pair of ebony high heels. Her brunette hair was elegantly coiffed, and the eyes beneath her clear, normal-vision glasses were jade-green like a feline's. She had Fortune 500 written all over her, a high-powered businesswoman out for a power lunch. But then again, she should have had the glow of money about her; only this morning an additional two million dollars had been quietly deposited into her numbered Geneva bank account, and by tomorrow, the amount would be doubled.

The door closed and the car turned right onto Seventeenth, quickly merging with the traffic. The man sitting next to Skyler opened a large suitcase so new it smelled of fresh leather. Without saying a word, she examined the contents: a navy-blue, one-piece SWAT-style uniform with a matching cap and jacket (the standard uniform of the FBI Critical Incident Response Group); a bullet-proof Kevlar vest, Glock 17 semiautomatic pistol with spare magazines, and Saber two-way radio (also FBI standard-issue); a pair of Leica laser-range-finding binoculars; an official CIRG controlled-access badge, pictureless and non-laminated; and a sealed manila envelope containing operational instructions. Skyler checked the badge to make sure the name was the same as last time; she would insert a picture and laminate the badge later. Confident she had everything required, she snapped the case closed.

"Any last minute changes?" Skyler asked.

The man looked down his nose at her. He thought she was an unimportant pawn, a middle-woman whose sole job was to run interference for Gomez. Though it nettled her, she knew it was best this way. The less he knew of her identity and role in the assignment, the better. But there was something else in his eyes, a salacious gleam. She wasn't important in her own right, but he still wanted to fuck her. That, more than his condescending air, pissed her off.

"Just one change—the firearm," he replied. "The Remington 700 is a no-go. It's to be a Winchester 70 instead."

Skyler frowned. *You've never fired a 70T.* "What kind of scope?" she asked, as the LeSabre turned right onto Broadway.

"Unertl 8X, externally adjusted. The rifle's been zeroed for five hundred yards."

You can fine-tune the setting in the field with the range-finder. "What about the stock?"

"Standard sportsman's," he said, eyeing her legs hungrily.

She ignored the indignity. "Suppressor?"

"Look, the details are in the packet," he said, tiring of her questions.

Skyler found his impertinence offensive and was tempted to smack him to show him some manners. But he was nothing more than an errand boy and she would be wasting her time. Besides, she had more important concerns on her mind—like the assignment.

She was not happy about the new conditions, but Plan A was still a damned good plan. True, there was now an added element of uncertainty since she would be using a rifle she had never fired before, and a model with which she was unfamiliar. But dropping a soft target from five hundred yards was not a difficult task for a shooter of her caliber. She would just have to make do.

"What about the cartridges?" Skyler asked.

"Explosive-tipped. Don't ask me what kind." He tapped on the suitcase. "It's all in there. Just get it to Mr. Gomez. *He'll* know what to do with it."

Skyler bit her lip to suppress her growing fury. "Will the target be wearing Kevlar?"

"Won't know until tomorrow."

The car turned onto Colfax, passed the Civic Center Plaza on the left, and took a right onto Fifteenth. "So it may take a head shot," she said, thinking aloud. "That will make things difficult."

"Not my problem," he said, looking at his watch. "Your guy's supposed to be the best. He can figure it out." His face took on a pernicious smirk. "And while he's doing that, why don't you and I go out tonight. I'll show you a good time—a *real* good time."

This was too much for Skyler to take. Turning her thumb into a weapon, she jabbed him in the eye.

He jerked back, groaning in agony.

The driver jerked his head around. "What the fuck is going on back there?"

"Nothing! Shut up and keep driving!"

He did as instructed.

She turned to the wounded man. "You must learn to treat women with respect."

"Jesus Christ, you could have blinded me!" he wailed, holding both hands over his eye.

God, you're pathetic. That was the thing about men: they could dish it out but they couldn't take it. As soon as a woman stood up for herself, men inevitably cried foul and exaggerated their own suffering. If only they knew how lucky they were, how much harder it was to be a woman—every day dealing with boorish, lecherous, overbearing men.

"Stop your whimpering—you're acting like a child," she scolded him.

He sat up and looked at her sheepishly, still covering his eye.

"I have one last question for you, and it's in your best interest to answer it honestly," she said, as the LeSabre turned onto Welton. "Who is my field contact—the same as last time?"

"That's need-to-know."

Skyler cut him a menacing look. The man's eyes flashed fearfully.

"Okay, okay. I'm dead serious—it really is need-to-know. Everything they want you to know is in there." He pointed to the suitcase again.

She squinted at him through disapproving eyes and called out to the driver. "Stop here!"

The car pulled to the curb. Skyler picked up the suitcase, opened the door, and stepped out. Before closing the door, she leaned in, her look hard and narrow.

"If I were you I'd learn better manners. That's no way to treat a lady."

And with that, she quickly vanished into the crowd.

CHAPTER 102

SHE HIT SEVENTEENTH and headed to her hotel. She was staying at the Brown Palace, the Mile High City's most historic lodging. It was built in 1892 when silver was king and the dusty old cowtown of Denver was a mere thirty-four years old and working mightily to live up to its new moniker as "The Queen City of the Plains." Soon the grand, triangular-shaped building came into view: nine stories of granite and red sandstone blending the ruggedness of the West with the sophistication of the East Coast Gilded Age.

Skyler crossed at Tremont and a dapperly dressed doorman opened the brass-handled door for her. Stepping inside, she walked past a small news shop and threaded her way through the soaring atrium lobby. Though lavishly appointed, it still exuded a certain rustic charm. Nine stories up, a stained glass canopy sparkled overhead. Important people had stayed here often, beginning in 1905 with Teddy Roosevelt. Inside the hallowed walls resided the whispered secrets of numerous presidents as well as powerful entrepreneurs, emperors, rock stars, and gods and goddesses of the stage and screen.

Skyler headed for the elevator carrying her suitcase in her right hand. She took the elevator to the eighth floor and walked down the hallway to her room, carrying herself with an air of importance befitting a high-level executive.

After securing both locks, she set the suitcase on the bed and took off her high heels. She pulled out her coded mobile and called Anthony at home. She longed to tell him how she felt about him, how all this would soon be over and they would be together again. She had spoken with him early this morning when she had touched down at DIA, but she needed to hear his voice again. She had already tried him twice today, but he hadn't been in.

The phone rang four times with no answer. She didn't want to leave her voice on Anthony's answering machine, so she hung up and decided to try again later.

She went to the bed and opened the suitcase, pulling out the uniform, raid jacket, cap, pistol, CIRG badge, and binoculars and setting them on the bed. Over the next few minutes, she affixed a color photograph of herself to the badge and carefully sealed the ID with colorless, self-laminating plastic. Then she pulled a Florida driver's license from her bag and compared it to the badge. Both ID's bore the name Carey Firestone and showed a physically fit, thirty-something woman with close-cropped, platinum-blond hair and a small scar on the chin. Both pictures also bore a striking resemblance to a certain female FBI agent from the Miami field office. Except the real Carey Firestone had no scar.

With the picture IDs in order, she donned the full uniform, including her false FBI creds, also in the name Carey Firestone. Examining herself in the mirror, she was pleased with the masquerade. She looked the part of a CIRG spotter perfectly. She would have no trouble making it through the checkpoints to her sniping position on the roof of the *Denver Tribune* Tower. The uniform, the binoculars, the creds—they made her look so official, so authorized.

Tomorrow I will be Carey Firestone from the Miami field office.

Of course, she would have to carefully alter her physical appearance to complete the transformation. After last night, the FBI would have put together a halfway decent sketch of her, or a computer-generated image of a female John Doe, although she had seen nothing on the Net or in the news yet. But changing physically—not just clothes but hair, eyes, and overall appearance—was never difficult for Skyler. Facial features could be altered with a simple actor's kit. Height could be added or taken away, as could weight, through the clever application of padding. Though she preferred wigs, hair could be manipulated through coloring, combing, or cutting.

From years of experience, she knew how to alter her appearance dramatically to achieve the desired effect. Male or female? Full-figured or slender? Old or youthful? Clothes were definitely a big part of it, but Skyler liked to think her facial expressions, contrived accents, and mannerisms were just as critical. Though people saw what they wanted to see in a person, she preferred to think of herself as an actress given the unenviable task of winning over an audience while handicapped with a horrendous script. She took pride in her own ability to *become* someone else, to transform herself and fool those around her with sheer skill and cunning.

It was a part of the game she would miss.

CHAPTER 103

DECIDING TO RECON the target area before lunch, she took off her uniform, put everything back neatly in the suitcase, and placed it under the bed. Then she put on her green jogging outfit and running shoes. Before going out, she tried Anthony once more, but he still wasn't in.

My God, have the police picked him up?

With this new source of worry weighing heavily on her mind, she took Welton to the Sixteenth Street Mall, hung a left, and jogged to the *Denver Tribune* Tower. The sky was dull pewter broken in places by white, wedge-shaped clouds with gray rims. The temperature had climbed into the midforties. She followed the walking ramp along the south side of the building until she reached a paved courtyard overlooking the Civic Center Plaza.

She stopped to study the line of fire from the Tower to the speakers' platform at the west end of the plaza, in front of the City and County Building. Five hundred yards plus, over trees, with a slight left to right crosswind if she made the shot today. It was unfortunate she had to use an unfamiliar rifle, but five hundred yards was five hundred yards. She could score ten-shot groups in a six-inch diameter circle, the equivalent of a head shot, with a .22 at that range—as long as the wind wasn't too strong. Wind was the one critical element, for humidity, driving rain, and rising heat waves were not in the forecast for tomorrow. A lot depended on whether Fowler wore Kevlar. If she had to make a head shot in a fierce crosswind, tomorrow could prove one tough assignment.

Resuming her jog, she headed south across Colfax, crossing at Lincoln. She passed a reddish-brown column with a sharp white point, the state's war memorial for veterans of modern wars. There was an eclectic assortment of people in the plaza: nattily-clad business drones, homeless people, joggers like Skyler, state employees heading off for two hour lunches, and the occasional out-of-place-looking tourist. Skyler headed through a copse of trees where squirrels foraged about and chased one another. Overhead she saw a squadron of geese, flying south in tight formation, a symmetrical V against the pewter sky.

Despite the chill, she was sweating now and her legs had found a pleasant rhythm. Soon she saw the newly erected platform where tomorrow Katherine Fowler would address a sorrowful nation. Standing in the same spot where William Kieger had fallen, Fowler would not only pay tribute to him, but defiantly protest the assassination. She would make a bold political statement, but Skyler knew it would be her last.

She stopped running to check out the platform. She had to do so from a distance because the area was cordoned off. There were a dozen cops and several plainclothed law enforcement people who looked like Secret Service. Bomb-sniffing German shepherds were being led to the platform. Banks of magnetometers were set up at all the entrances to the enclosed area.

Her mind drifted into the shooter's netherworld—to holding patterns, crosshairs, mil dots, and windage adjustments. She flashed back to last Sunday, to Kieger's exploding chest, to the spurting blood. She saw it clearly through her scope, as if he was standing right in front of her.

And then a totally unexpected thing happened.

She was suddenly overcome with lightheadedness. The world began to spin around her and she lost all sense of balance. Her mind went black and she swooned, falling hard to the pavement.

When she came to minutes later, there were three strangers standing over her, a businesswoman and two policemen.

"Are you all right there, miss?" one of the cops asked her, shaking her gently.

She had no idea where she was. "What?" she mumbled, trying to blink away the fog.

"Are you okay? You just fell down."

"Oh," she said, and then she remembered fainting. "I was jogging and...I...I just collapsed. My blood sugar must be low." She started to get up.

"Here let me help you," the other cop said, and he reached down to lift her up.

"Thanks," Skyler said, rubbing the back of her head. "I'll be fine—I just need to get some food."

"You sure you're okay?" the businesswoman asked.

"In perfect working order," Skyler said, giving an appreciative smile. "Thank you for helping me." Without saying anything more she walked off.

Heading towards Colfax, she wondered what was happening. *Am I totally losing it, or just having second thoughts because Fowler's a woman?*

When she reached the busy avenue, she stood dazedly at the crosswalk and was assaulted by the jarring cacophony of the city: groaning engines, screeching tires, beeping horns, the drone of a distant siren. Her body was bathed in sweat from exertion, but the sweat had turned cold.

After fainting, she felt diminished somehow, powerless to control her own body.

She crossed the street and went to the mall, trying to sort it all out. Slowly, the pieces of the puzzle began to come together. It wasn't that her target this time was a woman—she was repelled by the very thought of killing anyone!

Before she had always been able to rationalize the killings by convincing herself that the real murderers were the men who hired her. Before she had carried out her assignments with cold mechanical swiftness, which was enough to insulate her from shame. But now, because of Anthony, everything had changed. The feelings of guilt and remorse were overtaking her. They were making her physically ill, sapping her control over her own body. Now the demons came on during the day, as well as the night, and she was unable to fight them off.

Leaving her to wonder: *How can I possibly pull this off when I'm falling apart?*

CHAPTER 104

PATTON SPENT THE MORNING hunched over a desk at the L.A. field office, reviewing the files Lorrie Elert had emailed him while listening to Bill Monroe and the Bluegrass Boys on his iPod. Most people listened to something placid and soothing, like classical music or jazz, to focus their concentration; for FBI Special Agent Kenneth Gregory Patton, the only thing that worked was frenetically dueling banjos, dobros, and mandolins.

Spread out before him were NCIC case files, Interpol alerts, police reports, CIA memos, and dossiers from friendly intelligence services around the world. Lorrie had done a remarkable job. In less than three days' time, she had developed a computer code that queried hundreds of thousands of records—asking critical questions about murder weapons, bullets, firing distances, and tactical elements—and spit out thirty-nine cases similar to the Kieger assassination based on key elements. Of the thirty-nine cases, Lorrie had narrowed down the list to fourteen cases that had more than three common elements with the Kieger murder. This is where it got interesting: the fourteen cases involved only four different suspects.

Jack Hammond, former British SAS commando turned professional assassin.

Habib Mustafa, former gold-medalist shooter in the 2000 Olympics, now Islamic State gunman believed to be responsible for five killings since 2012.

McKinley Taggert, American, ex-Special Forces sharpshooter, formerly of right-wing group Red State Confederacy, now contracting out to various criminal and corporate syndicates as a hit man.

And Diego Gomez, no previous military experience, reportedly a member of the Basque separatist movement Euskara, but also an independent contractor.

All of them were reputed world-class shooters as well as masters of disguise, but most importantly, they were active and their whereabouts unknown. They were the best candidates based on a query of thousands of case files worldwide.

Going over the dossiers a second time, Patton found the Basque Gomez the most promising suspect. He was the most recently active, with seven credited kills in the past decade. More importantly, all of his sanctions involved distances believed to be in excess of 500 yards, as well as heavy-caliber weaponry, including, on two occasions, .50-caliber armor-piercing incendiary cartridges. Interestingly, the seven confirmed kills were restricted to Europe, the U.S., Canada, and South America.

Gomez certainly had the qualifications to take out Kieger. And he did work the U.S. But there was a problem: he had no apparent connection to John or Jane Doe. The two artist's sketches of Gomez, produced by the French and Italian intelligence services, bore only a vague resemblance to both. Not only that, the French sketch had little in common with the Italian one. There was one surveillance photograph, taken in Spain, but it was too grainy for a positive ID. Somehow Gomez had managed to stay in business for at least a decade without anyone taking a high-quality photo of him.

Closing the file, Patton decided to catalogue Gomez for the time being. He might prove important later, but for now he was just a mystery man.

Suddenly, Patton felt a hand on his shoulder.

He nearly jumped up from his seat, so intensely focused was he on the file in front of him. Turning around, he half-expected to see Diego Gomez standing there pointing a Glock at him.

But it was only Sharp, as usual looking none too pleased. The ASAC motioned for him to remove his earphones, which he did.

"What's up, Henry?"

"Turn off that hillbilly music and get your butt in gear. We have to get to the goddamned airport!"

Patton looked at his watch. "Jesus, it's nine already?"

"We'll meet you at the elevator. Hurry up!" and he was gone.

Patton scooped up all his paperwork and stuffed it in his briefcase along with his iPod. He and Sharp were flying back to Denver with Schmidt and Barr Hogen, Jane Doe's neighbor, who were scheduled to review the Union Plaza Building security tapes this afternoon. Taylor had flown back late last night to help with the security detail for Fowler's speech.

Rising from his chair, Patton turned off the light and shut the door. As he stepped into the hallway, he thought back to something he had seen on the security tapes of John Doe.

A fistful of breath kicked out his lungs as he was struck with a thought.

What if John Doe, Jane Doe, and Gomez are the fucking same person!

CHAPTER 105

AFTER BEING FINGERPRINTED AND PHOTOGRAPHED, Jennifer sat for over an hour on a cold steel bench in a dirty, stench-ridden holding cell. It could have been anywhere, but just happened to be the Colorado Springs Police Department at 705 South Nevada Avenue.

Soon a sour-faced Betty Davis lookalike in a sharply creased uniform called her name. The woman escorted her to a spartan interrogation room with a brown pressboard table, metal folding chairs, and out-of-place pictures on the walls showing flashy race cars barreling up Pike's Peak during the yearly mountain auto race. Seated at the table were two men who gazed at her accusingly as she walked in.

"Sit down," the older of the two men commanded gruffly. He was ugly as sin, with a crush of fissures lining his face and a nose that looked like it had been broken several times. He was dressed in a cheap jacket and tie and his hair was flipped over the top of his head, like a mop, in a futile attempt to cover his bald spot. The younger guy was African-American, late-thirties, with ballooning biceps his neatly pressed police uniform failed to conceal.

Jennifer fought back the urge to scowl at them as she took her seat. She distrusted cops ever since they had overreacted at a Dead show years ago, firing pepper spray at her and a bunch of other peaceful kids for no reason. In fact, she didn't like law enforcement types in general, though she was willing to make an exception in Ken's case.

"I want to make a statement," she declared straight off.

"There will be time for that," the older man said. "First we have to read you your rights."

He leaned across the table and turned on the tape recorder. Two minutes later, the Miranda warning was complete and Jennifer had agreed to answer their questions without an attorney being present. After all, she was innocent and as long as she told the truth, she had nothing to fear. She also learned their names: the older, fifty-something guy was Chuck Pinkerton, Captain of the Operations Support Bureau, Investigations Division; the younger, black man was Marvin Hayes, a detective within the division. When they were finished with the preliminaries, Pinkerton said, "Go ahead."

"First off, I had nothing to do with this. You've got the wrong person and all you're doing is wasting time. You should be trying to find the real guy who did this."

The two homicide detectives said nothing, staring at her through crocodile eyes. Everything about them was unsympathetic, suspicious, quietly hostile.

"Okay," Pinkerton said with mock courtesy. "Why don't you tell us exactly what did go down?"

She did. It took twenty minutes with the detectives stopping her occasionally to ask questions. Jennifer was pleased the younger guy seemed to loosen up a bit. He nodded a couple times, which she took as a good sign. But the older one, Pinkerton, was sullen as a clam.

When she was finished, Pinkerton said, "I gotta be honest with you, your story sounds pretty far-fetched. You expect us to believe that it wasn't you, but a policeman, who shot everyone? And after he did this, you wrestled the gun away from him?"

"I didn't say he *was* a policeman. I said he was dressed like one. And I didn't wrestle the gun away from him. I hit him in the arm with a toilet lid. It was the only weapon I could find."

"A toilet lid, huh? And after that, you just picked up the gun and walked outside, is that it?"

"Yes, that's exactly how it went down." *Jesus, I can't believe this is really happening.*

Hayes said, "And how does Benjamin Locke fit in to all this? You said something about how it was all his fault."

Jennifer didn't like the distrusting look in his eyes. "I believe he was the one behind the attack."

Pinkerton frowned. "That's a strong allegation. Benjamin Locke is a world-renowned religious leader and pillar of this community."

She shook her head in disbelief. *Pillar? Anathema is more like it!*

"Mr. Locke's take is a little different. And so are the eyewitness accounts from the other six people we've interviewed." Pinkerton paused to glance over his notes. "Three of the witnesses said when you walked out of the clinic carrying the gun, you looked like a zombie. Like you were in a trance or something. Now why would you act like that if you were innocent? I would think you would be in a state of emergency, running to get help as fast as possible."

"I don't believe this. Why would I lie to you? I told you I'm a professional journalist not some anti-abortion freak."

They just stared at her as if she were a violent, deranged woman. "Do you have any actual evidence Benjamin Locke's involved?" Hayes asked.

"Well no, but what was he doing there at the clinic? When Susan and I were at the hotel, she told her parents she was staying at a friend's house.

So he couldn't have known she was going to the clinic this morning."

"And why were you hiding out at the Marriot? I'm not sure I caught that," pressed Pinkerton.

"We weren't *hiding out*. Susan came to me for help after her father attacked her."

"Attacked her?"

"Okay, he didn't actually attack her—he spanked her—but she was still scared to death."

"So he...he *spanked* his seventeen year old daughter, is that it?" Pinkerton looked at his black partner with the bulging biceps. "What's the world coming to?"

Jennifer was irked by his dismissive, condescending tone and shook her head in frustration. "You're really not getting any of this are you, Detective? Locke forbade her from getting an abortion, but she was set on doing it—that's the whole point of all this. That's why we decided to rent a room for the night, so we could sort everything out. We decided that I would drive her to the clinic this morning and that we wouldn't tell her parents about the abortion. The parental notification age in Colorado is sixteen so we were fully within our legal rights."

"Why didn't the two of you just stay at your place?" asked Hayes.

"I didn't want them to find us...I mean me."

"Who are *they*?"

"Locke, Marlene Tanner, and the others. Just...just forget that part. It's not relevant."

Pinkerton's eyebrows jumped up. "Not relevant? When there are eight corpses at the Coroner's Office and two people in critical condition, we'll decide what's relevant. You'd better start telling us the truth."

For the next thirty minutes, they grilled her about her relationship to Locke and his family, her purported job as a freelance journalist, and finally her role as an employee at AMP. As the interrogation went on, she began to wear down, overcome with frustration at her inability to convey her innocence. Toward the end, Pinkerton brought the line of questioning back to the clinic attack.

"When you were first taken into custody, you looked at Susan and said, 'I'm sorry, Susan.' What did you mean by that?"

"That I was sorry for what had happened to her."

"You mean that you were sorry for killing her."

"No, that's not what I meant," Jennifer said, rubbing her forehead in weary frustration. "You're...you're putting words in my mouth again."

"Were you keeping Susan Locke against her will?" asked Hayes. "Is that why you were at the hotel?"

"Of course not—I was her friend. That's why I took her to the clinic and stayed with her in the waiting area. To offer moral support."

"But you weren't with her in the waiting area," Pinkerton said, his voice carrying an accusatory undertone. "You were in the bathroom."

"Just for a minute and that's when all hell broke loose. I didn't know what was going on at first, until I heard the screaming." Her face turned fearful. "You've got to believe me—it's the truth."

Pinkerton eyed her skeptically. "It's a tough pill to swallow. Here you are, the only person to make it through this bloody rampage unscathed, telling us you stole the gun from this so-called policeman. Well, I hate to tell you this, but no one interviewed saw any uniformed officers until after the shootings, when the squad cars arrived on the scene."

Hayes frowned. "What I can't understand is if all these people were being gunned down, why didn't you make any effort to help them?"

Jennifer's eyes dropped to the table. *I should have done more. I should have tried to save Susan.*

"It just sounds too convenient," Pinkerton said. "There's supposed to be some cop there, or a guy dressed like a cop, but no one sees him. Then everyone gets shot but you. And finally just as the guy's escaping, you manage to knock the gun from his hands. You really expect us to believe you could disarm an armed man. I mean, how much do you weigh, one twenty tops?"

Now Jennifer's head swam with fear and she knew she was in real trouble. She felt like the innocent guy in *The Wrong Man* or *The Fugitive*. The interrogation was not going at all how she'd expected. There seemed to be nothing she could say to convince them of her innocence. How naive to have thought she could simply tell the truth and everything would be properly sorted out.

She felt herself being swept into a riptide. Somehow, she had to get in touch with Ken. Hopefully, he would be able to vouch for her and clear up this mess.

Pinkerton fixed her with a prosecutor's glare. "You'd better just cut the bullshit, lady, and tell us what really went down. Because we're going to go over it and over it and over it—until we get it goddamned right!"

CHAPTER 106

AT 1:38 P.M., Benjamin and Mary Locke walked out of the El Paso County Coroner's Office. A flock of reporters quickly engulfed them, shoving microphones in their faces and bombarding them with questions. The attack on the Family Planning Group clinic marked the most gruesome episode in Colorado Springs history and the media was in a state of frenzy. It already had its angle on the big story: CHRISTIAN-RIGHT LEADER'S PREGNANT DAUGHTER SLAIN BY ZEALOT AT ABORTION CLINIC. The irony was not lost on Locke, but what made his blood boil was that there was nothing he could do to prevent the media from carelessly slandering him and staining the memory of his poor daughter.

With the help of four uniformed cops, Locke fought his way through the agitated crowd. Reaching his silver Cadillac, he helped his wife to the passenger seat and then bulled his way through the microphones and cameras to the driver's side. With reporters banging on the windows, they drove off, leaving the news people to scramble to their satellite vans and follow.

His wife had met him at the Coroner's Office a half hour earlier. Locke had already given his version of the story to the police downtown, in the reassuring presence of his top attorney. Because of his sterling local reputation and vast wealth, as well as his friendship with Police Chief Bill Hanson, the cops had only questioned him a short time. When asked about what he was doing at the Family Planning Group clinic, he reported that he had discovered his daughter had met with a Dr. Sivy about getting an abortion and when she had not shown up to school this morning, he had driven to the clinic. He had planned to dissuade Susan from taking the life of her child, he admitted, but was completely shocked by what had happened at the clinic.

When they had identified Susan's body, the unspeakable pain on his wife's face as the cold steel tray was pulled out and the sheet lifted would be imprinted in his mind forever. But what pained him most of all was that he could have prevented his daughter's death. He should have confronted Truscott and the colonel right away and called off the entire operation. It wasn't the Apostle's fault: he had only been fulfilling a contract.

He and his wife did not speak on the way home. However, during the long strained silence, Locke sensed that she was suspicious of him. To mask his utter shame and guilt, he reminded himself that Susan's death was only an accident and no one, not even Skull Eyes or the colonel, had intended her to die. All the same, he despised himself for not acting more swiftly and putting a stop to the contract the instant he had first learned of it. At the tender age of seventeen, his daughter's life had been prematurely snuffed out and he would never know the many mountains she would have climbed.

As they drove up to their Tudor mansion, Locke hit a button to open the heavy steel gate. He pulled into the drive, the electric gate swinging closed behind him, and parked in front of the house. Benjamin Jr. walked outside to greet them just as the satellite vans screeched to a halt at the curb outside the estate.

By the time Locke stepped from the Cad, his wife was already heading briskly toward the front door. Without saying a word to Benjamin Jr., she dashed into the house.

Locke was puzzled. *Why is she being so hostile? Benjamin hasn't done anything wrong.*

The kid watched her step inside before giving a shrug and turning toward his father. "Is it true?" he asked as Locke walked up. "Is Jennifer Odden really the one who did it?"

"She was caught with a smoking gun in her hand."

"I always knew she was no good. You can tell by a person's eyes."

Locke ignored the ludicrous comment and pointed to the manila folder in his son's hand. "What's that?"

"The background info on Jennifer Odden that Archie asked me to track down."

Locke took the file. "Let's see what you've got," he said, wanting to take his mind off the tragedy of Susan's death.

They walked inside.

CHAPTER 107

THEY WENT TO THE STUDY. Locke took a seat at his desk and opened the file. With Benjamin Jr. looking on like an expectant puppy, Locke read the two-page summary of Jennifer Odden's life. Much of the material was from her resume on file at AMP, but Locke quickly noticed three new details.

The first was that the FBI Agent Kenneth Patton was not just an acquaintance of hers, as she had claimed, but the two had been romantically involved in college. Not only that, Patton had apparently gotten her pregnant. After staying in a home for unwed mothers in Indiana, she had given birth to a son and given it up for adoption, apparently without Patton's knowledge. Finally and most importantly, she was not a Christian activist, but a liberal freelance journalist from the modern Gomorrah, San Francisco. She had published numerous articles under the pen name Stella Blue for both the *Examiner* and *Chronicle* as well as several magazine articles for liberal billionaire activist Aaron Stavros' *The New Constitution* and other left-leaning magazines.

Paper-clipped to the summary were a dozen or so reprints of her articles. Locke scanned several of the unflattering titles: "American Patriots: The Four Horsemen of the Apocalypse," "Benjamin Locke—Dark Shadow of the Christian Right," "God, Homophobia, and the Republicans' Not-So-Big Tent," "The Swindler Pat Robertson," "A War Against Christians? Yeah, Right," and "Meet the GOP—God's Only Party."

Putting the file aside, Locke twisted with rage. Partly, he was angry with himself for not seeing through her subterfuge and exposing her for a charlatan. But most of the blame he put on his staff. *How could they have hired such a fraud? Why wasn't her background checked more thoroughly, especially once she was hired full-time?*

At this point, the only consolation seemed to be that she would pay dearly for her treachery. She was in police custody as the prime suspect in a major murder investigation. With any luck, she would be tried, convicted, and put behind bars for the rest of her natural days.

Locke looked curiously at his son. "How did you come by all this?"

The smugness returned to Benjamin Junior's fleshy face. "I got her basic history from her resume. Then I started calling around…her college, her parents, her old friends. I said she was applying for a position as a corporate communications specialist for a company with high-level security. Part of the application process was to conduct a thorough background check on her past. I said I had to have a complete record, including medical history information. Most everyone I talked to bought it. It's amazing how gullible people are. Her father gave me a lot of info. I don't think he likes her very much."

Locke reappraised his son in a new light. He wouldn't have thought the kid had it in him to follow through on such an important assignment. *Maybe he does have the right stuff for intelligence work after all.*

"I did good, didn't I, Dad?"

Locke rewarded him with a smile. "Yes, son, you did very well."

CHAPTER 108

MOMENTS LATER, Locke heard a noise outside the office in the hallway. It sounded like someone walking downstairs, but something about it didn't sound right. There was stealth in the footsteps. He paused from talking to his son to listen. There was a clicking sound. *The front door?* Then he heard a slamming sound. *Definitely the front door!*

He rushed to the window.

He saw his wife walking hurriedly towards her white Mercedes, carrying two large suitcases.

What in God's name is she doing?

Benjamin Jr. came to the window. "She's...she's leaving!"

Locke's stupefaction turned to anger. *Where does she think she's going?* He tromped out the office and down the hallway, his beefy son trailing him like an overfed Labrador.

When they reached the front door, Locke heard the sound of the Mercedes firing up. He threw open the door and saw his wife start to pull away in the car.

As if on cue, the reporters crowding the gate went into alert mode. Cameramen climbed up on the stone walls and started filming.

"What's gotten into her?" wondered Benjamin Jr. "Has she gone nuts?"

Without responding, Locke charged the moving Mercedes. Coming up on the passenger side, he saw a look of determination on his wife's face. In his peripheral vision, he also saw the two packed suitcases in the back seat. He pounded on the window with his left hand while struggling to yank open the handle of the front door with his right, but it was locked.

The car skidded to a halt.

Locke peered into the car, puffing, as Benjamin Jr. came running up.

The front passenger window rolled down an inch, but no more. His wife leaned toward him and said, "I'm leaving you, Benjamin. I'm leaving you and that godless son of yours." There were tears in her eyes.

"Mary, you've got to believe me, I had nothing to do with Susan's death," Locke protested.

"Don't try and follow me. If you do, I'll call the police."

"Come on, we can work this out," he said, reaching into his pants pocket for his personal set of keys for his wife's Mercedes. "Please don't leave us in this time of crisis. We need to draw on each other's strength. God alone cannot navigate us through these perilous times. We need each other"—he turned toward Junior—"right, son?"

"What?" The kid's face was dumb as a cow.

Locke shot him a glare as he pulled the keys from his pocket. *One more second and I'll have this door open!*

"Oh yeah, right," Benjamin Jr. said. "You can't leave, mom. We need you here...to cook and clean and stuff."

Locke rifled through the keys on the ring, trying to find the one to the Mercedes. *Hurry, hurry!* But his normally deft fingers seemed made of brick.

Calmly, Mary reached up to the sun visor and hit the button to open the electric gate.

Locke was frantic now. *Oh no, she's opening the gate! Quick, which one is it?*

When the gate was half-open, she turned toward them, her expression a composite of disgust, sadness, and resolve.

There it is! Quick, stick it in!

"May God save you both," she said prayerfully, "because I've given up all hope."

And then, just as Locke shoved the key into the lock, she pressed her foot to the accelerator and sped through the open gate, leaving him and his son behind.

CHAPTER 109

PATTON SAW HER on an overhead TV monitor at Denver International Airport while waiting for Sharp to come out of the men's room. At first, he thought she was simply an amazing lookalike, so he stepped forward for a closer look, with Schmidt, Barr Hogen, and the two baby sitters from the San Francisco field office right behind him. But once he saw the face clearly and heard what the anchor was saying, he knew that his eyes hadn't fooled him.

It was Jennifer, and she had been arrested in Colorado Springs for...*murder!*

Incredibly, it was even worse than that. She had been arrested for the ghastliest massacre in Colorado since Aurora and the worst abortion clinic attack in U.S. history!

This is unbelievable!

He watched in silent horror as she was shoved into a police car, hands shackled behind her back. It was a nightmare straight out of Hitchcock. But it couldn't be true. Jennifer would no more launch an attack on an abortion clinic than Rush Limbaugh would become Chairman of the Democratic National Committee.

But he still couldn't figure out what she had been doing there. Was it an AMP protest? Was she there with Susan Locke? He remembered that Jennifer was with her last night.

He glanced at Schmidt and the others standing there with him, gazing up in shared outrage at this female version of Robert Dear and Eric Rudolph. The network was portraying Jennifer as evil incarnate. She was described as an "anti-abortion crusader" and "fanatical right-to-lifer employed by American Patriots." Patton imagined the shameful TV miniseries: I KILL FOR GOD: THE JENNIFER ODDEN STORY.

As Patton stared in disbelief, the pictures of the ten victims, eight dead, were flashed on the screen. His fears were confirmed when he saw Susan Locke among the casualties. No doubt Jennifer had been at the clinic with Susan. But what were they doing there? Maybe it wasn't a protest at all. Maybe Susan was there for an abortion and Jennifer was there for support.

Sharp pulled him from his thoughts. "What's going on?" the ASAC asked brusquely, having walked over from the men's room.

"Some nut attacked an abortion clinic in the Springs," Patton replied, as Captain Pinkerton of the Colorado Springs Police department appeared on the screen. Patton recognized him instantly. Pinkerton had attended an in-service training session on counterterrorism Patton had co-taught in Washington last spring. The FBI often gave joint training seminars to its field agents and high-level investigators from metropolitan police departments. Pinkerton stood behind a podium in a media room, answering questions, and was apparently in charge of the investigation.

"Henry, I need to make a call."

"It'll have to wait until we're back at the shop. I have to brief the governor."

Fuck the governor! This is more important! He pulled out his cell phone. "You go on ahead. I'll meet you there."

Sharp gave his patented frown and looked up at the screen along with the others. Jennifer's picture appeared again. "That's the murderer, a woman?"

Patton looked up at the screen. "She didn't do it."

"What, you know her?"

"Enough to know she's innocent." He walked a few steps away to make his call in private. "I'll meet you at the office in an hour."

"Don't be late." Sharp strode off with the others to the shuttle tram that would transport them from Concourse C to the Main Terminal and Baggage Claim.

Patton called the Colorado Springs Police Department and punched 911 to get the emergency connection. He gave the police operator the FBI equivalent of his name, rank, and serial number and told her he needed to speak with Pinkerton immediately. He said he had important evidence in the abortion clinic attack, evidence that Pinkerton would want to hear.

Three minutes later, Patton had him on the line. "Pinkerton here."

"Captain, this is Special Agent Kenneth Patton of the FBI. I taught a training session last spring in D.C. that you attended."

"Sure, I remember. You're working the Kieger case now."

"Twenty-four seven."

"Look, I'm real busy right now too. I understand you have something for me on this attack."

"I do. Now this may come as a shock, but the woman you're holding, Jennifer Odden, is innocent. She happens to be a crucial informant on the Kieger case. I'm working with her directly."

The phone was silent a long moment. When Pinkerton's voice returned, it was filled with skepticism. "She said nothing about being an FBI informant."

"That's because she's a good one. She's not allowed to say anything to anyone, not even police, without our approval. I'll bet she asked that I be contacted though."

"Yeah, but every crackpot we get in this joint asks for somebody. Look, ballistics has already confirmed the gun she was holding as the murder weapon. There are no fingerprints besides hers. Plus I got five witnesses who swear they saw her enter the building shortly before the killings."

"So you've questioned her?"

"Yeah. She waived her Miranda."

That was a mistake. "Who's the gun registered to? Not her, I can guarantee that."

"Serial numbers have been removed. We've got nothing there."

"How did she say she got the gun?"

"She claims she struck the assailant and knocked the gun from his hand."

"You got a description?"

"Just hers. She described him as male, early forties, dark hair, dressed like a cop."

"A cop, huh. What did she say she hit him with?"

"A toilet lid."

That's my Jennifer—tough and resourceful. "You must have usables on the lid then."

"Yeah, we got prints. They're hers. But she could have grabbed the lid after the fact."

Patton had heard enough. "Look, I understand your position, Captain, but she didn't do it. The key thing you're missing here is motive. That's how I can help you out. Jennifer Odden's not an anti-abortion crusader, she's a freelance journalist, as pro-choice as you can get. I'm sure she told you about the work she's done for the *Chronicle* and *Examiner*. She uses a pen name: Stella Blue."

Pinkerton said nothing.

"Susan Locke was her friend, Captain. There's just no motive."

"Maybe you don't know this informant of yours so well. Maybe she went crazy."

"Come on, Jennifer Odden's not a real American Patriots employee. She's a journalist who's infiltrated the organization. She's doing a piece on the hardball political practices of the religious right. And she's also a confidential FBI informant working directly with me."

"This is all fine and dandy, but there's not a chance in hell I'm going to release her. I hope that's not what you're asking me to do. The city attorney and media are in a frenzy over this thing."

Patton ignored the comment, though releasing Jennifer was precisely what he wanted Pinkerton to do. He decided to take a different tack. "Have you spoken to the two survivors yet? I'm sure they'll confirm she had nothing to do with the killings."

"I have two people standing by. The doctors won't let us near them."

"Are either of them going to pull through?"

"I don't know. They're both listed as critical."

"You've got to talk to them ASAP, Captain. And you've got to track down some witnesses who saw this so-called cop. Someone *must* have seen him."

Pinkerton's voice rose an octave. "I don't need you to tell me how to run my investigation."

"I'm not trying to tell you how to run anything. I'm only trying to warn you that this is all going to come back to bite you in the ass if you don't listen to me. Jennifer Odden didn't do it, and in the next two hours I'm going to prove it. I'm trying to help you out here."

"I have to get back to work."

"Okay, but here's what I'm going to do. I'm sending two agents from our Springs resident agency to your office. They'll bring you up to date on Jennifer Odden. I know I'm putting you in a difficult situation, Captain, but we *need* her released into our custody as soon as possible. She's a crucial informant on our case, which has just gotten a big breakthrough in California. I'll call you in an hour and see how things are going."

"You can send twenty agents for all I care. But I'm not guaranteeing anything—not a damned fucking thing."

CHAPTER 110

FORTY MINUTES LATER, Patton stood before a large video monitor at the field office. He was trying his best to concentrate on the image in front of him, but all he could think about was Jennifer. He could only hope that Pinkerton would check out everything he'd told him and realize that, despite the political pressure from the City Attorney's Office, he had no option but to release her.

In the bullpen with him were Charlie Fial, Dr. Thomas Hamilton, Wedge, Schmidt, Barr Hogen, and the two baby sitters. Schmidt and Hogen were seated in front of the screen, which showed a clear image of the UPS delivery person walking into the elevator in the Union Plaza Building.

"With the cap and sunglasses, it's hard to tell," Schmidt said.

"I have to agree," Hogen said. "It could be Jane Doe, but..."

"You're not positive?" Patton finished for her.

"I'm afraid not," she said glumly. Schmidt nodded his concurrence.

Patton turned to Fial. "Is this the best shot you have?"

"Yeah. I spent a lot of time cleaning it up too."

"Maybe if they saw the whole sequence, it would help," Dr. Hamilton suggested.

"Good idea." Fial popped in a new disc, rewound it to when John Doe first entered the building, and let it roll. The view showed shots of the subject from different vantage points: coming through the door, walking through the lobby, passing the security guard, boarding the elevator. Fial had spliced together the different camera angles into a continuous silent movie.

When they were finished, Schmidt said, "One more time."

Fial ran the disc again.

Patton's thoughts turned again to Jennifer. Feeling restless, he looked at his watch and wondered if he should call Pinkerton yet.

I said I'd give him an hour. It's still a little early. Better give him a few more minutes.

After the second run-through, both Schmidt and Hogen nodded. "That's her," Schmidt said. "That's definitely Jane Doe."

"How can you tell?" Patton asked, wondering what had convinced him.

"Because she moves like a panther."

Barr Hogen smiled, respectfully. "That there is one very clever, very dangerous feline."

CHAPTER 111

FIAL STUFFED another DVD into the machine and, again, the group turned its attention to the screen. What appeared was a bird-eye's view of a woman pushing a stroller up a parking ramp. As they watched, the perspective shifted position slowly; apparently the camera was fixed high on a building and sweeping in a slow arc onto the street and sidewalks below. The footage was grainy, the woman too minuscule in the frame to identify, but somehow the whole scene seemed oddly familiar to Patton.

"What are we looking at?" he asked Fial.

"The parking ramp to the Union Plaza Building. At 2:28 p.m. last Sunday, less than five minutes after the assassination."

"Where'd you get the footage?"

"It's from the Avery Insurance Building, twenty-five stories up," Wedge said, as the woman neared the top of the ramp. "The camera covers the Eighteenth and Broadway intersection. It's a new experimental security camera operated by the city. We just received the disc this morning."

Patton looked back at the screen. He watched as the woman pushed her stroller to the top of the ramp. She appeared only in the bottom quarter of the field of view. Suddenly, a man moved across the picture and came running up to the woman, halting her in her tracks. The man wore a dark uniform and cap and looked to be questioning the woman. The images were too small and grainy for Patton to make out the faces, but the exchange seemed uncannily familiar.

And then it struck him. *The woman with the baby!*

The one he thought he saw coming up the exit ramp. He had questioned her about it, but she had said something about how the wheel of her stroller got caught in a rut and she had turned it to get it out. He tried to picture her: blonde, vibrant blue eyes, a little pudgy but quite attractive, New England accent. He remembered the sucking sounds the baby had made, the way she had leaned over the stroller and reassuringly cooed to the child. Then he remembered Wedge radioing him about the two maintenance workers coming out the building. That was when he had let her go.

Now he knew his eyes had not fooled him. *She did walk up the ramp!*

"I wonder who that guy is talking to her?" Hamilton said aloud. "He looks law enforcement to me."

Patton stared at himself on the screen. As discretely as possible, he said, "Why don't we look this over in private," and then he had everyone but Hamilton, Fial, and Wedge leave.

When they were gone, Hamilton looked at him curiously. "We're all ears, Special Agent."

"Okay, motherfuckers, it's me," he admitted. "I'm the guy talking to her."

"You?" Wedge said. "But that would mean that…"

"I fucked up big-time," Patton finished for him. "I had her right in my mitts, but let her slip away, goddamnit."

Hamilton rubbed his hands together. "Do we know for certain that woman is Jane Doe?"

"That's what I'd like to know," Fial said. "Let's take a look at some pixels."

"While he's doing that why don't you tell us what happened," Hamilton said, seemingly amused.

Patton described the encounter as Fial did his thing. The spook's hands were in constant motion, pointing and clicking the mouse, punching the keyboard, all in an effort to fine-tune the image. When he finished, what the thousands of pixels showed was a clear picture of the woman's face.

"Damn," exclaimed Wedge. "If that's not Jane Doe, then I'm Alfred E. Neuman."

"I think we should get independent confirmation," Patton said, and he had Schmidt and Hogen brought back in the room. They quickly confirmed the match and were sent off again.

Fial said, "So Jane Doe goes in on Friday as a UPS deliveryman and comes out on Sunday— less than five minutes after violently murdering three people—as Super Mom with a newborn. She's not just an assassin— she's a goddamned ice woman."

"I think the baby was fake," Patton said. "I heard it making sounds, but we didn't find any baby articles at Jane Doe's apartment. It must have been some kind of robotic doll or something."

"A professional female assassin? Gives me the willies just looking at her," confessed Wedge.

I should've slapped the cuffs on her when I had the chance. Henry's going to go ballistic.

With a detached academic air, Hamilton said, "I think she's rather extraordinary, actually. This woman isn't just disguising herself or acting out the roles, she's *living* them."

"So how are we going to catch her?" Fial asked. "She's a chameleon."

"I wish I knew," said Patton. "I wish I goddamn knew."

CHAPTER 112

HE PICKED UP the phone to dial Chuck Pinkerton. He had no luck reaching him, so he decided to roll on with the case and call back every few minutes. He was awash with worry over Jennifer, but he forced himself to put her out of his mind temporarily while he sorted through the case. He needed to get everybody moving in the right direction.

He had two key goals now: first, to find out Jane Doe's true identity and history; and second, to find out who had hired her. Schmidt and Hogen could help with the first question, so he had them tell Dr. Hamilton everything they knew about the subject. Patton had briefed Hamilton over the phone from L.A., but he hoped the two witnesses could give more detailed accounts before they flew back to the West Coast later tonight.

When the separate interviews were finished, Patton and Hamilton retired to the profiler's office on the seventeenth floor.

"This woman puzzles me," Hamilton began the conversation, settling into the chair behind his cluttered desk. "She appears to combine multiple personality disorders."

"So clue me in on them, Dr. Freud."

"First of all, she's impulsive. Here she is a professional killer, a loner by design and necessity, and yet she goes to a nightclub, brings a man home to her lair, fucks his brains out, and steals strands of his hair in an orgasmic overture. Why? She could have obtained suitable hair by many means. Why this way?"

"Maybe she didn't know she was getting hair from a convicted criminal. Maybe she thought she was dealing with some average Joe who lived far away in Oakland and would never remember the incident. If she could get her hands on blond male hair, it would deflect suspicion from her, because her natural hair color is dark brown. The plan would have worked too if Schmidt hadn't done time."

"But why take such a big risk? Why is she on the one hand methodical, careful, and clever, and on the other hand so impulsive. It smacks of borderline to me."

"Criminology 101 was a long time ago, Doc. Refresh my memory."

"Borderline personality disorder. Displays a crisis in identity and unpredictably impulsive behavior regarding sex, drugs, or alcohol."

"Sounds like me in college."

"And yours truly as well. There's also the issue of the bondage. She was clearly trying to exercise power over Schmidt by handcuffing him to the bed. But it went beyond that: she was trying to hurt him."

Patton pulled out his iPad and thought back to what Jane Doe had said to Schmidt: *I'm going to hurt you, but you will like it.*

"That's one of the characteristics of the sadistic personality disorder. These are people motivated by power. They use cruelty to establish dominance and enjoy inflicting physical and psychological pain on others. They tend to discipline people under their control with excessive force or punishment. Oftentimes, their actions are a re-enactment of the way they were treated themselves. That's what I think Jane Doe was doing with Schmidt."

"So it's unlikely he was the first man she seduced to her apartment, handcuffed to the bed, and rode like a pinto."

"He was probably the only one she took hair from, but I suspect she had taken part in this ritual many times before Schmidt. And maybe since."

Patton nodded thoughtfully. *Sounds plausible.*

Hamilton's hazel eyes lingered on him a moment. "I see schizotypal elements here too. Such people have no close friends or confidants other than family and an amazing ability to change appearances and personalities. In the videotapes, her role changes are deeper than acting alone. The way she moved as the UPS deliveryman...the gestures were exactly what you would expect from a man. Based on the clothes you found in her apartment, I would venture that she not only dresses up and plays like a man regularly, but that she actually takes on a male personality. In any case, someone had to have severely mistreated her to make her want to dominate men the way she did Schmidt. I should think the seed was planted early, but there may have been later events that exacerbated her condition."

"So what we've got here is one crazy lady. How does that help us find her?"

"That's your job, Dudley Do-Right."

"Okay, how about this then, Doc? What would you say if I told you that I don't think our mystery woman's American? In fact, I think she comes from Southern Europe, probably Spain."

"She does speak fluent Spanish and her physical appearance is consistent with someone of Spanish, or at least Mediterranean, heritage."

"There's also her apartment. Everything I saw—the furniture, photographs, clothing, books—tells me we're dealing with an educated, worldly person. Then there's the multiple accents. They're all over the map. New England, Southern California, and of course the fluent Spanish. But you've got to consider it all together—Schmidt and Hogen's physical descriptions, the cosmopolitan feel of her apartment, her mastery of Spanish and English, the multiple accents, and the fact that most of the female terrorists these days are trained in Europe. It doesn't matter what country you go to, you have a huge number of women being trained to do bad things. But there's one other important thing. I think it's the clincher."

Hamilton leaned forward. "I'm all ears."

"Ever heard of Diego Gomez?"

"The Basque assassin?"

"He's actually supposed to be Spanish, though he's been linked to the Basque separatist group Euskara. He's mostly an independent contractor. Been on the international watch lists for years, but no one knows what he looks like. The one photograph from French intelligence is pretty shaky. And the two artist's sketches look nothing alike."

"Are you suggesting Gomez is actually Jane Doe?"

"It definitely fits. Gomez has seven kills to his credit in the last decade, mostly high-ranking political and business figures. All of his sanctions involved distances believed to be in excess of five hundred yards and all involved heavy-caliber rifles. On two occasions .50-caliber incendiary cartridges were used. And all of his reported hits have been in Europe, the U.S., Canada, and South America."

"Do either of the artist's sketches look like Jane Doe or John Doe?"

"There are vague resemblances, but nothing more. The fact that the photo and two drawings are so different leads me to believe Gomez is being protected."

"By whom? A foreign intelligence service? A dirty government?"

"Or an individual. Whoever or whatever it is, it would have to have the power to manufacture evidence, buy off witnesses, produce false suspect descriptions, that sort of thing. All in an effort to protect the true identity of the assassin."

The doctor scratched his chin, thoughtfully. "Gomez as Jane Doe. I have to admit I like the sound of it. It would explain why Interpol and every other outfit have had such poor luck tracking Gomez down. Gender and gender-specific activities invariably blind security, police, and military authorities. Men see women as nurturers, not killers. With the exception of Islamic female suicide bombers, an attack by a woman is so unexpected, so diametrically opposed to traditional cultural norms, the tactical advantages are limitless."

"Case in point: just look at how badly this woman has kicked our ass."

"If you're right about this, this is huge," Hamilton said excitedly.

"You're damn right it is." He looked at his watch. "Oh, shit. Jennifer." He jumped up from his seat. "Sorry, Doc, I have to make a phone call."

Hamilton looked at him with astonishment. "Who's...who's Jennifer?"

"The woman I aim to marry. But first I have to bail her out of jail."

CHAPTER 113

"MY DEEPEST CONDOLENCES to you and your family, Benjamin. This has been a terrible tragedy."

Locke was sitting at his desk in his home office, hunched over his speakerphone. He wasn't sure how to respond. On the other end wasn't just another grieving well-wisher paying her respects over Susan's death, but President-elect Fowler, the traitor who had betrayed him and his dream to resurrect America, the woman who tomorrow would die in front of twenty thousand unsuspecting spectators.

"I appreciate your taking time out from your campaign to call, Mrs. President-elect," Locke said with faked sincerity. "Words cannot describe the loss my family has suffered. Your call means a lot to us."

"Is there anything I can do?"

Locke stared off at his spectacular drawings of bronco-busting cowboys by Remington and Russell, but found nothing inspiring in the pictures today. "No, I don't think so. It's in God's hands now."

Thanks to the Net, the entire world already knew about the tragedy at the clinic. Locke had taken over a dozen calls from Susan's teachers, relatives, co-workers, and conservative leaders from around the country. He had revisited her death with so many different people, the faces and voices were becoming blurred.

"I know you had high hopes for Susan, Benjamin. There is perhaps nothing more unfair to a parent than losing a child. My heart goes out to you and your family."

"Susan shall dwell in the house of the Lord forever," Locke said wistfully, but his face betrayed his inner pain. The knowledge that he could have done more to prevent his daughter's death crushed him. Never again would he see Susan's happy face as she showed him her sterling report card, as she sang the hymns with him in church, as she triumphed on the soccer field. She was dead at seventeen because of him and there was nothing he could do to turn back the clock. Ultimately, there was no one to blame but himself; the Apostle hadn't known Susan would be at the clinic or even what she looked like. And even Skull Eyes and the colonel would never have allowed the attack to take place had they known his daughter would be there.

"I know this has to be awfully hard on Mary. How is she holding up?"

Locke had no choice but to lie. "She's doing as well as can be expected under the circumstances." It made him angry that he had to invent falsehoods about her whereabouts to everyone paying their respects.

There was a strained silence. Locke sensed Fowler had something important to say, but was hesitant. "Benjamin, I know you and I have had our differences of late. But I want you to know I view Susan's passing as a loss for us all. I only pray that the police can track down the culprit responsible. I understand they're going to release the woman they're holding."

Locke felt as though ice water had just been poured down his back. "W-What did you just say?"

"They're releasing the woman. Her name is Jennifer..."

"Odden! Jennifer Odden!"

"Yes, that's it."

"Good heavens, are you certain they're releasing her?"

"It's all over the news. You mean you haven't heard?"

"No, I've been busy taking calls."

"I don't know the details, but apparently there are eyewitnesses who said she didn't do it. They're saying the killer was a policeman, or a man dressed like a policeman."

The muscles twitched at Locke's jaw. "Has the man been identified?"

"No. Unfortunately, no one seems to have gotten a good look at him or the car he escaped in."

Locke felt the breath catch in his throat at this disturbing turn of events. *I need to call Bill Hanson.* "I appreciate your call, but I'm afraid I must return to personal matters."

"I understand. But before you do, there's something else I'd like to say. I know you'd like to give up on me, but please don't do that. I'm still hoping we may resolve our differences in the coming weeks. There is a middle ground here, and I believe you and I just need to work together to find it."

You imbecile! I didn't make you the next president so you could cozy up to the very social engineers who have ruined this great nation in the first place! America is in peril right now and you must step down— involuntarily—and give Senator Dubois his rightful throne!

"Benjamin, are you still there?"

"Uh, yes...I was just thinking."

"I want to try and resolve our differences. You have given me tremendous support in the past and during this election, and I want you to know how much I appreciate it. Will you give it another chance?"

"Yes, yes, that is the prudent course of action. But right now I must make this call."

"Is there anything I can do for you? Anything to help you and Mary through this difficult time?"

He thought for a moment and realized there was something he did want from Fowler. In his anger and outrage at being thwarted, he wanted to be there tomorrow when the fatal bullet struck. Like a Roman mob, he wanted a ringside seat to the bloody, triumphant spectacle.

"I'd like to attend your speech tomorrow, if I may," Locke said. "After everything that's happened this past week, it would mean a lot to me."

"Consider it done. I shall have a seat for you up on the platform with Senator Dubois."

Locke's jaw dropped. "The senator's going to be there?"

"Of course—I'll be announcing him as my vice-president-elect."

"What?"

"The party leaders have convened an emergency session and are recommending that I select Senator Dubois for my Veep. I have no objections with the selection. I thought Governor Jamison would have made a fine choice too, but given Senator Dubois' experience and outstanding devotion to this country, I agree that he is the better choice. And besides, I think Joe McFarland will step in quite nicely as head of the Senate Judiciary Committee."

She was up to something—Locke could feel it in his bones. *You little sorceress!*

"I'm so pleased, Benjamin, that you and Senator Dubois will both be there for my speech. It will be a historic occasion."

More than you can possibly imagine! "I agree it is time to put aside our differences and work together. There is much to be done."

"You don't know how happy I am to hear that. With your help, we shall do great things in this administration, Benjamin. Great things."

"I look forward to it. Goodbye."

CHAPTER 114

HANGING UP THE PHONE, Locke quickly dialed the chief of the Colorado Springs Police Department. Over the years, Locke had made numerous charitable contributions to police causes; accordingly, Chief Bill Hanson was a loyal supporter and friend.

"Tell me it isn't true, Bill. Tell me you didn't just release Jennifer Odden," he said without preamble.

Hanson sighed heavily. "I had no choice."

"You let the prime suspect in the case walk away? How could you do this to me? That woman took my daughter's life."

"Hold on, Benjamin. We had to let her go. She didn't do it. Before the college girl died, we showed her a picture of Jennifer Odden and she told us Jennifer was there with your daughter as an innocent bystander. She said some man dressed like a cop made the attack. The surviving nurse confirmed it. She ID'd the assailant as a uniformed cop too. She's in critical condition, but hopefully she'll pull through. I've also got three more witnesses who say they saw a man pull a young, wounded female victim back inside when she tried to escape. We think the young woman was Susan."

Locke was livid. "But Jennifer Odden had the gun in her hands! I saw her!"

"So did several other people, but she didn't fire the weapon. We swabbed her hands and ran neutron activation tests. We found no nitrates, so unless she was wearing gloves, which we haven't been able to locate, she didn't pull the trigger. Look, I would have liked to hold her longer too to question her some more, but the FBI pressed hard on this one. In fact, she was released on their recognizance. So as far as we're concerned, she's in the feds care now."

Locke was stupefied. "The FBI? Why are they involved?"

"I can't get into that. I know we're friends, but this is an ongoing investigation."

"My daughter's bullet-ridden corpse lies in the Coroner's Office and you're telling me you can't talk to me!"

Hanson groaned with frustration. "You're putting me in an awkward position."

"When I was in your office this morning, didn't you tell me to call on you for anything? Didn't you promise to keep me informed of any new developments in the case?"

"Yes, but I didn't mean—"

"I want to know on whose specific authority you let Jennifer Odden go!"

An acute silence on the other end. Locke rose from his chair and walked to the window, fuming. The television vans and trucks were still parked outside the electric gate. He saw reporters and cameramen flitting about as blue and yellow lights skipped across the street.

Damned liberal media!

Finally, Hanson responded: "All right, I'm only telling you this because I know how much Susan meant to you. The agent's name is Patton—Kenneth Patton. He's working the Kieger case. He said the Odden woman was a critical informant in the case."

"A critical informant? What could she possibly know?"

"I'm not sure. Agent Patton wouldn't tell me. Look, if you have a problem with her release, you'd better take it up with this Patton fellow."

"Since when does the FBI supersede your authority on a local homicide investigation?"

"No one's superseding my authority."

"You can call it what you want, but you no longer have a suspect in custody."

"We're working on that. But unfortunately, no one got a good look at the gunman. All they saw was a guy in a cop's uniform and dark sunglasses."

"I didn't see anyone matching that description."

"I know what you told us, but others saw him. We don't know if he was working alone. There may have been a driver. We're still trying to confirm it."

"So Jennifer Odden's under the protective custody of this Agent Patton. Where? In Denver?"

Another silence. *I'll take that as a yes.*

Hanson cleared his throat, rather officially. "I can't say anything more. I've told you too much already. Now if you'll excuse me, Benjamin, I have a press conference in five minutes."

I have what I need—might as well end on a polite note. "Bill, I know you're doing all you can and I want you to know I appreciate it. I just want to see justice done."

"I know, Benjamin. I've got to go now. I'm awfully sorry about Susan."

"Yes, thank you." Locke punched off and dialed another number. While the phone rang, he stared off at the polished Model 1873 Springfield rifle hanging from the wall. The .45-caliber breech loader had been affectionately dubbed the *Long Tom* by frontier infantrymen. It was no match for the long-distance rifle Gomez would use tomorrow, but it was the best of its day.

"Mr. Chairman," a baritone voice answered after the third ring. "I am sorry for what happened, sir. I just found out. I had no idea your daughter was there."

"Speak no more of it. I do not hold you responsible for her death," Locke said straight away. "But there's something you must do for me before tomorrow's assignment."

"Whatever you desire, Mr. Chairman," said the Apostle. "Consider me your obedient servant."

CHAPTER 115

PEERING OUT THE WINDOW of her bedroom, Jennifer felt like a prisoner. Television vans crowded the narrow residential street below, and blathering reporters with blow-dried hairdos covered the sidewalk and walkway leading to her front porch. The vultures had her surrounded and were using her apartment as a stage prop. She was part of a case that was important to the press now, and though she had been released from police custody, they would not leave her alone until they found the real killer.

He was out there, somewhere in the city or maybe the mountains, celebrating his ignominious crime in private, cackling at the bungling police. Or perhaps he was out front, furtively watching her this very moment, preparing to strike. The thought chilled her to the marrow.

Turning away from the window, she opened her closet door, pulled out her Gregory backpack, and began filling it with clothing. Outside her bedroom in the living room were two FBI agents from the Springs resident agency. They would be escorting her to Ken in Denver.

Ken!

She couldn't wait to see him. Thank God he had intervened on her behalf. She didn't know what he had said to the cops to expedite her release, but it had worked. The time spent at the stinking police station had been one of the most humbling experiences of her life. In retrospect, it was obvious that she should have requested a lawyer right off the bat even though she was innocent. The cops had been such assholes, treating her like a murderer, intimidating her with their silly mind games, twisting her explanations to fit their simplified theories.

But now, at least, it was over.

Now her biggest priority was to finish her story, the scope of which had now been greatly expanded. Benjamin Locke, it seemed, was not just a renowned right-wing activist, bending the rules to put hard-liners in power. Instead, he was a full-fledged psychopath. In all likelihood he was behind the Kieger assassination, the killing of the computer programmer in Berkeley, and the clinic attack. Through Locke all of these events had to be connected: all she had to do was find out how.

But first, she had to talk to Ken and find out what he'd learned.

Ken! She knew in her heart she wanted to be with him for more than just the short term. She thought he felt the same way—indeed he had said so—but she still felt uncertain. They had both changed so much in twelve years. She had her career as a journalist and he had his as an FBI agent; she distrusted law enforcement agencies and he worked for the granddaddy of them all.

How in the world would they ever work that one out?

She went into the bathroom and gathered her toiletries, placing them into a black leather Dopp kit. Closing the kit with an audible zip, she walked back into the bedroom and stuffed it in her backpack.

Her cell phone rang, startling her.

Thinking it was Ken, she reached down and snatched it quickly off her bed. "Hello, Ken?"

"No, it's Mr. Lampert. I need to talk to you."

Jennifer's heart sank. After everything that had happened today, the last person she wanted to talk to was Reid Farnsworth Lampert.

"We're going to do an exclusive on the abortion clinic attack. I have J.R. Welch conferenced in. He's standing right outside your apartment, ready to interview you."

"Hello Jennifer—J.R. here."

I don't fucking believe this! She went to the window. As if on cue, a pair of cameramen turned up and began capturing her on film. To the right, fully in the lamplight, she could make out J.R. Welch in his trademark tweed jacket and bowtie. He was staring up at her with his cell phone pressed to his ear. When he waved, she wanted to give him the finger.

"I know its short notice, but this story's huge," Lampert said.

I was almost killed, you callous fools! This isn't a story! This is my fucking life!

"You haven't spoken to any reporters, have you? We have to have an exclusive."

"No, I haven't spoken to anyone except the police."

"Good. We understand there are a couple of FBI agents there with you. Just tell them to let Mr. Welch upstairs so you can do the interview. It shouldn't take more than an hour."

"An hour would be perfect," J.R. Welch agreed.

Jennifer felt completely violated. Would they really do anything to get their exclusive, even if it meant trampling over her privacy in the process? "No way am I doing an interview right now."

"But you have to. We *need* this story. And you don't want to let Mr. Stavros down, do you? Imagine what it will do for your career. Especially when you follow up with the Kieger story."

"Your name will be known in every household in America," said J.R. Welch.

"Right now, my career is the farthest thing from my mind."

"Please, *Jennifer*—I'm begging you," groveled Lampert.

She couldn't help a sardonic laugh. "So now I'm Jennifer. What happened to *Miss Odden*?"

"What does it matter? The point is Mr. Stavros wants this story and we've only got three hours to deadline."

She shook her head. "You people—you truly amaze me."

There was a pause as Lampert seemed to formulate a new plan of attack. When his voice returned, it was flat-out desperate. "Okay, I've got a deal for you, a limited one-time offer. I'll pay you twenty thousand dollars for your story on the clinic attack, and I'll let you handle the Kieger story all by yourself. Right, Mr. Welch, isn't that what we agreed?"

"That's the deal. It's your baby, Jennifer. All you have to do is give me one hour of your time and tell me, in your own words, what happened. Think about it. Today was the biggest abortion clinic attack in U.S. history. The whole country—make that the whole world—wants to know what was going through your mind when it all went down. Real-life drama doesn't get any more visceral than this. This is a golden opportunity."

Golden opportunity? Is he for real? She was becoming infuriated and decided it was time to end the conversation. "I'm afraid I can't help you. I have to go now."

Now Lampert's voice turned threatening. "If you do this, the only publication you'll ever sell another story to is the fucking *Wichita Weekly*!"

Jennifer had suspected he would threaten her like this. "I don't think so, Reid. The *New York Times* just called five minutes before you."

"The *Times*? Are you serious? Listen to me, Jennifer, you've got to—"

"Bye, boys—gotta run," and she punched off.

After turning off the cell phone so it wouldn't receive calls, she grabbed her backpack and walked into the living room, feeling not just relieved to be rid of them, but a tad triumphant. The FBI agent with the pockmarked Noriega face put down the magazine he was reading and said, "Ready to go?"

"Almost. I have to grab one last thing."

She walked into the kitchen, grabbed her daypack from the chair, and headed into the living room. Reaching for the nylon case next to the CD player, she flipped through her Dick's Picks Grateful Dead CDs. After the horrible day, she needed some music for the trip to Denver. She felt like some early stuff, so she grabbed Fillmore East 2/13/70 and Harpur College 5/2/70 with the killer acoustic set featuring a wild romp of a *Don't Ease Me In.*

"All right, I'm ready to go," she said. "But can you big bad Hoover boys do me a favor?"

Noriega tipped his head in amused assent.

"Those media jackals outside—can you lose them for me?"

Noriega grinned through yellow smoker's teeth. "It would be our pleasure, ma'am."

CHAPTER 116

THROUGH HIS BINOCULARS, the Apostle watched with soldierly intrigue as the two men with the conservative suits, close-cropped hair, and stiff air of authority pushed their way through the swarming press, opening daylight for Jennifer Odden. *Damned Boy Scouts,* he thought to himself. Using their broad shoulders and sharp elbows, the FBI agents simultaneously shielded and escorted their package to the passenger seat of a green Subaru Outback. The pockmarked agent took the driver's seat; the other agent climbed into the metallic-blue Mercury LeSabre directly behind the Outback.

The Apostle waited until both engines fired and the headlights flicked on before pulling away from the curb. He knew the route they would take to Denver, as well as their final destination, so he drove down the street in the opposite direction. The feebs would drive fast to lose the satellite vans, which meant that the best approach was to allow them to overtake him before getting on I-25. Then he would fall back into position and follow them to Denver.

He took a right onto Wahsatch. When he came to the 7-Eleven, he took a right onto Platte and passed the august statue of William Palmer, the city's founding father, mounted on horseback in full military regalia. On his left he then drove passed Acacia Park, with its gently swaying trees and eclectic mix of loiterers, tourists, and businesspeople scurrying home from work. By the time he reached Cascade, he spotted his quarry coming up fast from behind.

He made his move.

When he crossed the two-way street, he turned right onto Bijou, taking the right-hand lane and slowing up to allow the two vehicles to catch up. Fountain Creek bubbled past as he crossed the steel bridge that would convey him to I-25 north. Just before the on-ramp, the cars overtook him. He eased in behind the Mercury with the lone FBI agent and merged with the traffic on the interstate.

It was a pleasant late afternoon for a game of cat and mouse, he thought. Though the sun had just dropped below the tops of the mountains and the air had turned cool, the western sky was streaked with beautiful watercolor hues of mauve and purple. There was nothing like a Colorado skyline except heaven itself—and even a professional assassin like the

Apostle took a moment to appreciate how precious it was.

His thoughts turned to his assignment. There was no question it would be a challenge. The FBI agent Patton was big and strong and knew how to handle a gun, and Jennifer Odden had proved earlier today that she was a more than capable adversary. But the Apostle wasn't worried. He liked the challenge of facing a formidable opponent. It made the ultimate triumph that much more gratifying.

He was hoping tonight's enterprise would be particularly satisfying. Special Agent Patton and Jennifer Odden were well above the standard fare, and he was feeling hot in the loins.

His skin prickled with goosebumps at the thought of how it would all go down. Before he killed, he often fantasized about it. He pictured the entire gamut of facial responses he could expect: first shock, then fear, then absolute panic, and finally revulsion as the victim realized the silent intruder about to kill him was about to cream his trousers. Or was he?

Though the consummate professional when it came to an assignment, he also knew he was a sick, sick man. But even sick men had to have their fun. Sex with women no longer gave him pleasure. The very cruelty of his job had left him impotent when it came to normal intercourse. He hadn't had a woman in years and had never really had anyone he could call a girlfriend. The only thing that got him off anymore was the fear in his victim's faces.

But then the trick was to hold back from climaxing. Now that was self-control.

Semper fi and praise the Lord Jesus Christ the Savior!

By the time he reached the Air Force Academy turn-off, he had worked out the entire murder in his mind. He would take out Patton first, Jennifer Odden second. He would take his time with her, so that she would know precisely what the euphoric grimace on his face was all about. And then, at the last second, he would restrain himself through his masterful self-control.

It was important that his victims knew what was really going on in those final, fateful moments. That was what got him off.

Tonight, he thought. *Tonight is going to be special!*

CHAPTER 117

"SO GOMEZ IS JANE DOE, and Jane Doe's our killer."

"That's my theory, yes," replied Patton to his boss, and he proceeded to lay it all out. It took him ten minutes. Unlike most meetings, Sharp didn't interrupt him once and nodded in agreement every so often. At one point, he even smiled. Patton found the ASAC's behavior peculiar but said nothing.

"The facts seem to fit your theory," Sharp said when Patton was finished. The tone was, for him, positively magnanimous. "Of course, it still doesn't prove Gomez is Jane Doe. And it still doesn't tell us who she's working for, if not the Brigade. But it does seem to make sense."

"I think she's working for Benjamin Locke. I can't prove it yet, but I will soon enough."

Sharp looked at his watch, and Patton wondered if he had a previous appointment. "Okay, suppose I buy into that theory. What evidence do you have to support it?"

Henry's definitely up to something. He's never this agreeable. But what could it be?

Putting aside his suspicions for the moment, Patton proceeded to chronicle the evidence for Sharp, without revealing Jennifer as his source. True, the assembled facts didn't prove Benjamin Locke was behind the assassination or its subsequent cover-up, but taken together they raised serious questions. Even Sharp admitted as much, which, again, Patton found surprising.

"I'm with you so far, Special Agent. But there's still a lot we don't know. Like where this lady comes from, who trained her, and how Locke got in contact with her."

Patton scratched his chin thoughtfully. "As I said before, Gomez has been linked to Euskara in Spain. But I think it's a front. Jane Doe, or a control agent acting on her behalf, is trying to deflect suspicion from herself to the fictitious Gomez. If I'm right, it's unlikely Jane Doe was trained by Euskara. In fact, she probably has no ties to the group."

"Then who trained her?"

"There are several possibilities. She could have been recruited by Russian intelligence or another Eastern European intelligence group. They were first to use female assassins on a wide scale. Or it could be one of the big terrorist groups in Western Europe or the Middle East. The Red Army Faction and Action Directe in Germany, the Italian Red Brigade, EXE in Israel, or a similar group. Most female operatives these days come from the former intelligence agencies in Eastern Europe, though. They've made career changes and become professional contract killers who sell their services to the highest bidder."

Sharp glanced at his watch again, which, again, Patton found vexing. "Jane Doe...the spy who stayed out in the field."

"Something like that. These types of groups routinely use women pretending to be pregnant as foils. They also use infants, real or mechanical."

"Like Jane Doe."

"Exact—" Patton was brought up short by the ringing phone. Sharp reached over and pushed the *Speaker* button. "Yes, Cynthia."

"Agent Nicholson is ready for you now."

"Tell him we'll be right over."

Patton gave a start of surprise. "What's going on, Henry?"

"We need to have a little talk with the boss," he said vaguely, rounding his desk.

They walked across the hall to the office of the special agent in charge, who had returned from his interrupted trek to Nepal late yesterday. Will Nicholson had long been a big supporter of Patton's, but that didn't matter now. Something was very wrong and Patton felt a sense of impending doom.

"Sit down, gentlemen," Nicholson said curtly when they walked in, waving them toward the exquisitely crafted mahogany table at which he was seated. With his statuesque frame and falcon's eyes, the top gun of the Denver field office conveyed a sense of authority, but without the hard edge of many an FBI careerist. He also had the look of an outdoorsman; he had climbed all but six of Colorado's fifty-two fourteeners. But today, Patton noticed an edginess he had rarely seen before. John Sawyer, the supervisory special agent of the DT desk, was also seated at the table. He looked away when Patton's eyes met his.

Once they sat down, Nicholson said bluntly, "Ken, I'm pulling you off the Kieger case."

"But why? We're closing in on Jane Doe."

Sharp rolled his eyes, as if listening to the rambling of a small child. "Agent Patton's latest theory is the killer is a woman posing as Diego Gomez."

"I have to take responsibility for this," Nicholson said. "I'm the one who put you in charge of the case."

"Over my objections," pointed out Sharp.

"Yes, over your objections, Henry. Duly noted."

Patton felt a wave of desperation. "I don't know what's going on here, Will. But whatever it is, I can explain."

Nicholson held up his hand, indicating that wouldn't be necessary. "You've put my ass and Henry's in a ringer. An hour ago, we got off the phone with the director, who had just gotten off the phone with Governor Stoddart. It appears that, since you've taken over this case, you've pissed off a leading religious figure and governor, shown insubordination to your superiors, overstepped your authority by meddling in Colorado Springs police business, and made improper use of Bureau resources."

Patton started to protest, but the SAC cut him off. "Now I understand you may have had reasons for some of your actions, but you have still embarrassed the Bureau and that is unacceptable."

Patton turned accusingly to Sharp. "Why are you doing this, Henry?"

"You did it to yourself."

Patton looked at John Sawyer, but the supervisor's eyes were glued to the table. *Sorry, Ken, but you're alone on this one,* he seemed to say. There was no option left but to plead with Nicholson. "Come on, Will, you know I wouldn't have done what I did without good reason. Benjamin Locke's an integral part of this case and so is Jennifer Odden. That's why I had her released. She has vital information. And she damn sure doesn't have anything to do with that rampage at the abortion clinic."

"Do you deny having had a romantic relationship with this woman?" Sharp asked accusingly, shifting the onus back onto him.

"What the hell does that have to do with anything?"

"I'll take that as a no."

Nicholson's frown deepened. "You violated standard protocols. Without John's or Henry's knowledge, you contacted our Springs residency and arranged for this woman to be escorted to Denver, where she'll be under your personal protection."

"I know I didn't follow procedure, but I needed to ensure her safety. She has information vital to the case. This isn't the first time a journalist has helped us dig up leads."

"I think you've forgotten how we operate. We don't stir up the pot with the locals, especially not governors. We don't strong-arm the police. And we never—and I mean never—give the bureaucrats in the Hoover Building or Boy Scouts at Justice a reason to put us under a microscope. We're under enough pressure to solve this case as it is."

"By pulling in this journalist girlfriend of yours," added Sharp, "all you've done is provide fodder for the civil libertarians and given the political-correctness police a reason to look over our shoulder."

"I haven't told her anything. *She* provided me with information, not the other way around."

"I don't want to hear any more," Nicholson said. "Whether this Odden woman or Benjamin Locke are involved or not, your conduct has cast embarrassment on the Bureau. You know the rules."

"Yeah, yeah, I know. J. Edgar's great legacy—don't embarrass the fucking Bureau."

"Get a grip, Special Agent. You are to bring John here up to speed and hand the case over to him. I'm putting you on white collar until I can figure out what to do with you."

Patton's heart sank. That was the ultimate low blow. In the Bureau, white-collar crime was the most tedious, least rewarding work. Convictions didn't come easy and few agents wanted to touch it. This wasn't just a demotion—this was fucking banishment!

"Jesus Christ, Will, why don't you just fire my ass. At least I'd have a reason to get up in the morning."

Sharp looked at Nicholson. "I don't think this is going to work. He needs time off to get his head straight."

Patton felt his blood boiling. "I don't know how you pulled this off, Henry, but I'm going—"

Nicholson's hand crashed onto his desk. "Silence! You're on a ten-day suspension, effective once you've briefed John and gotten him your 302s. You've given me no other choice."

"You can't suspend me without bringing formal charges against me. I've done nothing wrong."

"Oh, there will be charges all right," said Sharp menacingly. "I've almost finished the paperwork. It will be sent over to OPR by the end of the day."

Though Patton tried hard not to appear flummoxed, his face turned beet red and he was rendered speechless. The Office of Professional Responsibility, or OPR, was the branch that investigated allegations of employee misconduct within the FBI. Officially, it fell under the umbrella of the Bureau, but was in fact run by the Justice Department, like a police internal affairs division run out of the district attorney's office instead of the police department. The OPR investigators were not only painstakingly meticulous, but far from impartial, since the Justice Department and the FBI were often at odds with one another. This did not bode well for Patton.

"I'm sorry, Ken," Nicholson said with a note of regret. "But you're going to have to hand over your creds and sidearm."

Patton bit his lip. "This is going to look bad for you both when I'm exonerated," he said, his mind so filled with bile he didn't even realize the bridges he was burning.

"Hand 'em over," Sharp commanded. "Now!"

Keeping his eyes locked on Sharp, Patton pulled out his gold shield with the picture ID and then withdrew his clip holster with his Glock. He slammed them down hard on the desk, making a statement of protest.

"If that's the way it's going to be, I'll start serving that sentence right goddamn now!" he said angrily, and he stormed out the room.

CHAPTER 118

JENNIFER LOOKED across the kitchen table at Ken. For the last twenty minutes, he had quietly listened to her account of the rampage at the clinic. She could see the shared pain in his eyes. In his sober reflection, he seemed to be reaching out to her, telling her he understood what she had gone through and that everything would be okay.

He reached across the table and took her hand. "It's a miracle you survived. I'm sorry Susan didn't."

Her thoughtful expression hardened with resolve. "I want Locke to pay. I know he's the one behind the attack. We have to nail him, Ken. And I don't mean just for what happened at the clinic."

He looked away uncomfortably and she wondered what she'd said. "What is it?"

When he finally spoke, his voice seemed diminished somehow. "I'm afraid I'm not going to be of much help to you. They pulled me off the case."

Her first reaction was disbelief, followed swiftly by outrage. "But why?"

"It's a long fucking story."

Tenderly, she touched his face. "I'm sorry." And then it dawned on her that she might be the reason he was taken off the case. "Did this happen because of me?"

"Does it matter?" he temporized.

"To me it does. Did they do this because you bailed me out of jail and put me under your protection?"

"Partly," he said, still reluctant to blame her.

"Why didn't you tell me?"

"After what happened to you today, I could see no point."

"I feel terrible."

"You shouldn't. Sharp would have just found some other reason."

"What's going to happen to you?"

"I don't know. The Office of Professional Responsibility is conducting an investigation. Right now, I'm on a ten-day suspension. When I return, I suppose I'll be banished to white-collar purgatory for a few months, until I can work my way back to my old desk."

Jennifer was wracked with guilt. What could she possibly say or do to make up for all the trouble she'd caused him? If she'd known this would happen, she would have volunteered to be locked up in a cell for a month with nothing but bread and water.

"The most important thing is that you're safe."

Feeling a surge of affection, she rose from her chair and went to him. He stood up too and they wrapped their arms around each other and kissed. As they held one another close, she felt a delightful feeling inside, a pulse of warmth to take away the edge of sadness.

He started to say something.

"Don't say a word," she whispered gently in his ear. "Just hold me."

CHAPTER 119

MINUTES LATER, they decided to have a beer and put on some music, to further the healing process and put some distance between themselves and what had happened today. Jennifer went to the stereo cabinet to work on the tunes while Patton pulled a pair of Fat Tires from the fridge.

She saw right away that his musical taste hadn't changed: bluegrass still predominated to the exclusion of just about everything else except a little classic rock and blues. She was pleased to see he had a good collection of Dead CDs. She pulled out *American Beauty* and popped it in the CD player. A nice strumming acoustic intro then Phil was singing the opening line to *Box of Rain*.

Patton returned with the beers. Like condemned prisoners sharing a final ironic joke, they clinked bottles and sat down on the blue corduroy couch. He propped his feet up on the antique pine coffee table and loosened his tie. Outside, the autumn wind whistled through the massive oak, pine, and elm trees standing watch like sentinels over Wash Park. A thumbnail moon shone down on the lake, where a hundred honking geese quarreled over which route to take in their annual sojourn south.

They talked for a while about the old days and ordered Indian take-out from a new joint that had opened up on Alameda. After dinner, Patton turned on the TV to catch the news. A meticulously made-up anchorwoman who looked like a younger, prettier Diane Sawyer was doing her spiel.

"*...woman wanted for questioning by the FBI in connection with the Kieger assassination. She is described as being in her early- to late-thirties, five foot seven to five foot nine in height, with varying hair color. Her identity is unknown at this time, but the FBI have given her the name Jane Doe. She is considered armed and extremely dangerous...*"

As the anchorwoman rambled on, a color image flashed up with a caption that read "Jane Doe." Patton saw instantly that it was the picture from the city security camera Fial had put together for the new wanted poster.

"So is this Jane Doe an accomplice?" asked Jennifer, staring at the TV.

"No, she's the assassin. There is no John Doe."

"You've got to be joking? That matronly woman is the killer?"

"Don't let her fool you—she's a goddamned La Femme Nikita with some serious mental hangups."

Jennifer turned up the volume with the remote. The shot of Jane Doe dissolved and Henry Sharp appeared on the screen, looking FBI-ish in his perfectly pressed navy-blue suit. A bleached-blonde reporter with puffy, collagen-enhanced lips stood next to him with a microphone.

Patton recognized the backdrop as the media room on the sixteenth floor of the field office.

"At this time, we believe Jane Doe may have been an accomplice," Sharp declared, holding his head in a self-assured, patriarchal tilt.

"So you have no reason to suspect her as the assassin?" the reporter asked.

"Not at this time. A woman doesn't fit the profile we've established."

Patton was livid. *This is bullshit! Sharp's making a mess of my case!*

"Are you saying the killer couldn't be a woman?" the reporter asked Sharp.

"Well, it's certainly possible," he allowed. "But we believe our prime suspect, John Doe, has certain paramilitary experience that would be unlikely for a woman to possess. Not impossible, mind you, just unlikely," he added, with a patronizing smile that made Patton cringe.

"So both John Doe and Jane Doe are still at large?"

"For the moment. But we'll catch them."

"What is the FBI's current take on the Green Freedom Brigade?"

"The Brigade is our leading suspect group at this time. I am pleased to report that an hour ago, a task force from our San Francisco field office arrested four members of the group outside Truckee, near Lake Tahoe."

"So is it known whether Jane Doe or John Doe are members of the Green Freedom Brigade?"

There is no John Doe, you moron! And the Brigade has nothing to do with the assassination!

"That has yet to be confirmed. But you can rest assured we are working diligently on the case and hope to have all the perpetrators in our custody soon. That's all I have to say at this time."

"Thank you, Agent Sharp." The reporter turned back toward the screen. "Back to you Karen. From the FBI field office in downtown Denver, this has been Mary Elizabeth Schumacher reporting."

Enraged, Patton flicked off the TV with the remote. He wanted desperately to break something—anything, it didn't really matter. "I don't believe this shit."

Jennifer smiled with apparent amusement. "Don't get mad, Ken, get even. Let's pool our resources and figure this thing out. Together."

"Okay, but we're going to need java," he said, looking like a downhill racer at the starting gate. "Gallons of it."

CHAPTER 120

THEY WENT OVER THE CASE frontwards and backwards. They set up shop at the pine kitchen table, with aromatic Seattle's Best roasted coffee, notepads, and the playful picking of Doc and Merle Watson in the background. By the time they were finished, they had developed a plausible conceptual model of the assassination and its cover-up. But in Patton's mind unanswered questions still remained.

It was clear an organized group was behind the assassination. But how many people were in the group, or attached to it? There was Locke, the probable ringleader, and Jane Doe. There was the hacker who had infiltrated Anders Houser's computer. And there was Houser's killer. But was the group a large one with grandiose objectives or a small coterie of like-minded men? Did it consist primarily of AMP members, a mix of members and outsiders, or all outsiders except Locke?

There was also the matter of Jane Doe. Was she really Gomez, or was Patton grasping at straws? If she was the mysterious killer, this meant the world's best sniper was, in fact, a woman, an embarrassing revelation for the macho international intelligence community. It also meant that Gomez was nothing more than a phantom killer, a ghost of the files. Which, in turn, meant Jane Doe had to be under the protection of someone with powerful intelligence connections. The French intelligence service had the most complete dossier on Gomez. Was there someone high up in that body feeding Interpol and the world's law enforcement community false information?

Another difficult question was whether Jane Doe had received inside help. Did she infiltrate the Union Plaza Building and decommission the elevator and two security cameras on her own, or did she have inside support? Perhaps someone in intelligence or law enforcement? Could this be where Sharp fit in? It would explain his erratic behavior. What about Will Nicholson? Why had he been so eager to take Patton off the case so soon after returning from Nepal? Had he even been in Nepal? And what about that viper Governor Stoddart?

But in Patton's mind, the most intriguing question was the true identity of Jane Doe? How accurate was the profile Dr. Hamilton was developing? Did she suffer from real personality disorders, or was the good doctor working in the realm of conjecture? Why did she take unnecessary risks, like stealing Schmidt's hair? Why was she so methodical and professional yet so impulsive? Most importantly, how was he going to catch her now that Sharp and Nicholson had taken him off the case?

The thought of Sharp left a nasty residue in his mind and he decided to call John Sawyer. He had left the office in such a huff he had forgotten to brief his replacement. He called him at the office, but he wasn't in, so he dialed his home number and reached him there. He offered to come in tomorrow to go over the case in detail. Sawyer accepted and said he was already lobbying hard to get Patton back on the job in at least a supporting role. Patton believed him. John Sawyer wasn't a bad guy; he was just in an impossible situation.

When Patton hung up, he sat back down at the table and started jotting down notes again. Jennifer leaned across the table and took the pen from him. "I think we've done enough for one night," she said, resting her hand on his suggestively.

Patton saw a familiar look in her eyes that made his blood turn warm. "What did you have in mind?"

"I don't know," she said coyly. "I was wondering whether you'd learned anything these past twelve years. You know like tricks?"

He felt himself blushing. "Are we talking dirty here?"

"Does it make you feel uncomfortable?" Her foot gently rubbed his below the table.

"No, but I do feel like Dustin Hoffman in *The Graduate*."

"Uh-huh," she said devilishly, still stroking his foot. "And is that good or bad?"

He leaned across the table and kissed her. Her lips tasted like wild mountain honey. "I'd have to say, it's pretty damned good."

"Shall we then?"

He was hard as a hammer, but pretended to be the chaste one. "You don't waste any time, do you?"

"I believe it's been twelve years, Ken."

"Too damned long," he said, and he picked her up and carried her into the bedroom.

CHAPTER 121

THE APOSTLE quietly exulted as he saw the bedroom lights go out. *If you hurry, you can catch them in the act!* He had been spying on them for over an hour now and had seen them kissing through the half-drawn curtain of the kitchen window. From his dossier, he knew they had been lovers once; obviously, they were rekindling the old flame. It would be absolutely titillating catching them just before they climaxed, when they were completely vulnerable. His intrusion would be so unexpected, he would get the best possible reactions from them both.

He pictured them in the heat of passion as his shadow loomed above. The FBI agent Patton would be on top and Jennifer would spot the shadow first, peering over her lover's shoulder. Her nubile, sweaty body would tense, her red lips would part in horror, and she would scream, but it would take a second or two for Patton to stop thrusting inside her. Adrenaline would seize hold of their naked bodies and they would become prey animals. They would try desperately to disengage, to flee, but by then it would be too late. Instead of swimming in the ecstasy of an orgasm, they would be gunned down at point-blank range.

What a sudden twist of fate. One moment rapture—the next Nightmare on Franklin Street!

The moon radiated a restrained, eerie brilliance—like a freshly burnished silver candlestick in a dark, ghostly mansion. The Apostle had already worked out his approach so he made it to the backyard quickly, keeping to the shadows of the towering blue spruce. He slipped quietly over the white picket fence and headed for the back porch, his booted feet swishing softly through the grass. A dog howled, but he could tell it was far down the street.

He carried his black Beretta 92F cocked and locked. One round in the chamber, the hammer cocked, and the safety set so he wouldn't blow off his foot. The leather sheath about his ankle bore a six-inch, serrated, double-edged knife that would have made Jack the Ripper proud. He also wore a Kevlar bulletproof vest, knowing tonight he would be dealing with an armed, and therefore dangerous, adversary.

In the Apostle's line of work, one could never be too careful.

When he emerged from the shadows of the trees, the moon caught him momentarily. One-half of his face basked in the glow of the fluted light, while the other remained masked in darkness.

One-half good, the other evil, he mused. *No, no, no, you're all evil— pure unadulterated evil!*

A cloud passed in front of the moon, throwing his face into complete blackness. He gave a crooked smile: it was like a sign from above.

He continued to the back porch. A dim outdoor light illuminated the steps and a third of the small yard beyond. When he reached the door, he withdrew his Beretta. Boasting a 15-round magazine and with a muzzle velocity of 1,280 feet per second, it was a truly lethal piece of ordnance. He plucked a custom-designed suppressor from his pocket and threaded it into the nose of the gun. Stuffing the gun in his fatigues, he checked the door to see if it was locked, and, finding it was, he proceeded to pick the lock. It took him less than thirty seconds.

His body twitched with excitement as he pushed open the door and slipped inside.

He moved swiftly but noiselessly down the hallway, keeping the gun pointed straight ahead. His excitement grew when he heard the squeaking bed and moaning voices, one gentle and female, the other husky and masculine. His eyes were adjusting to the darkness faster than he had expected. When he passed a kind of study, he undid the safety on the Beretta.

Inside his pants, he began to throb. This was going to be very special indeed.

His breathing turned heavy. The pistol in his pants grew harder still.

This wasn't his first time in this situation. He had caught lovers in the act on two prior occasions, and both dalliances had been intensely gratifying. He felt like an unseen killer in a slasher movie, about to catch the unsuspecting teenagers in the heat of passion.

He came to a halt outside the door. The voices inside the room were practically screaming, the bed banging at a fever pitch.

This was it—time to kill.

Knock, knock, the Apostle's here. It's time for you to meet your Maker.

CHAPTER 122

PATTON WAS IN THE THROES OF RAPTURE.

He had waited twelve years for this and the world spun in a pleasant way, as if he were on a merry-go-round. He arched his back and kissed Jennifer's lips as she slid back and forth on top of him. A churning euphoric sensation took hold of his lower stomach. He kissed her on her hard, slippery nipple as they continued to thrust in unison. Her womanly scent was sweet and thick, like tropical air. His arms reached out like tentacles, clasping her smooth bottom, and he pulled her to him, plunging upward, deeper. She let out a moan and he could feel himself about to let go.

I want to come with you; it's always best that way.

He had waited twelve years for this. Twelve long years.

And then he heard the sound.

It wasn't much, a scarcely audible squeak, but something about it didn't sound right. He glanced over Jennifer's shoulder toward the door. It opened slowly and he saw a partial shadow creeping along the wall, growing in size.

He stopped moving beneath Jennifer and searched frantically for his Glock. Then he remembered that Nicholson and Sharp had confiscated it. *Damn!* What about his backup piece? No, it was locked up in the spare bedroom. *Shit! What else is there?* His eyes darted to the side table next to the bed. There were three lead miniatures and the alarm clock. *Is that it?*

He looked back at the door. Now the outline of a large figure was visible in the doorway.

"Is something wrong?" Jennifer asked, wondering why he'd stopped making love.

"Shh," he whispered, keeping his gaze fixed on the door.

The figure slinked back deeper into the shadows.

Patton knew he had to act now. There was no time for anything but a desperate move.

In a fluid motion, he pushed Jennifer off him, eliciting a shriek of surprise, and reached for the closest lead soldier on the side table. Then the former Wolverine quarterback leapt to his knees and hurled the figure with all his might.

It was one in a million, but Elway himself couldn't have heaved one better.

There was a grunt of pain, a manly sound, as the impromptu ballistic missile crashed into the intruder's face, disorienting him. A shot rang out, but the bullet drove harmlessly into the headboard.

Patton seized his opportunity and charged the intruder. He knocked him into the wall, driving hard with a solid shoulder. The man grunted again and crumpled to the floor, his heavy boot jerking forward and crunching the toy soldier.

Patton reached out to grab the intruder and felt something solid and bulky in his mid-section. *Jesus, he's wearing a fucking bulletproof vest!* He knocked him again and the gun dropped to the floor. He kicked it to the side, toward Jennifer.

"Pick it up!"

He took a vicious kick to the ribs. He staggered and felt another punch hammer the side of his face. The intruder pulled away and leapt for the gun. Luckily, Jennifer reached it first, but the intruder jumped on top of her and tried to wrestle it away.

Patton grabbed him in a headlock and pulled him off, dragging him to the other side of the room.

"Shoot him!" Patton screamed. "Shoot the motherfucker!"

The intruder twisted his body in what seemed like a predetermined military maneuver, and suddenly Patton found himself thrown to the floor, judo-style. He let out a heavy grunt as he hit and felt a sharp pain shoot through his back.

Jennifer fired, the bullet tearing a hole in the carpet at Patton's feet. "Not at me! At him!"

"I'm trying to!"

The man's hands reached out and clasped Patton's throat in a vice-like grip. Patton's windpipe was completely closed off and he felt the life being choked out of him. For the first time, he got a good look at his adversary. The guy was scary as hell: he was built like a Special Forces commando, his eyes were as cold as agate, and his teeth were clamped over his lower lip like a werewolf.

How in the hell am I going to stop this monster!

He felt one hand pull away from his throat. The hand reached back, and he heard the crisp sound of a knife being removed from a sheath. He threw his arm out to block the man's hand as it swung around with a horrifying double-edged dagger. He gripped the man's wrist, preventing a stabbing impact, and watched helplessly as the blade inched slowly toward his face. The jagged edge glimmered hideously in the moonlight. It would be only a matter of seconds before the cold steel pierced him; the man was so strong he could see no way to overpower him.

He realized, in that strangely kinetic instant, that the man was a professional killer, well practiced in the art of extreme violence. *Mano a mano* against this guy, Patton knew he was badly overmatched.

Shit, he thought. *I'm going to fucking die.*

CHAPTER 123

JENNIFER TOOK CAREFUL AIM and squeezed the trigger. This time she was rewarded for her composure as the assailant emitted a heavy grunt and released his grip from Patton's throat.

A direct hit to the chest! But why isn't he going down?

She fired again.

This time the man howled and dropped the knife. When it fell to the carpet, Patton reached for it, but his hand was knocked aside and the knife flew under the bed. The two men tangled, twisting and fighting on the floor. In the weak illumination of the bedroom, Jennifer couldn't make out the intruder's face very well, but she could see enough to know it was the same psycho who had tried to murder her this morning at the clinic.

Jennifer moved closer, following their back-and-forth movements with the gun like a spectator during a tennis match. She tried to draw a bead on the intruder, but he and Ken were interlocked and she wasn't about to risk killing Ken. She would have to wait until they pulled apart again and she could get off another clean shot.

She wished she was confident enough in her aim to take the shot and put an end to it now. But she had never fired a gun before and the kick was surprisingly strong. She had always loathed women in the movies who stood there paralyzed with fear or screaming in panic when they should just pick up the damned gun and shoot the bad guy. But it wasn't easy to keep one's head straight in a desperate situation like this.

The intruder broke free for an instant and knocked Patton to the floor with a heavy thud. He then swiped an elbow across Patton's face, drawing blood from his left nostril. Patton kneed him in the balls and they wrestled for a moment before breaking free.

As they staggered to their feet, Jennifer thought she had a clean shot. But at the last second Patton crossed into her line of sight, and she held back.

Patton head-butted the man in the face, receiving three stunningly quick jabs in return. Jennifer tried to draw a bead on the intruder, but still didn't have a clear shot.

Patton dodged the fourth punch and clutched the man by his uniform. He drove upwards with a right, catching the intruder in the chin. The man responded with a hard fist to Patton's gut, doubling him over.

Jennifer could stand it no longer. *I have to take a shot!*

She aimed at the intruder and squeezed the trigger twice in rapid succession.

The man jerked back with a loud grunt.

She fired again and he staggered from the room. She heard running footsteps receding down the hallway, the back door jerk open, and the sound of feet thumping on a hard surface. Then the sound disappeared and there was nothing.

She felt along the wall for the light switch and flipped it on. Blinking into the bright light, she looked at Ken. He was slowly climbing to his feet, his heaving chest covered with sweat, his face red, tender, bleeding.

"Jesus, you're a mess. Here let me help you."

She went to him. He took the gun from her as she wiped blood away from his eye. Behind the house, an engine roared to life and tires squealed. They both looked anxiously in the direction of the sound. Slowly, their expressions relaxed as the sound of the getaway vehicle faded away.

He turned to her. "I feel like I just went through a meat-grinder. Are you okay?"

"Scared shitless, but still in one piece."

"That was nice shooting by the way."

"I just reacted. I didn't even have time to think."

"Well, you got him." He stepped towards the door and pointed at the droplets of blood on the tan carpet leading out of the room like a trail of breadcrumbs.

Jennifer was puzzled. "Why is there so little blood? I must have hit him three or four times."

"Bulletproof vest."

So that's what it was. Looking down at herself, she suddenly felt self-conscious being naked and pulled the edge of the quilt over herself.

"That was the same maniac who attacked the clinic this morning," she said. "We were lucky."

"Not lucky enough, I'm afraid." He bent down to pick up something next to the wall.

"What do you mean?"

He held up a one-armed lead soldier. "That son of a bitch just made a cripple out of my great-grandfather, General George S. Patton."

CHAPTER 124

SENATOR JACKSON BEAUREGARD DUBOIS tilted his head, tossed back three ounces of the finest Tennessee sour mash whiskey known to man, and set the glass down on the desk. His face shone harshly, like a cruel desert sun.

"I don't give two damns and a jar of cold piss about my personal safety. When I hear that first shot, I'm going hell bent for leather to Fowler's aid. That, Mr. Chairman, is what will make the American people revere me like old George Washington."

Leaning back in his chair, taking the pulse of the man before him, Locke knew that, despite the obvious risks, the senator was onto something. There was a very good reason to handle the matter this way. Performing a feat of remarkable bravery in front of millions of TV-viewing Americans would forever enshrine Dubois as a national hero.

"All right, Mr. Vice-President-elect," Locke allowed, "but if we go through with this, the plan has to be foolproof."

The Prince of Darkness's lips parted into something so crooked, so splendidly diabolical, it only vaguely resembled a smile. "Why Mr. Chairman, consider me your obedient servant in this matter."

SATURDAY

CHAPTER 125

ON THE MORNING OF THE ASSASSINATION, a warm wind rose up and chased the cool air from the Great Plains. The indigo sky and puffy clouds of yesterday afternoon had, like Dorothy, drifted back to Kansas, leaving behind a canopy soft, cloudless, and periwinkle blue. The sun was strong for mid-November, which would be something the citizenry of the Mile High City would long remember when they recounted the tumultuous events of this day. By mid-morning, the mercury was already in the sixties and the day promised to be a gorgeous one.

Peering out at the city from the eighth floor of the historic Brown Palace Hotel, Skyler went over the plan once more in her mind. On paper it was simple, but, in her experience, seldom did a plan, even a perfectly concocted and methodically executed one, go off without a hitch.

Today, she would face a combined Secret Service and outside law enforcement detail in excess of one thousand individuals. They had already secured the Capitol Hill and Civic Center Plaza areas. With meticulous care, they had swept every nearby building and set up perimeter checkpoints in a twenty-block radius. They had identified every conceivable line of sight, studying and restudying trajectories, angles, windage, and the like. They had fastened every window overlooking the speakers' platform. They had set up magnetometer checkpoints and x-ray machines all around the plaza. They had set up triple the usual number of countersnipers and spotters on the rooftops. Finally, they had sent an army of bomb-sniffing German shepherds to do what humans could not.

These careful preparations should have been more than enough to prevent an assassin from succeeding in a mission.

But Skyler was no ordinary assassin, and her plan was no ordinary plan.

Even so, she had second thoughts. Not about whether the plan would work, but whether she wanted to go through with it. This morning after calling Anthony she was gripped with lightheadedness, just as she had been yesterday during her reconnaissance. Even now, waves of anxiety, coupled with a deep longing to be safely in Anthony's arms, lashed at her like storm waves upon a beachhead. She had not felt this confused and uncertain since her indoctrination as a freedom-fighter under Alberto.

After a light workout to clear her head, she took a long hot shower.

Drying herself with a towel, she put on the plush Taylor of London terrycloth robe provided by the hotel and drank two full glasses of cold artesian tap water. Then she went back into the elegantly appointed bedroom. Though she felt better now, she couldn't seem to shake the guilt. It continued to gnaw at her.

She decided to call Anthony again. She punched in his number on her coded mobile, reaching him after two rings.

"I've been worried about you," he said straight away. "God, how I miss you."

"I miss you too," she said softly. "But it will all be over soon."

"Let's not kid ourselves, Skyler. It will never be over. You're CIA. There will always be guys like this looking for payback. Because of information you obtained about some important person, some technological innovation, some state secret. It's all right—I can deal with it. Just don't pretend the risk will simply vanish once this is over."

Though his tone was stern, Skyler realized that he was deeply worried about her safety, and she was touched. "If I were to quit the Company, there would be no more threats. I've told you I've been considering it."

"Would you really do that?"

"For you I would," she said, and she meant it.

"Skyler, the way I feel about you...it's like I'm in an old black-and-white directed by Billy Wilder. I've never felt this scared, or alive, in my whole life. And the thing is I like it. I like my stomach being twisted up in knots. I like waiting by the phone wondering if you'll call. I like not being able to think straight when I hear your voice. I like worrying about you instead of the traffic on the 405 or some stupid production schedule. Am I rambling on like a Pat Conroy novel or do you feel the same way?"

Skyler was choked with emotion. "I feel the same way. And like you, I am powerless to stop it."

"So I'm not crazy after all?"

"No, of course not." She was so deeply moved she thought she would cry. "I love you, Anthony. If anything happens to me, it's important you know that."

"Don't say that. Nothing's going to happen to you."

"But if something ever did, please remember that these last few days have been the best of my life. And that I love you."

"Why are you even saying this? Nothing's going to happen, okay."

"Just tell me you love me. I want to hear you say it."

"I—LOVE—YOU."

He pronounced each word slowly, passionately, and Skyler felt a longing as never before. Suddenly, it dawned on her that if the plan didn't work out, she might never see him again. She might be wounded, killed, or captured. She might be forced to run the rest of her life. Anything could happen, and these intimate words between them might be their last.

"I have to go now, Anthony," she said, feeling like an astronaut about to be launched into outer space. "Goodbye, and remember I love you."

She punched off before he could say another word. A tear trickled down her cheek and into her mouth. She wiped away the wet trace, pulled out her rosary, kneeled down, and prayed. When she was finished, she made herself a promise.

Whether you live or not, Angela, this is the very last job.

CHAPTER 126

HEADING NORTH ON I-25 in his Cadillac, Locke was on a mission from God. In his mind, what would transpire today in the Civic Center Plaza was most assuredly not murder, and he was no murderer. He was simply the instrument of God's will. The Heavenly Father had deemed Fowler unfit for the nation's—indeed the world's—highest office, and it was up to Locke to execute His wishes. Fowler's death would be an end, true, but it would also represent a new beginning.

The era of President Dubois. The very thought made Locke's skin tingle.

He imagined the new Chosen One being sworn in before the Chief Justice, taking the oath of office: "I, Jackson Beauregard Dubois, do solemnly swear that I will faithfully execute the Office of President of the United States, and will to the best of my ability, preserve, protect and defend the Constitution of the United States..."

A feeling of euphoria swept through him as he pictured the historic scene.

It lingered in his mind for several minutes, bolstering his resolve and filling him with a patriotic fervor.

And then the fantasy drifted off like a cloud as he peered out his car window. Everywhere he looked he saw God's magnificent handiwork, and it reinforced the view that he was on a righteous path. To the west, rising high above the naked plains, stood rocky escarpments and spiny ridges and perfect pyramids, the rocky precipices filled in along the flanks by shaggy forests of ponderosa pine. Clear-water creeks sliced through the rock and fed the pebbly rivers forming delicate lattice works across the Great Plains. Closer to the highway, he could see copses of still-leafy cottonwoods, their branches waving to him with melodic movements. There were also spectacular conglomerate monoliths and gently-dipping cuestas, shrouded with sweet-smelling sagebrush.

God's handiwork—how magnificent!

His reverie was interrupted by his ringing coded mobile. He picked it up from the seat next to him and took the call. "Hello?"

"Benjamin, where are you? We need to talk."

Skull Eyes! Locke wished he hadn't answered his phone. But he wasn't about to let the ex-CIA man or anyone else spoil his fine day. "You have some nerve calling me after what you've done. You murdered my daughter in cold blood. Believe me, you are going to pay dearly for that."

"Come on, Benjamin, you know damn well we had no idea she would be there."

It was Colonel Heston, and by his hollow, distorted voice, Locke could tell that both he and Skull Eyes were talking into a modulated speakerphone.

"You have overreached, gentlemen. You took matters into your own hands and acted without the Coalition's authority."

"We told you it was an accident," protested Skull Eyes.

"An accident? That's all you have to say for yourselves. Have you gone completely mad? Don't you understand what you have done? You killed not just innocent people, but my own daughter! All so you could oust me as chairman!"

"Words cannot describe the sorrow we feel over Susan's death," said the colonel. "But it was an accident."

"No, it was a flagrant abuse of your authority and has perhaps drawn unnecessary attention to the Coalition. Do you have any idea the damage you've caused?"

"You're the one to blame for everything that's happened," snarled Skull Eyes. "When we elected you chairman, you took an oath that you would hold yourself to the highest standards of personal conduct, competence, and leadership. But you have failed us completely. You have violated our trust and must step down once and for all."

"So I'm the one who's being punished for your crazy scheme?"

"The Committee has voted and you are hereby relieved of your duties as chairman."

"Without my vote or that of Senator Dubois? Everyone on the Committee knows I wouldn't kill my own daughter. I'm afraid your plan to overthrow me has failed, gentlemen."

"The vote was by a quorum of the Executive Committee and cannot be overturned. We're still deciding whether to remove you from the Coalition altogether."

Locke could care less; once Dubois was in power, he would be restored to his rightful place as chairman. "If I may be so bold as to inquire, who is the new chairman?"

"I am," affirmed Skull Eyes.

"Well then, enjoy your new position while it lasts, Mr. Chairman. I give you, at most, one week to live. And that goes for you too, Colonel. Mark my words, your days are numbered, gentlemen."

There was a strained silence. Locke could tell that he had put the fear of God in them both and they didn't know how to respond. The lopsided smile of a slightly unhinged man took hold on his face. The death of his beloved daughter and his wife abandoning him had sent him into an emotional tailspin, and all he truly cared about now was lashing out in a momentously Biblical-like fashion at his mortal enemies.

He expelled a little sigh. Then, rolling down his window, he embraced the earthy fragrance of sagebrush and needle pine. Again, he absorbed the drowsy beauty of the landscape, the sun ricocheting off the quartz-rich sandstone and conglomerate spires.

God is truly with me today!

"Where are you, Benjamin?" asked Truscott. "We need to meet with you in person to discuss this situation."

"What, so you can terminate me? I'll be the one doing the terminating if you don't mind, gentlemen."

"Where are you, Benjamin? Just tell us so we can help you," pleaded the colonel.

"Oh, let's just say I'm out for a drive, taking in the pleasant fall air."

"Come now, Benjamin," pressed Skull Eyes. "We need to know where you are. We know things have not turned out as planned and that you're upset. We want to help. Where are you?"

Locke's grin widened. "I'm afraid I can't tell you that. I bid you *adieu*, gentlemen. I have to sign off now."

"Benjamin, please!" the colonel pleaded. "You must tell us where you are!"

Silence.

"You wouldn't really kill us," sniffed Skull Eyes. "You don't have the stomach for it. That's why your time as chairman is finished. You've become not only incompetent but gutless."

"All I can say to that, gentlemen, is one thing. By the end of the week you shall both be no more."

"Not if we get to you first, you bastard!" hissed Skull Eyes.

"Then let the contest begin," pronounced Locke, and he punched off.

He smiled with saintly self-confidence as he set the phone back on the plush Corinthian leather car seat. Skull Eyes and the colonel were going to die all right, but not quite yet. Locke had more urgent business to attend to first.

All he needed was a single bold stroke.

And today, at 2 p.m. Mountain Standard Time, he would get his opportunity.

CHAPTER 127

IT WAS TOO LATE FOR BREAKFAST, so Patton concocted a huge Swiss cheese–porcini mushroom omelet and called it brunch. Pan-seared potatoes, English muffins, and piping-hot coffee rounded out the meal, which he and Jennifer ate in front of the curved bay window overlooking the park. With the FBI evidence response team cloistered in the apartment until the wee hours of the dawn, they had gotten only a few hours' rest, so the meal and coffee provided a welcome spark.

After breakfast, they went over the case again with John Sawyer. He had come by last night with the ERT and police, but Patton had not had time to go over the investigation with him in detail, focusing instead on the break-in. Patton was still disappointed about his removal from the case, but at least Sawyer was keeping him on unofficially. They had agreed to keep Sharp out of their little secret for the time being, although Sawyer had briefed the ASAC on last night's attack.

It was noon when Sawyer left the house. Five minutes later, one of the two FBI agents posted outside walked into the kitchen. "You have a visitor," he said to Patton.

"Who?"

"Mary Locke. She said it's urgent and she'll only speak to you."

Patton went straight to the front door and, after a minute's worth of uncomfortable preliminaries, showed Mrs. Locke into the living room. At that moment, Jennifer walked out of the bathroom. Her mouth opened wide with surprise.

"Mrs. Locke!"

The silver-haired woman stiffened, and said nothing.

Jennifer walked over to her quickly. "I am so sorry about what happened to Susan," she said. "I feel horrible about the entire..." Her words trailed off sadly.

Mary Locke acknowledged the consoling remark with a tilt of her head, but Patton could tell she was deeply troubled by Jennifer's presence. Obviously, she blamed Jennifer, at least partly, for her daughter's death.

"Would it be better if we spoke in private?" asked Patton.

Before the woman could answer, Jennifer said, "I'll be in the bedroom." She started off.

"Wait," Mary said, her lower lip trembling.

Jennifer stopped and turned around, slowly.

"Before I talk to Agent Patton, I need to know what happened to Susan. You must tell me everything."

CHAPTER 128

IT TOOK JENNIFER ten minutes to tell the story. As she spoke, she felt a host of conflicting emotions: guilt, anger, sadness, outrage—each vied for space inside her, twisting her like a washrag, leaving her emotionally drained. She hadn't talked Susan into having an abortion, but she still felt responsible for her fate at the clinic. She wished she could have somehow saved the poor girl and felt guilty for surviving the ordeal when so many other innocent people had perished.

When Jennifer was finished, Mary Locke covered her hands with her own. "I was angry at you," she said, her voice choked with emotion. "I thought you had planted the seed of having an abortion in Susan's mind. I thought, if only she hadn't befriended you these past few days, none of this would have happened. Now I realize my anger was badly misplaced. It is my husband, not you, who has acted unconscionably."

Patton leaned forward in his chair. "Are you saying he had a hand in the attack at the clinic?"

"No, I'm sure he tried to stop it. But that's not the point. The point is that he *knew* about it."

"Is this what you've come here about—the incident at the clinic?"

She shook her head and her eyes turned down to the floor.

"You have to trust me, Mrs. Locke. I'm here to help."

Mary's lower lip trembled again. Jennifer could see the emotions running amok through the poor woman as she struggled to speak. "I think my husband's involved in something...something terrible," she said finally, her voice faltering.

Patton tried to draw it out. "Something terrible?"

"The Kieger assassination."

"You think your husband was somehow behind it? Or involved in some way? Is that what you're telling me?"

"Yes, but there's more."

"More?"

She reached down, opened her purse, and pulled out a small leatherbound book. "It's Susan's diary. I went through it after she...she...please just take a look at the page I marked."

Patton took the book from her and opened it to the page with the yellow Post-it note. There, in Susan's own hand, he and Jennifer saw the startling revelation.

"My God. Your daughter thinks your husband…but how did she—?"

"I don't know, Special Agent. But we have to do something."

"We've got to get down to Civic Center Plaza right now," said Jennifer, feeling a sudden sense of urgency.

Patton slowly nodded. "The speech—so that is the plan after all."

"Yep, and we have to stop it," said Jennifer. "We have to stop it right now."

CHAPTER 129

PATTON DIDN'T WASTE A SECOND. He sprinted into the kitchen, grabbed his cell phone, and dialed the number for the Denver field office dispatch center. "This is Special Agent Patton. I need to track down John Sawyer. Is he in?"

"Yes, but he told me to forward all calls to Agent Sharp's office. I'll connect you."

"No, wait!" Patton cried, but he was too late. The call was being transferred.

Shit, I don't want Henry involved in this. What should I do?

"Sharp here."

Though Patton wanted to hang up, at the last second he decided against it. "Henry, this is Ken. I need to talk to John. Is he there?"

"You're on a ten-day suspension, Special Agent. Whatever you have to say, you'd better say it to me."

Patton looked at his watch. *Damn! There's no time to argue.* "Okay, Henry, here's what I've got." He quickly gave him the rundown of the situation.

"Where are you?" Sharp asked.

"At my house. Look, Henry, we have to cancel the event. Fowler's life is in jeopardy."

"Now just hold on. We can't shut this thing down based on a dead teenager's diary entry or the word of some emotionally distressed woman. Mary Locke probably holds her husband responsible and is trying to—"

"No, it all fits, goddamnit! Locke had Kieger killed and now he's going after Fowler!"

"That doesn't make sense. Why would he do that?"

Patton told him all the reasons.

"All right, I suppose these allegations *do* warrant looking into," Sharp conceded. "But I'm not going to embarrass the Bureau by inciting panic. I'm going to have to speak to the Locke woman myself to verify this. I'll be there in twenty minutes."

"Twenty minutes? By then it could be too late!"

"No, it won't. The speech doesn't start until two. That gives us plenty of time to call off the event, if necessary. But you are in no position to make that call. Capiche?"

"No, we need to alert the Service now."

"You are to remain at your house until I get there to question the Locke woman myself. Is that understood?"

Patton looked at his watch. "I'll give you until one thirty. After that, I'm going—"

"I am ordering you to stand down and wait for me, Special Agent! Then we'll settle this matter once and for all!"

CHAPTER 130

A HALF HOUR EARLIER, at 12:30 p.m., Skyler walked out of the Brown Palace Hotel and headed for the Sixteenth Street Mall. She wore a conservative blue concierge uniform with a red tie, the same attire worn by the staff of the Adam's Mark and a half dozen other hotels downtown. A brunette wig and clear, normal-vision glasses rounded out her blandly official costume. She carried an overnight bag on her shoulder and a purse in her hand. Denver police and federal agents were posted in front of the barricades at every intersection, but they paid her little mind.

She walked inside the public restroom near the corner of Cleveland Place and Sixteenth, a location she had scouted on two prior occasions. She quickly glanced beneath the stall doors; all four were empty. She entered the last stall, closed the door behind her, and changed clothes, exchanging her hotel staff uniform for two other uniforms.

The first was the white uniform of a paramedic for Lifecare Ambulance Service, a national emergency transport company with offices in Denver, Colorado Springs, and Boulder.

The second, which she slipped over the paramedic's clothing, was an FBI critical incident response group uniform, complete with all the accouterments that went with it.

With the uniforms complete, the only thing left was to apply her actor's makeup. This took her several minutes. When she was finished, she examined herself in her compact mirror.

The transformation was so effective, she bore only a vague resemblance to the brunette concierge who had entered the restroom a few minutes earlier. With the wig gone, the hair beneath her gold-lettered FBI cap was close-cropped and platinum-blonde. Last night, she had cut and dyed it to give herself a butch law enforcement look. Her skin was now alabaster rather than olive, with the prominent freckles of a fair-skinned woman of British Isles decent on the nose and around the eyes. Her irises were now as blue as the Caribbean, and a thin pink scar had been painted onto her chin, to give her that single imperfection all eyes would be drawn to like a magnet—and people would remember. An identical scar was evident on the ID cards she carried on her person.

She was now Special Agent Carey Firestone from the Miami field office, with FBI creds, a controlled-access CIRG badge, and a Florida driver's license to prove it.

And when the time came, she would be paramedic Jackie Chorney, a veteran driver with Lifecare Ambulance Service in Denver.

She was ready to move out. After making sure the restroom was still empty, she climbed on top of the toilet, popped one of the ceiling tiles, and stuffed her carrying bag behind a sheet metal vent. Climbing back down, she put on a pair of dark Ray-Ban sunglasses, opened the stall door, and stepped onto the mall with an air of authority befitting an FBI agent. She crossed Broadway and walked into the *Denver Tribune* Tower. A security check-in desk had been set up in the lobby in front of a bank of elevators. Two neatly dressed U.S. government agents manned the desk.

Skyler held her breath. *The moment of truth.*

The agent on the left spoke first. "And you would be Agent..."

"Firestone. Miami field office, spotter."

She flashed her creds. The man gave her a conspiratorial look unseen by the other agent. *So here is my first helper.* She wondered if the guy was FBI or Secret Service.

He made a big, cumbersome show of cross-checking her identifications. Then he handed them back to her and the other agent checked her name off a list, all part of the plan.

"All right, Agent Firestone, you're good to go. I'll radio you're coming up."

"Thanks." She headed for the elevators. When she reached them, she blew out a sigh of relief. At the same time, it occurred to her that she would miss this: the high-wire tension and clever masquerades. The actual shooting wasn't the big deal; it was the planning, infiltration, and escape that were most exciting.

She took the elevator to the twentieth floor. When the doors opened, a man in a SWAT uniform just like hers was waiting. He introduced himself as Agent Patrick Hughes, checked her IDs, and led her down a hallway, past a half dozen staff writers hammering away at computer keyboards. When they reached the west stairwell, he pushed open the door and they walked up a flight of concrete stairs. He opened another door and they stepped onto the rooftop into the bright sunlight.

Three men stood near the edge, staring down at the Plaza. They turned around as she and Agent Hughes walked up. Right away, she recognized the big, distinguished-looking man in the blue suit.

"Agent Firestone," the man said, "we've been expecting you." He held out his right hand. "Frederick Taylor, United States Secret Service."

It was the same voice that had warned her last night to get out of her apartment. She shook his hand, noting his lack of surprise that she was not a man.

So you've figured out I'm Gomez. You're a clever one, Agent Taylor.

"This is Agent Rostello, and this is Agent Lufkin," Taylor said, introducing the other two men.

Skyler repeated the handshaking ritual with them, unaware that the second hand she shook belonged to...*the Apostle.*

CHAPTER 131

AT HALF PAST ONE, Locke greeted Senator Dubois and they took their assigned seats next to the speakers' platform. The crowd—at least thirty thousand strong—spread across the grassy lawn in front of them like a newly sprouted colony. There was a frisson of anticipation in the air: Locke felt as though his whole life led inexorably to what was about to happen.

He gave a sidelong glance at Dubois, sitting directly to his right like Alexander the Great. With his close-cropped white hair, perfectly pressed charcoal-gray suit, and crimson tie, he looked exquisitely presidential, as if he knew this moment belonged to him. Soon, he would come face to face with his destiny—and America would once again rise to the glory she had once known.

Yes, it would be a bold future all right. There would be a new commander in chief in Washington. He would institute his own special brand of political reform in short order, for here was a man who brooked no opposition when it came to protecting and defending the Constitution. It would be a paradigm shift, a change in economic, political, and social policy that would reverberate for decades. By God, there would be law and order in Washington, and there would be honor and integrity. But most importantly, there would be a return to American hegemony and a reawakened respect for the nation's sacrosanct institutions.

The great ship would be righted and America would be born-again.

Nothing could stop them now.

Feeling a patriotic stirring inside, Locke looked over again at the supreme commander who would lead the charge.

On the soon-to-be-announced vice-president-elect's craggy face, he saw a little smile of triumph.

It was then Locke knew: God had truly spoken.

CHAPTER 132

"WHERE THE HELL IS HE?" cursed Patton, pacing in front of his bay window overlooking Wash Park. "Sharp should have been here five minutes ago. Something's wrong. I don't like it."

"I don't either," echoed Jennifer. "You have the phone number of that Secret Service big shot? What's his name?"

"Fred Taylor."

"If it gets down to the wire, you can call him, right?"

He saw the look of worry on her face and knew it was a mirror image of his own. "I'd rather talk to him in person. Either way, we've got to stop this."

"There's more at stake than just Fowler. We both know who takes the White House if Locke pulls this off."

"Senator Dubois."

"The Prince of Darkness himself. It's looking more and more like he's Fowler's pick for VP. It's crazy when you think about it—he could very well be part of all this."

The thought of the Prince of Darkness in charge of the country sent a chill down his spine. Though Patton leaned a little to the right on many issues, and was a self-described "fiscal conservative," a future with Dubois as president was a future he wanted no part of.

Suddenly, Jennifer's mouth froze half-open as she stared out the window.

"What is it?"

The agents guarding the house were running for their car.

What the hell? Patton dashed to the front door, swung it open, and leaped down the brick stairs. "Hey, where are you going?" he called out, waving his arms.

The Crown Victoria screeched away from the curb and tore down the street, leaving behind an acrid stench of burnt rubber.

"Why would they just leave like that?" asked Jennifer from the front porch.

"Sharp's up to something. I should have known."

They walked back inside just as Mary Locke came out of the kitchen carrying a glass of water. She took one look at them and said, "What's wrong?"

"Our protection detail just left. I think it was ordered away."

"By whom?"

"My boss, most likely. Don't worry, everything's going to be okay. But you should both collect your things. We need to get out of here."

He went into the spare bedroom, unlocked a drawer, and grabbed his personal Glock. Walking back into the living room, he chambered the first round and stuffed the pistol in the small of his back.

When he looked up, he saw Jennifer and Mary Locke staring at him.

"It's okay," he said to reassure them. "I know what I'm doing."

In truth, the last time he had fired a gun was his annual re-certification training nine months ago. The vast majority of FBI agents went through their entire careers without ever firing a single shot in the field—and, thus far, Patton was one of them.

Now the faint rumble of car engines was discernible; the sound seemed to be growing louder.

Jennifer looked worried. "That doesn't sound friendly to me. We'd better go now."

Patton listened a moment, nodded, and spoke in a voice of calm urgency. "Go to the garage, open the sliding door, and climb in my Explorer. Leave the driver's seat open and just wait there. I'll be right there once I see who it is. It's possible we're being paranoid over nothing."

"I don't think so," Jennifer cautioned. "You said yourself Sharp could be involved. Suppose he's sending in a team to arrest you—or all of us."

"If that's the case, I still need confirmation. So please get in the car."

Jennifer nodded grudgingly and led Mary Locke to the back door.

Patton darted to the bay window looking out on the street. Three vans screeched to a halt out front. Doors flung open and a dozen hard-looking agents poured from the vehicles, wearing raid uniforms and brandishing assault rifles.

Assault rifles! Jesus Fucking Christ!

This was no peaceful mission to question Mrs. Locke or a simple arrest—this was a goddamned raid! And there was Sharp, the bastard, barking out orders like his great-grandfather, General Patton. There was no longer any doubt Sharp was deeply involved in this thing and would stop at nothing to keep anyone who might suspect his involvement quiet. *The bastard!*

But there was no time to dwell on that now.

Patton turned and ran down the hallway, flung open the back door, and cleared the steps in a single bound. He sprinted across the lawn to the garage and jumped into the Explorer, tossing the Glock between the seats. Sticking the key in the ignition and throwing the jeep into drive, he slipped into the alley and floored it, looking in his rear view mirror for signs of pursuit.

There was no one.

Good, he thought. *Now all we have to do is get our asses downtown in time to save the day!*

CHAPTER 133

PEERING DOWN FROM THE ROOFTOP of the *Denver Tribune* Tower, Skyler felt a prickle of tension as the procession of Lincolns came into view. For the past hour, she had scanned the upper floors and rooftops in quadrant six, as Taylor had instructed her to do, but now her attention was riveted on the street below. From Colfax, the sleek black Town Cars turned right onto Bannock and began pulling to the curb in front of the City and County Building. Beyond the motorcade, there was scarcely a ruffle in the giant American flag at the steps of the marble-gray government building. A police chopper circled lazily overhead, making its way slowly around the perimeter of the Civic Center Plaza. Somehow, the world seemed deceptively serene to Skyler, like the calm before a storm, which made her even more anxious for what was yet to come.

She pulled down her binoculars and let them hang from her neck. Surreptitiously, she studied the four men on her right as they watched the procession of Lincolns. Two of the men gave her the willies: Secret Service Agent Taylor, the hero who had saved Reagan, the man who was sworn to protect presidents and presidential candidates, but who was, in fact, a traitor; and Agent Lufkin, the spotter with the jackal's smile. She suspected Lufkin wasn't Secret Service at all, but a freelance killer, like herself. His being here could serve only one purpose—to eliminate her when the assignment was complete—and she was determined to keep a close eye on him.

The other two uniformed men, Agents Hughes and Rostello, didn't concern her. Neither would leave the rooftop alive, and one was her ticket out.

Or at least that was the plan.

Down on the ground, Katherine Fowler filed from the car with her handlers. Behind a protective wall of Secret Service agents, the president-elect made her way to the speakers' platform, where soft orchestrated music drifted from the loudspeakers. The large crowd was, as expected, more subdued than last Sunday. The event was intended as a tribute to Kieger and protest against the assassination, not a political rally, though Fowler's handlers, no doubt, didn't see it that way.

Skyler felt a twinge of guilt knowing she was about to drive a stake through the nation's heart for the second time in a week. *But you are a professional,* she reminded herself. *And a professional has to go about her job with emotional detachment.*

Fowler shook hands with Governor Jackson Stoddart and the mayor before taking a seat a few feet back from the podium. The governor stepped forward to make the scheduled opening remarks; he was to be followed first by the mayor and then Fowler. The fatal shot was to be delivered when Fowler stepped to the podium and the police helicopter was farthest away in its elliptical flight path around the plaza. At that moment, Skyler would have a clear line of sight to the president-elect and the helicopter would be effectively neutralized.

As the governor launched into his opening remarks, Taylor issued instructions for the team to resume its survey of quadrant six. Skyler raised her Leica range-finding binoculars again and studied the countersniper positions. Taylor had chosen their current position well. There were teams posted on every building around the plaza, but not one had a clear line of sight to her position. The countersniper squad on the dome of the State Capitol almost had a clear shot, but as long as she kept crouched behind the wall, she'd be out of harm's way. The Petroleum Building and Union Plaza Building would have provided perfect lines of sight, but the stairwell and two ventilation structures on the rooftop of the *Denver Tribune* Tower where Skyler stood obscured a direct view.

She would be most vulnerable right after the shot, when she rushed for the door to the stairwell. At that moment, she would be exposed to long-distance fire from at least three stationary positions and, less likely, from sharpshooters in the mobile chopper. But hitting a moving target from across the plaza or from a moving helicopter would be a challenge for even an expert marksman.

After a couple of minutes, Skyler swung the range finder back toward the podium, locking the laser ranging dot on the governor's head. Though he wasn't the soft target, he served as an excellent gauge of distance. With the press of a button, she sent an invisible ray of laser light that struck the test target and bounced back instantaneously. Skyler read the red digital readout superimposed, in standard U.S. units, in the upper right-hand corner of the image.

Five hundred eight yards.

Ordinarily this distance, though substantial, would pose no problem for a shooter of her pedigree. But according to Taylor, Fowler was wearing a Kevlar vest equipped with a ballistic trauma plate, so she had to go for a headshot. This cut her target area by more than half. All the same, Skyler had no doubt she could get the job done. She would just have to be methodical in her calcs and remain true in her hold.

Picking up her Winchester 70T sniper rifle and sighting the target area through the scope, she quickly computed the drift and drop. There was no breeze, so she wouldn't have to correct laterally for windage. But the drop was substantial, given the distance. Last night she had memorized the specs on the Winchester and the Unertl 8X scope. She would have to hold on the third mil dot below the reticle to account for the bullet's drop over its lengthy flight path, which meant she had to hold three dots higher than at short range.

As she resumed scanning her quadrant through the scope, her thoughts returned to Anthony. Once the assignment was complete, they would be reunited. She visualized them nestled together in front of a log fire somewhere in the Swiss Alps, lounging on an endless beach of white sand on a reclusive island in the Lesser Antilles, making love in a lavish hotel room in some exotic region of Asia. It was all going to work out for her. She was going to quit the game, have minor plastic surgery performed, obtain three fresh sets of identity papers and credit cards, and go on to live a life of luxury.

Ideally, Anthony would be a part of that life, but if not she would find another man like him. She knew now there were men out there worth loving. Being helplessly in love was the most important thing in the world to her now. She was sick and tired of the conflicting emotions, the surges of guilt and nausea. She hated the ghosts of men she'd killed haunting her subconscious, coming at her in her dreams. Not just Kieger, who had floated through her mind all week, but Don Scarpello and all the others she had murdered. She didn't want to spend the rest of her life living like this—wandering around strange cities, biding her time until the next hit, surrounded by people she did not know or care about.

It was time for a change. It was time to *live.*

All you need is one last hit. Then you shall be free.

CHAPTER 134

"CAN'T THIS THING GO ANY FASTER?" Jennifer cried from her shotgun seat as they blazed down Speer Boulevard toward downtown. "We're going to be too late!"

"Mario Andretti at your service!" Patton slapped his foot down on the accelerator of the Ford Explorer.

"That's more like it," Jennifer said. Behind her, Mary Locke held on for dear life to a handgrip.

Steering with his left hand, Patton yanked out his cell phone from his pocket and tossed it to Jennifer. "Get Taylor on the line!" he cried as they shot through the yellow light at Logan.

Jennifer punched it in. "It's ringing," she said, and she handed the phone back to him.

He took it in his left hand and held it to his ear as they came upon Lincoln Street. He jerked the wheel to the right, screeching onto the one-way street. The engine roared like thunder.

"Agent Taylor here."

"Fred, its Ken Patton." He quickly explained the situation over the roaring engine.

"Where are you now?" Taylor asked.

"I'm heading north on Lincoln. I'll be there in five minutes."

"Is Mrs. Locke with you?"

"Yeah, and Jennifer Odden too. Look, Fred, you've got to shut this thing down. Call your people and get Fowler out of there now. Her life's in danger."

The phone was silent a moment. "I want you to listen to me very carefully, Special Agent. I'm going to do what you ask, but I have to follow the proper protocols. I want you to go to the parking structure beneath the loading dock at the *Denver Tribune* Tower. The address is 1560 Broadway. The parking structure is on the north side, on Sixteenth. I'm here with my team now. From there, I'll take you to Bob Riley, the SAC in charge of the personal protection detail. In the meantime, I'll call him and ask him to delay Fowler's appearance, but he's going to need to talk to you and Mrs. Locke in person before he can order a full-scale shut-down. This event's just too damned big. Fowler and her people will go ballistic if we cancel without justification."

"You'll get a temporary postponement until we can speak to Riley?"

"Just as soon as you let me off the line."

"All right, we'll be there in five minutes."

"Lincoln's closed off at Fourteenth. You'll have to swing east of the Capitol and come in on Sixteenth. That will take you a little longer." In fact, Taylor was banking on it.

"Roger that."

"And Ken."

"Yeah."

"You did the right thing to call me."

"I know I did, Fred. See you in a few."

CHAPTER 135

THE TRAITOR PUNCHED OFF his secure mobile, quietly seething under his breath. Every plan had its exigencies, its unavoidable breakdowns, but this one was monumental. He had badly underestimated Patton. IQ-wise, the Bureau brat wasn't Harvard Law or Wharton Business School material, but that meant little in the realm of crime solving. This kid was something far more dangerous: he was as doggedly persistent as a bloodhound. He had been yanked off the case, but he just wouldn't let go.

Damn him!

Now he had to be dealt with—once and for all. So did his two compatriots.

But there was the rub. Taylor couldn't very well take out Mary Locke, the wife of his employer, without his employer's consent. But if he was going to prevent Patton and that damned journalist from warning the Service or DPD, there was no way around it. He would just have to hope Locke would never know who was behind it.

His mind working in overdrive, Taylor scanned the speakers' platform in the far distance through his binoculars. The mayor was on the stage now, speaking to the large crowd. Behind him and to the left, Taylor could make out Locke and Senator Dubois, who looked as hard and tough as a steel drill bit. Yes, the senator was the perfect choice to pick up the conservative torch; he would get the beleaguered country headed in the right direction in no time at all.

Taylor turned his binoculars to the glimmering dome of the Capitol and other buildings across the plaza. The countersnipers and spotters were in position, but all he could see was their upper chests and the tops of their heads, like little Roman busts along the balustrades. The police chopper hovered above the Art Museum, across the plaza.

Time for the opening act.

Taylor walked over to his companions crouched along the edge of the rooftop. The stairwell structure, a few feet from the wall, covered them in shadow. He choreographed the next few seconds in his head; everything had to be handled with swift, violent efficiency.

He made eye contact with the fictitious Agent Lufkin and touched his nose in a prearranged signal.

The Apostle didn't waste a millisecond. He withdrew a small plastic pistol from his coat pocket and locked onto Agent Hughes. There was a subtle pop, like a valve releasing compressed air, and the victim collapsed on the rooftop, rifle still in hand, a hypodermic dart sticking from his neck.

Agent Rostello's mouth opened and he raised his rifle to shield himself, but he was too late as a second dart spit from the gun. He toppled over like a stringless puppet, the Apostle snatching the rifle from him as he fell.

Skyler backed away a step. She had known what was coming, but was still taken by surprise.

Taylor thought how much he would like to have one of those guns. *So compact and efficient.*

In fact, the Crossman repeating .22-caliber air pistol was still in the experimental stage. It was favored by international intelligence and terrorist organizations because it was as small as an old-time Derringer and both the gun and ammo were constructed solely from plastic, which facilitated easy smuggling through airport metal detectors.

The Apostle pulled out the toxin-coated air darts and propped the bodies against the wall, giving the appearance of spotters crouching down to peer over the edge. Because of the heavy shadow from the stairwell structure, this would be enough to fool the spotters on the rooftops and the police observers in the helicopter.

Taylor looked at his watch. "Everything's set. Fowler will take the podium any minute now. I have to take care of something, so the success of the mission now depends on you two." He looked at Skyler. "You are to take the shot once the target is standing at the podium and the helicopter is at apogee. Is that clear?"

"Crystal," Skyler said dryly.

"Good—happy hunting then." He disappeared into the stairwell.

CHAPTER 136

LOCKE'S left leg twitched with anticipation. *Almost time.* From his first row seat on the speakers' platform, he studied the Secret Service agents posted at the stage. They stood still as statues behind their dark sunglasses, each and every face stolid as granite. They were honorable men, consummate professionals, who took pride in their jobs and their country; and yet, even the most stalwart among them could not prevent what was about to happen.

Locke wished the mayor would hurry and finish his speech so Fowler could take center stage for her last—and most memorable—performance. But the man was a typical politician, unable to give his jaw muscles a rest once a huge crowd had assembled before him.

Locke's steel-gray eyes swept the audience, taking in the solemn yet hopeful countenances in the first few rows. These people were gravely mistaken if they believed reformers like Kieger or Fowler would make their country a better place to live. No, what they needed was the regal Southern gentleman sitting next to him. With a conservative majority in the House, Senate, and Supreme Court, Dubois would put an end to this rancid era of American weakness in the form of regulatory suffocation, moral relativism, and tax and spend liberalism. Of course, to appease the moderates, he would promise to govern from the middle, but it would be nothing more than window dressing. When he took office, he would rule proudly from the far right, and there wasn't a damn thing anyone could do about it.

True, this was only the first step, but one day goodness really would overtake evil and America would truly be born-again.

Locke could almost taste the rebirth, sweet as apple butter.

He was pulled from his reverie as the mayor introduced the president-elect. The crowd responded with polite applause befitting the sober occasion as Fowler rose to her feet. Time seemed to stand still as the young, charismatic woman shook the mayor's hand and took the podium.

When Fowler cleared her throat, Locke felt his body tense with anticipation. He imagined the bullet ripping through the traitor's head, the crowd's terrified shriek and ensuing pandemonium. He looked over at Dubois and saw his jaw tighten. When they made eye contact, Dubois gave a little nod.

The new Chosen One knew what to do.

CHAPTER 137

AS THE CHOPPER passed over the Adam's Mark Hotel, Skyler brought the stock of the Winchester 70T slowly to her shoulder, placing the third mil-dot beneath the crosshairs on her soft target. She wore ultrathin leather gloves to ensure her fingerprints would never be found on the weapon. Through the Unertyl 8X scope, Katherine Fowler looked remarkably similar to how Governor Kieger had looked during the final moments of his life. Her fists hammered at the air, her face sparkled with passion, and her commanding voice rose stridently over the loudspeakers.

Skyler forced herself to think of her not as a woman, not as a terrestrial being with blood coursing through her veins, but as a means to an end.

One more soft target and you are free. Just one more hit—the very last hit.

She pulled the stock tightly against her shoulder and held the mil-dot there on her target with the cool, collected discipline of an expert professional assassin. Her right index finger slid forward and curled around the trigger. Her hands were steady, her muscles tense but precisely controlled. She was as ready as she would ever be.

And then she lost it.

A wave of nausea seized her, followed by a sudden throbbing in her head like a migraine. The rifle started to slip from her hands.

My God, not again?

"What the fuck's the matter with you?" the Apostle snarled, pointing his SIG-Sauer at her temple.

Skyler slumped against the wall, the rifle sliding carelessly to the gravel rooftop. She tried to draw a breath, but the air refused to enter her lungs. She grasped her head in her hands, rocking with pain.

"Shoot goddamnit or I'll blow your fucking head off!" He shoved the pistol against her temple.

"My head...it...it feels like it's trapped in a vise."

"I don't give a flying fuck! Take the fucking shot!"

Skyler willed the rifle back in her hands. "Okay," she gasped, still short of breath. "I'll do...I'll do it. Just give me a second."

The Apostle grudgingly backed up, giving her some room but still keeping his pistol trained on her.

Skyler took a few controlled breaths and thought of Anthony. Slowly, her head began to clear and she felt a renewed strength. It would be a precious waste not to suck it up and carry out the assignment. Then she would go on to share a real life with Anthony.

You can love, she exhorted herself. *You can really love!*

And that's why you have to go through with this.

CHAPTER 138

AS SENIOR SECRET SERVICE AGENT TAYLOR stepped from the parking garage elevator, his coded mobile rang. He debated whether to answer it, but it could be Patton, so he took the call.

"Taylor here."

"Special Agent, we know what's going on," Joseph Truscott declared. "And we're here to tell you there's been a change of plans."

"Change of plans, sir?"

"Yes, Agent Taylor, we have a new target."

CHAPTER 139

SKYLER LIFTED THE RIFLE until the crosshairs were centered on the new soft target's face. The professional shooter's discipline had returned. All reservations were pushed aside, leaving her with perfect concentration.

There was not the slightest tremor in her grip, only supreme confidence.

She took a moment to study the target's face. The image through the scope was clear, unwavering.

Her nerves hardened. Her breaths came in a steady rhythm.

She felt in complete control of her destiny.

You can do this. Just finish the job and get out of here.

She raised the rifle a hair and the third-mil dot locked onto the new soft target's face.

The perfect hold: no anger, no guilt, no doubt, no fear.

The perfect way to end a remarkable, if unorthodox and sanguine, career.

The mil-dot became one with the target as she entered her own private world, the sniper's cocoon, for the last time.

The field of fire turned noiseless. No one and nothing moved.

Her mind was as clear as a mountain lake as her gloved right index finger curled softly around the trigger. All her resolve, all her professionalism, all her energy, would go into this final shot.

"Bless me Father, for my last sin," she murmured in her native tongue.

And then, she sighted and squeezed the trigger—three times in rapid succession.

CHAPTER 140

"SO WHAT ARE YOU SAYING, JENN?" Patton asked as Fred Taylor approached the car on the driver's side, from fifty feet away.

"I'm saying can you really trust this guy?"

"Of course I trust him. He's been working the case with me all week. He's the one who got hold of the security disks and tracked down Jane Doe. Him and Charlie Fial."

"Yeah, a Secret Service agent and a spook. They don't work for the Bureau, Ken. You don't really know them. And look how much trouble your own people have caused you. Look at Sharp."

Taylor continued walking forward.

Patton studied him closely. *He's wondering why I'm not driving up to him. But he doesn't seem anxious or hostile and his gun isn't drawn. Then again, he's Secret Service. That's how he's trained to be: cool, calm, and collected. And the parking garage is empty, the perfect place for an ambush.*

"I don't like it," Jennifer said. "I've got a bad feeling again."

"I'm learning to trust your feelings." Patton smiled and waved to Taylor as if everything was okay. "Let's see what he does."

He jammed the Explorer in reverse and made for the exit ramp, keeping his eyes on Taylor. As if on cue, the Secret Service man's look narrowed and he jerked out a black pistol equipped with a noise suppressor and opened fire.

Patton slammed his foot down on the accelerator and turned his head around so he could see behind him. "Get down!" he yelled as perfect circles suddenly blossomed on the front windshield, radiating outward into branching spider webs of fissured glass.

With bullets peppering his windshield, Patton lost his bearings.

He collided with a parked minivan. Then the engine stalled.

"Damn!" he cursed.

Taylor came on, firing rapidly, his piece spitting out piping hot brass casings.

"Oh my God!" Mary Locke cried, and she began to pray.

Patton turned the key. The engine wouldn't turn over.

"C'mon! C'mon!" exhorted Jennifer.

He tried again; this time the engine caught.

Taylor charged, teeth clenched, shooting. Patton reached for his gun between the seats, but in the confusion, it had slid to the floor of the passenger seat, out of reach.

Shit!

He decided their best chance was to go forward into the maw.

"Hold on tight and stay down!"

He slapped his foot down onto the accelerator and, keeping his head down as low as possible, he charged the traitor.

Taylor stopped in his tracks, calmly popped in a new magazine, and raised his arm to fire.

Patton brought the jeep up to thirty miles per hour, tires screeching across the concrete.

Taylor just stood there, firing his semiauto like an M-16.

Patton guessed which way the senior agent would dive. He chose left.

Taylor ripped off three more rapid bursts then dove left.

The Explorer drove into him and pitched him violently against a Toyota hybrid, his head smashing like a cantaloupe on the rear fender.

Patton slammed his foot on the brake and jumped up in his seat to get his bearings.

He was almost too late.

A concrete support closed in on them without warning. But at the last possible second, he was able to swerve to the right and screech to a halt before hitting the wall.

There was a moment of stunned silence.

"Whew, that was close. Everyone okay?"

"I'm all right," Jennifer said.

"Me too," echoed Mary Locke. "Is he...?"

Patton looked at the lifeless form of Agent Frederick Taylor. "Yes, he's dead." He unbuckled his seat belt.

Suddenly, he heard gunfire and a mechanical whirring sound. He was hammered with a realization. He reached down, grabbed his cell phone and Glock from the floor of the passenger seat, and thrust the phone at Jennifer.

"Call in the cavalry!" he barked, chambering the first round.

"Where are you going?"

"To the roof!" and he jumped out of the Explorer.

CHAPTER 141

WHEN THE LAST OF THE THREE BULLETS STRUCK, Skyler saw only the tiniest puff of smoke, followed by a wet pink cloud of spurting blood, brain-matter, and bone as the head was literally pulped. The body was driven back, the arms flung out helplessly, like someone being thrown off a cliff, and the victim collapsed to the wooden platform. It was a gruesome sight, a cinematographic-like experience that would be indelibly etched into Skyler's mind for as long as she lived. But there was no time now for guilt.

"Wait," exclaimed the Apostle, staring through his high-powered binoculars, "you weren't supposed to—"

"So I changed my fucking mind." She took the stock of her rifle and drove it into his binoculars, smashing his face like a hydraulic ram. Then she swatted him a second time, downward, knocking the pistol from his hand. With a third swing of the rifle, she delivered another crushing blow to his head. He crumpled to the roof with a blank look on his face. He was out of commission, at least for the time being.

Skyler grabbed his pistol with her gloved hand and threw it over the edge. Then she shoved the Winchester into his arms, picked up the dead Agent Hughes, heaved him over her shoulder, and ran for the stairwell door.

That's when the chopper appeared.

It came out of nowhere, a monstrous dragonfly with spinning rotors on the top and tail of the aircraft, its white-and-blue frame glistening in the sunlight as it roared in from the east. The side door slid open and two SWAT sharpshooters opened up on her. Stirred into action, the countersnipers on the rooftops across the plaza and the dome of the Capitol quickly joined in the fusillade.

Bullets danced all around her, ricocheting off the wall and metal door to the stairwell. Skyler ran as fast as her legs would carry her, straining under the weight of the small but suddenly very unwieldy Agent Hughes. Every stride took tremendous effort, but finally she made it to the door, throwing it open with a free hand while balancing the dead agent over her shoulder like a circus act.

Then she plunged down the stairs, two steps at a time.

CHAPTER 142

SHAKING HIS HEAD CLEAR, the Apostle crawled to the wall for cover, holding a warm Winchester 70T without a round in the chamber. Bullets rained upon him from all directions, like a shooting gallery with him as the central target. He might have laughed at the sheer craziness of his predicament if he had any energy to spare. The bitch was clever, he had to admit. She had fulfilled—no she had wildly exceeded—her contract and then, without pause, she had ensured her own survival. She was good— damned good—a worthy adversary in a world where there weren't enough of them.

But she was of no concern to him now, at least until he got off this motherfucking rooftop. If he could just pull himself together, he might be able to get out of this. He and his platoon had been in just as tight a pinch during a Desert Storm raid in Kuwait, and he had come out of that one alive.

You can do it again!

But he had to hurry. His chances of escape were dwindling with each passing second.

He pulled out his backup gun, the compact Beretta in his ankle holster. Releasing the safety, he took aim at the chopper. He fired five times and was answered with twenty rounds of blistering counterfire, not just from the chopper, but the sharpshooters on the surrounding buildings. They were moving into position, trying to get a clear line of sight, a better angle.

The helicopter swung around, and suddenly the Apostle was exposed, the wall now offering no protection. He retreated to one of the ventilation fans, protruding like a blob of coral on a sea floor. The wail of the rotors and blazing gunfire were deafening. For a fleeting instant, he imagined himself back in Kuwait firing at ragheads. He felt a strange warrior spirit sweeping through him, an unexpected and unusually pleasant sensation. Suddenly, he burst out with maniacal laughter, jumped up, and opened fire at the chopper in a rapid burst, completely emptying his magazine.

It was then he met with a stroke of good fortune.

The last shot sailed through the front windshield of the helicopter and drove into the helmeted pilot's forehead. As his hands slid from the controls, the huge machine shuddered, pitched wildly right, and nosed downward toward the edge of the roof. When the front two wheels of the undercarriage clipped the wall, the helicopter bounced up, bucking and swaying like a rodeo bull. Then the aircraft stalled as the top blade slowed its rotation.

Again, the front tires smashed into the wall. Only this time, the helicopter plunged over the edge.

Down the chopper plummeted, a free fall nosedive.

A terrific explosion shook the building. The next thing the Apostle knew, smoke leapt up along the edge of the roof in a black mushroom cloud.

There was no time to celebrate. He ran to the door of the stairwell, threw it open, and plunged down the stairs. The thick black smoke rose like a plume of volcanic ash, covering his retreat like a stage curtain.

The bitch! I still have to kill the bitch!

He might not make it out of this, but he would damn sure take her out before the feds swarmed the building. It would be like a final cigar for a man condemned to a firing squad. The Apostle certainly wasn't going to be taken alive. If he couldn't manage to escape, he would at least kill the bitch before making a last violent stand. He had long ago decided that when his time came, he would go out like Butch and Sundance.

With his pistol blazing, laughing in the face of his enemies.

CHAPTER 143

"AGENT DOWN! GUNMAN ON ROOF! CLEAR THE AREA!" Skyler shouted as she ran toward the elevators, lugging the limp Agent Hughes over her shoulder like a sack of potatoes.

The twentieth floor of the *Denver Tribune* Tower was already in a heightened state of alert. Editors, graphic artists, staff reporters, and administrative assistants were peering worriedly out the office windows, wondering what the commotion was about, when the black cloud of smoke shot past them. But Skyler needed more. To get out of the building alive and avoid capture, she needed to incite a complete panic.

"Agent down! Gunman on roof! Clear the area!" she yelled again, louder this time.

Now the employees heeded her warning.

The floor turned into the deck of the Titanic in the final fateful minutes. People fled the offices, cubes, and workstations in panic, choking the hallways like salmon during a summer run. Running, stumbling, colliding, screaming. The bedlam spread with the speed of a computer virus, and people were knocked down as they merged into the traffic flowing toward the fire stairs and elevators.

It was complete pandemonium.

Skyler was nearly bowled over by a wave of people as she made a mad dash for the bank of elevators. A silvery-long-haired man who looked like a cross between the Grateful Dead's Bob Weir and Yosemite Sam— whom Skyler recognized as illustrious veteran political reporter Mike Littwin—was frantically punching the *Down* button. Around him stood a dozen or so people, muttering to themselves and quaking in their shoes.

"Take the stairs!" Skyler commanded them as she dashed up. "This man needs medical attention and the gunman is after me. Save yourselves and get out of here! Go now!"

Everyone but Littwin obeyed her command and instantly scrambled for the fire stairs.

"Why aren't you going with them! If you stay here you will die!" she shrieked at him.

"After Columbine, Aurora, and Colorado Springs, I think I'll take my chances with you," he said, showing not even a modicum of fear. "My forty-yard-dash time isn't exactly in the Demaryius Thomas range."

"But he'll kill you!" she cried as the doors to one of the elevators started to open.

As if to prove her point, a bullet whizzed past Littwin's left ear, crashing into the heavy steel doors as they parted. Turning, Skyler saw the Apostle running down the hallway toward her, teeth clenched, Beretta firing.

"Okay, maybe I was wrong—call it a Bernie Sanders moment," said Littwin, and the veteran political reporter made a desperate dash for the stairwell, running every bit as fast as one Demaryius Antwon Thomas, the blue chip wide-receiver of the Denver Broncos.

Skyler stepped into the elevator, dropped the dead agent to the floor, and jerked out her Glock as the Apostle charged toward her. Her arm swung up and she fired three times. Then she reached out and hit the button for the garage.

A bullet drove into her, sending a burning ripple of pain up her arm. Then she was hit again.

The Apostle came on like a demon, but he was not swift enough.

The elevator doors closed.

CHAPTER 144

PATTON WAS SUCKING MEGAWIND. Running up the fire stairs, his thigh and calf muscles felt like lead, his breath came in ragged gasps, and his lungs burned like an icy fire. He had only two floors to go, but he was fading badly.

Then he heard shooting, coming from above. It sounded close.

It was all he needed for a second wind. He charged up the last two flights of stairs and threw open the steel door.

There loomed the professional killer from last night! Thirty feet away, loping toward him like a big, scary Sumatran tiger!

The Apostle's right hand flew up, and he let loose with a rapid burst of gunfire. Patton dove into the cubicle next to the door. The bullets whizzed past, slamming into the door.

The firing stopped for a moment and Patton quickly surveyed his surroundings, his muscles tense as brick. He definitely couldn't stay here. The flimsy pressboard and synthetic fabric offered no protection. He had to keep moving, stay on the offensive, seeking cover behind large stationary objects like desks and credenzas.

But he also had to be cautious. He was dealing with a trained assassin.

The same son of a bitch who had come within a millimeter of slitting his throat last night!

Suddenly, a fusillade of bullets tore through the walls of the cube. Patton scrambled to the side as the little light-filled holes moved from left to right like a buzz saw carving through pressboard.

Patton ran from the cubicle. The Apostle was standing up on some object and firing down at him from two cubes away.

Damn! How did he get there so fast without making a sound?

Patton gave a head fake to the left, in the direction of the cube across the hallway, turned, and ran down a short hallway until he reached an open area with clustered desks. He dove behind one and peered cautiously out from the side. From his Quantico training, he knew you were never supposed to look over an obstacle when under attack. You were supposed to remain in a crouched position and look around it, so as to avoid counterfire. He didn't see anything, but he heard sounds to his right.

Now he saw the Apostle again, standing next to a gray file cabinet, his pistol pointing straight at him. There was a crazy glaze in his eyes like a rabid dog as he pulled the trigger. Patton ducked down and returned fire twice, but both shots missed as the Apostle dove behind the cabinet.

Another shot rang out, sending splinters of oak airborne from the desk behind him.

Again, Patton returned fire and low-dashed to the next desk over.

The movement was a mistake. There was a third shot, and this time he felt a burning sensation along his right side. He fell back heavily and slumped against the desk, feeling a rush of warm blood inside his shirt. Looking down, he saw a growing red blot.

"Target down!" the Apostle gloated from twenty feet away.

Now Patton thought of his adversary in a new light, one of roiling contempt. *You machine! You crazy murdering machine! I'm going to blow your head off, you son of a bitch!*

He heard movement again, a light footfall on the carpet, to his right. He felt his antagonist pressing closer, heard his light breathing. He swung the gun up and leaped out from behind the desk, the already hot gun blazing in his hand.

There was a look of astonishment as the Apostle took a hit in the left shoulder. He fell back with a grunt. Patton squeezed the trigger two more times, but the bullets drove harmlessly into a cube.

The Apostle crept away, noiselessly.

For a half minute, there was a standoff. No one moved or made a peep.

For diversion, Patton grabbed a stapler and tossed it a few feet away, hoping to draw return fire.

There was none.

But there was something else: shuffling feet and voices, coming from the stairwell.

The cavalry! It's about fucking time! Now he felt emboldened. "It's over, asshole! They're coming for you!"

His bravado was answered by a burst of gunfire. Then he heard feet thumping across the carpet, followed by a loud metallic banging sound.

Fire stairs!

Wincing in pain, Patton staggered to his feet and ran for the exit. He heard the hollow echo of the Apostle's dashing footsteps in the stairwell. When he reached the landing, he raised his gun to fire, but the man had vanished like Houdini, the door swinging shut behind him. Now Patton heard loud voices, nearby. He looked over the railing and saw Henry Sharp running up the stairs, glowering at him from several floors below.

"Agent Patton, what the hell are you doing? Stop!"

Sharp? You've got to be fucking kidding me? What should I do?

He popped in a fresh mag and ran up the stairs, bursting through the

413

door shoulder first.

The Apostle was there, dancing on the wall, mumbling incoherently as long-range sharpshooter bullets whirred past him like hissing snakes. A dead federal agent in a SWAT uniform and a sniper's rifle lay at his feet next to the wall. The Apostle held a pistol in his right hand, but it was pointed down in a nonthreatening position.

"Care to dance with me, Special Agent?"

A bullet ricocheted off the wall behind Patton. "I think I'll sit this one out." He crouched down low to avoid another stray bullet.

"Don't you want to know who fired the fatal shots?"

With an unsteady arm, Patton drew a bead on the Apostle. Blood poured from his side, but he ignored it. He was tempted to just shoot the bastard, but he had him talking now. "I already know the answer—it was you. Why don't you just step down from there, so the world can hear your story?"

"You really think it's that simple?" the Apostle shouted, moving along the wall, back and forth, a cross between a pacing zoo tiger and a high trapeze artist. He just managed to avoid two bullets as they screeched overhead, kicking up gravel on the north side of the roof. The guy had to be insane, Patton thought, dancing along a rooftop with unfriendly fire pouring down on him, indifferent to the fact that with one false step he would plunge two hundred feet to his death.

Patton waved his arms, hoping to discourage further fire from the countersnipers. "I don't think it's simple at all. So why don't you put down the gun and come down from there. Then you can explain it to me and the rest of the world." He stepped cautiously toward the Apostle, gun trained on his chest. "You want the people out there to know the truth, don't you?"

"You just want me alive so you'll have a neat and tidy case. That's the way it is with you G-boys, isn't it? Always just one guy who did it, one nutcase. Oswold, James Earl Ray, Sirhan Sirhan, Hinckley. Always a loner, a social outcast, a loser."

Patton continued moving toward him, keeping the Glock locked on his chest. The shooting had stopped, which was a huge relief. The spotters must have seen him and given the order to hold fire. "I don't believe for a minute it was one guy. So who, besides Locke, was behind it? What's the name of the group? It was the same one behind the Kieger hit, wasn't it?"

"I believe you're catching o—"

The words died in his mouth as multiple rounds of gunfire pierced the air. Suddenly, the Apostle's face and upper chest opened up like an egg, squirting blood. He wobbled for an instant before his bandy legs came out from beneath him. His hands reached out and clawed at air, but the effort was half-hearted as only his brain was alive. Over the edge he flew, his high wire act brought to a swift and violent end.

Patton wheeled to see Henry Sharp and a half dozen CIRG sharpshooters with rifles in a horizontal hold.

"Goddamnit, Henry, he was about to tell me who was behind all this shit! Why the fuck did you have to shoot him?"

Sharp said nothing. He went to the edge to have a look. Patton stumbled after him, dripping blood.

Twenty stories down, splattered against the pavement like a run-over squirrel, lay the Apostle. One of his arms was wrenched back at a grotesque angle. Crimson blood poured from his head like a ruptured fuel line.

A triumphant smile took hold of Sharp's leathery face. He reached down and picked up the Winchester sniper's rifle. "Good job, everyone— we got our man!"

"We don't know that for sure," pointed out Patton.

"Like hell we don't." Sharp's eyes widened, as he took in Patton's wound. "Jesus, Special Agent, you're bleeding like a stuck pig."

"I'll live." He wobbled in his stance. "Is...is Fowler dead?"

Sharp looked at him like he was an idiot. "What the fuck are you talking about? That assassin down there just killed President-elect Fowler, Benjamin Locke, and Senator Dubois. I guess he wasn't taking any goddamned chances!"

CHAPTER 145

"GO—GO NOW!" cried the U.S. government agent helper that had navigated Skyler through the security checkpoint two hours earlier. He banged on the driver's side door of the ambulance to get her moving before turning and barking into his two-way radio.

Feeling woozy from extreme blood loss, Skyler flipped on the siren and flashing dome lights, pressed her foot down hard on the accelerator, and charged out of the *Denver Tribune* loading dock onto the street. The squealing tires left behind a trailing plume of smoking rubber as she swung right onto Sixteenth Avenue.

She had fulfilled her own personal assignment and killed Fowler, Locke, and Dubois. At the last second, the contractors had officially switched the target from Fowler to Locke—she had received confirmation from Xavier—but she had decided to handle things in her own way. She had no problem with what she had done. Fowler was an idiot—anyone who flip-flopped their positions like that didn't deserve to rise to the pinnacle of American power; and Locke and Dubois—well let's just say that the two fire-and-brimstone right-wingers were plain fucking nuts and good riddance to both of the felonious bastards. In any case, in all the frenzied excitement she had been damned lucky to pull off the three insanely difficult shots.

Despite her grave wounds, she had managed to transform herself from FBI spotter Carey Firestone into veteran paramedic Jackie Chorney of Lifecare Ambulance Service. Strapped to a gurney in the rear of the ambulance was the unlucky, but extremely useful, Agent Hughes she had lugged down to the loading dock.

The light at Sherman turned green. To her surprise, it looked as though she might actually get away after all. But how far could she possibly get? She was leaking blood like a sieve and already woozy. She doubted if she would be able to make it out of the city before she passed out. And even if she did make it, she would probably die before she could get proper medical attention.

Then she thought of Anthony.

Goddamnit, Angela, you must live! You must live so that you can go on to live your life as a real person!

Fighting against the excruciating pain and blood loss, she blazed down the street and took a screeching left onto Sherman, the lights of the ambulance striping their way across the jungle of glass and steel, the siren shrieking.

Like a wounded lioness, she had a desperate will to live.

The devout Catholic then prayed to the Heavenly Father and drove on.

CHAPTER 146

IT WAS LIKE A STRANGE DREAM. The lips of the agents around him moved, but no sound came out. Arms reached down to him, but they were not like human appendages, more like tree branches viewed from the slipstream of a fast-moving train.

What had just happened was not at all clear.

He tried to get to his knees, but was held down. With blood soaking through his shirt, he felt as weak as a baby. He touched his fingers to his stomach and felt the warm blood. The pain he felt was dull instead of throbbing, which he knew was bad because that meant the wound was serious. Someone pressed something against his stomach to clamp shut the flow of blood.

Moments later, he was lifted onto a stretcher and carried away by paramedics.

"Hold on, Ken—hold on," he heard a familiar voice say.

"Jenn, is that you?" he asked, squinting up at the fuzzy face.

"I'm here, Ken. You're going to make it—just hold on."

"Where's Little Ken? Is he...is he all right?"

"He's okay. Little Ken is okay."

"They didn't come and take him, did they? They didn't take *our son* away from us."

"No, Ken, they didn't take him. He's fine—we're going to see him now."

"Good, I want to see him. I want to see our boy."

"You will see him, Ken. Just hold on!"

He felt a sensation of being hoisted up. Then he was moving and there were other blurry faces peering down at him.

He felt lightheaded, ethereal, and the sensation reminded him of a football game twelve years ago against Michigan State. Dropping back to pass, with his primary receiver open on a crossing pattern, he was driven hard to the turf by a blitzing 250-pound linebacker named Lamont Hendricks. He lay there on the frozen ground, muddled and dazed, and the world all around him seemed curiously surreal. He felt that same sense of semi-consciousness now. He could hear someone—Jennifer?—crying softly beside him, and there were other voices, deeper and slower, like a tape playing at reduced speed. His sensory intake was coming in fuzzy, like a weak radio signal.

He thought of something from Psalms, a lingering vestige of his Methodist upbringing. It came to him in the voice of a country preacher, and his mind reached back to the old Westerns he used to watch with his dad, the John Ford, Howard Hawks, and Sam Peckinpah classics.

He imagined a gathering of settlers standing over the grave of some luckless cowboy, their faces hardened from sun and wind and hardship. They were listening to a black-hatted preacher, Good Book in hand, as he recited the Psalm in a sad voice that mingled with the whipping wind. It was a stark scene, but somehow comforting, with rolling tumbleweeds and a curtain of dust in the background and the stoic faces of the hardy but weary pioneers in the foreground. It all came to Patton clearly, like a dream just before one awakes, as he listened to the preacher's solemn words.

The Lord is my shepherd, I shall not want
He makes me lie down in green pastures
He leads me beside still waters, he restores my soul
He leads me in paths of righteousness, for his name's sake

Even though I walk through the valley of the shadow of death, I fear no evil
For thou art with me; thy rod and thy staff, they comfort me

Thou preparest a table before me in the presence of my enemies
Thou annointest my head with oil, my cup overflows
Surely goodness and mercy shall follow me all the days of my life
And I shall dwell in the house of the Lord forever

That was his last thought as he slipped into unconsciousness.

EPILOGUE

SIX MONTHS LATER

WITH WARM SUNLIGHT slanting through the windows and Flatt & Scruggs whirling in their ears, they drove up the craggy mountain, past the quaking Aspen and Rocky Mountain juniper into lush forests of Douglas fir and ponderosa pine, from the montane into the alpine, toward the jagged crest where the bighorns bounded and golden eagles nested. Soon they were above timberline, zig-zagging up the road cut through the imposing granite batholith named for Zebulon Montgomery Pike.

Patton smiled over at Jennifer. They were having fun, frivolously toying with Lady Death, churning up the steep grades and skittering around the hairpin turns where a mistake could mean tumbling down thousands of feet of sheer cliff and talus. Nearing the crest, they gasped in awe at the big black mountain crows and even larger ravens gliding past the window, dodging and darting, flapping their wings occasionally as sudden gusts of wind jarred them from their flight paths.

Reaching the summit, they stepped out of the car into the cold mountain air, walked to the large viewing platform, and gazed down onto the Great Plains to the east. It was a spectacular panorama, as it should have been, considering they were atop one of the tallest mountains in North America—14,110 feet above the world's oceans and 9,000 feet above the seemingly boundless plains below.

"God, it's beautiful up here," Jennifer exclaimed.

"It certainly is." He smiled as he stared down at the rusty-gray steel tracks of the old cog rail line. Slowly, his face took on a more serious expression. "The Kieger Report's finished, Jenn. It's not what I expected at all. After six months of rigorous investigation, the Justice Department's concluded that Benjamin Locke, Frederick Taylor, and Kenneth Cutler, a.k.a. the Apostle, acted alone. I don't know about you, but it strikes me as a little too convenient when the three lead actors of the country's biggest melodrama since 9/11 are all dead."

"I thought you got a positive ID on Jane Doe. Not only at Union Plaza, but at the Trib Tower."

"The powers that be claim it's not necessarily the same person. They concede she may have been an accessory to the murders, but there's no mention of her possibly being the assassin. And there's no mention of my Diego Gomez theory either."

"But that isn't what was in your report. What happened? Why did they make up their own story?"

"It's simple. The Justice Department—and every other government agency with any connection whatsoever—wants closure. Especially the Treasury Department. Apparently the big shots in Washington lobbied hard to make sure Taylor was the only one named in the report. They're conducting their own internal investigation into other agents, but I wouldn't hold my breath."

"I can't believe this. There's been no sign of Jane Doe?"

"It's like she's disappeared from the face of the earth. She's still on the Ten Most Wanted List and the Interpol alert is still in effect, but inquiries into her whereabouts have taken a back seat to more pressing cases. We're also in somewhat of a turf war with the CIA over jurisdiction. We're supposed to be sharing information, but it seems to be moving only in one direction."

"So everyone just wants it all to go away."

"Everyone but congressional Democrats. Three rogues end up on a cold slab and the case is wrapped up all neat and tidy like a birthday gift."

Her brow wrinkled disapprovingly. "So that's it?"

"Not for you it isn't. I made copies of Justice's report for you. And mine too. They're in my car. Just remember, you didn't get them from me."

"My lips are sealed." She blew on her cold hands. "You know what. I think your macho fed cohorts just can't admit they've been duped by a woman. That's why they refuse to acknowledge your theory."

"Might be some truth to that. The bottom line is Jane Doe fooled everyone."

They fell into silence, staring out at the peaceful world around them: the Continental Divide to the west, the towering Sangre de Cristos to the south, and the Great Plains to the east, the direction from which explorer Zeb Pike had come in the early 1800s. After a few minutes, they walked into the Summit House to get a cup of coffee. When they came back outside, they walked north and climbed around on the rocks.

She blew on her coffee. "What about Governor Stoddart?"

"We don't think he had anything to do with the conspiracy. All that time I thought he was trying to derail me, he was simply trying to protect AMP, his biggest Stealth PAC contributor. Still, his career is effectively over. You killed any chance he had for reelection with your series. The

Locke campaign finance connection did him in. The whole State of Colorado owes you a debt of gratitude."

"I'll make sure not to let it go to my head. What about Sharp?"

"He wasn't involved either, but like the governor, he was brought down a few notches. OPR conducted an investigation and found that they didn't particularly like the way he handled the case. He was forced to take early retirement and they cut him some kind of deal so he'll retain his pension. Where I work we have two basic rules: overwhelming force trumps all, and never tarnish the Bureau's reputation. Apparently Sharp's early retirement falls into the latter."

"Jesus, Ken, how can you work for these people?"

He stared down at the endless plains below, taking a moment to marshal his thoughts. "The Bureau may be a dysfunctional family, but it's my dysfunctional family. You don't just give up on your family, Jenn. You try and change it."

"You're only saying that because of your promotion," she ribbed him playfully. "Domestic Terrorism desk supervisor. You're a big shot now, part of upper management. Pretty soon, you'll be just like J. Edgar himself, putting together secret blackmail files to keep public figures in line and subverting civil liberties at the drop of a hat."

Patton laughed and sipped his coffee.

"That wasn't meant to be funny, Ken. You know I just don't want you to become a crusty government agent with an eye patch, protecting your beloved Bureau at all costs. I care too much about you to let that happen."

"So you *have* decided to move in."

"Why is it always the woman who has to move? Why can't you come to San Francisco with me?"

"You know the answer to that question."

Jennifer mimicked a previous conversation they'd had about this. "I know. I'm the freelance journalist, so I can go anywhere. Whereas you're the DT triggerman with the Federal Bureau of Intimidation in Denver, so I have to come to you. I think it sucks."

God, you are beautiful, and the best thing about it is it hasn't gone to your head. "We could live in the Republic of Boulder. It's pretty much the same as San Francisco, except that I've heard they're experiencing painful tofu and alfalfa sprout rationing."

"Oh, so now you're trying to appeal to my leftist sensibilities."

"An obvious sign of desperation," he said, and they shared a good laugh.

Finishing their coffee, they walked back to the viewing platform and stared at the columns of granite sprawling to the south. The ancient weathered Precambrian rock was riddled with joints and flanked by vast slopes of gray scree. He came up from behind and took her in a gentle hold. They stood there, swaying for a minute, staring out at the ruggedly spectacular landscape.

"Do you really think it can work out between us after everything that's happened?" she asked.

"I can't see myself with anyone else. Whether you and I will end up happily ever after is another question. But I'd like to give it a try."

"What about Little Ken?"

"He belongs to others now. All we can do is move forward and make our own little critters."

"Is that a marriage proposal, Agent Patton?"

"I believe the choice is yours, not mine, in these progressive times. All I know is I've waited twelve years for you to come back into my life and I can't picture myself with anyone else. Ever."

Jennifer turned around. "Oh, Ken," she said, and they kissed tenderly.

"If you'll have me, I'm yours. I've never loved anybody like I love you."

"Oh, Ken," she murmured again, and this time there were tears in her eyes. "How can a girl turn down a proposal like that, freezing her butt off atop a fourteen-thousand-foot mountain?"

"We're a match made in heaven: the macho FBI agent who routinely subverts civil liberties—and the left-wing journalist who exposes all his dirty little secrets."

"Oh keep quiet, you handsome rogue, and give me another kiss."

He swiftly delivered. Then they walked to the edge of the platform, collars turned up against the wind. Gazing out at the jagged-edged landscape, she said, "Now that it's all over and done, are you sure Jane Doe is the assassin?"

His eyes were drawn to the sky, where a pair of dark ravens glided gracefully along the edge of the big mountain. "She's the killer all right," he said, picturing how the great bird dispatched its prey. "And she's out there right now, probably laughing at us."

"But are you certain?"

"Yes, I'm sure," he said, his expression hardening with resolve. "She's out there somewhere. And one of these days, I'm going to find her."

AUTHOR'S NOTE

The Coalition was conceived and written by the author as a work of fiction. The novel is ultimately a work of the imagination and entertainment and should be read as nothing more. Names, characters, places, government entities, religious and political groups, corporations, and incidents are products of the author's imagination or are used fictitiously and are not to be construed as real. Any resemblance to actual events, locales, businesses, companies, organizations, or persons, living or dead, is entirely coincidental.

There is indeed an FBI Field Office, a Civic Center Plaza, and a State Capitol Building in the Mile High City; a Broadmoor Hotel, Colorado Springs Police Department, U.S. Air Force Academy, and Old North End residential neighborhood in Colorado Springs; a Castle Café in Castle Rock, Colorado; and a nifty beach town overlooking the Pacific Ocean called Venice Beach, California. However, to the best of the author's knowledge, no one bearing any resemblance to the fictional characters portrayed in *The Coalition* has ever engaged in close-quarters gunfights, long-distance sniping, desperate foot chases, workplace harassment, abusive interrogations, illegal raids, or sadomasochistic sexual activities similar to the events dramatized in the novel at these inspiring locations. Furthermore, the author holds the utmost respect for the FBI, U.S. Secret Service, and the Denver and Colorado Springs Police Departments portrayed in the novel and has not made any attempt to present any government law enforcement agency in a bad light. In fact, both the FBI and U.S. Secret Service were instrumental and generous in answering questions and providing assistance to the author. Thanks are given to the FBI and Secret Service personnel in the *Acknowledgements* in the subsequent pages.

There are no religious and/or political organizations known as American Patriots or The Coalition in Colorado Springs, Colorado, or anywhere else, at least that the author is aware of. Therefore, the illicit, shadowy, and ultimately murderous activities carried out in the novel by the representatives of both American Patriots and its hyperviolent, far-right counterpart, the Coalition, have been entirely fictionalized and, in reality, would likely not occur in the real world of even a militant U.S. religious-political organization. There is, of course, no prominent Christian political leader known as Benjamin Bradford Locke and no Dr. Sivy or Family Planning Group clinic in Widefield, Colorado. All employees of American Patriots and the Family Planning Group portrayed in the book have no real-life counterpart and are wholly the creation of the author's imagination.

ACKNOWLEDGEMENTS

To develop the story line, characters, and scenes for *The Coalition*, I consulted hundreds of non-fiction books, magazine and newspaper articles, blogs, Web sites, and numerous individuals as well as visited each and every real-world location in person. These locations included numerous physical settings in Denver, Colorado Springs, and Castle Rock in Colorado, and San Francisco, Oakland, Los Angeles, and Venice Beach in California. All in all, there are too many resources and locations to name here. However, I would be remiss if I didn't give credit to the critical individuals who dramatically improved the quality of the manuscript from its initial to its final stage. Any technical mistakes, typographical errors, or examples of overreach due to artistic license, however, are the fault of me and me alone.

I would personally like to thank the following for their support and assistance. First and foremost, I would like to thank the many professionals from the FBI Denver Field Office and U.S. Secret Service in Washington, D.C., for patiently answering my questions on agency protocols, firearms, DNA testing, ballistics, fingerprinting, and interagency task force procedures as well as for describing what every work day life is like for both senior-level staff and field agents. *The Coalition* greatly benefitted from the expert advice given by the numerous professionals at these agencies. Any technical mistakes or inaccuracies due to artistic liberties, of course, belong to me and not the helpful professionals from the aforementioned governmental agencies that assisted me.

Second, I would like to thank my wife Christine, an exceptional and highly professional book editor, who painstakingly reviewed and copy-edited the novel.

Third, I would like to thank my former literary agent, Cherry Weiner of the Cherry Weiner Literary Agency, for thoroughly reviewing, vetting, and copy-editing the manuscript, and for making countless improvements to the finished novel before I chose to publish the novel independently.

Fourth, I would like to thank Stephen King's former editor, Patrick LoBrutto, and Quinn Fitzpatrick, former book critic for the *Rocky Mountain News*, for thoroughly copy-editing the various drafts of the novel and providing detailed reviews.

Fifth, I would like to show my appreciation for author James Patterson and author-literary agent Donald Maass for their positive reviews and constructive criticism of the novel. They took the time to give me genuine feedback and, without their encouragement, I might not be as determined and resilient an author as I am today.

I would also like to thank Austin and Anne Marquis, Betsy and Steve Hall, Fred Taylor, Mo Shafroth, Tim and Carey Romer, Governor Roy Romer, Peter and Lorrie Frautschi, Brigid Donnelly, John Welch, Link Nicoll, Rik Hall, George Foster, Margot Patterson, Cathy and Jon Jenkins, Danny and Elena Bilello, Charlie and Kay Fial, Peter Brooke, Vincent Bilello, and the other book reviewers and professional contributors large and small who have given generously of their time over the years, as well as to those who have given me loyal support as I have ventured on this incredible odyssey of suspense novel writing.

Lastly, I want to thank anyone and everyone who bought this book and my loyal fans and supporters who helped promote this work. You know who you are and I salute you.

ABOUT BESTSELLING, AWARD-WINNING AUTHOR SAMUEL MARQUIS AND FORTHCOMING TITLES

"Marquis is brilliant and bold…It's hard not to think, "What's he going to come up with next?"
—SP Review - 4.5-Star Review (for *The Slush Pile Brigade*)

"A promising thriller writer with a fine hero, great research, and a high level of authenticity."
—Donald Maass, Author of *Writing 21st Century Fiction*

"*The Coalition* has a lot of good action and suspense, an unusual female assassin, and the potential to be another *The Day After Tomorrow*."
—James Patterson, #1 *New York Times* Bestselling Author

"With *Blind Thrust* and his other works, Samuel Marquis has written true breakout novels that compare favorably with—and even exceed—recent thrillers on the *New York Times* Bestseller List."
—Pat LoBrutto, Former Editor for Stephen King and Eric Van Lustbader (Bourne Series)

Samuel Marquis is a bestselling, award-winning suspense author. He works by day as a Vice-President–Hydrogeologist with an environmental firm in Boulder, Colorado, and by night as an iconoclastic spinner of historical and modern suspense yarns. He holds a Master of Science degree in Geology, is a Registered Professional Geologist in eleven states, and is a recognized expert in groundwater contaminant hydrogeology, having served as a hydrogeologic expert witness in several class action litigation cases. He also has a deep and abiding interest in military history and intelligence, specifically related to the Golden Age of Piracy, Plains Indian Wars, World War II, and the current War on Terror.

His technical scientific background and passion for military history and intelligence have served Marquis well as a suspense writer. His first two thrillers, *The Slush Pile Brigade* and *Blind Thrust*, were both #1 *Denver Post* bestsellers for fiction, and his first three novels received national book award recognition. *The Slush Pile Brigade* was an award-winning finalist in the mystery category of the Beverly Hills Book Awards. *Blind Thrust* was the winner of the Next Generation Indie Book Awards in the suspense category, an award-winning suspense finalist of both the USA Best Book Awards and Beverly Hills Book Awards, and a *Foreword Reviews'* Book of the Year award finalist (thriller & suspense). His third novel, *The Coalition*, was the winner of the Beverly Hills Book Awards for a political thriller.

Former Colorado Governor Roy Romer said, "*Blind Thrust* kept me up until 1 a.m. two nights in a row. I could not put it down. An intriguing mystery that intertwined geology, fracking, and places in Colorado that I know well. Great fun." Kirkus Reviews proclaimed *The Coalition* an "entertaining thriller" and declared that "Marquis has written a tight plot with genuine suspense." James Patterson compared *The Coalition* to *The Day After Tomorrow*, the classic thriller by Allan Folsom. Other book reviewers have compared Book #1 of Marquis's World War Two Trilogy, *Bodyguard of Deception,* to the spy novels of John le Carré, Daniel Silva, Ken Follett, and Alan Furst.

Below is the list of suspense novels that Samuel Marquis has published or will be publishing in 2015-2017 along with the release dates of both previously published and forthcoming titles.

The Nick Lassiter Series
The Slush Pile Brigade – September 2015 – *The #1 Denver Post* Bestseller and Award-Winning Finalist Beverly Hills Book Awards
The Fourth Pularchek – 2017

The Joe Higheagle Series
Blind Thrust – October 2015 – The #1 **Denver Post** Bestseller; Winner Next Generation Indie Book Awards; Award-Winning Finalist USA Best Book Awards, Beverly Hills Book Awards, Foreword Reviews' Book of the Year, and Next Generation Indie Book Awards
The Cluster – September 2016

The World War Two Trilogy
Bodyguard of Deception – March 2016
Roman Moon – January 2017

Standalone Espionage Thriller Novels
The Coalition – January 2016 – Winner Beverly Hills Book Awards

Thank You for Your Support!

To Order Samuel Marquis Books and Contact Samuel:

Visit Samuel Marquis's website, join his mailing list, learn about his forthcoming suspense novels and book events, and order his books at www.samuelmarquisbooks.com. Please send all fan mail (including criticism) to samuelmarquisbooks@gmail.com.